EVERLASTING SKY

A Novel of the
First Empress of China

Kajira Wyn Berry

KAJIRA WYN BERRY

This is a story based on real people and real events.
It also includes some fictional characters, dialogue, and scenes
that are solely from the author's imagination.

Published in the United States by
EYE/WEST, Vashon Island, Washington
kajirawynberry.com

ISBN: 978-0-9800020-1-0

Printed in the United States of America

Author photograph by Douglas Mesney
Book design by David Steel/Sy Novak

I DEDICATE THIS BOOK:

To The Three—David, Bonny and Duncan,
my children who have so enriched my life;
To my sweetheart David,
who brings sunshine into each morning;
To my beautiful sister, Gwen,
for sharing our life's adventures;
And to my many friends
who have sustained me all these years

Contents

Book One

BOOK TWO

BOOK THREE

The Tang Code Of Law

This coiled, four-toed dragon is the symbol on *The T'ang Code of Law*, the project that Emperor T'ai T'sung initiated and that Empress Wu completed after his death. It was the basic code of law in China until the 20th century.

A NOTE TO THE READER

BOOKS ARE A WONDERMENT TO ME. I mean beyond the words. What's the story behind the story, the impelling moment beginning with a sheet of paper or a blank computer screen ending in the birth of a book? So I thought you might like to know—although I'm not sure I have all the whys and wherefores completely clear myself—how I came to write and rewrite this story for almost 40 years.

I *can* tell you when it began—January 1968, my home in Portland, Oregon. After a brisk walk, I sat down with a cup of hot coffee in front of my friend Sanje Elliot's freestanding two-paneled painting. Within minutes, I was *inside* the painting, myself as a different person, walking across a vast and lovely garden, experiencing sights and sounds quite foreign to me. Perhaps the painting served as some kind of mandala that led me into another time/space quite unfamiliar. The architecture—a peculiar type of roofline in the ornate, three-story building behind me—the palace wings on either side, on the left where one son's wife was yelling at her kids while he had his head in the stars; within the right wing, silence, where I knew that the other son and his carousing buddies were sleeping off an evening of Sassanian music; two words—tie and sun, and I, dressed in sheer lavender cotton tied with ribbons on the sleeves, felt that something wonderful was about to happen that breathless spring morning.

The next day I went to the library and looked up these clues of images and a few words. There they were—the architecture, music, names could be identified as those of Emperor T'ai Tsung (the tie and sun words), and of the 7th century T'ang Dynasty which borrowed architecture and music from Sassania (ancient Persia)—a history and culture that I had never studied or read about, before. What followed was more than two years of living this story and verifying specific events, as they occurred, through research in libraries throughout the world. Whenever it seemed like a dead trail, just the right information or book (most often in Powell's or Berkeley or London) would appear. Talima and Empress Wu Chao T'se Tsien became an inseparable part of my everyday life.

I wrote some of this story, then put it away. Even after I had picked it up again and put it away several times, having decided I was done, Talima or T'se Tsien would pop up to say, most emphatically, "Finish the book, I want my voice heard."

So there you have it—the story behind the story of *Everlasting Sky.*

Denis Twitchett writes, in *The Cambridge History of China, Volume 3,* "Casting her shadow over most of Kao-tsung's years on the throne, and indeed over the rest of the seventh century, was the beautiful and enticing Wu Chao. Everything concerning this remarkable woman is surrounded by doubts, for she stood for everything to which the ideal of the Confucian scholar-official class was opposed...From the very first the historical record of her reign has been hostile, biased and curiously fragmentary and incomplete. Less is known of the details of political life during her half-century of dominance than of any comparable period of the T'ang.

"However, in spite of the venom and hostility of the Confucian historians to this woman who dared to overthrow the Li-T'ang house and had the effrontery to rule like a man, it is nevertheless apparent that she was exceptionally gifted, with a natural genius for politics and brilliantly adept at manipulating the power structure at court."

Nothing is known for sure of Wu Chao T'se T'sien's early life before her Tai Yuan family; this book fills in that gap according to the experience of my imagination.

Perhaps now, that gifted, adventurous, headstrong woman will let me be, at last. Her voice and history can be heard. I'll miss her.

I would like to thank those who also believed in her story and helped get it into print: my sister Gwen, and my sweetheart David, who painstakingly edited and corrected the manuscript, line by line; Sy, whose considerable skills made David's book and cover design become real; my nephew, Collin, for a splendid web site, kajirawynberry.com; my best friend, Hita, who helped me keep things in perspective; my beloved daughter Bonny, who hatched a plot to make it happen; my splendid sons David and Duncan and dear daughter-in-law Melany, who literally made the book possible; my granddaughter Arielle's willingness for her sweet face to be the basis of our cover Talima; thanks to Sanje for his painting and long friendship; hats off to my inspiring and superbly discriminating writers' group, Ann, Jean, Jill and Rachel; and to close friends who will be glad not to have to hear about the progress, year after year. With gratitude and love and laughter to all.

Vashon Island, Washington, September 2007

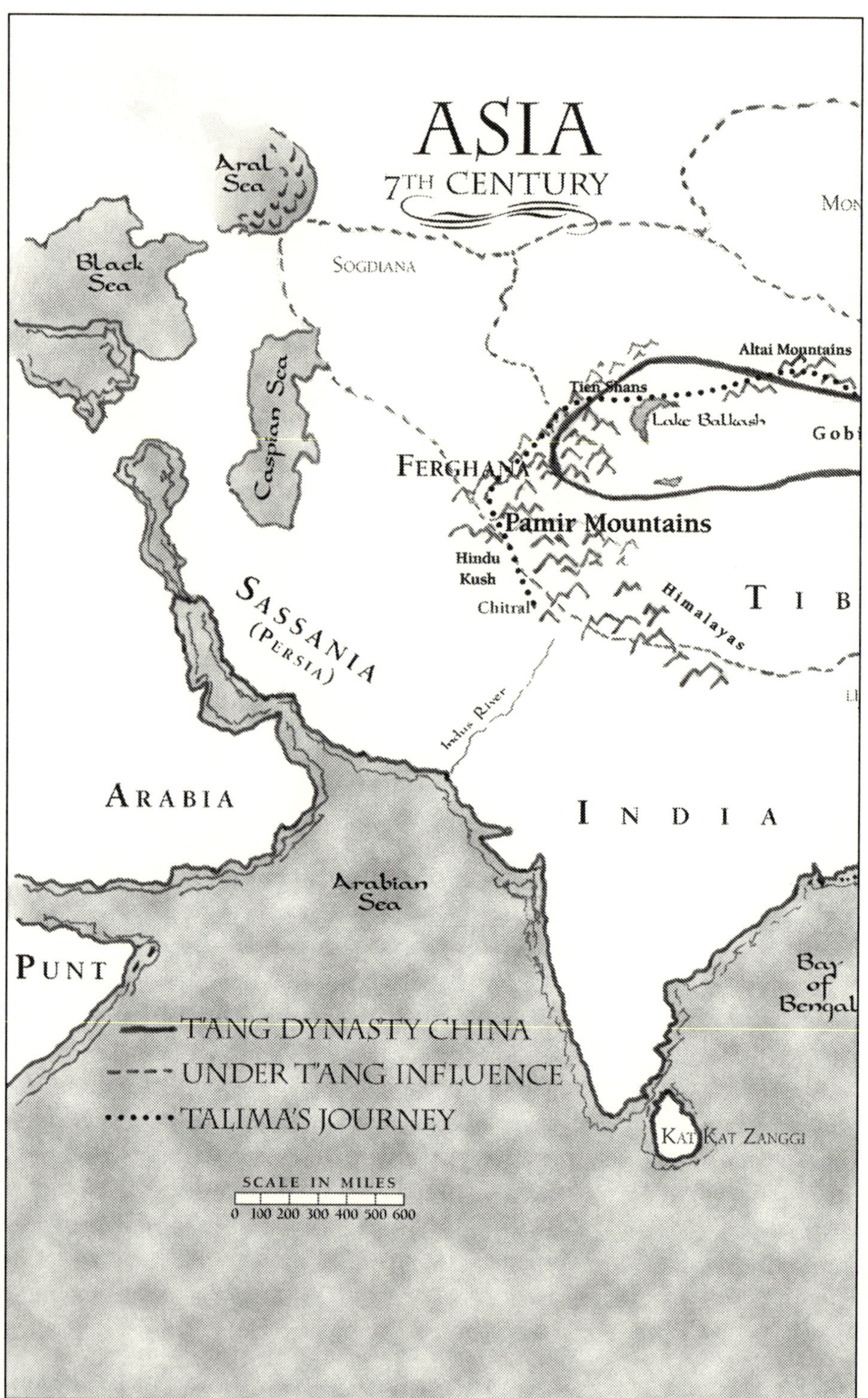
ASIA
7TH CENTURY
Aral Sea
Black Sea
Caspian Sea
Sogdiana
Altai Mountains
Tien Shans
Lake Balkash
Gobi
Ferghana
Pamir Mountains
Hindu Kush
Chitral
Himalayas
Sassania (Persia)
Indus River
Arabia
India
Arabian Sea
Punt
Bay of Bengal
T'ANG DYNASTY CHINA
UNDER T'ANG INFLUENCE
TALIMA'S JOURNEY
Kat Zanggi
SCALE IN MILES
0 100 200 300 400 500 600

N
W
E
S
Mon-Barbarian land
Lake Baikal
Altai Mountains
Lake Balkash
Gobi Desert
CHIAN
(CHINA)
SILLA
(KOREA)
tains
Great Wall
Yellow River
Tun-Huang
Caves
Loyang
TIBET
Wei River
Changan
Shaolin
Mountains
Himalayas
Lhasa
Yangtze River
East
China
Sea
ASSAM
Irawaddy River
DIA
ANNAM
BURMA
South
China
Sea
Bay
of
Bengal
KHMER
EMPIRE OF
CAMBODIA
CHAMPA
Celebes
Sea
KAT KAT ZANGGI
SRIVIJAYA

Book One

BRONZE WINGTIPS FEATHERED AIR SHIMMERING *with ice crystals as a golden eagle hovered, then screamed, and plummeted earthward toward an unsuspecting mouse.*

Like an echo of her hunting cry came the raw wail of a woman's birth ecstasy and the shrill, reedy mew of a newborn's cry. A girl-child was born to the wife of Tashih Shaymak, Great Chagan of the Golden Igren.

Again, the eagle climbed soul-blue skies above the Pamir Mountains and soared along cliff rims and canyons, far out over high mountain valleys. Her jubilant "scr-eee-ee-e-!" rang out on the banner of wind for all the steppe-land of Central Asia to hear.

1
In Which An Heir Is Born
626 A.D.

In the Igren birth-tent, lantern light flickered around the encircling painted and embroidered felt walls. A midwife bathed the glowing baby with mare's milk, rubbed her with warm sheep's fat, then wrapped her snugly in soft woolen blankets.

"See how strong, how healthy she is!" The midwife said, laying her in her mother's arms. The baby turned her head, looked around her and smiled at this world of light and air.

"Look, beloved husband," said the mother proudly. "Our beautiful daughter, our first child. Is she not wonderful?"

"She is, well, wonderfully little!" The Chagan lifted the baby and shifted her around in his arms until her head was cradled in his left hand. Tentatively, he touched the silken skin of her wrinkled fingers, tiny fingers that instantly clutched his rein-hardened forefinger.

"She holds on so tightly!" He laughed with delight, "I think, though, it is not my finger, but my heart that she has really taken hold of!"

People gathered outside their leader's tent. There were only a few dozen family members still in this permanent winter camp, most were with the vast horse herds, trailing up to summer pasture.

Tashih Shaymak smiled tenderly at his wife. "Honey of my life," he said, "it's time for us to share our blessing."

Cradling the baby beneath his embroidered, scarlet cloak, he lifted the tent flap and stepped outside. "Behold, my friends! I bring you a new child of the Blue Wolf—my daughter Talima!

"Hear my prayer, O Everlasting Sky! May my daughter's days be filled with the sunlit sounds of happiness! May she ride the winds bravely!

May her spirit dance on the mountains like a flame! Grant these boons, O Sky, to my daughter, Talima!

"As you have made me Chagan-sha, Keeper of the Igren Hearths, I now proclaim Talima, my firstborn, heir to all my rights and titles.

"May she drink the dew of night's wisdom, moon's wisdom, preserving *The Yasa*, our sacred law, all the days of her life. Witness the birth of my heir Talima, O Great and Everlasting Sky!"

The Chagan held the baby high over his own head, her swaddled body silhouetted against the star-pricked sky. His clansmen's cheer reverberated against twilight-purple hills, echoing an ancient joy.

A NEW MOON CRADLED THE VENUS STAR. The eagle still circled above Igren valleys that intersected trade routes that radiated in all directions like spokes of a great wheel—the many trails of the Silk Road. Traders endured hardships that the high Gobi Desert and ice-crested mountain ranges imposed, and hazarded their lives against immense odds, answering the demand for silk, the shining cloth prized above gold. Every country along this far-flung trading route, great or small, came under the hegemony of China, or Chian as it was then called, the wealthiest most brilliant culture of the time.

In the capital city of Chian, far to the east of the mountain valley where Talima's birth was cheered and celebrated, in Changan, at the beginning of the Silk Road, other people celebrated, other people cheered. Multitudes from a far-flung empire gathered to swear allegiance to their new emperor at the commencement of the dynasty called T'ang in this year, 626 A.D. The vast wealth of China was spread at the feet of his Peacock Throne, and as the Chagan's people acclaimed Talima, so the Chinese people acclaimed Tai Tsung.

On this spring evening of his inaugural, Tai Tsung, that great warrior, did not know, nor would have cared, that a girl-child had been born to a vassal nomad chieftain three thousand miles to the west. Concerned with royal rituals, processions and speeches, he did not dream how intertwined his life would be with hers.

2
AN AMBASSADOR'S ULTIMATUM
643 A.D.

Glacial mists swirled a shawl around the shoulders of Burkhan Kaldun, the Igren's "Mountain of Power". The sunny wind sent lenticular clouds, oval cloud-saucers, spinning out against a sapphire sky. Wind sang as it blew over the domed dwellings that sprouted like so many gaudy, painted mushrooms on the high dusty plain below.

Wind, now a visible force as it gathered unto itself dry grass and fluffs of hair shed from thousands of grazing horses, whooped into the vast tumult that filled the valley bowl. Camels brayed. Cattle and sheep bawled and baa-ed. Men and women called to each other. Children shouted and ran and laughed. Ponderous yaks moved peacefully in the midst of it all.

The People were gathered for Kuriltai at the summons of their great chieftain, Chagan Shah, Tashih Shaymak. Kuriltai, the joyous celebration that marked an end to another achingly long winter of storms and snow. Winters when no caravans passed through this hub of East/West trade on the Silk Road. Winters isolated in the heart of ice-spawned winds, the ever constant wind, at home in this Pamir mountain valley, the only constant in the lives of the nomad Igren, People of the Ger.

WITHIN THE WIDE CORRAL, THERE WAS A WILD MELEE OF POUNDING hooves and flying manes. Twisting and bucking, horses caromed against each other. Bareback riders, nearly invisible in the whirling saffron dust, swung long curved mallets, hit at a hard, leather-wrapped ball no bigger than a fist, raced against each other as they leaned far out toward the powdered earth.

Talima, her copper braids flying, hit the puck between the legs of an opponent's horse that tried to come between her and the goal. The horse reared, pranced backward and fell, as its rider flew off. She leaped down to help him get safely away from other excited horses.

"Are you all right?"she asked the fallen rider.

"Whoo-ee, yes, but that wild horse of yours is formidable!" her younger brother, Jalco, sat up and rubbed his shoulder.

"Bagatur isn't wild, little brother, just well-trained, foolish boy!"

"I'm only two years younger than you, my ancient almost 17-year-old sister, so you'd better watch out! I'll beat you at alabolo one of these days! Just you wait!" He grinned,and slapped yellow dust from his wide-legged, woolen pants.

At that moment a series of wavering whistles shrilled into the suddenly quiet air. Slotted arrows, shot by lookouts stationed outside the valley, signaled an approaching caravan.

"Sky! Father will need me at the Greeting Council...Jalco, will you rub down Bagatur? Please? I'll need to hurry!"

"Wish I could go with you...oh, well, of course, I will." Jalco agreed.

Talima walked quickly across the broad valley, crossing a stream that sparkled with the icy rush of newly melted snow. She passed many kibitkas, great wagons drawn by oxen, assembled for Kuriltai. She saw slaves unloading household gear from the immense platforms, while others stretched felt covers over bent-willow boughs, creating the traditional round tents, the ger, in which the assembling Clan lived.

Kuriltai...what a wonderful time it is! Talima thought, smiling and waving to friends she hadn't seen since the summer before. *No one wants to miss the feasting and dancing, to say nothing of comparing their favorite hunting birds with kinsmen! Nor are they willing to be absent from voting on important Clan decisions—what tolls to charge for the protection of passing caravans or where to graze the herds for, as father says, every Igren's born with a firm idea of what's right and what's definitely wrong. The only problem is in getting them to agree*!

Camel bells, faint at first, grew louder as the caravan wound its way down from the rocky pass. Talima watched its progress as she hurried toward the Chagan's pavilion. First came men on horseback, followed by camels heavily laden with chests and sacks of provisions. Beside the camels marched short men wearing padded shirts and pants beneath leather armor. Either a long or short sword hung at their sides. Eight taller warriors walked between the bamboo shafts of a swaying palanquin. Its red silk curtains billowed out in the dry wind.

It looks like scarlet wings of a many-legged butterfly, she thought.

Igren outriders kept the moving line together, threading it through the noisy melee of animals and children toward the Chagan's ger. By their extreme care, Talima knew that this caravan must contain persons or goods of unusual significance.

A man astride a black and white gelding rode up beside her, "The Chagan is waiting for you, Talima-sha, an important personage is arriving!"

"I know that, Pirjhan. I heard the arrows," she answered curtly. *How like him, telling me what Father wants, as if I didn't know! Father gives him too much authority.* She smoothed her hair, slapped the dust from her tunic, cinched her blue-and-red-striped sash more tightly, and ran up the hill.

The Chagan and his three brothers had assembled. With each totem flag flying behind them, they sat on thick felt pads on either side of Tashih Shaymak. They were lean, raw-boned men, skin tanned like old leather, shoulder-length hair bleached almost white from years of strong sun and stronger winds. Chief among the Igren nomads, they were the resourceful, tawny men of the Golden Family.

"Ahatou, my father, 'hatou, uncles," Talima said breathlessly, then quickly sat down on the empty mat at her father's left, under his carved white falcon.

The Igren horsemen directed the caravan camels and men into a half-circle facing the Chagan's snapping flags. The bearers set down the palanquin and opened its fluttering curtains.

A slight, elderly man with long, black mustaches that drooped nearly to his waist, stepped down and straightened his shoulders. His flaring coat and pants of blue-green silk were embroidered.

He looks like a jeweled beetle shining in the afternoon sun, Talima thought.

Arms tucked into his flowing sleeves, the stranger bowed from his waist and began to speak, "Tashih Shaymak, Great Wolf of the Far Mountains, your name is known and esteemed by men. Pardon, if you will please, my unworthy appearance before you, but the way has been long. Cold, too, and dusty."

His words are somewhat understandable but more like the twitter of birds than the speech of men, mused Talima.

"Please seat yourselves," the Chagan gestured to him. "I'll have refreshments served." He rang a small silver bell for slaves to bring sweetmeats and chai, the hot, spiced drink served on all special occasions.

"Talima, please see that our riders care for the pack animals and men," the Chagan murmured to her quietly. She jumped up to carry out his request.

Then Tashih Shaymak began to speak in a rapid, singsong pattern. "I am the Igren Chagan, Tashih Shaymak, head of all the Golden Families. May I know your name, shining one?"

"I am Chang Chun, ambassador to you Western Mon-barbarians from His Most High Majesty, Tai Tsung, glorious emperor of Chian, who sits the Peacock Throne, inherits the wind, and commands the known world." His silk robes swirled around him as he bowed.

"My brothers and I," Tashih Shaymak gestured to the men seated on his left and right, "welcome such an august ambassador as yourself to our valley. Have you been traveling long?"

"Since the harvest moon, nearly half a year ago, honored sir. We took the longer, southern route, it being winter, to avoid the highest mountains. Even so, had it not been for well-provisioned post-stops, we would have been in greater travail." His black eyes sparkled, belying the timidity of his words.

Talima came back into the circle and sat down.

"If all these men," the ambassador's wide sleeves fluttered in the mountain winds as he gestured toward the Chagan, "are your brothers, Great Chagan, who then, if I may be so bold, is the one who sits beside you? Your beautiful wife perhaps?"

"No, not my wife," the Chagan smiled at Talima, "This is my heir, my only daughter, Talima."

Chang Chun seemed oddly satisfied, placing each jeweled hand into his long sleeves, nodding imperceptibly, "Aaaah, so... just so. I wonder, most gracious one, if I might seek shelter here with you until I am able to intercept the Red Hats from Hrom as they come through? It should be only a few weeks at most, now that the passes are open. You see, I must continue on to my appointment at the Sassanian Court in Persia and I thought—no, the emperor thought—that it would be wise to ah, educate these Red Hats about the current state of their indebtedness for silk. It has grown to quite alarming proportions, I assure you!"

"You are most welcome, of course, Chang Chun. It's true that much of the known world is madly in love with the silk whose secret Chian guards so carefully. I was told," the Chagan said tentatively, "that your silk is spun from ice worms deep within northern glaciers—does that idea have merit, d'you think?"

The ambassador leaned back and laughed, a high whinny of a laugh, "La! Who knows? But that is certainly an intriguing idea!"

There followed a formal conversation of flattery and verbal fencing in the trade language that Talima found difficult to understand. She drifted into daydream. *I'll wear my best silk tunic to the dance tonight, I love the way silk feels on my skin when I move—it makes me feel so alive...*

"And so, the great emperor Tai Tsung, will insist on bringing all men of the known world under one banner, enriching each clan with the shared wealth of the other," continued the stranger.

"We would agree that the trade routes are essential, Chang Chun, but it is unclear how your lord sees the Igren in that respect. We are independent of your hat-and-girdle townsmen of the lower valley, you know," said Tashih Shaymak.

I wonder who'll be at the dance tonight—maybe one of the faraway families with a tall, strong son I've not met before...

Talima's attention drifted in and out of the conversation. She was unaware of the Chian man's long and flowery explanation of his emperor's plans for the Igren. She came back from her daydreaming only when her kinsmen's outrage exploded.

"One thousand horses! One thousand horses—and half of them perfect white? He must be mad!" shouted the brothers.

Chang Chun's silken voice answered calmly, unaffected by their anger. "Yes-s-s-s, one thousand warrior horses from the most famous herd in all of Asia. And, as final tribute to the Son of Heaven, a virgin daughter of the great Chagan to be wed to the Shining One, binding the contract by blood as well as words. Yes s s..." his sibilant voice trailed off.

A stunned silence followed. A red-tailed hawk screamed above them, then stooped swiftly down on its prey.

"But Father, I ..." Talima began.

"Not now, Talima," her father warned sharply as he stood up, indicating an end to the meeting.

"Batu, will you conduct the envoy to his quarters please?" The Chagan's voice was tightly controlled. "We will consider your request, Chang Chun, and meet again to let you know our decision."

"This humble, ah, this humble person would not offend, Great Wolf, but I must point out to you that the emperor does not request. He commands. When you consider, consider that his mighty arm reaches to the ends of the Earth. Consider how his wrath devastates whole peoples. Consider his position, seated on the Peacock Throne, chosen Son of The Everlasting Sky. Consider carefully, great Chagan!" He nodded, smiled, and followed Batu toward the guest gers.

"An amiable man, but ominous! What think you, Jamui?" said the Chagan to one of his brothers as they watched him walk away.

"But Father! I am your only daughter! I cannot leave, he cannot mean..."

"You are my heart's delight, I'd give anything—a winter's furs—a caravan of silk, not to lose you. But I'm not certain whether or not we have a choice." The Chagan's silvered eyebrows pulled down so tightly, his mouth was such a grim line, that he looked as though he'd put on a mask carved from stone. "Let me explain, this man brought with him a golden Tablet of Authority—did you notice it hanging from his belt, Talima?

"For the past seventeen years, ever since you were born, actually," he continued, "since Tai Tsung became emperor, his armies have continued to conquer and consolidate the world. The few who have resisted him have been annihilated, their men killed, their women and children taken as slaves. But those same armies have kept the trade routes safe for all caravans, from any country, to travel along, a connecting lifeline for us all.

"As you know, these caravans are an essential part of our lives, for furs and horses that we provide, as well as the salt and silks and metals that we trade for. So, for our continued existence at the crossroads center of this vast trade, we must be woven into this net of relations ruled by the emperor of Chian. Is that clear?"

"Yes, father, it's clear. Clear as boiled yak fur!" she teased as she had when little, trying to lighten the dark web they both felt caught in.

"All right," he smiled at their long-familiar joke, then continued patiently, "Chang Chun says—weren't you listening? That the emperor decrees that all clans and tribes participating in this far-flung wheel of trade must pay tribute to him, to the Peacock Throne? From us, from the Igren families, he demands a banner of horses, one thousand warrior horses, half to be of precious, pearl-white in color..."

"By the Everlasting Sky! We won't do it, will we father?"

"We really have no choice, Talima, as I've just explained, not if we want to maintain our borders in peace. The emperor could destroy us—we aren't mighty enough to stand against Chian. Besides, it won't be so hard—one banner of horses, split between our four main families won't reduce the breeding stock too much."

'But Father! It's unthinkable! It does not seem fair! Why don't we..."

"It isn't the horses I mind, my dear," he said sorrowfully. It's the second condition of the required tribute. The emperor wishes to bind all clans by blood, by children.

"His command is that a virgin daughter of each clan's chief be sent to his court in Changan, to become one of his many wives or concubines, to bear his children, thus assuring that clan's loyalty by blood relationships. It's meant to be an honor."

"But I'm your only daughter! Who can you send? You can't mean ...I'm your eldest child! Your heir! You can't send me!"

"I know, little love, but I don't see any alternatives that are honorable."

"Jamui and Kit Boga both have daughters. Send one of them! I belong here! My place is beside you, Chagan! You can't send me away! Send one of my cousins. You must!"

"One of your cousins is not *my* virgin daughter. I would be deliberately lying with intent to deceive the emperor if I sent one of them in your place. That would violate one of our three most basic laws, as you know." He looked out across the glowing foothills. "Besides, I am the Hearth's Keeper, I cannot give over that responsibility to my brothers when something happens that I don't like.

"You know this, Talima-sha. You've spent your life by my side, learning *The Yasa* and the responsibilities that are part of leadership. The position of Chagan is one of power, my dearest child. Power is both pleasure and pain. I shall consult with the Bequi. Perhaps she'll be able to find an honorable way to..."

Talima felt suddenly in danger of being cut off from all that she knew and loved. "No! I won't go! I'll go into the hills by myself! You can disinherit me, disown me! Then I wouldn't be your daughter anymore!" Talima flared up, standing tall as a torch.

"Your uncles have already sent men to bring the horses from their home herds." He continued as if he had not heard her. "It will take several weeks to gather the full banner of horses—for Changan is at least a three moon journey, even for us."

"Please, Father! Please think of something, anything! I know you can!" Her breath came in short, ragged gasps. "I *won't* go! "She whirled away.

"I'll go now to the Bequi, there may be another way. Will you come?" He called after her. But she didn't hear. Blinded by tears of fear and frustration, Talima ran toward the distant corrals.

3
TALIMA DREAMS AND WITNESSES SEDUCTION

TALIMA WHISTLED FOR BAGATUR. SHE LAUGHED WITH DELIGHT AS SHE SAW HIM leap over the corral gate and hurtle toward her. As he skidded to a stop in front of her, she reached up and fondled his velvety ears, looped her sash through his braided-leather halter and jumped onto his back.

"Like the wind, my valiant one, fly!" And fly they did, up into the greening foothills at a drumming gallop as if, in that flight, she could leave all her fears and doubts and anger behind her.

Her red-gold braids streamed out in the wind of their passing. Marmots dived into their holes to avoid being trampled. At a mile-devouring gallop, they rode the ridge into the next valley, walking more slowly along a stream that rushed and burbled through rushes and watercress and small, woodland flowers.

Soon they came to a grove of cottonwoods, leaves turned silver side out by the ice-edged wind. A lonely girl-child in a family of men after her mother died when she was three, it was a place of reverie and solitude that Talima cherished as her own secret hiding place.

Within this wide circle of trees was a secluded haven open only to the everlasting sky. She slid off Bagatur and fed him a handful of wild barley from her pocket. He whickered and nuzzled her shoulder as she brushed sorrel winter hair from his withers. They lay down together in the sun-dappled shade. Talima pillowed her head on Bagatur's belly and stretched out on the mossy ground. She watched clouds take shape, dissolve, and change; she made up stories of the creatures she imagined there until she drifted off to sleep.

And sleeping, dreamed. And dreaming, knew she had dreamed this dream before…

She dreamed she rode a gold and scarlet dragon whose wings spanned the heavens. She smelled the acrid incense of his fiery breath. She felt his power, the lifting surge as he climbed, great talons scattering stars as they went …higher, ever higher, spiraling above the earth until mountains and rivers and valleys were mere shapes in the mists below.

She dreamed…of flying nearer, ever nearer to the moon. Her senses filled with the moon's haloed presence, drowned in its pearly radiance… until a comet flared past, gathering up moon and dragon and rider as it swept the sky with its long tail, and they all, all instantly dissolved in its starry skirts like bubbles in a stream…leaving only one small pearl, glowing in the night sky.

SHE WOKE FROM THE DREAM AS SHE ALWAYS DID, abruptly, half-awake, confused by feelings she did not understand.

Even before she opened her eyes, Talima heard small bird-like cries that she could not identify. *No animal or bird sounds like that*, she thought. The breathy sounds became harsher, faster. She looked around the glade cautiously and almost laughed aloud as she realized where the sounds came from.

On the far side of the clearing, a girl and boy were on the ground with their arms around each other. The squeaks and squeals came from these two as they twisted and writhed together. Talima didn't want them to know she was there, so she lay very still.

She recognized her cousin, Tulari, but the man who was kissing her was a stranger. Judging from the skin coat that lay beside them, and the burnt-ash color of his half-naked body, she thought he probably came from Skyfire country, up north.

Bagatur fidgeted under her. She scratched behind his ears to keep him quiet.

Mmmnnn, it might be nice to touch and be touched, to kiss, to feel another person's body along mine and then…but I'd want more of a man than that scrawny one my cousin has there! Someday I'll have a lover though, tall and sweet. I wonder who he'll be?

As she watched, she felt a shimmer of excitement in her body, centered in the swelling heat of her own *precious gate*. Her breath joined that of the lovers. Her legs wrapped around each other and squeezed rhythmically, pulsing the muscles between her thighs. The liquid heat of her body gathered into itself, creating a trembling, poignant sweetness. Intense pleasure held her taut as the string of a bow for a few moments, then released her gently. She sighed and continued to lie still, unseen in the deep shade of the cottonwoods.

Talima watched their joined bodies separate. The stranger stood and began to dress.

"Did you really mean what you said, before…before we, well, you know?" she heard Tulari ask.

"I could speak to your father, Tulari. I came for a bride you know. I'm a rich man's son! I can pay for what I want, but…" He swaggered around her.

"And do you want me?" she said coquettishly.

"I *have* you," he said. "No, I've changed my mind. Before I offer for you, I'll compare you with other girls of your clan before I decide which one I want."

"But, Kurt! You promised! If I let you, if you—if we…" Tulari murmured something Talima could not hear.

Their voices bickered back and forth, finally fading into silence as they finished dressing and walked away. Their disagreement seemed to be resolved as they began to leave the glade.

"Did I tell you that I'm racing the Chagan's sons this afternoon? I challenged them," he boasted, "wagered that I'd beat them by six lengths. I'll do it, too!"

"You can't!" Tulari answered defiantly.

"Oh? You'll see! I'm the best rider in the whole North Country! No one can beat me!"

"Don't be silly! You can't really believe that that short-legged, shaggy pony of yours can beat one of *our* horses!"

"I'll bet you!" Kurt flared, "I'll bet you a gold piece that I win by six lengths!"

"Do you really have a gold piece?" asked Tulari cautiously.

"I told you, I came to buy a bride. I have a bag of gold pieces!" he declared proudly.

"I have no gold to wager," Tulari said.

"That's all right, you have something else I'll take against the bet." He looked at her, calculating her response.

"What's that?"

"Your total submission. You will do anything I tell you to—for a whole night!"

"Well, if ever there was an easy bet! How could I lose? Done and wagered!" Tulari held out her hand to seal the bargain. They shook hands and left the grove.

When she was sure they were gone, Talima stood and stretched, feeling the familiar roughness of felt on her thighs and breasts, satisfied with the pleasure of it.

Bagatur scrambled to his feet, shaking moss and leaves from his head and mane. They wandered out of the cool shade into the warm afternoon. Small frogs sang spring songs along the riverbank.

The hills had worked their magic, and Talima was no longer angry, no longer desperate. She was however, resolute in her determination to find a way out of the emperor's edict, and deeply troubled by the recurring dragon dream. Mounting Bagatur, she set off to seek advice and explanations from the Bequi, grandmother and elder shaman to the whole clan.

SHE RODE INTO A COPSE OF LACY, TAMARISK TREES WHERE DRIED BIRDS SPUN, their feathers curing in the dry wind. Willow baskets were heaped with drying flowers and leaves, aromatic in the strong sunshine. Small, furry animals scampered in and out of gnarled, bleached branches that the Bequi had brought down from timberline.

"'Hatou, Bequi?" Talima called. "How quiet it is, where could she be?"

"'Hatou, Talima-sha," the Bequi answered quietly, gliding out from her ger. She was as wispy and willowy as the grasses that blew around her, as bone dry as the earth she walked on. Her skirts were stained with odd patches of bark dyes—yellow, blue-green and maroon. Her pet raven hopped after her, speaking in deep chirrs and squawks that sounded like the Bequi herself.

"Won't you dismount and come in? The Chagan and I are *reading-the-bones*. And what we read concerns you. Deeply," she smiled her crooked smile.

"I won't interrupt, Bequi, if you and father are..." Talima wanted to run again, wanted only to understand her dragon dream, wanted to stay as far away as possible from decisions the Chagan might be making.

"As you wish, Talima-sha, but you must, you know. You must know. You cannot deny your destiny. Come, join us. Sit. Listen."

Reluctantly, Talima dropped her reins and slowly, silently, followed as the Bequi commanded.

In the center of the ger, a small, hot fire burned, its smoke curled up through an open hole. The curving, felt walls were hung with a shaman's paraphernalia. The air smelled of smoke, sweet herbs and dusty mystery.

On the other side of the fire, Tashih Shaymak sat cross-legged, his heavy riding boots standing on their own beside him. He looked up, unsmiling, as Talima entered, and gestured for her to sit beside him.

Across from them, the Bequi coiled her long, grey hair over one shoulder as she began turning a sheep's shoulder-bone in the fire. She pulled it out now and again to examine the pattern of cracks that appeared as it charred.

"Mmmnnn-hmmnnn, eeeh ya so...the winds of fate blow cold," she whispered, nodding.

"What do you see?" the Chagan asked. "I must know the truth! What does this jagged, broken line mean, Bequi?"

"Patience, my brother. We will see the pattern of the whole, in time. In time." The Bequi rocked back on her heels. Her tongue clicked an accent to her words.

Over and over again, the two consulted the oracle burned into the still-smoking shoulder-bone. The map of the future seemed clear. As always, the prosperity and honor of the Igren depended on obedience to *The Yasa*, the sacred, ancient law. Truth in all dealings was of paramount importance, else the very fabric of society would be shredded.

Talima realized her father's grief as he looked up, tears streaming down the furrows of his cheeks. She saw him stand, resolute in the clear understanding of what must be done. Resolve was written on his face, the knowledge that he could send no other than herself, his only daughter.

He looks as if his heart were breaking, she thought. She wanted to reach out, to touch him, but he turned, his tall body bowed with sorrow, and walked slowly away from her out into the sunshine.

Stunned, Talima remained. "But, Bequi, what about...?"

"Ya, so, little one, your dream of dragons, that you would understand, is it not?"

"Yes, but how did you know?"

"Because the bones foretold your destiny, my dear. And riding the great dragon of your dreams is part of that. You'll fully understand it only when a blazing star sweeps clear across the Everlasting Sky. Only then. Only...then..." Her voice trailed off.

Talima leaped up impatiently. "All you and Father ever do is speak in riddles! How am I supposed to understand riddles! One moment I think I know, the next, I'm totally in the dark!" She ducked under the low door and once more gathered up her reins, to ride, fast and furious, back into the home valley.

4
Talima Hears the Truth: Wolves Dine

As Bagatur and Talima crossed the valley, mountain shadows grew long. Newly-hatched insects poured out of the grass at every step. Fountains of minute, iridescent wings spangled the air.

Kuriltai hullabaloo had begun early. At the center of each circle of ger, skewers of seasoned meat dripped juice onto glowing coals. The day's bets were being settled. Weary falcons flew to their covered stands. Night's fires flared anew as shadows lengthened.

Men who had been drinking *kumiss*, fermented mare's milk, for hours, danced the whirling men's dance. Their riding boots stomped into dry, red earth. Skin pipes skirled, fiddles sang, drums and cymbals beat and clanged. The day's gaiety was rapidly progressing into uproarious debauch.

Leading Bagatur, Talima wound her way through the throngs of merrymakers. She felt almost invisible.

Lathered horses jostled around her. She realized her brothers had been racing, and judging by their jubilation, had won. The sour-faced northerner on his richly-decorated, shaggy pony plodded behind them.

A poor loser, Talima thought. *He looks like an evil earth-kelet, glaring at everyone. What a mean-spirited fellow he is! Ah, well, live and let live.*

"'Hatou, little brothers!"

"Come ride with us, Tam," Jalco said.

"Thanks, but I want to change before dancing tonight. I'll meet you there."

Talima continued on to the corrals, turned Bagatur loose with the herd, then walked to her own small ger that stood beside her father's splendid one.

Two clay pots, one of water, one of milk stood outside her door. She drank from the water jug and, with her mouth full, slowly squirted the stream of water over her hands, washing them vigorously, a habit she had learned as a child. She took off her boots, lifted the felted door flap and ducked inside.

The setting sun made her ger a translucent dome. Flowers and vines painted on the walls looked almost real. A shaft of rose-colored light poured down through the central fire hole, making a lantern unnecessary. Talima's treasures hung from the willow framework: beaded sashes, bright-colored woolen tassels, and woven lariats. Furs were heaped beside a wicker backrest on a blood-red rug.

Talima took off her woolen tunic and shirt and folded them into a basket. She rubbed soured cream into her wind-tanned face and hands, brushed her braids out into a shining waterfall that fell below her knees. Over her head, she tossed a shift made of creamy silk, reveling in the feel of it on her skin. She tucked full, magenta silk pants into soft, red-leather boots, wrapped a purple sash around the waist of her best blue-brocaded tunic, then turned 'round and 'round, hair flying, tunic swirling until she was dizzy. For the moment, she put cares aside and was ready to celebrate. She slipped next door to her father's ger just as her cousin, Tulari, burst in upon his conversation with the ambassador.

"He promised me!" Tulari wailed. "And now he says he never did! It was a bargain, Tashih! A bargain!"

"All right, lass. Slow down. Who promised you?" asked the Chagan.

"He did. Aah, Kurt did!" Tulari wiped tears away with the back of her hand.

"And who is this Kurt?" Tashih Shaymak asked patiently. "Hush now, dry your tears."

"He's a man from a clan up north, from Skyfire Land."

"And what's he done to you, my young filly?"

"He bet that his horse would beat your sons' horses—by six lengths! Of course it was foolish, but he *did* bet me a gold piece!"

"Father, I might be able to clear..."

"One moment, please, Talima. Now let's see if I have the straight of it, Tulari. A man named Kurt bet you a gold piece that he'd win a race with your cousins by six lengths. He lost the race and now won't honor his debt?"

"That's right."

"What did *you* bet, Tulari?"

"Well," she fidgeted. "Well, I agreed to do anything he told me to do. For a whole night."

"I see," the Chagan said softly. "Yes, well, I think we should hear the young man's side of this story, don't you?"

He beckoned to one of his companions. "Fetch a guest from the northland, Kurt by name. Bring him here, please. We have some business to settle before we feast tonight. Honored Ambassador, would you wish to leave?"

"With your permission, I might find a formal hearing interesting—to see how the Great Blue Wolf deals with situations of this sort. Who knows? I might be able to learn something, yes?"

Within the hour, the Chagan's ceremonial totem was in place; nine yak tails wound with tasseled wool fluttered from a ten-foot pole. At the top, the traditional white falcon spread its protective wings over the man below.

Jamui and Kit Boga, still relatively sober, sat on their brother's right, Talima on his left as befitted the heir. A half dozen Cup-Companions and the Chian ambassador sat around the open fire. Tulari sat on one of two felt pads opposite them, her back to the main encampment.

The northerner arrived, standing between his lanky Igren escorts. *He looks smaller and darker than ever*, Talima thought.

"You wanted to see me?" the stranger said, neglecting the simplest of courtesies.

"We have asked for you to come so that you may answer a charge made by our kinswoman, Tulari," answered the Chagan. "Please be seated."

"I have better things to do—wine and wenches, Grandfather! I'll talk with you tomorrow. Sorry, but I'm not interested in stories of Tulari's, or anyone else's for that matter!" He stood, thumbs hooked in his waist sash, legs apart, trying to look older and taller.

"You *will* sit!" thundered the Chagan, "Your name and clan. Now. Be quick about it."

"I'm Kurt Charigar, the Black Eagle, eldest son of Mazar, chief of Tagh Clan," he boasted. "I'm not one of your soft-mouthed men! My father will hear about this!"

"Indeed he will," Chagan said intently. "Meanwhile, since you have chosen to join our Kuriltai, Kurt Charigar, you must abide by our laws and customs. If you do not wish to do so, you may take your slaves and baggage and leave. Immediately."

"Oh, no! I came to buy a bride and I'm not leaving without one to warm my backside on the way home. So let's get on with it."

"Very well. I believe you know Tulari, my kinswoman?" The Chagan's stone-blue eyes pierced the distance between them.

"Sure, I know her," Kurt leered, "Why?"

"Tulari charges you with dishonoring a debt, specifically with reneging on a wager. We would hear your side of the story so that trust between persons may be restored in the camp."

"But first, we must convene the hearing. Kit Boga will recite *The Yasa*, the Code of Right Conduct by which civilized people live. Kit?" The Chagan gestured to his brother and leaned back.

"In the time when the Blue Wolf still roamed the Mountain of Power," Kit Boga began to chant the ancient Law. "In the time when She gave birth to the first of the Blue-eyed Men, She saw their power, saw them as strong, unbroken rocks and rushing torrents, saw their need for Law.

"Our ancestor, the wise Blue Wolf, Mother of Igren, gave her children The Wand of Power, *The Yasa*, spindle around which our lives are spun," Kit Boga swayed slightly as his singsong voice rumbled on. "*The Yasa* says that every man, woman, and child must live each day by honoring the Everlasting Sky in thought and deed.

"*The Yasa* says there are only three great wrongs. Each are punishable by death. The first is practicing black magic. The second, acting sexually with animals. The third and greatest wrong is lying—lying deliberately—*with intent to deceive.*

"This is *Yasa*. This is *The Law*," he remained standing for a moment, then, hand over heart, saluted the Chagan's standard and sat down. Chang Chun sat with lowered eyes, his thoughts hidden, nodding, as if asleep.

"Tala Tulari, state your accusation, please," the Chagan nodded to her. Talima listened, listened for the color of truth in all that was being said.

"Thank you, Tulari. Now Kurt, what have you to say?"

"I say she's lying Chagan. You know women, they'll say anything to get back at you!" Kurt smiled at the men. "Plain fact is, Tulari's a disappointed female. She wants me to marry her and I won't. So now she's trying to discredit me.

"You know how it is, give 'em a little kiss and they think they own you! *Our* women know their place better. They'd never dare to accuse me like this stupid wench!" Kurt sneered at the unhappy girl.

"So. You deny having bet on the race? Deny having wagered a gold piece?" asked the Chagan. Talima began to speak, then thought better of it.

"Well, I ask you, Tashih Shaymak, would anyone in his right mind wager against your famous horses? Much less bet a *gold piece?* It wouldn't make sense, would it? Why, all the world sings praises of the Igren horses. I'd be a fool to bet against them—and I'm no fool!

"As I see it, you have to decide between the words of a chief's son, of Mazar Tagh's son, and that of this druze-girl. Not much question of who's in the right, is there?"

"How do you say then, Kurt Charigar? Do you declare yourself guilty or innocent?"

"Oh, innocent, Chagan, most certainly innocent!"

"Very well," said the Chagan, troubled, "remain here. Both of you. I will hold counsel."

Talima went with her uncles and father into his spacious ger.

"It's as the boy says, a ridiculous thing to bet on. You're Tulari's father, Jamui, d'you trust her word?"

"Father," interrupted Talima, "There's something I think you should know."

"Aye, daughter, I'm glad you were here to hear both testimonies. I trust your ability to hear what a person's heart is saying, regardless of their words. Can you tell which one is truth-saying?"

"Yes, Father, only this time I don't need to rely on the color of truth behind their words, for I have other knowledge." Talima spoke formally in keeping with the seriousness of the occasion.

"You see, I overheard their conversation. I heard Kurt bet Tulari a gold piece, just as she said."

The four men, like tall trees around her, stood very still as the full impact of her words sank in. The boy from Skyfire Land had told a deliberate falsehood. *Had lied to them…with intent to deceive!*

Guilt or innocence of the charge was unimportant now. The wager was unimportant. Even the gold was unimportant. But the truth *was* important. For they all knew that without truth between persons, no one, nothing, could be trusted. Lacking this honesty, the whole fabric of society fell apart.

Talima felt the men's resolute strength as well as their horror at the lies, the deliberate lies, that Kurt Charigar had told them.

"We have no choice then, do we?" the Chagan said with deadly quiet. "It is *The Law*. We must obey it."

Without another word, they went back outside to those who waited.

"Kurt Charigar! Tala Tulari!" Jamui called, "Stand and hear the Judgment."

Tulari stood, wavering as if blown by strong winds. Kurt brushed back his black hair and got to his feet with insolent slowness. *He must be mad as well as wicked, to so provoke the Council,* Talima thought.

"We have found that Tulari is telling the truth. This leaves us no choice but to charge you, Kurt Charigar, with the great wrong of lying with intent to deceive," the Chagan's deep voice intoned.

"We find you guilty of deliberate lying, Black Eagle of Tagh Clan. You have violated one of the *Yasa's* fundamental laws. I deeply regret to inform you that you must be punished by death."

Talima saw Tulari's eyes flare like a frightened antelope's. The northerner seemed to shrivel. He shook as if chilled. He began to make mewing sounds; his face twitched in a sly, one-sided smile.

"Who said? It's not my fault! She's the one who lies! You just want to get my gold! You're thieves! All of you!"

The Council clapped, clapped their hands in disapproval, derision, disgust at his continued lying.

"Stand like a man! If you can!" the Chagan thundered. "Talima witnessed your wager with Tulari. You deliberately and falsely accused another. You declare yourself innocent when you are truly guilty." The Chagan continued as if the boy's whining were no more than a whisper on the night wind.

"As you tell us that you are a person of superior birth, we will not spill your blood, but..."

"Right! I'll pay you the gold to let me go! I'll go first thing in the morning. You can have it all!" Kurt scrabbled around in his pockets.

"We have a proverb that says, 'We have no whip but a horse's tail.' By tradition, you will become *zulgur*, will be wrapped in felt,and tied behind the tails of two horses.

"Those horses will run through the herd until you no longer exist in your present form. Until the life you have disgraced is trampled out and you are as the felt you have been wrapped in. You are condemned to die as zulgur."

At the word zulgur, horror bleached all living color from Kurt's face.

"With the exception of one gold piece paid to Tulari in just settlement of your wager, your gold, horses, and baggage will accompany your slaves back to your father. May your spirit be cleansed of its falseness before it comes again to this earth. Take him away!"

The leader of the Golden Family had spoken. Men jumped to obey.

"When the zulgur, the mess-that-was-a-man, is complete, take it to the High Place as an offering to our brothers, the wolves, who will feast tonight," the Chagan instructed.

Talima turned away. *I know the harshness of the sentence is appropriate, but I can't help wondering if there might be another way...such a terrible way to die.*

Talima saw Chang Chun, standing in front of her, gather his furs around him as he muttered, "How very interesting, how innocent mon-barbarians are. Why on earth *would* anyone lie *without* intent to deceive? If the truth be told, the fabric of life at court would unravel completely if lies were not used!"

Talima heard him murmur as he walked away, "It may be difficult for the court to properly train this odd young woman, given her background. How would you go about civilizing someone so uncouth? I'm glad it won't be up to me to do so!"

Before she could call out to him, the ambassador wandered into the star bright night toward the Kuriltai pavilion, alone.

Outside, two horses pawed the ground and whinnied irritably as the lumpy bundle, wound round and round with felt and ropes, was tied to the base of their tails. At the Chagan's command, whips snapped, and the horses took off over the rocky ground at a heart-pounding run.

An eerie, muffled sound came from the bundle, half moan, half scream, all animal, that grew fainter and fainter as the horses raced in circles. Soon there was no sound at all, and the horses were allowed to slow to a walk.

Three slaves cut loose the zulgur, the blood-sodden bundle that had once been Kurt Charigar. They carried it up to the High Place where wolves waited patiently.

5
THE CHAGAN DECIDES: A REED IS BROKEN

FLAGS SNAPPED IN NIGHT WINDS OFF THE MOUNTAIN. Tashih Shaymak, his daughter, brothers, and Cup-Companions walked down toward the sounds of music and revelry that came from the pavilion at the center of the valley. The weight of power and judgment was heavy. Their hearts were filled with sorrow that evil had existed, even for a little time in their midst.

Their boots scrunched dry grass thick with frost-flowers that sparkled in the moonlight. They held together in silent regret and looked forward to the solace of friends and family.

Jamui held open the pavilion's door flap and beckoned them inside. The Chagan hesitated, then took Talima's arm and held her back, "Let's talk for a few moments before we go in, my dear, "

"Have you found a way for me to stay?" she said, hoping still, though she knew the answer before he spoke.

The Chagan gently brushed back the hair from her forehead, "You are my own brave girl. You must fulfill the emperor's command. You must go to Chian with our banner of horses. We have no choice."

Oh, Great Tengri, she thought, *help me to bear this, help me to live up to what father expects of me! Help me to stay strong... I don't think I can... but I must... but how? There's no turning back now, no other choices to be made. But oh, how hard it is!*

"I'm not sure I can manage a whole banner of horses by myself, " Talima said, tears sparkling in her eyes as she abruptly changed the subject.

"I'll send several men with you, a few *chapars,* someone to lead, to make decisions on the trail. Not your brother, he's too young. Jalco must stay anyway—I must begin teaching him to take your place. Maybe Pirjhan?"

"Pirjhan! He's not much older than I am! I can make any decisions that are necessary, Father. Why would you choose someone like Pirjhan?"

Tengri, Pirjhan! It's always Pirjhan between me and father these days. I wish Pirjhan would pay attention to me, instead of pretending I don't exist! Why does he always make me so angry?

"He's a good man, Talima. Resourceful, loyal, intelligent. And although he's only a few years older than you, he's vastly older in experience on the trail and in strange or dangerous situations. He was only a boy when slavers ripped him from his mother's arms, you know. And he lived with that caravan, hard traveling for ten years, until they came through here, and I bought him to get him away from their brutality. He's proved himself a thousand times since then.

"You see, daughter-mine, I have few talents, therefore I am fond of intelligent men. I am fond of Pirjhan. He can be relied on to bring you and the horses safely across the Great Desert."

Suddenly the world doesn't look quite so bleak—leaving home to be empress of a faraway land is too hard to imagine. Riding the trail for three months with Pirjhan could be an entirely different matter 'cause he'd have to notice me then and, well, that just might be—a grand adventure!

"I suppose we could make decisions together, Pirjhan and I," she said. "All right, Father, I'll show Chian what a daughter of The Blue Wolf can do! I'll go to Chian...but I'll be back!"

"There's my good girl. You've always loved a challenge—think of this as the biggest challenge of your young life. We'll be together for yet a little while, for the Kuriltai hunt tomorrow, and to feast and dance tonight. Shall we go in?"

He lifted the painted felt door and they stepped inside exchanging mountain freshness for air thick with smoke from oil lamps. Arms around each other's waists, the Chagan and Talima stood together and looked at their joyful people. Several hundred boisterous clansmen were there, eating, drinking and dancing. Their shadows cavorted over the curved ceiling.

The women wore furs and embroidered vests over supple silk or woolen shifts. Gold and silver bangle bracelets chimed on their arms;

heron feathers plumed their looped and braided hair. Little girls and boys looked like bright hummingbirds in their embroidered tunics and soft boots. Men wore fur-trimmed boots and their finest woolen tunics wrapped with many-colored belts; their conical white felt hats made them appear even taller than they were.

Arms entwined around each other's shoulders, three Cup-Companions greeted their Chagan by holding out a foot-long ram's horn filled with kumiss.

"Drink, Chagan! Drink...drink...drink!" They stomped the heels of their boots in time with their words.

Tashih Shaymak took the spiral horn, tossed his head back and drank it all in one long swallow. Rising and falling like streams from the mountain, dozens of voices rang out in welcome to their Chagan and his daughter.

His usual good nature restored, Tashih Shaymak swept Talima into his arms and spun her into an ebullient dance that ended only when they fell, laughing and breathless, on his own waiting carpets.

"Tam! Come join us!" A group of young people called. Talima bowed to her father and joined them.

"You're just in time to settle a bet!" Jalco declared.

"Spare me, little brother," Talima smiled. "Tonight I've had enough of wagers. Tonight I would be merry. Come dance with me!"

Fiddlers struck up a lively tune. Talima shut her eyes and let Jalco lead her into wordless, joyous movement, dizzy with a delight she felt throughout her lithe body.

Everyone danced. Women danced with girls as well as men; boys danced by themselves as well as with girls or grandmothers. Little children danced standing on their father's boots. Singly or together, they danced, boots kicking, tunics flaring, hair flying.

Then a chaining circle-dance began—lines of dancers intertwining, meeting, greeting, changing partners, circling back. As each pair of dancers met, their eyes held, their hands clasped over their heads, and they sang an osun chorus: "Hai! You are in I, am in me, am in we! Hai!" Then each would kick high, skip two steps and start all over again with the next dancer.

It was Talima's favorite; she felt part of each person she met, felt she could see through their eyes. She lost her sense of self, and turned through a circle of familiar, gray and blue-eyed souls. She felt feather-light, moved only by the music's will.

Suddenly, green-gray eyes, brown hair, the strange smell of smoky perfume, another kind of intensity, a different sort of person. Talima felt jolted out of a dream as she realized that it was Pirjhan, but a different Pirjhan than she had known before.

As head horseman, a slave from the Land of Lions, Pirjhan had seemed merely another of her father's men. This man was a compelling, attractive stranger whose warm, rein-rough hands vibrated against her own.

"Hai, Talima! You are...in I...am in..." Pirjhan sang, smiling across at her.

"'Hatou, Pirjhan!" Talima's heart beat faster as she danced on, her lungs filled with his scent.

As the night wore on, couples drifted out into the moon-frosty night and returned later, smiling in an intimate way. Children fell asleep on furs, fat little bodies tangled together. Older children played jokes on grownups by sneaking around under tent flaps and jumping out at them unexpectedly.

At last, the lanterns were burnt out, and night's fires burned low. The first light of dawn bloomed on Burkhan Kaldun's peak. A rosy light suffused the ice fields.

The Chagan stood. At his signal the music stopped. Everyone still capable of doing so, stood with him and joined hands. They formed a wide circle within the dim and dusty pavilion. The sudden stillness woke children who clung, wide-eyed and staring, to their mother's hems.

Talima watched as a figure glided out of the shadows into the center of the ring. It was the Bequi, Speaker-to-Heaven, who seemed tree-tall, graceful rather than forceful. Her thin greying hair was twisted with feathers and sparkly stones and a white fur cloak swept the ground behind her. Her bony face was chalk-white, her full, pouty mouth red from berry juice. As she came, she swung a smoking censer and sounded a shrill, whining "Ya-ya-ha-ya" over and over.

The encircling clans swayed and hummed as they waited for the traditional closing ceremony of the first of Kuriltai celebrations.

Talima found herself standing between her brother and Pirjhan. His presence made her oddly happy. She watched as the Bequi picked up her carved speaker staff and tapped the ground four times, once for each direction of the winds.

The Bequi began to chant an Igren litany of creation, "Behold, oh Sky, thy blue-eyed children! Born of the Blue Wolf, their hands strong as bears' paws, their voices like thunder in the mountains! They sleep naked by a fire of mighty trees. They feel the sparks no more than insect bites. They feel the cold no more than a summer breeze.

"The blue-eyed ones have heads of bronze! Their teeth gnaw into rocks. Their hearts are iron. Drinking the dew of night, they ride on the wind!" The circle swayed right and left, humming accompaniment.

"Possessing only their shadows, they are possessed by no one! Their strength is in the power of their blood. Their freedom is everlasting under one Sky, one Family, undivided!

"I have read the stars!" continued the Speaker-to-Heaven, "The Wolf Star is strong in its statement for the coming year. There can be no doubt in our minds of its auspicious nature.

"The time is at hand for the Igren to reach out and take what rightfully belongs to them, riches beyond what we have know before! Riches from the Land of the Rising Sun, power from a Snake-That-Flies. New roads, new ways! A time of change. Be strong. Be assured. The stars proclaim the truth of it!"

She put down her staff and picked up a bundle of tightly bound, dry reeds, then beckoned one of the children and Jalco to come to her. She gave the bundled reeds to Talima's brother.

"Break this bundle…if you can."

Try as he might, strain as mightily as he was able, Jalco was unable to break the bound reeds.

Then the Bequi pulled a single reed from the bundle and gave it to the small child, who snapped it with ease.

"Thus is the strength of the family assured in the year to come. Bound together we are unbreakable!" She waved the reeds overhead. Her triumphant cry rang in quavering shrillness…thrilling, jubilant.

"Be ye of the same mind and hold together!" Her voice trilled. She picked up the bundle of reeds again and unbound them. "And now…"

She gave one reed to each person, blew a white powder over their heads as she moved around the circle, saying, "Be ye of the same mind…"

"…and hold together," Talima answered. The Bequi leaned close to her and whispered, "Keep this reed with you always!" She feathered Talima's head with the sacred white dust and moved to the next person.

When everyone had received a reed, and responded to the oath, the Bequi smiled her crooked smile and shuffle-skipped out of the tent.

Women gathered up their sleeping babes. Men extinguished fires. The Igren filed out into the freshness of a mountain morning. They drifted off toward their own ger through rising, roseate mists. Wolves sang to each other from high places.

Talima pretended not to notice that Pirjhan still held her hand. She smiled at him with a new shyness, then walked away alone. The dawn was full of promise.

BY NOON THE NEXT DAY, NEARLY FIFTY EAGER RIDERS GATHERED at the meadow's edge for the traditional hunt. They courteously maneuvered their horses into trail position behind the Chagan. Dressed alike in baggy, felted pants stuffed into sturdy heeled boots, their knee-length, fitted felt coats spread over high-pommelled, wooden saddles. Woven sashes secured knives and coiled lengths of twisted hemp around their waists. Men wore wide-brimmed felt hats; most women wore caps with embroidered earflaps that covered their coiled braids. Capless, Talima's hair shone in the strong sun.

"Early this morning, I sent a dozen beaters out with Pirjhan, into the next valley to start the animals moving. We should find game a-plenty waiting for us," the Chagan announced.

As they waited, some hunters stood in their stirrups in order to test whether the short, double-curved bow that hung over their left hip was free. Some drew imaginary arrows out of tightly woven arrow cases to make sure they'd be easy to reach during the frenzy of hunting.

Many hunters carried their own birds—falcons or hawks, an eagle or two—hooded and jessed, on their shoulder or forearm. In time-honored fashion, they bantered and bet amongst themselves: wagers on the changing weather, the outcome of the hunt, their horse's speed, or their bird's prowess.

The Chagan rode a silver-dappled stallion whose saddle was covered with scarlet felt on which his name and titles were emblazoned with gold-wrapped yarn. He leaned forward, crossing his arms on the pommel, iron-still, observing everything that happened, everything that was said.

"Are you ready, my swift one, my Merket? This is our last hunt, you know. We must do well," Talima whispered to her falcon as she smoothed neck feathers from under its indigo-blue hood. She hitched the strap of her bow into a more comfortable position on her hip, tucked a horn-handled knife into her sash, pulled bridle tassels from under Bagatur's mane, and moved through the crowd of horsemen. Proudly, she took her place at the Chagan's side.

On the leather-wrapped, left forearm of the Chagan and each of his three brothers, golden eagles sensed, despite their hooded eyes, the excitement around them. They moved restlessly, lifting a taloned foot, stretching a thickly feathered bronze wing, readying for flight.

When it seemed as though all who wished to hunt had arrived, the Chagan lifted his arm. Talima took a rose-lipped conch shell from her saddlebags and blew a throbbing sound that reverberated across the valley and into the forest ahead. The sound tore at her heart, reminding her of all she held dear, all that soon would be gone.

Not now! I must not think of this just now...only the hunt, my last hunt. The last notes wavered as her eyes filled with tears.

At this signal, they moved out, singing and joking as they climbed the ridge that led onto the mountain's flank. The well-worn trail led to the headwaters of two sacred rivers that burst forth, full-sized, from Burkhan Kaldun's bowels.

It always seems a miracle to me, Talima thought, *these two rivers flowing full force from the earth...the "Jun" and "Barun", the left and right arms of the mountain, holding our home valley. I wonder how far they flow, if they ever stop. Bequi says they flow into a "sea" somewhere beyond the Lands of Eternal Snow, I wonder where that is...in Chian perhaps?*

As their horses waded the Barun River, each rider took his drinking flask and spilled a few drops of whatever it contained, water or kumiss, into the stream to placate the water-spirit-*kelets*. Masters of Flowing Water, they knew, were always thirsty.

Talima squirted an offering of milk into the river. Then she tipped her head back and squeezed a thin arc of milk from the goatskin into her mouth. Without swallowing, she lifted Merket and, girl's lips to falcon's beak, gave him a drink too. She savored this small act, savored each precious moment of this glorious hunt.

The horsemen reached the top of the ridge and looked down over another plain. The fields had been burned weeks before, an immemorial practice to renew the grass for grazing. Now, bright green blades of grass pushed up through black stubble. Gusting winds flurried the ashes.

A solitary horseman galloped toward them. He rode an odd-looking horse, front half black, rear half white—the Chagan's head horseman who sat tall, riding with the ease of a man who has spent most of his life in the saddle.

"Ahatou, Tashih-sha," he greeted as he reined up between Talima and her father.

"You have game waiting, Pirjhan?" the Chagan asked.

"'Hatou, Pirjhan," Talima greeted, but he ignored her.

How like him—pushing in between father and me, riding that ugly brute of a horse, Caraco, pretending that I don't exist. I thought, after last night...well, we'll see.

"Aye, sir, that we do, game a-plenty! Large herds of antelope in a box canyon just beyond that far butte," Pirjhan grinned.

"The Everlasting Sky is good to us!" Tashih Shaymak exulted. "Lead on, Pirjhan, let's *ride!*"

Igren horsemen plummetted down—raptors riding into the updraft wind, their full-throated hunting cry rippling before them across the prairie. Spread out from ridge to ridge, no one horse rode ahead of another.

This is what life is all about! Riding out with your own people as the grass turns green—hunting on a fine, fast horse—holding a falcon on my wrist. How good it is!

At full gallop they spurted through the narrow canyon mouth into thousands of antelope that dashed every which way in mounting panic.

The afternoon passed swiftly in the wildest, bloodiest, most chaotic hours Talima had ever experienced. Single scenes, instant, intense, burned themselves into her mind: the burnt-gold flanks of antelope, shifting, turning like shoals of fish flashing in the sun; golden eagles beating at the antelopes' heads with their stiff wings, blinding them until the deadly arrows found their mark; horses colliding, falling, their riders miraculously unhurt, scrambling to their feet in the midst of antelope that leaped and bounded wildly, unable to escape.

She never knew whether she had killed or not. Her arrow case was lighter, but she could not remember bending her bow. In the rapidly changing melee, she was aware of only one thing, of staying just behind and to the left of her father, becoming his shadow in this as in all things, wheeling, rearing, charging, matching his movement, moment by moment, time without end.

And then suddenly, as if by some signal, the hunt ceased. The remaining antelope were allowed to stream from the canyon. It was over. The Chagan waved her away.

Talima flung herself out of the saddle onto a grassy knoll. She watched her brothers and their friends rolling around her, wrestling and laughing. She felt older, separate, already a stranger.

What will all this seem like when I'm in that world so far away? Even though I know I must, how can I bear to leave? Great Everlasting Sky, give me strength! She leaped onto Bagatur and readied her gear for the night ride home.

Gradually, everyone gathered—youths, older men telling stories of other hunts, heavily laden animals and slaves.

As a lop-sided sun sank slowly into its jagged mountain bed, the full moon, like a great bubble, bounced into the sky from an opposite ridge. For a few moments, the light of the world balanced between them, holding off the night. Twilight, green and glowing, suffused dark pines. Purple mountain skies paled and pearled.

Talima, first to ride around the last bend of the trail, stopped, her delight kindled as always, when she looked down and out across her beloved home valley. Moonlight silvered icy air that smelled like snow. Campfires on the dark earth below sent showers of sparks into the sky.

Earth-kelets spitting fire...one more night, one more day, one more, no more, never more...

She shivered with a brooding premonition of change too great to name. She leaned forward, lifted her reins, and flew down the trail, leaving mysteries to the night behind her.

6
On The Trail

THE *BANNER* OF A THOUSAND HORSES FLOWED OVER THE LAND like a multi-colored river. They streamed out of the home valley at dawn as effulgent sunlight shafted through the mountain pass.

At the river fork, Talima turned Bagatur, in order to look back, to gather the whole familiar scene into her memory and store it away like precious treasure to carry with her into the unknown world that lay ahead. As wind feathered strands of copper-colored hair blew around her head, Talima listened to the singing wind that sang songs of all she held dear, all she was leaving in the valley below.

Talima looked up at the Mountain of Power where glacial mists whirled like a shawl, where haloes of ice-crystals spun out against a sapphire sky. She thought of this Burkhan Kaldun Mountain, of how its constant presence, its moods of storm and mist and sunlight had given her strength and lifted her spirits on even the loneliest days, all the years of her life.

How will I live without it? I must not think about this now. Now I must ride. And not think of tomorrow. Only ride. "Like the wind, like wind from the mountain—fly, Bagatur!"

She leaned forward, her head against his streaming mane, loosed the reins and let her stallion carry them both into the current of horses pouring through the pass, out of the home valley, along the northern Silk Road, into the three thousand miles of desolate Gobi Desert that lay ahead.

Talima rode up beside Pirjhan, three chapars—her old horse trainer, Juchi,and two younger Igren—Tulak and Kilar—all of whom were shouting across the undulating river of horses, bunching them up as they rode north.

"Ho, Juchi! Let's give the horses some room, let them spread out.

We've a ways to go and you know they don't like such tight quarters, next to the camels 'n all," Talima directed.

"No. It's better this way," interrupted Pirjhan. "Until we get safely away, I don't want them turning around and heading for home—let them be, Juchi."

Talima smothered an icy retort and cantered off, thin-lipped and silent. They kept their quick, tight, riding pattern all day. Well away into the rolling hills, they moved more slowly, stopping frequently to check the loads on pack-camels, allowing the animals time to grow accustomed to the inflexible rhythm of riding trail.

Daily, they scrabbled up mountain passes and slid down the other side, causing minor rock avalanches. Often a valley would be flooded by snow-melt streams. They forded icy torrents by hanging onto their horses' tails as they swam across. They stayed wet and cold. They continued on, ever on, covering the country as only Igren horsemen could.

As she rode, Talima felt the sorrow that had consumed her days gradually lessen, soothed by the steady drumbeat of horses' hooves, scoured by the ever-present wind, diminishing the rebellious anger that had poisoned those last days at home.

Talima thought back on the last afternoon she'd spent with her father, the afternoon when they'd brought millet and milk to the outstretched hands of a stone statue that stood by her ancestors' hillside graves. They had placed their offerings on her mother's grave, the mother who had ascended into the Everlasting Sky when Talima was so young. Then they'd said goodbye, while Talima thought her breath would stop and she'd never be able to breathe again. Her father had cried and the hills had echoed his grief.

She thought of the gift her father had given her—Shira, the star-bright mare that now followed Bagatur like a shadow, even as she had been the Chagan-sha's shadow. *Until now. Now, who am I, now?*

Father says that the first days on the trail are the hardest, but this is ridiculous. I hate Pirjhan, he's an arrogant, rude bully, he contradicts anything and everything I say! Talima muttered as she urged Bagatur across a marshy stream. With heart-straining effort, Bagatur gathered himself and leaped up a muddy bank made slippery from the passage of all the horses before them. The mare, Shira, slithered behind them.

It doesn't matter what I say, high-and-mighty Pirjhan disagrees with me. Here I am, riding at the back of this caravan when I should be leading it! It is not any safer back here, Pirjhan, you just want to impress us all with how wise you are! We'll see about that!

She leaned onto Bagatur's neck, standing in her stirrups, balancing her weight to help him up the hill. They topped the rise and looked out over another valley, another ridge of hills that became yet another range of mountains lit by the last of the sun. As far as she could see, the backs of horses rippled across the plain, creating its wake, like a river that coursed through a greening meadow.

Trouble began their ninth day out. Ahead, at one side of the moving herd, Talima saw two horsemen standing still.

Something must be wrong! That's Pirjhan and either Tulak or Kilar. I wonder why they've stopped—come on, Bagatur, let's go! She cantered toward them.

"Quicker, Tulak. You must be quicker! That mare could've drowned while you coiled your lariat! You should've been in that water with your bare hands!"

The men barely nodded to Talima as she reined in beside them. "And what is wrong with your throat, Tulak? D'you have some sort of growth?" Pirjhan pointed with his short whip at the rangy young horseman's neck.

Tulak's neck does look funny—thick, sort of, and lumpy. Why doesn't he say something? He just sits there dumbly while Pirjhan yells at him.

"Speak up, man! Do I have to look for myself? To get an answer?" Pirjhan moved his horse up beside Tulak's.

Tulak hung his head as if to hide his throat with his chin, but he did not respond. In exasperation, Pirjhan reached over and tore open the collar of Tulak's shirt. A bunch of grapes popped out and fell to the ground. Pirjhan and Talima looked down in amazement as scattered grapes rolled against tufts of grass and patches of snow.

"Grapes? In your shirt collar? Where did you get them?" asked Pirjhan.

"From the Chian man's provisions, Pirjhan-sha," Tulak said, his back straight as an arrow.

"But why did you..." began Talima.

"Be quiet, Talima. Let's get to the bottom of this before you begin to ask questions. Now, Tulak, you *stole* these grapes? Carried them all this time?" Pirjhan shook his head as if he couldn't quite believe what he saw.

"Yes, Pirjhan-sha. I stole them before we left," said Tulak. "He had plenty, from his journey in the south. I was hungry and..."

'No, no one is ever hungry when the snows are gone. There's always food, Tulak. Dismount. Take off your shirt. "

"Pirjhan! What d'you think you're doing?" demanded Talima.

"Ten lashes of course. As punishment for stealing, Talima," Pirjhan uncoiled his whip. "We might as well get it over with. Now. "

"No, Pirjhan! That is too harsh! It was only a little bunch of grapes!" Talima pushed Bagatur between them.

"It's the usual number of lashes for theft. Stand aside. We're wasting daylight," Pirjhan said. "Stealing is stealing. You know that. A bunch of grapes today, a horse tomorrow. Move away."

"I can't watch you do this!"

"Then leave."

"Talima-sha," Tulak said softly, "please go. I'm all right and it will soon be over. Just go on...we'll catch up with you shortly."

"Very well. I'll go, but I won't forget this!" She reined Bagatur and galloped off.

Several times, as they rode, Pirjhan dropped back to walk his horse beside Talima's. "Listen, listen, please," Pirjhan entreated. "I'm sorry you're angry with me, Talima-sha, but you must see that I had no choice!"

"I see a hard man, Pirjhan. A man not much older than myself who has set himself up as some sort of superior being that we all must obey. Or else," Talima retorted, biting off each word through clenched teeth.

"In experience, I am older. Not much older in actual years, you're right, but in the time I've spent dealing with life on the trail, surviving under dangerous conditions, I'm worlds older."

"By the Everlasting Sky! You forget who you're talking to!"

"No, oh, no I don't. I couldn't forget who *you* are, Talima-sha. That's part of the problem—I owe so much to the Chagan. He's honored me by giving me command of this caravan, of getting you safely to Chian. I must be true to his confidence in me. Don't you see?"

"I see that you're too impatient with the faults of others, Pirjhan. Too quick to judge. Having a hard childhood hardly justifies that."

"It's you! *You're* too quick to judge, Talima-sha! I should've known better, I suppose, than to try to be friends with the Chagan's beautiful daughter!" Pirjhan drove his horse to the right, heading off a colt that had wandered from the herd.

Talima yelled after him. "Friends? You don't know how to have friends. You have to give of your time and your attention, in order to have friends. Friends stand with you, forgive you, help you to endure.

You never have enough time for silly things like that, do you, Pirjhan?"

Pirjhan's horse skidded across a granite outcropping as he came back beside her. "I've never had the luxury of time, Talima. You've never feared anything or anyone, but I'm careful about making friends, I've had to learn caution, my life's depended on it. Yours too, now. Please try to understand."

"I understand that you're selfish. That you only think of yourself."

"Enough! I've had quite enough! Let me know when you've grown up enough to carry on a reasonable conversation. A real conversation!" Pirjhan wheeled his horse and rode off.

That man will make me crazy! Why do I even care? One minute he seems so wonderful... the next, he's completely impossible!

ALTHOUGH THERE HAD BEEN BRIEF STOPS FOR CHAI AND QUICK MEALS boiled over a quick-burning juniper fire, days and nights were spent in the saddle, moving along increasingly unfamiliar trails, constantly traveling north-northeast along the rim of mountains.

Late one afternoon, they rode into a meadow where spring had arrived early; the grass was ankle deep. Grey bones of rocks were crowned with vivid pink and yellow flowers. Sparse, sturdy pines sprouted bright, new growth. Snow-covered mountain peaks shimmered reflections across a jade-green lake.

Pirjhan called a halt beside the lake. Talima contested his decision, insisting that they continue while good weather held. Patiently, he explained that the men and animals were tired, that they needed a rest. Scornfully, she answered that they were Igren men and animals and could rest as they marched.

They stopped and made camp. It was the first real camp in over a week.

Talima slid stiffly to the ground, unbridled Bagatur and let him join the other horses in a mane-tossing, snorting gallop down to the water's edge. She watched Juchi, Tulak and Kilar unload the pack animals, then noticed Pirjhan striding toward her. She stood rigidly as she waited.

"According to the map, the Chagan's map that the Chian ambassador gave him, this lake is the last before we come into Skyfire Land and rougher country. A good rest, some fresh meat perhaps, makes sense at this time," Pirjhan said. "Stay in camp, Talima-sha. This is strange country—we don't know its hazards. Strange country from now on."

"How long do you intend to loiter here, Pirjhan? To stay in camp?"

"No longer than necessary. I assure you,"

"Excellent. I'll go help the men." She walked away feeling peculiarly conscious of hard ground, the earth dizzyingly close after many days on horseback.

"Juchi! Tulak! Kilar! Hai!" she called. "Where've you all gone? You're like a bunch of marmots, darting into your holes whenever Pirjhan and I get near each other! Well, you can come out now, it's safe."

"I'm here, Talima-sha," said a raw-boned, gangly young chapar. He swept off his hat and slapped dried river mud from his sheep's-hide leggings.

"Ah, Kilar, don't be shy, I won't bite, you know. We're going to camp here for a day, so let's get the horses corralled beside the lake where they can get to water on their own."

Soon a temporary corral was completed. Small traveling ger, fastened around willow poles brought from home, were set up quickly. A cooking fire, half above, half below the ground, blazed. Each of them worked in his own fashion efficiently setting up a comfortable, secure camp.

After work was done, twilight lingered. Talima walked away through islands of small trees twisted by fierce winds, bleached white by a harsh sun. She breathed deeply of the scented air, of juniper, tamarisk, and dry resinous plants. Along the lake there were wildflowers—purple and magenta hyacinths. She sat down on a rock beside the shadowed lake and thought of home.

I feel as though I've been on the trail all my life. Her breath plumed out in the still, frosty air. She chewed a piece of tender grass and thought of all that had happened in the past weeks, the waterfalls and steep passes, the companionship of the trail, the loneliness. *How hard it's been, but how good! I couldn't ask for better companions—even Pirjhan is as resourceful as father said he'd be. And he's good to the others...but I had hoped it might be...different.*

She jumped up, ran down to the lake, and splashed icy water over her head. *I hope lake-kelets like being splashed and played with.*

Suddenly, as naturally as if the sun had come out from behind a cloud, Talima felt the weight of grief and anger lift. She was simply glad, glad to be alive. Excited about the challenges in a strange country, of seeing things she had never seen before, moving on. The last lavender light faded. Against the gathering dark, she watched as fireflies flickered the souls of those departed, then joined the others around the blazing campfire.

They ate a succulent stew of dried meat and fruits as their thoughts and memories danced in the flames. Kilar sat a little apart, skirling a wild melody with his skin pipes. Tulak and Pirjhan sat together, mending camel harnesses.

"Talima-sha, that young mare of yours, Shira, is comin' into season I think. She's gettin' mighty tail-twitchy. What d'you want to do about it? Let her breed with one of the white stallions?" Juchi asked as he lit his long pipe with a coal from the fire.

"Shira? 'Sky! I hadn't noticed. Well, we'd better, I suppose, she'd foal truer from a white sire, if Bagatur hasn't already claimed his rights!" Talima laughed.

"At the rate these mares are foalin', we'll bring in half again as many horses as we started with, maybe fourteen, fifteen hundred for his high muckety-muckness in Chian—barrin'misfortune on the trail, o' course," Juchi grinned his snaggle-toothed smile, the smile that had made Talima laugh ever since she was a baby.

"Juchi, you bandy-legged, old coot! You've always got your mind on women, haven't you? Well, if that's the way the talk is going, I'm going to bed!"

At that moment, a loud commotion from the corral ripped the night. A horse screamed. Hooves pounded the earth.

Shira, white tail arched over her back, stood at the center of a storm of stallions that raged about her, necks snaked out, ears flattened against their skulls, slashing at each other with bared teeth.

Talima watched as a Bagatur she had never seen before bit and kicked the other horses away from Shira. Having beaten the rest into frustrated retreat, he wheeled on the trembling mare. His eyes rolled white in the starlight. He reared over her, snorting and snuffling, his stallion's power evident, erect, great as a man's arm.

Talima seemed to feel his teeth on the back of her own neck, hear his rasping breath in her ear. She became the young mare, waiting for Bagatur's great seed in her belly, bracing herself against his thrust.

Then it was over. The mare and Talima shook themselves. Shira whinnied and rolled in the dust. Talima laughed self-consciously, bade the men goodnight and fled to the privacy of her own ger and the dreaming night.

7
PIRJHAN SCOLDS

TALIMA ROSE BEFORE DAWN WHILE THE CAMP STILL SLEPT. Her boots scrunched frost crystals as she walked to the corral where Shira stood dozing beside Bagatur.

"How peaceful you look this morning," Talima said, slipping a bridle over her head. "Now Bagatur, Shira and I are going for a walk and I want you to stay here. All right? Good." She shinnied onto Shira's back and rode off into ribbons of fog made incandescent by the setting moon. Talima let Shira wander along the lakeshore as she wished.

She felt vaguely irritable and unsure of herself. For the first time in her life she felt truly lonely, longing for family and familiar friends. The exhilaration of the night before seemed as unreal as vapors rising from the satin-surfaced lake.

Even the Everlasting Sky seems far away today. Since Kuriltai everything has moved so fast... I need time to think.

An image of summer lightning, jagged and intense, joined simultaneously by earth-shaking, bone-rattling thunder, crackled into her mind. *That's just what it feels like. I feel as if my life has been struck by lightning. Shattered by some force I can't even name, much less control. 'Sky! I don't want to be a victim of life! I want to be a part of its mysteries, fully alive!*

Shira whickered and tossed her head as if to answer in some wordless way.

I thought this was going to be a grand adventure... that I might fall in love. But instead, Pirjhan's still impossible! Well, I'll not let him bother me anymore!

She leaned over against Shira's mane and scratched between her ears. *I keep wishing I were riding through my own valley, toward my own hearth, wishing I'd hear words of love I've never heard. I'm as restless as grass that blows this way and that in a gusting wind...*

The rushing sound of wings overhead put an end to Talima's reverie. *Ahhnng-haa..loo-ahng..whoop-whoop.* Birds skeined endlessly across the sky, their cries, bittersweet and fluting, echoing between the hills. Some landing; some lifting off; a tide of birds, rising and falling.

A rippling mass of wingtips...and migrating swans lifted into the air just as the sun popped over the mountain's ridge. The sudden flood of sunlight turned the birds' snowy bodies into gold, spread a silken dazzle over lake and marsh.

Talima looked down on a marshland of nesting swans flapping and feeding on wild grains in the shallow water. Newcomers were greeted by resident swans whooping and bobbing their long necks. The journeying swans rested, great wings outstretched, black heads relaxed along round white backs.

As she watched, she became aware of movement in the reeds below, a pattern disconnected from that of the swans. The peaceful gabble of feeding birds continued. They didn't seem to sense danger, but she was sure that something, somehow, threatened. Then she saw seven figures moving toward the feeding swans.

"Those people look like tiny dolls in a puppet show...what d'you suppose they're doing, Shira?" Talima idly braided strands of her horse's mane.

She saw two of them stand and throw something into the air. Sunlight illumined webs that spread out into gossamer circles. As the nets fell, swans bugled and wailed. Again nets were thrown, and again and again swans' clamor shrilled the morning. The air was thick with frantic birds flying to freedom, leaving behind many that were held fast, ceaselessly beating their broken wings against the hunters' nets.

Talima spurred her horse downhill, slipping and sliding toward the tumult below. Hundreds of swans flew in chaos about her as they streamed into the safety of the sky.

By the time she reached the edge of the marsh, only the hunters and captured swans remained. Three skin-clad women and their children held the nets tight while men with heavy sticks thumped into the birds' bodies over and over.

As the swans died, air forced itself from their blood-speckled breasts. This last breath of life that flowed from the swans' throats quavered a reed-like melody into thick, wet mud. It was the very sound of death itself, haunting, never to be forgotten.

"No! Oh, no! Stop!" Talima yelled ahead as Shira galloped toward the men. Appalled and angry, she rode pell mell into the midst of the bloody hunters. They looked up in surprise, having been too engrossed to notice her before. They seemed fearful, but began shouting to each other in short guttural sounds that Talima could not understand. They ran toward her.

One grabbed Shira's bridle, others tried to pull her off by grabbing at her feet. She kicked wildly at them. Another picked up the club he had been beating swans with and started swinging. Talima howled with rage as Shira screamed and reared.

They glared up at her from under thick brows and matted hair. Blocked from running away by the men who hung onto both her and Shira, Talima began to be afraid.

Stupid, you're an idiot, Tam! You never go out without a weapon, you learned that years ago! Not even a knife!

As Shira shied and jumped from side to side, Talima lost her balance and was flung to the ground. Instantly, the men let go of the horse, and tried to capture her. Talima's screams shrilled at them in the same way the swans had screamed as they died. She tried to get a foothold amongst the heaps of blood and feathers where she had landed, every muscle tensed for escape.

She leaped up, but one foot slid on the slippery mass and she felt one of the men grab her ankle as she went down. She twisted over to see a shaggy man standing over her, his club rising into the sky above her.

At that instant, a whistling sound, a thunk, and the man with the club collapsed next to her, an arrow protruding from his neck, his blood a fountain pouring over her.

Another whistling arrow and the man nearest her fell. A black and white horse galloped up, and Pirjhan jumped off beside Talima.

The two remaining men hurriedly picked up their nets and, struggling under the weight of their kill, ran and stumbled after the fleeing women into the hills.

"Tengri, Talima! You'll be the death of us all!"snarled Pirjhan. "I told you never to leave camp without one of the men! You even left Bagatur behind! Dangerous foolishness!"

Talima stood up, shaking, stepped quickly away from the dead man, and whistled for Shira.

'Sky, I'm glad to see him...I don't know what I would have done! She said, "Oh, Pirjhan, it's none of your business who I ride with!"

"It is my business! I'm responsible for you. Whatever you may think, or may wish." Pirjhan's dark eyes blazed at her. "Fortunately I woke early and decided to go hunting. Then I heard your scream, so I....

"Yes, yes, and I'm grateful, naturally, but..."

Talima stomped over the trampled feather-strewn ground, trying to reach her skittish mare. Through a sudden mist of tears, she saw smashed eggshells and bits of newly-hatched swans spattered on blood-soaked feathers all around her.

In the midst of all that blood and mud, she saw an undamaged ball of fluff. She reached down and picked up an egg, still warm, as large as her cupped hand.

"Come on, Talima, we must get back to camp, don't dawdle now." Pirjhan turned his back on her, leaped onto his horse and rode away.

She held the creamy-white egg to her ear, hearing the smallest sound inside. *It's alive!* Quickly, she picked up a ball of swans' down, put the egg inside and carefully tucked it inside her sheepskin vest. Shira pranced up, whickering. Talima swung up onto her sun-warm back and set off, following Pirjhan back to camp.

As she rode, she could hear a *tick-pick, pick-tick* coming from inside her vest. She took the egg out and saw that a tiny bit of shell had loosened and cracked off. Talima picked at the shell with her fingers as the swan chick picked from the inside with its soft beak. Soon the hole was large enough for a wet, bobbly head to poke out, breathing air for the first time in its life. Together, they broke away the rest of the shell.

Talima held the sticky newborn swan in both hands. Its translucent webbed feet bent backwards beneath black, stick legs.

"Oh, you *are* beautiful, even without all your feathers. What shall I call you? What d'you think, Shira?"

The mare shook her head and kept on walking.

"Kara would be a good name for you, birdling. Kara means white one, you see, and someday you'll be a great white swan! And you shall have me as your mother and Shira the Golden as a sister, and Bagatur the Valiant for a bold, brave brother, and Merket the Swift as a friend!" Talima snuggled the small bird next to her throat.

"And we'll be a family, Kara!" Tiny white feathers fluffed quickly in the hot sun. Talima tucked Kara under her hair on her shoulder and held her there as the baby swan quickly learned to balance.

She took a drink from her skin flask and, holding the milk in her mouth, put the bird's beak between her lips as she had done for Merket many times, then gradually spit small spurts of milk into the swan's mouth. Kara flapped miniature wings and peered at Talima with black, bead-sized eyes.

"You know, Kara, I'll wager that you're the very first swan since time began to be born on horseback!"

To catch up with Pirjhan, Shira began a slow canter, whinnying to the horses left in camp. As they rode closer, Talima gave a shrill whistle to summon Bagatur. He ran once around the corral, mane and tail flying, and leaped into the air, easily clearing the makeshift fence. Neck arched, he pranced up to them and whickered a greeting.

"'Hatou, Bagatur, wait till you see your new little sister!" Talima said as he rubbed against the mare's side.

Wordlessly, Pirjhan dismounted.

"There you are Talima-sha! At last. You shouldn't be out alone!" Juchi said as he met them.

"Well, Juchi, as you can plainly see, I'm not alone. Don't scold!"

"This isn't Igren country and you've no idea what sort of spirits are prowlin' about out there!" the old chapar grumbled. "It's more of your headstrong ways, lass, goin' off without tellin' us. You, without even your arrow-case and bow! The Chagan wouldn't like it one bit! !"

"All right, just for you and father, I'll be more careful." She grinned.

"Bein' careful is not enough, Talima-sha. You're a young lady now, not a wild young mountain goat."

"Oh, Juchi, do stop fussing at me! Come see what I found." Talima held out the wobbly swan-chick.

"By the Blue Wolf! You can't keep it. I mean, it's a dear little thing, surely, but on a journey like this it doesn't stand a chance!" Juchi sputtered. "A newborn chick belongs in a nest on the ground, not on horseback!"

"I'll manage. You'll see, Juchi, I'll keep Kara alive!"

"Kara is it now? Plain foolishness, I fear." He saw her fierce determination, and reconsidered. "'Tis a fair, sweet creature, to be sure and 'twould be a comfort for you to have somethin' to cuddle, I wager. Well, I c'd make some sort of carry-case for it maybe..."

"Oh, Juchi, would you?'

Bagatur nuzzled Shira's flank, making her step from side to side to avoid him. When the stallion playfully nipped at Shira, she shied, and then reared. The bundled chick rolled out of Talima's vest onto the ground. Talima dropped her reins, jumped down and gathered up the nestling.

"What is *that?*" Pirjhan asked as he saw the small ball of fluff for the first time. "A new-hatched chick? Well, get rid of it. We're ready to ride."

"I'll do no such thing, Pirjhan. I shall keep Kara" she drew in a deep breath and held it, her heart pounding.

"It'll die, of course. The point I must make," Pirjhan said calmly, "is that you must not, *must not* go off alone."

"Yes, yes, yes!" Her breath came out harsh and strong. She dropped Shira's bridle and strode off, cradling Kara.

THERE FOLLOWED MANY LONG DAYS AND NIGHTS IN THE SADDLE as they pushed into new country along old trade routes. Game was still plentiful, sweet water sprang from the earth at convenient intervals.

Talima found a way to feed and care for Kara, who ate anything and everything as long as Talima touched or chewed it first. The cygnet adored her human mother. More accustomed to riding than walking, Kara distrusted the unmoving ground. She'd lift one floppy, webbed foot and wait for the earth to come up and meet it as a horse's back would do. When that support failed, she'd fall over on her side, repeating the whole ridiculous procedure with her other foot, falling and flapping pin-feathered wings.

The men laughed and called her "little drunkard". Talima merely smiled indulgently and picked her up. There Kara would nestle on her shoulder and chirr companionably. Rocked by the steady rhythm of the horse's rolling gait, she'd fall asleep.

Caring for Kara relieved Talima's loneliness. She felt she had created a family, a traveling family, dependent only on her love. She and Pirjhan avoided each other, spoke courteously when conversation was necessary and kept a careful distance the rest of the time. Personal considerations fitted themselves into the larger framework of riding on, ever riding on.

The nights grew shorter as summer came on. But still the sky-fire blazed and rippled across the stars, shaking out banners of green and gold and blue. The Great Bear stars walked through shimmering soaring lights of the far north. As they rode the night trail, Juchi taught Talima star lore—where the Archer pulled his bow, where the Serpent twisted through the heavens, showed her how the Twins replaced the Bull at mid-heaven this time of year, where to find the Wayfinder Star and the intense White Metal star at dawn.

On good days, they covered more than a hundred *li*—a hundred miles. A late blizzard slowed them for no more than the time it took to prepare and eat a meal or tend to a foaling mare for an hour or two. They lived up to their reputation. Igren, as they reminded themselves, never even knew the place of their birth as each was born as the Clan marched. Except for a few weeks of deep winter, they were always on the move from one grazing place to another, from one family rendezvous to another.

Their caravan passed occasional way stations, simple huts of dried mud packed around twigs. A lone monk might scurry out, ask for news, offer a cup of hot tea, astonished at the great river of horses. He would gesture blessings, hoping they would stop. But they poured past, flowing over stony ridges and down deep valleys ever onward toward an unimaginable, fantasy life in faraway Chian.

8
THE BURAN BLOWS

ONE DAY THE WIND TURNED COLD, SO COLD IT FROZE THE MOIST HAIRS OF their nostrils. The animals' breath blew out in frosty plumes. Black-purple clouds shrouded the sky.

During a brief halt, Talima sat on a rock outcropping, breathing warm steam from a cup of chai as Kara bobbled around her feet.

"Looks like we're in for a blow!" Juchi said, tucking his weather-wrinkled chin into his collar as he stopped beside her. "Reckon we'd best round up and make camp."

"Let's go a little further, Juchi, see if we can find a more sheltered spot. We'd blow clean off this rocky flatland if a storm really hit!" Her words whipped away on the wind.

"I dunno, Talim-sha," Juchi shook his head, "Don't look to me like there's shelter of any sort as far's eye c'n see! Besides, there mightn't be time enough to get anywhere else—I've been watchin' the camels... they've been snarlin' together all day, and the instant we stopped, they buried their mouths in the dry earth—looks like a sign of the *Buran* to me!"

"Did you ask Pirjhan whether we should round up here?"

"Naw, thought I'd try you out first, lass. He always wants to keep going. He's that hard to stop. You'd think a devil was drivin' him!"

"Perhaps you're right. Perhaps we should stop. It's bitter cold all of a sudden!"

Without further warning, a stinging wind roared around them. Thick with snow pellets, a blinding white wall howled across the barren ground. Talima grabbed Kara before she was blown away and stuffed her inside her fur-lined cloak.

"'Tis the Buran!" Juchi shouted above the screaming wind. "It's the

Great Devil Wind, the killing wind—the Buran! Cover yourself! I'll see to the horses!" He galloped away to help the others who were throwing packs off lurching camels and trying to bunch the frightened horses.

Talima looked in desperation for Shira, who carried her furs and felt ger covers. She put her head down into the powerful wind...and found herself walking steadily in the same place. She tried to whistle for Bagatur but could not feel her lips. The wind coiled coldly around her.

She could not see which way to go. She dropped to her knees, hunched away from the stinging blizzard in order to protect Kara. She grew colder. Time slowed, freezing the moment into a crystalline eternity.

After what seemed like forever, Talima felt a weight settle over her. And Pirjhan was there, piling furs on top of them both to shut out the wind-driven ice. He pulled her inside the warmth of his greatcoat and began to rub her briskly all over. Kara wriggled and strained between them, bursting out of his embrace.

"Tengri, the swan! You have kept that foolish swan alive at the risk of your own life!" Pirjhan said and then began to laugh. He laughed as if he'd never stop. His laughter shook the three of them.

"Pirjhan, please don't scold. I'm so cold my toes hurt, I thought I was, I didn't know what to..." Talima's teeth chattered.

"See? You can't always look after yourself! I was so afraid—afraid I'd lost you completely!"

"The storm came so fast! I didn't know..."

"That's Buran! It sweeps down from the highest mountains, winter-killing everything in its path. Your father warned me. We're in for it, for at least a day or more, I fear."

"I'm all right now, Pirjhan. You can let me go."

"Yes, good. We need to make this shelter more livable before the snow gets too deep for us to move."

They rearranged furs, sheepskins, and felt covers that Pirjhan had brought, and made a snug space around themselves, not much room for moving about, but sufficient air for breathing. Sticks and pebbles battered at the outer layers of their shelter. The first snow pellets sifted beneath the shell's edges.

Talima, Kara, and Pirjhan, snuggling in their fur cocoon, were warm. And with the immediate crisis over, silent.

Talima lay and listened to the wind. She was piercingly aware of

Pirjhan's body beside her, the smell of him, incense and horses, that filled their space. She could feel the heat of his thighs on her legs, the heavy warmth of his belly against her back, warming her whole body, bringing her back to life.

In a sudden reversal of all she had thought these last days, she understood how good and kind he really was. She couldn't even recall why she'd been angry with him for so long. "Talima…Tam…" he began. "I'd almost given up hope of finding you. I am so grateful…"

Kara chirred. They both laughed into the enveloping darkness. "I'm glad…" they said at once, together. And that set them laughing again.

"Ahnng—looo, haa-aa-a." Kara sighed.

"She's hungry. I don't suppose you have anything to eat, do you?"

Pirjhan searched his pockets and brought out a drawstring bag that held dates and strips of dried meat. They took turns chewing food for the hungry cygnet before feeding it to her.

"Watch how well she can drink directly from my flask now!" Talima said proudly. "If we're careful—and Kara will cooperate, she *is* a growing bird, you know—this much food should last at least a day or two."

"Well, tell her not to grow. Growing takes food." Pirjhan teased.

"Pirjhan, that's silly, might as well tell the Buran to stop blowing!"

"Silly, yes, I've been silly. You too, Tam. I really don't want to quarrel with you ever again."

"I know. How did we…when did it start? I thought, before we began this journey, that you sort of well, liked me."

"Liked you! You? Didn't you understand? I mean, surely you must have known!" Pirjhan was at a loss for words.

"You seemed so cold and…"

"I wanted to be near you. All I could think about was you!"

"As if you thought I was a nobody. Not worthy of your time."

"You're the Chagan's daughter…his *heir!* And I'm only a freed slave!"

"It's not right you know, Pirjhan, to treat me this way."

"I had no right, I knew, Tam, to want you the way that I do."

Talima smiled into Kara's feathers. The wind that wuthered and whined outside sounded, somehow, like a song. "Hold me, Pirjhan, please hold me."

He put his arms around her and held her close. "You smell of grasses, milk and lovely bees."

She nestled against his shoulder and sighed contentedly. Kara shifted next to her, shook herself, and settled into sleep.

Pirjhan hummed for a moment, then began to sing, *"Into the house made of dawn...into the house of twilight, into the house of stars above..."*

"I like that," yawned Talima.

"I bring flowers to my love," he sang. "Tam? Tam, my little love?" But she had fallen into an exhausted sleep. He lay awake, smiling.

The *Buran* howled, undiminished.

THEY HAD NO IDEA HOW LONG THEY SLEPT. A pale light glowed through thin places in their body-shaped tent. Outside, the storm spread its wild, freezing power over all the land.

Talima stretched, and immediately regretted it, for her movement woke Kara who began flopping around on top of them, whooping and sighing cheerily.

"Kara! get off me, settle down, do!"

"She can't get off you, Tam. No room here for a swanling, I'm afraid."

"True. Oh, Pirjhan, I slept so well. Did you? What shall we do now? How long must we stay here?"

"We'll stay right here. Safe and dry and warm, until the storm blows itself out. However long that may be."

"Of course. Well then, this is an adventure! Together after all! You know...I'm hungry."

"Yes? We'll eat and drink only a little from our drinking skins, and that'll take up some time if we do it slowly."

"Listen to that wind! 'Sky, it's wild! Am I glad to be inside! It's so peaceful here, with you, 'Jhani. Is there any more barley cake? Kara ate all of mine."

"A little, here."

"Jhani? Would you tell me more of what you remember of your childhood? I mean, you know everything about me, but I know nothing about you or the land you came from."

"Well, first of all, it was a warmer land, golden under a hot sun. Palm trees that rattled in warm winds, fountains, gardens filled with flowers and singing birds. And my mother singing, always singing." he said.

"I remember the black, sticky dates and ripe melons—pale green and apricot melons, running with juice. Red melons with jet black seeds, sweet on your tongue. I remember liking melons so much that I was caught once stealing melons from the neighbor's garden!"

"Was that one of your mother's songs that you sang last night?"

"Yes. She sang songs that her mother and grandmother sang, those songs that sing in me now."

"Sing us a song...tell us a story?"

"I'll sing you a song of Inanna. I used to think it was a song about my mother, another name for her. Maybe it was—she was so beautiful. You remind me of her, Talima—of Inanna."

"Do I? Was Inanna your mother's name?"

"No, Inanna is one of the Goddess' names."

"Goddess? Isn't that just an old superstition?"

"Well, there are those who think differently. Few people think about Inanna now, but I've always believed in Her."

"Well, sing me the song of Inanna, then. Come here, Kara, come listen."

Pirjhan's deep purple voice filled their cocoon, *"Mighty, majestic and radiant, You shine brilliantly in evening, you brighten the day at dawn, Radiant Lady of Morning, Hail!"*

"I like that. It's a much different song than our Igren songs—slower and sweeter. I do like it.

Pirjhan's voice was filled with longing, *"In the pure places of the Steppe, on the high roofs of dwellings, the people sing Your praises, celebrate You in song."*

"When I have babies of my own, I'd like to sing them songs like that."

"You aren't thinking of having babies already, are you, Tam? You're too young!"

"I'm not too young! I'll be seventeen in one more moon!"

"Really? What an old woman you are! I had no idea!"

"Old woman, am I? I'll show you, Pirjhan-sha!" Talima pounced on him, searching under his clothes for a good spot to tickle.

Taken by surprise, Pirjhan was vulnerable. "Don't! No, no! Get away you rascally old woman!"

"Oh! You'll pay for that, you, you..." Talima was used to teasing her brothers and was quick to seize her advantage. She tickled him until he became weak from laughing. She crouched astride his chest, holding his arms down on the skins beneath. "Give up? Take back what you said, or I'll tickle you some more!"

"Yes, yes! Whatever you say, oh merciless one," he gasped, laughing still.

Talima looked down into his face so close to her own, looked into the dark well of his eyes, saw his heart smiling up at her.

White wind, white sound without. Within, all was still. Even time seemed to hold its breath. Slowly, she sank down on him. His arms enfolded her. Their joined breath flowed between them, fragrant, compelling.

"Jhan, Jhani," she murmured, hardly able to breathe her own air, breathing only him. She felt his thick, strong tongue thrusting into her mouth, prodding her tongue to respond, tasting her, drinking the sudden liquid of her body.

His kiss dissolved her. Talima spun into limitless desire that swept her into the center of a universe called Pirjhan. She abandoned herself to pleasure and melted into that stream of stars, swiftly rushing, burning, singing her blood with a high sweet song.

Breath returned. She was curved like a bow against his side, floating into an everlasting sky. "Jhani?"

"Mmnnn?"

"I just wanted to say your name," she murmured. Her mouth moved along the muscles of his throat. "I can feel your blood, your heart beating here. I can feel it with my lips."

"I must be alive then—thought I'd died and gone to heaven."

Talima giggled.

"Tengri! You are so lovely. In this dim light you shine like the moon, my sweet." He rolled her over onto her back.

Talima closed her eyes and felt his weight the length of her body. Again they kissed, and kissing, lost themselves in each other. Long, lingering kisses, sweet as ripe melons.

"Tam, little love..."

"I think I love you, Jhani."

"I think...I've always loved you," he said hoarsely, smoothing her hair back with his hand.

"Are we going to undress now?" she asked.

"Wha-a-a-t?" Pirjhan sat up abruptly.

"You know, silly. Take off our clothes!"

"Wherever did you get that idea?"

"Well, isn't that what comes next? Like Bagatur mounting Shira, like that?"

"Talima, you amaze me. One minute you're a woman, wise and knowing. The next, you're as wanton, as impertinent, as a caravan urchin! No! No, that is definitely *not* what comes next!"

"Why not?"

"Because. The Chagan is sending his *virgin* daughter to the emperor. We must respect his orders."

"But, Jhani, I want to make love with you! Here. And now."

Pirjhan chuckled and hugged her, "Listen, my little dove. Now pay attention to me, please. Tengri knows I want you. But we mustn't. Only kissing—and even that..."

Kara woke and shoved between them. She nipped and nuzzled their hair and ears until they gave in and sat up.

"She's hungry again," Talima sighed. "Well, I find it hard to accept, Jhani—what you just said. It seems to me that you or father, or the emperor, are always deciding what I must or mustn't do! Maybe you're right, I'm not sure. Of course I'll do whatever is necessary to protect my people, but there must be another way that I can accomplish that and still have you, can still touch and kiss and love you. I'll have to think about it."

"I, too, find it hard. Perhaps, if things were different, if...Tengri! Let's think of other things while you feed that swan child of yours. Shall I tell you a story?"

"Yes, do."

So Pirjhan began. He spoke of sunny lands and fragrant gardens, beautiful princesses and bold, handsome princes. His slumbrous voice enclosed them in a realm of fantasy, a fantasy wherein Talima lived an imagined reality skillfully woven by a Pirjhan she hadn't known existed. Finally, they slept again.

An unusual stillness roused them.

"The wind! The wind's died!"

"The storm's over?" asked Talima in dismay. "I'm almost sorry."

"Don't worry, little sweetheart. It's not the end of our world. We still have time to be together. Let's see what it's like out there."

Cautiously, they poked their heads out, squinted against brilliant light. A shower of snow from the top of their shelter sifted over them, powdering their hair and eyelashes.

They stood up. Snow crystals flurried around them. The sky, blown clear of clouds, was blue, intense, vibrant, mountain-midday blue. Sun sparkled a frozen earth, shimmered a million minute rainbows around each dazzling snowflake.

"It's lovely, Jhani! So still. No wind at all. Nothing's moving!" She blew snowflakes from her sleeve and watched them float down. "The whole world's different! Nothing's the same. Magic, isn't it, love?" she danced in circles, dry snow eddying around her.

"The air smells like mountains!" she breathed deeply. "It's so good to be alive!"

"So very good, yes. Let's see where the others are, they'll be worried, I know."

Kara wriggled her way out of the shelter into the snow where she flapped her half-grown wings wildly, sending iridescent, snowflake fountains spilling into the sunlight.

"Jhani? Thank you for coming after me, for finding Kara and me."

"I will always find you, always," he replied. His look caressed her. "Wherever you are, I will always come to you." He held her hand as they set off through snowy drifts together.

Hopping clumsily, Kara lurched behind them as she bugled into the frosty air.

The sound of camel bells answered.

9
HONEY LEADS TO DISASTER

TALIMA AND PIRJHAN WERE GREETED BOISTEROUSLY BY THE CHAPARS, who had sheltered safely within the herd. The animals were snorting and blowing at the snow, pawing in order to get at the sweet, sparse grass growing below.

Talima stayed close to Pirjhan. She felt oddly shy, as if these men whom she knew so well, were changed somehow into strangers.

Juchi and Kilar were digging packs out of drifts. They had already made a small, smoky fire of dry dung from camel packs and were tending two pots that hung above it. As the chai began to boil, Tulak went to one of the horses and untied a skin slung as usual beneath its belly. The milk it contained was thick with clotted cream that foamed as he whipped it into the hot drink. Wild barley, millet and strips of dried meat simmered in melted snow. It was a meal fit for the gods and they were ready for it.

They had lost nothing to the Buran except a few days. Once more they had survived. The storm proved to be the high mountains' farewell for, as they rode down from the icy plateau, an empty land stretched out endlessly before them. They had reached the fringes of the Gobi Desert. They began forced marches between oases.

Days lengthened until only a few hours of frosty nights remained in which breathing was cool enough to be comfortable. By day the sun beat down on constantly shifting sands. Many-colored, wind-eroded canyons dropped out from flat tableland, creating habitat where wild pigeons nested, where gazelles, wild asses and mountain sheep managed a precarious existence.

Often the shallow, marshy wells they found were completely filled with sand, yielding a scant cup of brackish water over an hour's time. Abandoned huts crumbled beside dried-up waterholes.

Trying to keep blowing sand out of her eyes and throat, Talima wrapped her head with a length of sheer muslin, a veil that twirled around her in the grit-filled wind.

With all its hardships, Talima was content. She enjoyed easy companionship with the men she rode with, worked with, loved. She rode hard, slept in the saddle and woke each day to the desert's harsh beauty.

The arid land they passed through was not unchanging—some of its wrinkled hills were ribboned with bands of ochre, maroon and ash, some were wholly black—black sand, massive black boulders, black twisted plants. They rode cautiously through this desolate land where evil spirits might lurk. Kilar's steady drumming accompanied them, drum-sound to drive demons below ground.

Sometimes they thought they heard human voices calling from all directions, trying to lure them into the wilderness. They began to feel watched by invisible eyes. They longed for the cool night and were afraid of what the darkness might bring. They lived with fears they had been taught from childhood.

Water became scarcer. The mares' milk began to dry up, depriving both humans and young foals of a staple and necessary food. In order to save the littlest and weakest horses, they lifted them onto the bulging packs of camels and tied them there, their tiny, bony legs flopping in rhythm to the camels' swaying walk.

Mirages shimmered over hard-scrabble hills. Wavering visions of trees, of violet mountains, of castellated towers just ahead, tantalized them with promises of water and shade, mirage promises that drained into the sand as they drew near. They kept the herd bunched for safety, slowly moving on toward the north and east.

Days later, they drove the herd up yet another steep slope. But instead of the hard rattle of hooves against parched earth, they heard only a sibilant sound of hooves sinking into spongy soil. They rode over the ridge and stopped in astonishment.

A rushing winding stream sprang out of the ground below them, disappearing into a field of reeds in the distance. Golden eagles, falcons and a few buzzards hovered and hunted the broad valley. Fields of wild iris spread out before them. The carpet of blue, only a few inches tall, looked heaven-high to travelers weary of the desert.

Shouting and whistling exuberantly, they rode down into the valley and drank the clear cool water. The Igren caravan—horses, camels, humans, a few falcons and a young swan—drank their fill. Packs and provisions were unloaded and the animals turned loose to roll and kick their heels. They all rested and ate, drank some more, ate again, and thus whiled away the afternoon.

Kara had never experienced a body of water like this before, the first water that hadn't come from Talima's waterskin. She was confused at first, but soon waddled in and floated off.

It was a time for play and they exulted in it. Pirjhan scooped out a series of small holes on the sandy shore, filled them with multi-colored pebbles and showed Kilar and Tulak how to play Wari, a game from his childhood.

Juchi and Talima lay on the flowered slope and watched them. Juchi dozed off into an old man's dreaming. Talima day-dreamed fantasies.

Funny, she thought as she watched Pirjhan, *I'm so used to seeing him on horseback, I never noticed how beautiful he is when he walks. I like the way he moves, the way his dark hair curls over his shoulders like a great hawk.* She gazed after him as he finished the game and walked downstream toward the horse herd.

Bees hummed in the flowers that surrounded them, bees, gathering nectar. *Bees!* Talima sat up. *Where there were bees there must be honey!* She had an overwhelming craving for some sweet sticky honeycomb. Without disturbing the sleeping Juchi, she jumped up. She ran down the valley and found Bagatur and Shira, whose belly had begun to swell, grazing together. Pirjhan was nearby, grooming his horse.

"Jhani, listen! Hear the bees? I'm going to see if I can find them, get some honey, want to come?"

Pirjhan caught her excitement, "Honey? Makes my mouth water! You bet I'll come...can't be far!" He slung saddlebags onto his horse and mounted.

She saddled Bagatur and shooed Shira away. They set out. Kara, who had followed along as usual, set up a whooping holler, half running, half flying after them. Finally, Talima reined in, put Kara up on her shoulder and they were off.

The flower-scented breeze ruffled Kara's feathers and blew Talima's hair in an arc around her face.

"You look half bird, half woman," Pirjhan smiled at her. "Or even more, like a radiant princess astride a winged horse. You're the princess in *my* life. Just looking at you fills me with delight."

They cantered onto a sweeping mesa cut at intervals by steep canyons. They were silent, happy in this moment, riding through an azure afternoon.

They explored several canyon walls for signs or sounds of bees—dark wax dripping down rock walls or the low hum of a hive. Small caves held nesting birds, but no bees. They didn't mind searching. Being alone together was sufficient.

"Sing me a song, Jhani, like the ones you sang during the Buran, one of the songs your mother sang. Teach me the words?"

"Songs. My mother's songs? She used to sing this one as a lullaby, though it's not. It's a love song really."

They rode close enough that their stirrups touched. Pirjhan's low, resonant voice held them in a world removed from reality.

"As I was shining bright and dancing, singing praises to the coming of the night…my beloved met me…"

The day's heat lessened. Lightning zigzagged from dark clouds on the horizon. The wind freshened. They wandered on, singing, oblivious to everything except each other.

"He laid me down on a fragrant honey-bed, he took his pleasure of me…sweet is the sleep of hand-to-hand, sweeter still the sleep of heart-to-heart…."

They sang it over and over until Talima had memorized both words and melody.

A few large raindrops spattered the dust. It had been so long since they'd seen rain, they hardly recognized it for what it was—the forerunner of a fast-moving thunderstorm.

Lightning shattered the clouds. Thunder rolled, shaking canyon walls. Kara bugled. The horses snorted and bolted. Black clouds roiled over them and created night where none had been before. Only an eerie afterglow remained.

Talima and Pirjhan rode out their horses' panic, turning them in a tight circle within narrow canyon walls to bring them to a halt. Joined thunder-lightning ripped the air around them. Raindrops became pellets of ice. Hail the size of bird's eggs hammered at them.

"A cave! I see a cave at the far end, Tam," Pirjhan shouted over the gusting wind. "Let's ride for it!"

They galloped past giant boulders into the mouth of a cavern. The sound of their horse's hooves was drowned by the storm.

The cave, open to the sun's arc all day, had stored up warmth. They unsaddled their horses, spread their outer, wet gear to dry and prepared to wait out the storm. Kara was exhausted from the excitement, and like a child, wriggled under a saddlebag and fell asleep.

Pirjhan and Talima were exhilarated by their wild ride, and by the violence of the storm itself. They sat on their saddle blankets, laughing. The cave absorbed all sound. Gradually, even their laughter stilled.

"I think I'll explore, see how far back the cave goes…" Talima stood up. "It'll be completely dark soon, and then…"

She started to walk—and felt the quiet settle around each step. She thought she could hear the cave breathing. She felt, rather than heard, Pirjhan stand behind her. Close. Intent. The hairs on the back of her neck prickled. She turned toward him…

For a moment she wondered if she had really moved or was the air between them shrinking, pulling them closer, dissolving space that separated them? She felt herself flow forward, moving like thick syrup.

And in that movement, a strange panic swept through her, panic of the young dove as she catches sight of the hawk above her. She lifted her hand to her breast as if to guard her heart and felt it flutter in inevitable surrender.

Soft, crooning sounds breathed themselves in and out of her mouth. In one swift flying gesture, she twisted away from him. But it was too late. She only danced the circle 'round and faced him closer at the end, enveloped by his scent.

He loomed above her now in the half-light. With one stride he pinioned her, encompassed her wholly, not to be eluded or flown from, or escaped in any way.

His heart beat the rhythm of hers. His breath breathed hers. They stood, their bodies molding together, swept away by a passion so overpowering that the storm, raging outside, faded into insignificance.

He swooped her into his arms, and carried her to their nest of blankets. There were no words in the world of their longing, only eyes that spoke of love. Only eyes that drank the other's beauty, swimming their senses with desire.

Their tongues seemed made only for tasting, for exploring an inner curve of ear, sipping nectar from an eager mouth, touching heartbeat from another's throat.

Slowly...he unwrapped her from her clothes. Gently...he let his hands glide along her breasts and belly. His eyes held her, compelled her into him, enveloped her in the heat of his body.

His hands beneath her arms commanded her to stand before him. He turned her, touched her body unexpectedly, feather-touches that tingled her skin. She trembled.

She saw his smile, a slow-dawning, lingering smile, and knew that she pleased him. Her breasts seemed to push themselves into his hands. She saw herself naked, for the first time, in the mirror of his eyes—a slim, high-breasted woman, part child, part goddess, shining in new-moon curves against the velvet dark.

He unbound her hair. The sea of it flowed around her slender body. Her knees dissolved and she sank to the cave's floor. She knelt before him, waiting for his touch, longing for his touch. Scarcely breathing...

THE STORM SLATTED AGAINST ROCK WALLS OUTSIDE THE CAVE. Pebbles rattled downhill. Silhouettes of men stood briefly against the cave's entrance before all hell broke loose. Kara bugled. Horses whinnied, their hooves striking sparks off the cave floor as they struggled to rise. Hoarse, guttural commands were shouted by the attackers.

In that instant, as she opened her eyes, Talima felt a heavy net settle over them. She and Pirjhan were gathered swiftly into the net's loop, their own arms and legs tripping and tangling their efforts to escape.

She counted only six men, but was awed by their size. They were not unusually tall, but simply huge—black, matted hair, great sloping shoulders, heavy bodies shining with grease, thighs as big as her waist.

"Tam! Get Bagatur!" Pirjhan wrestled against the ropes that held them. "Ride for help! Get out of here!"

"I can't! They've got us all!" Talima cried, trying to gesture through the net. "Even Kara's caught!"

Pirjhan threw himself at the nearest man, dragging Talima behind him. She watched in horror as the man clubbed Pirjhan without a flicker of either effort or emotion,

They took his unconscious body out of the net and slung it over the rump of his horse. Then they bundled Talima and a squawking swan onto the other horse, tied on the rest of their gear and led them outside.

Talima hung, head down, over Bagatur's side. Her hands and ankles had been tied painfully tight. They threw skins over her naked body, but it was night in the desert, and very cold. She tried to see Pirjhan.

They've killed him! Oh, please, Great Tengri, don't let him be dead! Let my love be alive!

Bound and helpless, she felt a blackness overwhelm her. When consciousness returned, she realized that, even though their speech was different, she *could* understand much of what their captors said.

"Mazar Tagh be pleased," grunted a man who seemed to be the leader.

"Yes!" The rest chorused in agreement. "Be too pleased!"

And later, "Man be strong slave in mines. He dig us gold."

She found herself looking directly into the small, close-set eyes of a mountain-sized man who walked beside her.

"She has sun-hair. Has watery sky-eyes."

"She not a *person.* Maybe not a *druze?*"

"She be druze all right," one chuckled, as he lifted up the skin that covered Talima and poked with his thumb at the soft hair between her thighs.

Talima fainted again and dreamed of Pirjhan's touch, thinking she was still in his arms, warm and safe. Bagatur plodded on, carrying her faithfully into the unknown.

10
MAZAR TAGH LEARNS THE TRUTH

SOME TIME LATER, AS ECHOES OF HORSES' HOOF BEATS BOUNCED BETWEEN steep walls, Talima awoke. She heard Pirjhan moan and called to him, "Jhani! are you all right?" Her voice sounded loud as it reverberated against the darkness.

With an oath, one of the men covered her face with his hand. "She calls out spirits against us!" he said fearfully.

Another man tore a piece of greasy cloth from his tunic, wadded it up and stuffed it into Talima's mouth, gagging her. "There. Be still. No voice now. We'll be safe from spirits." Reassured, they continued on.

The short, moonless night grew light with the coming dawn. Talima saw rocks that rose like pillars from the flat plain they crossed. Wind-weathered towers that seemed carved by demon hands stood sentinel against intruders.

By midday, they climbed through a maze of these watchtowers, winding up and around to higher ground. They passed through a narrow gate of piled stones and were met by a pack of yipping, snarling dogs. Instantly, they were surrounded by dozens of men and boys, some fat, all heavy and slow-moving. Talima saw other, smaller figures that knelt beside cooking fires or peered from skin-covered huts.

She heard a shouted command. The hubbub of village voices subsided. Men and boys silently drew back, making way for an immense man, a giant who walked toward them with heavy strides as if the earth itself belonged to him. He was dressed in fringed skins with silk scarves wrapped in bright colored bands around his bulging belly. A grinning bear's head covered his skull. The bear's skin flopped stiffly from his wide shoulders to the ground.

"Mazar Tagh! You see!" their captors said, gesturing to Talima,

Pirjhan, Kara and the horses.

"We got good prize, Mazar Tagh," they said, vigorously nodding their heads while they looked down at the ground as if afraid to look directly at their clan's headman.

"Where did these horses come from? What sort of carrion did you bring back this time?" Mazar Tagh rumbled, squinting down at them.

Two of the men grabbed Talima and threw her into the dirt at his feet. Her hair, filled with sunlight, swirled over her bound hands and spilled onto black sand.

"She have sun-hair, great Tagh," one explained. "She be rare druze. Good for breeding, eh?"

"Your great seed would split her, Tagh!" another sniggered.

Mazar Tagh rolled her over with his boot and said nothing. But his black eyes narrowed as he looked down at her. His gaze slid over her naked body. With one quick gesture he took a knife from his waist and cut the ropes that held her ankles. Then he stepped between her legs, forced them apart, and without a moment's hesitation, slid two of his thick fingers into her.

Talima's scream mewed weakly through the rotten cloth gag. She arched away from him.

"Faugh, a worthless druze!" he spat at his men. He turned, leaving Talima where she lay.

"Here be good mine-slave, mighty Tagh!" Pirjhan, conscious now, but also bound and gagged, was thrown down for their leader's inspection.

"Not too bad," Mazar Tagh admitted grudgingly. "Put the person and druze in cages. I'll decide what to do with them, later. Hobble those horses. Take that damn, shrieking swan away! And you, Oyin, Truk, come with me."

The men scrambled to obey. They cut the ropes that bound Talima and Pirjhan, ungagged them, and shoved each into a separate, wooden cage that was too low to stand in.

Talima pulled herself into a corner nearest Pirjhan's cage. She huddled there, giving in to despair and fear. Tears of anguish and helplessness flowed over her cheeks onto the dirty skins they had wrapped her in.

Pirjhan crawled as close to her as he could and stretched his arms through the bars. His fingertips brushed her arm. She looked up through a haze of tears, reached out and touched his hand, held his hand, felt his strength, held by his love.

"Oh, Jhani, what shall we do? How will we get out of here?" she wailed. "Can you think of something? Anything?"

"Yes, I will, Beauty, hush now, don't cry," he stroked her hand. "I'll think of something, never fear."

He tried to reassure her, but he spoke no words that comforted. There were no words that gave even the beginning of hope.

The next day, Mazar Tagh emerged from his hut. The bearskin still hung from his shoulders, but now Talima's blue-silk sash adorned his belly. Pirjhan's bow hung from his belt and curved against his hip as a sword would. "Bring me my bear!" he bellowed.

Several boys ran off and returned leading an enormous she-bear, grey and grizzled, restless at the end of a braided-leather leash. The bear stood and pawed the air before Mazar Tagh. Chains of wrought silver hung around her shoulders and neck, gold earrings swung from her ears. The bear put her great paws on her master's shoulders and pulled him into a few dancing turns. He pummeled and patted her affectionately before they strolled off together.

In the village square, Talima and Pirjhan were the objects of torment. Old women and boys prodded them with sticks, threw garbage into their cages, jeered, pinched, and poked them mercilessly. More wornout, mouldy skins had been thrown in for them to cover themselves with. One child had offered water to Pirjhan, but the cup was knocked from his hand by her mother.

Talima saw that they were caged in the open center of what must have been an ancient city. Patched huts leaned against crumbled-stone walls. Carved pillars stood along wide, once-paved roads. The air smelled of rotten eggs. The desert wind scoured old spaces and sang stories of past glory between the stones.

"Where is this place, d'you know, Jhani?" she whispered.

"I've no idea. Not on your father's map. Juchi and the others'll have no idea this place even exists, will have no idea where to look for us, won't be able to find us."

"They'll continue the drive to Chian though, we'll catch up to them on the way, don't you think? When we escape?" She looked out then, and saw a strange apparition—an enormous, bear-clad man, and a dressed-up bear lumbering toward them.

They approached Pirjhan's cage first. Mazar Tagh motioned for the cage to be opened. His men dragged Pirjhan out, tied his wrists together behind him and forced him to his knees.

Mazar Tagh took the leash from his bear and looped it securely around Pirjhan's throat. He gave the other end of the leather rope to the bear. "Here, my pretty, a man-person to play with," he said, waving in a grand gesture to an old woman, who led the joined pair away.

Pirjhan resisted. The bear pulled on the leash that bound his neck, tumbling him onto the cobbled street. Then she dragged him along behind her as he twisted and fought for breath and balance. The Tagh's laughter resounded against stone walls as he watched his bear cavort with the captive man.

Talima looked up as this bear-like man hunkered down beside her cage. "What's your name?" he demanded. Talima did not answer. He reached in, took her arm and twisted it back against the bars. "Your name!"

"Talima."

"Who are you? Who are your people? Don't wait for me to break your arm—I will break it, you know. Tell me. Now."

"I am an Igren," she said proudly.

"I thought so," he said quietly. "What man d'you belong to?"

"I belong to no man!" Talima said defiantly.

"You belong to me now!"

"Never! What do you intend to do with us? Our men will find us soon, you know."

"Never," he echoed her. "We've been safe in our city since the time of Old Ones. Here we be protected from all harm! Ours is the First City. You...will never... escape!

"I had a son," he went on, "A good son, as sons go. He was Black Eagle son. Old enough to take a bride, but not wise. You two met, I think. Tell me!" he commanded, his voice harsh and raw with pain.

"I never met your son," Talima stated.

"You lie!"

"I never lie."

"Who be your head man?"

"I...I'm the Chagan's daughter."

"I knew it! Knew you to be barbarian! Everything about you stinks barbarian," he shouted and spat into her cage. "Now you will remember my son. My Black Eagle son, my Kurt Charigar son! The son your Father destroyed—nothing! For a little lie to a filthy druze. Nothing! And now I have no son," he growled.

"Kurt Charigar! Ah, yes, I do remember," Talima said softly. "I'm truly sorry about your son. But he broke The Law, he deliberately lied with intent to deceive."

"Why else would he lie?" Mazar Tagh wondered aloud.

"Don't you see," Talima said earnestly, "he declared himself part of our Kuriltai—we warned him, but he kept on lying and lying! You must understand...we had no choice!"

"No choice. No. Tagh have no choice, either, Kurt Charigar must be avenged. Gods angry! Hide our gold farther and farther down in evil depths of earth. Slaves die digging underground. Gods make our lives bitter. Make our wells dry! We thirst for sweet water. Children grow sick, swell up, die! All this, Tagh knows, is punishment for letting death of Black Eagle go unavenged. We need great sacrifice to make up for Kurt Charigar's stupid death! Hear me!" He bellowed then spat again into Talima's cage.

"And here you are, a barbarian druze," he continued more quietly. "It would be fine revenge—watching you split open like a ripe melon from seed I would plant in you. But I am the Great Tagh! I must think first of my men.

"You will be sacrificed to please the gods. You'll be the tool that opens a way to better times for my men!"

Talima stared at him, unbelieving, thinking he must surely be completely mad.

"But," he said thoughtfully, twisting a strand of beard around his ringed finger. "Best time for sacrifice be the longest day—coming soon. Full moon of summer coming soon. Sun-god work long hours then, be most hungry. You must be rounder, fatter, fuller like moon, so you will please gods. You must grow fat quickly, quickly.

"No moon now, but by full-moon-time you must be fat, moon-round, moon-full, to feed gods, to satisfy their hunger for revenge. Then will come good times for us. Good times at last!" Mazar Tagh shouted, pleased with such a simple solution to all his problems.

"Come! Come hear me!" he barked into the village. "A plan! A plan to please the gods! To bring water back! To bring gold! Hear me now!"

Among the people who came at his summons was his bear, still dragging Pirjhan behind her. An old crone disentangled the she-bear's bruised and bleeding plaything and shoved him into his cage.

Pirjhan heard Mazar Tagh's announcement through clouds of pain, "What? What does he mean? Are you all right, Tam?"

Talima told him everything she had learned, how crazy it all seemed, how helpless and trapped they were. Pirjhan agreed that they must escape somehow...and soon. They began to make plans, fantasy plans, unreal elaborate plans for impossible escape.

11
A Bear Service Girl

MAZAR TAGH'S PLAN BEGAN IMMEDIATELY. PLATES PILED WITH FOOD OOZING congealed fat, were shoved into Talima's cage. As unappetizing as it looked, Talima ate because she was hungry. She shared with Pirjhan until the women caught her passing food into his cage. Then they pushed his cage away, too far for her to reach.

Soon she was no longer hungry and then the horror began. Old women, fearful for their lives, force-fed Talima. When she would not eat, they took her out, bound her, forced open her mouth, stuffed it full, held her nose and stroked her throat until she simply had to swallow. Gagging, kicking, she ate. All day she ate. During the night, they waked her frequently with more food and thick, rich drinks.

Pirjhan's nightmare was different. Each day he was taken out and given to the Tagh's playful bear, to be returned hours later, bruised and battered, barely able to stand. At times Mazar Tagh would play with the bear first, tickling her, arousing her bearish sexuality until she teased him to play more intimately. Then he'd haul Pirjhan over by his leash and tell him to satisfy her. Little boys with stinging whips made certain that Pirjhan stayed within reach of the bear's hug.

Pirjhan, fed on scraps slimy with mould, grew weaker every day. Whenever he was allowed, he slept, exhausted.

Denied sleep, unable to touch or talk to Pirjhan, Talima lost the sense of time. She saw the days lengthen, watched the moon swell, felt herself bloat and thicken. Nothing seemed to matter. She felt powerless to think or plan. She had always had someone to turn to. Now there was no one.

In the endless procession of women who fed her, she noticed one who was different. *She's very young,* Talima thought, *not more than ten or eleven perhaps, and small for her age. Her bones stick out, welts and scars cover her arms. Her skin's dirty, but lighter-colored than the others, her tangled hair seems to be blonde—I wonder where she came from...*

Talima saw that the girl served everyone—children, women, and of course, any man. This girl invariably fed Talima on moonlit nights. Talima asked her why it was always she who came on these nights.

"When Skywalker-Moon walk the night, she lasso souls. Steal soul-seed, steal man-seed so man can't breed babies. Skywalker never give seed back! No one care about bear-girl's soul, no one mind if my soul be gone, so I walk the night."

"You seem different from the others. Who are you? What's your name?" Talima asked with the first spark of interest she had felt in days.

"My name be Faina. I be in *bear-service,*" she answered simply.

Faina, at Talima's insistence, told her story. She had been captured from a passing caravan as a young child, and because of her yellow hair, had been named as a future sacrifice to the Sun-god. Therefore she was in bear-service until she began her moon-flow.

"When I begin to bleed," Faina said shyly, "I be offered to the gods. Only, Mazar Tagh's angry with me I not show blood yet. He say too long in coming. So now, you be sacrifice before me."

"How horrible! Faina, tell me, do you know how they do it? How the sacrifice is done?"

"Only Tagh know for true. But old women say they see sacrifice once, longtime before. They say..." Faina looked around and lowered her voice to a whisper.

"What do they say, Faina?"

"They say on longest day, when sun rises, gods will eat. Eat living heart from sacrifice," she finished softly.

"They eat a person's *heart?* My heart?" Talima gasped.

"No, only eat heart of sacrifice," said the bear-girl, matter-of-factly.

"*Where,* Faina, do you know *where* they hold the sacrifice?" Talima asked urgently.

"No. Old women know. You eat now—not struggle?

"All right, if I promise you not to struggle, will you do something for me? Will you find out where this sacrifice will take place?"

"You not struggle? You not lie?"

"Faina, I *never* lie. I want to be your *friend.* Do you know what friend means?"

"Friend? When I was little, before I be a slave, word called friend. Nice sound. Yes, friend," Faina smiled. Her face became delicately beautiful.

"Yes, I will be your friend. I will *care* what happens to you, I will *listen* to you. I'll help you, if I can," Talima promised. "I must know how and where the sacrifice is going to happen. There isn't much more time, is there? Can you help me?"

"Can do...for friend," Faina whispered. "Can do!"

"One more thing—could you..." Talima spoke to Faina for a few minutes more, then watched her slip away, in and out of the crescent moon's shadows.

By her looks, Faina might even be an Igren, but anyway, she is a friend, a friend who might, somehow, someway, make a difference. If I can just figure out a way! Talima felt hopeful for the first time in what seemed like a hopeless lifetime.

Talima watched and listened with renewed attention, hoping to piece together enough information to escape. She yearned for Pirjhan's strength—and saw him weaken daily.

The days grew longer, the moon grew fuller. She knew that time was terrifyingly short before the scheduled sacrifice.

Each day she saw young women and slaves walk out of the village in long, dreary lines, to return much later with heavy loads of earth which were sifted for gold. Little girls tended sickly babies. Men came and went, often carrying an assortment of loot from passing caravans.

Talima had a rough idea now of the pattern of their lives—which directions led out of the village, where the men slept. She wondered where their animals were kept, whether Bagatur and Kara still lived. Perhaps Faina would know. Now that increasing moonlight kept most of the villagers inside their huts, Talima almost enjoyed the nights. It was quiet. She began to think more clearly.

Days, however, were agonizing. Mazar Tagh roamed the ruins constantly. Often he stopped by Talima's cage. There was no way she could avoid his jeweled hands. He poked and pinched her face and arms, kneaded her breasts, felt to see how full her flesh was growing. When pleased, he'd have her brought out and stripped, so he could inspect her more thoroughly. Talima had fought only once, kicking him on the shins and scratching his face. He had cuffed her head with idle power, setting her ears ringing, making her nose bleed. After that, she endured silently, saving her strength. She dreaded his visits, hated his touch, loathed the way he made her feel. She shut her eyes and tried to imagine being somewhere else. Visions of loving times with Pirjhan swamped her senses and she felt betrayed by her own healthy body.

Today, Mazar Tagh seemed to be in a particularly good humor. Talima could hear his laugh rolling before him as he came down old streets. She saw Faina, chickens scattering before her, hurrying across the open square. Mazar Tagh swaggered from an alley just as she passed.

"You there, bear-girl! Stop, don't run away! Too scrawny chicken-girl to be honored with bear-service. You bleed yet?" Mazar Tagh grabbed her arm.

Talima thought that Faina looked like a small rag-doll in the grasp of a giant bear.

"No, Great Tagh. No blood yet," Faina cringed from an expected blow.

"Take too long. Tagh make you bleed sooner. Make you do it *right.* I show you many times, stupid druze. Tagh must show you again. Over... bend!"

Talima watched in raging helplessness as Mazar Tagh casually flipped aside the meager skins that covered Faina's buttocks and held her there with one hand on her back. He searched through his tunic, brought out a ball of stuff that he popped into his mouth, chewing it with obvious pleasure. He grunted, and holding Faina's hips, impaled her. He pumped his immense organ into her, lifting her thin body off the ground with each thrust.

He grunted once and shoved her off him, sending her sprawling on the stones. Then he covered himself and ambled toward Talima without a backward glance.

"Bear-girl not good yet. Be better someday," he explained kindly to Talima.

"Better! You'll kill her, you beast!" Talima spat at him, shaking with anger. *I'll find a way to get back at you, I'll do something! I'll get us out of here...I will!*

"Ha! Druze feeling strong today, eh? Maybe Tagh show her, too?" he said, smiling ominously as he untied her cage door. He pulled her out into the sunshine.

She stood as tall and straight as she could. Her eyes flashed blue lightning. *What will I do if he treats me as he does Faina?* "You're evil! You can't abuse a person that way!"

"A person? What person?" Mazar Tagh was puzzled.

"You know very well what person. Faina...she has a name, you know!"

"Ah, bear-girl! Bear-girl not a person. Tagh a *person*," he thumped his chest. "I, Mazar Tagh, am a person! If druze a person, be like me!" he explained. "Person have this!" He waggled himself at her.

Talima felt her knees weaken and was afraid she'd fall.

"So. Bear-girl is not a person," he continued reasonably. "Druze never a person, is animal made by Old Ones for persons to use."

"*You* are the animal!" Talima flared.

"Enough! Shut your mouth! Stinking barbarian druze!" Mazar Tagh slapped Talima across her mouth, first with one enormous hand, then the other. His rings cut her cheek. She sagged to the ground.

"Stand!" he commanded, forcing her up again.

She stood warily, weaving slightly. He squeezed her thighs and breasts, measured how far his finger could poke into her navel, turned her this way and that to see what results the forced feeding had had.

"Something's wrong. Not fat enough. Two more days and still not fat enough. Good, but not enough." He sat down to think.

Talima, afraid to speak, gazed up at the Everlasting Sky and silently implored its blessing. She looked over at Pirjhan's cage. He was not back from his daily round with the bear. *Bring him again to me, Tengri... keep him alive a few more days, until I can figure out...*

Mazar Tagh thumped his thigh and shouted, "Now Tagh know why druze not fatter! All food is going to her head! Food's making hair grow, not body, ha!" He leaped up and yanked a knife from his sash.

He grabbed Talima by her hair and threw her to the ground between his legs. Her hair spread out around his boots, shining in the sunlight with a life of its own. Talima was terrified that he meant to kill her.

Mazar Tagh grabbed a fistful of her offending hair and hacked at it. He threw handfuls of her hair behind him, grasped more and cut that off. Then he pulled her up, grunted his satisfaction and pushed her back into her cage.

"Now druze'll grow fat like moon. Now food can make body fat for sacrifice." He stomped off.

Dry wind sent eddies of Talima's hair curling after him. Tufts of it caught on twigs and drifted against crumbled steps making the barren, squalid streets look oddly gay.

Around the far corner, whooping and bugling, a swan came. Her wings outstretched, her black head snaked forward, she flutter-hopped into the square.

"Kara! Kara, over here—here I am!" Talima sang out. The swan swung around and swooped toward the beloved voice.

"Kara, oh, Kara, I thought you were gone forever! What have they been doing to you, feeding you the same as me?" Talima reached through the bars and stroked her swan, her beautiful, *fat* Kara.

"They clipped your wing feathers, too, didn't they? Never mind, they've almost grown out again." She comforted.

For awhile they slept, Talima's arms through the bars, curved around Kara's back. When the women came to feed Talima, Kara hissed protectively. They didn't seem to mind having her there. It made their job easier. They simply shoved food down both girl and bird at the same time.

So Kara stayed. Talima drew strength from her presence. A plan began to take shape in her mind. *I'll need Faina's help, a lot of luck and every bit of strength I have, but Kara and Pirjhan are still alive...the Everlasting Sky is beginning to answer my prayers...and now, for the first time, it may be possible to...*

12
A Winged Horse Flies To The Moon

THROUGHOUT THE LONG, LINGERING TWILIGHT, TALIMA WAITED for Faina to come. Kara slept against her cage. Pirjhan, too, slept, moaning. When they brought him back that afternoon, he had not been conscious long enough to notice that Talima's shorn hair haloed her head in short, ragged curls.

Talima yearned to touch him, to tell him of her plans, to give him hope. She began to sing the song he had taught her on that golden afternoon so long ago, ".... *he put his hand in my hand, he put his hand to my heart...*" Tears streamed down her dirty cheeks. "*Oh, my dearest dear...sweet is the sleep of hand-to-hand, sweeter still the sleep of heart-to-heart.*"

She thought she saw him smile and her heart filled with a fierce resolve. She would save him. She must.

The full-circle moon rose. Shadows, as if cut from the light, became crisp black shapes, devoid of detail. A warm wind spoke of mysteries and magic. Mists writhed like ghostly dancers, accompanying Faina as she ran through deserted streets.

"Faina come, for friend," she said proudly. "Friend have name? Like me?"

"Yes, Faina. I have a name, too. My name is Talima, but you can call me Tam. Because we're friends." *And because I'd like to hear someone call me Tam again.* She looked longingly across at the cage where Pirjhan lay in darkness. "Did you find out where the sacrifice is going to be?" Talima asked urgently.

"Yes. Old women talk. Faina listen. They say sacrifice be made where earth talks. Where old stones stand."

"Where the earth talks? Where old stones stand? Do you know what that means, Faina?

"Once bear-girl see a place like that. Look for goat once. Find goat near place where earth-spirits whisper and blow hot mud from many earth mouths! They try to catch bear-girl! If catch me, cook me with spirit-breath!" she shivered, remembering.

"Think, Faina! What else was there?"

"Stone giants. Old Ones. Taller than Tagh! Old Ones dance in moonlight they say, dance in circle. Become stone by sunlight." Faina spoke with a rush, as if fearful of the moonlight itself.

"How do they...how is the sacrifice made? Did the old women talk about that?"

"Old women say it be one fine time, Tam," she said shyly. "All will be happy! Druze for sacrifice be happy more than all...drink god-seed-juice. Black seed-juice from poppy flowers, to make happy." She passed food to Talima, who ate with resignation.

"So. Everyone is either drunk or drugged? How does it happen, Faina?"

"You will know," Faina smiled. "Pretty bowl for god-seed-juice. Drink...dream...be happy...happy when Tagh cuts out heart for sun-god's food. They say this is for true, Tam, not lie!"

"I see. Faina, listen, we had two horses when we came. D'you know if they're still here?"

"Yes. Horses be just fine. They stay in a place outside village near mud-spirits. Boys try to ride them. Horses kick, run. Boys fall off!" She giggled.

The two girls laughed together, forgetting fears for a moment. Faina picked up the empty bowls and started to leave.

"Listen to me, Faina," Talima then spoke long and earnestly. "All right? D'you think you can do this?"

"Faina can do, Tam!"

"Thank you, my friend," Talima said. "Oh, and one more thing, will you be sure to bring..."

"Will bring! Tomorrow, Tam," she said shyly. "Tomorrow we be happy."

THE SHORTEST NIGHT PASSED; THE LONGEST DAY DAWNED. Not one villager left for the mines. The streets were thronged with men and women, boys and girls and slaves, all together.

Mazar Tagh, dressed in odds and ends of hoarded finery, was abroad early, joking with his men, tasting foods offered to him, play-wrestling with his bear. He carried a silver-handled lariat with which he lassoed little children, laughing when they fell. Good humor prevailed.

Men made a platform in the center of the square and covered it with furs for their Tagh. They brought Talima to the platform, took off her tattered skins and covered her with oil and rubbed her naked body until it shone. Someone produced a carved, wooden comb with which they feathered her cropped hair. Then they pushed her to her knees before the Tagh. Around her neck he fastened a collar of gold that was attached by a chain to the handle of his lariat. From the pile of furs he chose the softest and whitest ones and wrapped these around her, fastening them at her shoulders with long, gold-tipped pins.

He gestured with his lariat. Talima was jerked to her feet by the collar. From under his multicolored sashes, he took two woven bracelets, cuffed them around her wrists and tied them securely together in front of her. He called for his bear and chained and dressed her as he had Talima. Even Kara had a gold chain around one black leg which, when yanked, caused her to shriek and flap wildly, creating more merriment for the celebrants.

Millet and honey beer was set out in large gourds. By midday, no free person was sober. The Tagh's bear was let loose. She lumbered from group to group, getting drunker, upsetting pots and people, multiplying the confusion.

Mazar Tagh generously allowed each of his men a turn leading Talima around. Some of the men insisted on sharing their beer with her, spitting it ceremoniously from their own mouths directly into hers.

Talima seethed with anger and humiliation. But she was quiet, knowing she must wait. Wait to make any move lest she alarm her captors. She had not seen Faina all morning and hoped that that meant she had been able to do what she had asked of her. It was a terrible gamble, but one essential to her plan.

Pirjhan, too, was brought out to share in the celebration. Talima was shocked to see how thin he had become. Old crones tried to lead him as Talima and Kara had been led, but they left him where he had fallen while they went for more beer.

Talima's heart cried for him. Involuntarily, she started in his direction when he fell, only to be pulled up short by her chain. Mazar Tagh, suddenly alert, looked from her to the crumpled body of Pirjhan. He gestured for Pirjhan to be brought before him.

"So this is the kind of man-being you like, eh, druze? This small scrap? It might be amusing to..." Mazar Tagh grinned malevolently. "After all, what matters? Tomorrow you be god-meat. Today you have what you want. Tagh give all good things today. Give man-slave to druze for happy coupling! Yes!" Mazar Tagh nodded, impressed by his own generosity.

Before he could act on this idea, three drunken hags reeled into the square leading a black-and-white horse. Cackling and chortling, they picked up Pirjhan and, with some difficulty, hoisted his limp body up onto its back, tying his feet together around the horse's tail. Then they wound a rope around Pirjhan's neck and arms, tying them to the horse's neck. All three slapped the horse's rump and stepped back to watch the results of their buffoonery as the horse, spooked by noise and confusion, dashed wildly every whichaway and Pirjhan's body, arms flopping, bobbled ridiculously.

One thing led to another. Mazar Tagh went on to other entertainments and forgot his threatened generosity. Talima patiently endured the afternoon's eternity.

After a few more hours of revelry, Mazar Tagh summoned his musicians to play. Three men drummed, two blew long horns, one clanged cymbals. They began to play beside the Tagh's platform. To Talima's ears, their music sounded wildly discordant, tuneless, weird.

Buzzing with excitement, the villagers swarmed together. The drum's pulse quickened human heartbeats. Cymbals flashed and clashed. The long-drawn-out, haunting notes of rams' horns echoed against the stones of fallen walls.

Mazar Tagh motioned to his closest men. They brought him a two-handled urn decorated with black and white dancing figures, a delicate relic from an age beyond memory. He stood and held it above his head. "Today be the end of bitter times. Long time of no water, no more gold, will be gone now! Great Tagh has cared for you all. Has made good things happen for you!"

Pirjhan and his horse, no longer the focus of attention, stood in the shade of a ruined wall. Talima, at the Tagh's feet, held as still as she could. She breathed slowly and gathered strength into herself for what, she felt sure, was soon to happen.

"Tonight we take this druze," he pointed at Talima, "to sky-walker. She will eat the soul of druze. Then horned-mother will be happy. Will give us sweet water!

"At dawn we take the heart of this druze for sun-god. We take her heart and we eat! Become strong like the heart of sun! Strong with gold. No more troubles! Yes, your great Tagh sees this. Gives you all this!" His arms swept out in an expansive gesture.

"Now we drink. Be happy. Dream..." he finished amidst loud, drunken cheering. He picked up a small gourd, decorated with burnt-in designs and poured the thick, black-purple liquid it contained into a large urn of beer. With great solemnity, he stirred it as the crowd watched. Not one word broke the expectant silence.

The Tagh scooped up a dipperful. With slow ceremony, he offered it first to Talima, who pretended to drink but only swallowed air. She held the drugged liquid in her mouth until she could spit it out without being noticed.

Then Mazar Tagh drank and passed the libation to his people. As the dipper emptied, it was refilled. The air hummed with murmurs of appreciation. When all had drunk, the Tagh mixed up more of the poppy-juice in a tiny, porcelain cup and placed it beside Talima.

"Drink this. All of it" he commanded in a low, hoarse whisper. She swallowed a bit, but again she pretended, letting the poppy juice spill onto the platform when he wasn't looking.

Mazar Tagh stood. The black bearskin swung from his wide shoulders, the bear's skull crowned his head. He lifted Talima, clad in white furs, and carried her off the platform and into the square. Quietly, people parted to make room for them.

Musicians took their places. Mazar Tagh, holding Talima effortlessly before him, came next. Following him came his tipsy bear, the men and the boys. After them came women who balanced baskets of food and flagons of beer on their heads. Everyone else straggled along behind. Kara and the black-and-white horse, carrying a barely conscious Pirjhan, brought up the rear.

The procession wound through carved pillars that held up empty sky on either side of the road, out of town, and into the countryside. The stench of rotten eggs enveloped them, growing stronger as they went.

Talima, partially shrouded by the Tagh's bearskin, surrounded with its rancid animal smell, was carried on inexorably. She willed her body to lie very still in Mazar Tagh's arms, but her mind was racing.

Where is Faina? I wonder how much farther we have to go? She tried to visualize exactly what she would do when she got to the place of sacrifice, to the Old Stones, but couldn't. She had no idea what she'd find there. Terror threatened her will.

What if I can't get away? What if I die here? They'll never even know! I wish father were here, or the Bequi, she thought. Doubts of her own ability hammered at the walls of her resolve as the men who marched with them chanted words she could not understand.

An image of the Bequi shuffle-skipped into her mind. She saw her as she had been at Kuriltai, singing, *"Hold to the highest"* and blowing her magic white powder on each of them. She could almost feel that powder shimmer around her, sift into her blood. She felt, pressed under her arm, a bit of the slim reed that Faina had brought to her from her arrow case, from the heap of other confiscated things outside the Tagh's hut.

The rhythmic beat of drums thrummed her body and patterned itself into words in her head, incongruous words, words of love that Pirjhan taught her, *"...as I was shining bright and dancing, singing praises to the coming of the night...he met me, my beloved met me, we rejoiced together."* And suddenly she felt clear and strong and filled with light.

I will survive! I will free us! Like the waters that sprang from Burkhan Kaldun Mountain, she felt a certain power surge into her being.

A new sound now intruded into the caterwauling of horns—a fervent, seething sound. Talima felt hot steam against her bare legs. She opened her eyes.

She saw that they wound their way through a field of mud springs. Black mud with a life of its own, dark blood of the earth itself. It pulsed into the evening sunlight, wheezing, sighing, flopping down again in shining circles, releasing spirals of rank-smelling steam into the dry air.

Slowly, ever so slowly, Talima turned her head to see what lay ahead. Beyond the fuming mud field she saw a raised mound crowned with monolithic stones standing in a circle.

There they are, there are the Old Stones that Faina told me about. That's where it all begins...or ends! No! I'll get us out of this, I know I can. I hope you're ready, Faina!

The music stopped. Now Mazar Tagh moved ahead, holding Talima as an offering before him. Talima felt weightless, as if her flesh was whisper light, obedient to the air's will rather than the earth's whim.

The Tagh walked inside the circle of standing stones. People flowed around them, filling space between the massive rock spears. Mazar Tagh carried Talima to the center and gently stood her up on a flat stone slab. He turned her around so that all could see and appreciate their sacrifice.

Talima realized they were on the edge of a cliff, for she could see, over the villager's heads, a rumpled plain that spread eastward, far below. She turned to look at the setting sun. It glowed, incandescent as it sank toward the jagged horizon. There was no sound. Nothing moved. The world seemed to be holding its breath. Waiting for the sun to die, waiting for the moon to rise. Time hung suspended in the still air.

Faint, warbling cries pricked the stillness. Talima recognized the sound instantly. Her pulse quickened. As if it were the signal she'd waited for, she lifted her head. Like a wild creature, she smelled the wind for information she sensed it carried.

Moments later, the first migrating swans flew above them. The rushing sound of wings, the cries, honks, whoops and sighs, became clearer and louder. A multitude of swans flew above them in a tapestry of sound.

Kara bugled, answering their ancient summons. Unable to join their flight due to her clipped wings, she lurched and flapped through the throng of people. She reached Talima and leaped onto her shoulders. Balanced there with outstretched wings, her neck curved over Talima's golden head, she sang out her longing for freedom.

This was the moment Talima had prayed for, the moment she had known, that somehow Tengri would send her. She whistled, adding her own shrill call to that of the swans. Her whistle went unnoticed, unnoticed by all the dreaming people. Noticed only by those it was meant for—Bagatur and Faina, who waited at the village corral by the edge of the mud-springs.

Hearing his mistress' whistle, Bagatur bolted away from Faina's hold on his bridle, and cleared the fence in one soaring leap. All the other horses surged after him. With water bags slung over her frail shoulders, Faina ran after them as fast as she could.

Bagatur led all the horses in a turbulent gallop toward Talima's whistle-summons as they raced along the same narrow trail that the villagers had taken. At times they slipped off into steaming mud but, without slowing their pace, pulled their hooves from the ooze and raced on. Finally, they galloped up onto the mound. Bucking and snorting, they ran into the crowded circle-stones.

Mazar Tagh stared in disbelief. Everything seemed without sound, without significance to him. Eternally slow—but still he held Talima's neck-chain.

As Bagatur charged up to her, Talima got ready to jump. Before she could, Mazar Tagh yanked on her chain and sent her tumbling and Kara whooping, onto the ground. Bagatur reared, pawing the air above the Tagh's head.

In that instant, as undulating rivers of swans whistled overhead and horses scattered the dreaming people, Mazar Tagh looked up at death.

Bagatur's great hooves moved out of the sky inexorably, inevitably. They pounded Mazar Tagh. His hooves hammered into flesh, smashed his bones against the stone until only a bloody bearskin covered the pulpy mass that was left.

Bagatur trumpeted to Talima. She scrambled onto his back and wound her braceleted hands into his mane. Kara screamed onto her shoulders, her wings stretched skyward for balance. Talima searched the milling horses for the one that carried Pirjhan and, finding him, turned Bagatur in that direction.

She grabbed Pirjhan's lead-rope as they ran by. Together they thundered out of the crowd and down the trail that led back toward the village and off the mountain to freedom.

As a bubble rises to the surface and floats, the full moon popped above the plain and soared into the summer night's sky. All that Mazar Tagh's people ever remembered was a swan song that swallowed their sacrifice...and a winged horse that flew into the moon.

Talima saw Faina when she was only a speck ahead of them. Holding her arms out to her she shouted, "Stand still, Faina! Grab hold of me...I'll swing you up behind...now! Jump!

Faina obeyed. As the horses ran toward her, she stood by the side of the path, her thin arms raised, ready. Talima braced herself with her knees as she had done in games at home. At full gallop, she leaned to one side and scooped Faina up onto Bagatur's back.

"Hang on! Take your knife. Cut loose my hands. You were perfect, Faina. You did everything right! Now hang on. Tight! We've a hard ride ahead!"

She looked back over her shoulder at Pirjhan and saw that he was conscious. *Good,* she thought, *I'll have to stop and untie him, as soon as I can—as soon as it's safe.*

The wind sang in Talima's ears. She felt clear and resolute. She saw the barren rocks and hills glow with an inner light, rainbow-rimmed. Each sound—night bird's cry, rattle of racing hooves, her own breath—pierced her heart with its sweetness.

She felt her head brush the sky. A high, keening cry pushed up out of her throat. Exultant. Electrifying. Echoing, as she rode, against the toppled walls of past glories.

Moonlight lit their way out of the ruins, down through the twisting canyon passage and out onto the plains. Only then did Talima stop. She untied Pirjhan and caught him in her arms as he slid off his horse.

"'Hatou, Beauty," he smiled wanly as she hugged him. "You did it! I don't know how, but you did!"

Fears from the past and problems of the future were unimportant for a few moments. They had each other. They were alive. And free.

13
THE SINGING SANDS

BUT, THERE *WERE* PROBLEMS, SOME SMALL, SOME SERIOUS. THE MOST SERIOUS was the scarcity of water. Faina's water-bags would last a day or two at most. Talima hoped that would give them time to find an oasis, but knew she couldn't count on it. She reassured Faina's fears by telling her that Bagatur had often found water for her in the past, that he would most likely do so again. To herself, she added *I hope!*

The immediate problem was food. Talima felt that she and Kara could go for months without more to eat. But Pirjhan, Faina, and the horses were another matter. Talima doubted they would be pursued. Mazar Tagh was dead and his entire herd of horses had followed Bagatur, but she knew too, that the Tagh's men ranged far and fast on foot. It was wise to be as far away from the village as quickly as possible. It was difficult to forage for food at their distance-devouring canter.

The moon was in mid-heaven when they first halted their wild ride down onto the plain. Talima put on a tunic that Faina had brought and tied the furs in which Mazar Tagh had wrapped her around Pirjhan's wasted body.

A recurring problem was that of keeping Pirjhan and Faina on the back of their horses. Faina had never ridden before, and Pirjhan was too weak to ride without a saddle to cling to. And they had no saddle. They stopped often for one or the other to be pushed back on again after sliding off. Whenever they stopped, Kara whooped and bobbed excitedly, spooking all the horses, who then pranced and cavorted in terror, making Faina's and Pirjhan's seat even more precarious.

Talima's major worry was for Pirjhan, who was desperately weak. She knew he needed time to rest, time to heal his body and spirit from the long ordeal. But they could ill afford to stop.

She wondered where Juchi and the others might be, whether they'd waited at the blue iris river, or continued on. She reasoned that, since they were honor-bound to take the horses to Chian, they would have continued eastward.

It's just possible that we might intersect the caravan route further on, if they continued traveling in the same direction as before. And if I've reckoned where we are, with any accuracy...

It was worth a try. So she kept the Wayfinder star, that bright star that Juchi had taught her to recognize, over her left shoulder, and let the horses slow to a steady walk.

They pushed on erratically, silently, through the moonlight. The night seemed interminable. Talima knew it was all too short.

As the summer sun bolted into an apricot sky, they came to cliffs where pigeons nested in hollows that honeycombed the rock face. Below the rose-colored rock, groundwater seeped into shallow puddles. They spent the day following the sun's shadow around the walls, napping in turns, drinking their fill.

While Pirjhan slept, Talima and Faina dug into cracks and crevices to find wild carrots and other edible roots. They climbed up to ledges where they found pigeons' nests filled with small, round eggs. Carefully, they carried the eggs down and, one by one, fed them all to Pirjhan.

Toward evening they set out again. Talima noticed a few traces left from passing caravans: dried camel dung, a broken pot, scraps of outworn leather. "You see, my dears? Others have come this way before us! It won't be long now before we catch up with our chapars and the banner of horses." *Please, Great Tengri!*

They found no more water for several days. Their water -bags were empty. Talima showed Faina how to cut open flat-leaved cacti for a few drops of life-giving liquid. They plodded on all through the next night and well into the morning without finding water or shelter again. Talima picked up a small pebble for each of them to hold in their mouths, warding off the worst thirst. Constant wind shifted the dunes they traveled and blew shining veils of sand off every crest, sending sand-spume slithering down the lee side in feathered patterns.

Talima walked beside Bagatur, on whose back Kara perched. A straggling line of the Tagh's horses followed them, their legs sinking almost knee-deep in blowing sand. On all sides, barren, lifeless slopes ranged, ridge after fluted ridge, boldly etched against a burnt-orange sky.

Late one afternoon, Talima thought she saw a burnished island that rose from heat haze shimmering before them. A pure white, pillared temple, misted by clouds, seemed to rise out of the blazing sea of sky. *It looks,* she thought wearily, *like a place that gods might live, oh, Everlasting Sky, see Thy children! Hold us, bring us to safety!*

As they plodded through time, she witnessed the island and temple dissolve into nothingness, one more illusion in an unreal world.

The next morning, Talima led Pirjhan's horse as they began to climb a particularly steep, forbidding ridge. Breathing became more difficult as the sun grew hotter. Sand sucked them down with every step. The horses frequently floundered and fell in flurries of sand. Pirjhan was conscious less and less.

Helping to push Pirjhan's heavy, limp body back onto his horse was an obstacle that Faina's strength was no longer equal to.

"Tam? I can't go on, can't hang on anymore." Faina's thin face was gaunt.

"It's going to be all right, Faina, we'll just take one step after another. *Tengri, if I can just keep them moving, one agonizing step at a time! One day and night at a time, and pretty soon, we'll be fine, I'm sure there is something good waiting for us—there has to be! We've come so far!* Come on...we can do it! We escaped from Mazar Tagh, remember, so we can do anything we need to do, right? *I'm Igren, I can do this!*

Close to exhaustion herself, Talima reached the crest of the ridge. She looked down the other side and...saw a miracle...and dared to hope it might be real this time—not one more mirage.

What she saw, hundreds of feet below, was another crescent-shaped lake curved into the hollow of warm dunes like a new moon cut from the clearest turquoise. Trees ringed the lake and beyond, a vast herd of horses grazed spring-green fields. White horses beneath the noonday sun dazzled her eyes. Near the horses, small-domed gers stood. *It has to be, it is—an Igren camp!*

"Jhani! Faina! It's a lake! I'm sure it's a lake! And I think...it looks like...come and see!" She led them to the top, held each one as they slid from their horses. They lay on the ridge and looked below.

They saw swans and small black ducks that speckled the lake's mirror surface while along the water's edge familiar looking people walked. With a bugling whoop, Kara leaped over the edge and tumbled down. As she did so, the hillside sands shimmered and sang. Whenever she landed, a humming sound thrummed the air. Talima, Faina, and a wobbly Pirjhan joined her, falling and sliding down the singing sands.

As the horses followed, the whole slope trembled and reverberated. Echoes rang a welcome from surrounding hills. By the time they stumbled, breathless and laughing, into the valley, Juchi was there to meet them. Talima thought his snaggle-toothed grin was the most beautiful sight in the whole world.

"Talima-sha! Great Tengri! I thought never to see you again!" Juchi pranced stiff-legged around them. Tears streamed down his weathered face.

"Oh, Juchi, I am so glad to see you!" Talima could only stand and smile, her heart overflowing with joy.

"Where have you been? What happened to you?"

"In a moment...first help me get Pirjhan into the shade. Some water first, then stories, Juchi."

Tulak and Kilar ran up shouting and laughing. They carried Pirjhan into the cool and fragrant shade of a grove of cottonwood trees.

"'Sky! It's so good to see you all, just to be here, together again. Juchi, Kilar, Tulak, I want you to meet my friend, Faina. Without her we wouldn't be...well, it's a long story!"

Friends clustered around them as Talima began telling their tale, interrupted at intervals by a proud and smiling Pirjhan.

DAYS PASSED, SOMNOLENT PEACEFUL DAYS, ORDINARY HEALING DAYS. Only the comforting, homely tasks of caring for horses, hunting, preparing and eating food, were necessary. The rest was play. Kara preened and swam with her own kind while Faina's merry laugh charmed them all. Pirjhan grew strong rapidly and Talima was, quite simply, happy.

Perhaps it was the lake that held them in thrall, all that glinting, rippling, dazzle of water in lives that since birth were enured to arid, wind-riven, dust-dry mountain meadows. It seemed a paradise that the Great Blue Wolf herself had conjured for their ease and pleasure. Except for two old monks who tended their garden on the far shore, no other travelers arrived to break the spell. This wonderland was all their own. Time held them in its sunny days and star-reflected nights.

Willows curtained a shallow pool wherein Talima played. She rolled and splashed and dived as if she, too, were one of the rose-speckled fish that darted beneath her in clear water. She lay still and reveled in the silken feel of sun-warm fresh water along the length of her body. Minnows, their tiny sides like iridescent ribbons, gathered around her floating breasts, and suckled at stiff, pink nipples and the little ridges surrounding them. When she moved, fish flashed away for an instant, then returned. Her laughter was as liquid as the pool.

She stood, smoothed water from her arms and belly, shook her hair out to dry, and walked through rushes onto the shore where she climbed onto a flat rock that held the heat of morning. She dozed and dreamed.

And dreaming, once again felt the great, green-gold dragon between her thighs, its awesome power as it scaled the sky, sensed the earth unroll beneath them as they flew, saw an immense stone snake that defined the mountains' horizon as it undulated along their flanks, felt a tumbling terror that had no name, knew sorrow that rose, like the cloud of lemon-colored dust below, to shroud the dragon's wings. She heard a singing in the wind as she woke.

Through the pale, green lace of willow branches she saw Pirjhan running down the hill of singing sand. Quietly, she watched as he stripped off his clothes and waded into the lake. *Still too thin,* she thought, *but beautiful and strong again.*

His throat and arms were deeply tanned, his body creamy white and muscled, the fine, delineated muscles of a horseman. She smiled as she noticed his flesh gather inward, his jade stalk shrinking within its tight wrinkled sack as he waded into cool water. The hairs around her precious gate prickled. She rubbed herself softly. She could smell the peach-flower smell of her body's own juices. Drawn by an ancient summons, she slipped soundlessly into the water.

Unaware of her presence, Pirjhan dove into the lake, then exploded into the air shaking showers from his dark, curly mane as a stallion, filled with good health and frolicsome spirits, is wont to do. Then he stretched out on a flowered island-tussock, put his arms behind his head and squinted into the sky.

Talima swam soundlessly toward him and tickled his toes with a grass stem. He idly kicked at whatever it was. As she twirled the grass between his toes, he twitched all over in annoyance and sat up abruptly. Talima's laughter rippled over them.

"Oh, it's you, Beauty! I thought it was a water-kelet come to nibble my vitals," he chuckled.

Talima smiled. It was a smile that spoke the words she could not say, a knowing smile of woman's mysteries, a smile of promise. Slowly she pulled her wet body over him. Warm length of throat, breasts, belly, thighs slithered over cool, hard thighs, erect and pulsating stalk, taut belly, broad chest and waiting mouth.

The sun on her back was cooler than the joined heat of their bodies. Her desire imbued his body with an answering life of its own. His desire quickened her and called her into being, a new being of woman, first woman of creation, all women from the source of all beginnings.

As one body, they tumbled into the lake. They swam into the shallows, touching, gliding, separating and coming back together, a ritual dance of loving. Sunlight through willow leaves stippled their bodies, light and dark, making flesh insubstantial, a reflection of water and light.

As he pulled her to him, she saw him smile, a slow-dawning smile that seemed to take possession of her. His eyes held her, flooded her senses until she became buoyant, afloat.

He cradled her head amongst flowers: tiny white stars of watercress that echoed the stars in her eyes, lupines the same mauve of his manhood, fringed mouths of water hyacinths as rosy as the swelling nether-mouth of her sex. She writhed in rising ecstasy. Waves rippled against the shore.

Along the length and heat of their bodies, their skins melted, fused. Tenderly, he slid into the deepest wellspring of her body. He filled her... her womb, her belly, her lungs, her throat, her mind, her heart. He came into her in full flood. Inundated by his seed, there was no part of her he did not quicken.

They floated free and swam together through blue-silver space. Higher and yet higher, breathing eternity's instant... hovering...holding, breaking the bonds of watery earth, they burst beyond dimension. Rapturous. Ecstatic. One.

And slowly, slowly, settled into separate skins, shook themselves into their own bodies, opened their eyes...and saw each other. Two now. Joined only in the circle-song of loving.

"For you are...in I, am...in you," she murmured. "D'you remember, Jhani? The Kuriltai dance? So long ago?"

"Yes, I remember," he smoothed hair from her shining face. "For I am, in you, and you are...in me," he finished the litany.

"I love you Jhani. I didn't know what that meant...before."

"Beauty, I love *you*. There is nothing else in all the world except my love for you."

They dressed then, slowly, reluctant to move away from each other, reluctant to put more skins than necessary between them. Hand in hand, in the fullness of a summer afternoon, they wandered into the hills together.

JUCHI STOPPED SCRAPING OUT HIS HORSE'S HOOF AND WATCHED as they walked, arms around each other's waist, Talima's head on Pirjhan's shoulder. He saw them almost float through long grass, saw the smile of lingering rapture on her face. And recognized that an ancient alchemy had taken place.

My wild young mountain filly's gone and gotten herself to be a woman, he murmured. *Aye, bound to happen, those two, sure's the sun comin' up in th' mornin'. And right now it's all right but...ah, Tengri, I'm fearful for them! For when we leave this spirit-blessed place and come into Chian...what then? What can two lovers do then? And what will happen to the Igren when the emperor finds out that the Chagan's word is broken?*

He sighed, heavy with worry over the future, and went back to the familiar comfort of cleaning the frogs of his horse's hooves.

14
Li Jho Recognizes Talima's Destiny

It had been a morning of patience and frustration for Talima, trying to teach Faina to launch Merket, a falconry skill so familiar to Talima, so foreign to Faina. But Faina, with her usual merry attitude, kept them both laughing even when they failed to get meat for dinner.

Talima and Faina were just returning from hunting in the hills north of Half Moon Lake when they saw a gaudy procession. The caravan, the first that had come since they had arrived, was jingling and ringling down the sand hills.

"Those people aren't from our part of the world, Faina. Those foot soldiers, in their leather greaves and short sabres, look like those that accompanied Chang Chun," Talima remarked. *How long ago the Chian ambassador came into my home valley, it seems like a dream...or is this the dream?* "I know, let's go visit with them after we turn the horses out, all right with you?"

"Oh, yes, Tam, see how beautiful those persons are. It would be good to talk to more friends like us."

"Faina, try to remember, we are all persons, not just men. But you're right, those men do look remarkable."

As the group rode closer, they saw that the men wore high, fitted boots and full-sleeved tunics, elaborately embroidered across their shoulders. Enameled, jeweled dagger handles protruded from belts slung low on their hips. Three wore black hats with wide leather brims. One man, taller than the rest, wore a turban of striped silk. They came, laughing and joking, riding horses hung with silver trappings. Oxen, camels and asses followed, laden with wicker hampers, bulging carpetbags and baskets of every shape imaginable.

Three women in the center, riding creamy-white horses, wore slender shifts over full, gathered pants. Wind from the hills fluttered their shining silk tunics. *They look,* Talima thought, *like butterflies drying their wings—just as Chang Chen did.*

LATER, TALIMA, FAINA AND PIRJHAN WANDERED AROUND THE LAKE to the cottonwood grove where the strangers had set up camp. They were greeted enthusiastically in a mixture of gestures and trade language. One young woman, slimmer than the others, wore her gleaming black hair braided with ribbons, fastened high on her head with silver hairpins. She held out a traditional mountain welcome—palms open, raised shoulder high.

"Hatou, strangers," she greeted them. "Do you live in this lovely valley?"

"No, we are Igren, on our way to Chian. I am Talima, daughter of the Great Chagan, Tashih Shaymak, and this is Pirjhan, our head horseman, and Faina, a dear friend."

"And are all these animals yours?" the woman swept her arms out to indicate the thousand grazing horses and pack-camels.

"Yes, they are tribute to the most illustrious Emperor Tai Tsung," Pirjhan said shortly. "And who might you be?"

"I? I am Wu Shih Ssu, third daughter of the Duke Wu Shih Huo, and of my mother, Wu Shih Yang, who is a daughter of the royal family of Sui. We come from the Imperial City and are following the Great Silk Road west to the land beyond Samarkand."

"Why?" interrupted Talima.

"Why? Well, you see I am betrothed to a Uighur Qaqhan, Chinghis Qhan. My family accumulates great honor by this alliance as well as riches," she explained with pride, "...for the Qhan sent marvelous gifts—sable furs, girdles of jade, a hundred horses, twenty camels and a hunting-leopard—just for me!"

"Oh!" said Talima. "Like me! You're traveling to a strange land to be wed to a man you've never seen for purposes that are not your own. How terrible!"

"Not terrible at all, wonderful! Exciting! To be so honored by my emperor is a great privilege. What more worthy act, could I, a mere third daughter, ever accomplish? I'm only in the position of fourth-mourning to our Most Luminous Illustrious, yet he chose me, and the children I will bear, to be a bridge that unites two countries. It is most excellent for me!" Shih Ssu shrugged gracefully.

Her curving, crimson fingernails make her pale hands look like the talons of an eagle after a kill, thought Talima. "But Shih Ssu, don't you mind leaving your family and friends?"

"Why no," Shih Ssu said, as if it were the first time the thought had ever occurred to her. "I left my family in Tai Yuan long ago when my first moon-flow came. I've spent the eight years since then in the imperial court as a lady-in-waiting to the most gracious aunt, Li Tien Phu, who only passed on into the Celestial Realm a few months ago.

"Besides. I brought my friends, some of them anyway, with me," she smiled at her countrymen. "These two girls are now *my* ladies-in-waiting and these three fine horsemen are cousins and younger brothers. We bring our culture to the mon-barbarian court of the Uighur Qaqhan.

"And I," the turbaned man stepped forward, smiling, "...am Li Jho, counselor to Princess Ssu. We are glad to make your acquaintance in this spirit-forsaken land."

"Oh, Li Jho, I didn't mean to leave you out," laughed Shih Ssu, "I just left the very best till last. He's more than my counselor," she confided, "...he's an astronomer, a dream interpreter, a soothsayer, a magician! Aren't you, dear Li Jho?"

"When the occasion calls for it," he answered serenely, "But now, tell us please, of your country."

"Yes, tell us what the trail west is like!"

"Is there water all the way?"

"What dangers did you encounter?"

Questions came fast. While Talima and Pirjhan answered them, Shih Ssu's people laid out wine and other foods: lychee nuts, sticky, sweet buns, rice balls stuffed with dried grapes and almonds, apricots, and dried fish.

Filled with freedom and high adventure, the young people exchanged stories of home and the trails they had traveled. The convivial afternoon drifted into a glowing twilight.

Talima was groggy the next morning. *Too much wine, too much talk, probably,* she told herself. Before she was really awake, Shih Ssu and Li Jho were suddenly beside her.

"Talima, Li Jho has discovered something important that we want to discuss with you." Ssu spoke in a rush.

"Important? Me?"Talima tried to pull her muddled thoughts into more coherent order.

"With your permission, I must ask a few questions," Li Jho said, as they sat down facing Talima.

"All right, but I can't think..."

"Let me first tell you what has occurred." He ran his hand through his midnight-black hair, unbound by his turban this early morning. "I was unable to sleep last night. The new moon beckoned me down to the lake. There, I sat and meditated on the ripples lapping at my feet, the silver shoon of them that seemed to speak in liquid words I could almost understand.

"Mists rose into the moonlight and within those mists I saw forms that began to take shape. As I watched, a green and gold dragon writhed up from the depths...and stared at me! Yes, stared right into my eyes!"

Talima gasped.

"I leaned forward to more closely see this most auspicious creature," Li Jho continued. "Closer and closer toward me it came, and I could see that it wanted to tell me something."

Talima shivered as from a swift-chilling wind.

"And it was then I heard, heard the dragon's fiery breath breathing out at me with these words, 'Riding a comet that sweeps the azure Everlasting Sky, she is the Prince of Wu, the future emperor of all Chian!'

"As this dragon sank down into the seething waters, it whispered, 'Look around you, she is here now. The glorious prince, herself.' And I must ask you, Talima, for it is your face that lingered in the glowing aftermath, do you know what this means? And more to the point, are you perhaps familiar with this dragon?

"Oh, dear, I don't know...I can't say for sure, but..." Talima held her breath, and tried to think of what, and how much, to tell them.

"It has been written that a comet will herald a Prince of Wu. It has been known, also, to many scholars like myself, that there is a high mountain lake in which the images of future rulers can be seen. A lake wherein great sages and great kings are foretold. To find this lake is one of the main reasons I accompanied Shih Ssu on her travels," he said, his words sliding like smooth pebbles underwater. "Are you, Talima, this

Prince of Wu?"

"Li Jho...Ssu...no, I am only Talima. But..."*Great Tengri! What can I say?* "I do dream of a dragon, a green and gold dragon...once in awhile... since I was little, actually."

"Talima, this is so exciting!"Ssu sparkled. "And Wu is my family name, so maybe..."

"And what does this dream dragon do, only-Talima?" his velvety voice seemed to crackle the question at her.

"Nothing, I just ride it while it flies high into the sky,"she explained. "And I've never finished the dream because I'm so in awe of the dragon's power—and I just wake up, you see."

"I think I do see, only-Talima, I believe I have witnessed your destiny, your Chian destiny." He took Ssu's arm and pulled her to her feet. "I must ponder this event carefully. Come along, Shih Ssu, we shall all meet soon again."

"Oh, Talima, I want to get better acquainted with you!"Ssu exclaimed. "Will you meet me after first meal so we can talk?"

"Yes, I'd like that, I'll be there." Talima watched the two tall Chianese, heads bent toward each other, talking as they walked quickly away.

How did he know about my dragon dream? I wonder what he meant by my "Chian destiny". All in his imagination, I suspect, or perhaps it was a mirage, a vision. Funny, he looks like such a sensible man, too! It makes no sense...except it does sound a little like what the Bequi said. Well, I won't think about it right now.

15
SHIH SSU SHOWS MAGIC

"HOW MANY DAYS' TRAVEL BEFORE WE REACH CHANGAN?" Talima asked Shih Ssu as they walked their horses down to the lake.

Talima, with Merket on her left gauntlet, rode Bagatur beside Shih Ssu on Shira. Talima had initiated an excited Ssu into the wonders of hunting with a falcon, and the hunt had been successful, for their saddlebags held six wild pigeons and an unwary rabbit.

"Changan? Well, we've been traveling nearly a moon now. We left during the Lotus Moon, and now the moon is almost into the Moon of Hungry Ghosts. We're in no hurry. We want to experience everything along the way, you see," Ssu said. "Oh, Talima, you must go by the Tun Huang caves if you can.

"Monks live there, each in his own little cave, who worship The Mother, most Merciful and Compassionate One bless us, and they paint their visions, feathered fairies and birds, in reds and purples on the dun-colored cave walls!"

"Are these caves on our way?"

"You've been traveling along the Tien Shan Nan Lu, the Northern Silk Route, haven't you?"

They dismounted, stripped off saddles and bridles and turned the horses out to graze.

"We've been riding eastward through high desert keeping a range of mountains to the north, if that's the route you speak of, yes."

Talima picked up her bag of game and gave it to Tulak for skinning and preparing for dinner.

"You'll soon head up into the mountains again. You must, in order to reach Chian, you know. Then you'll trail down through the Jade Gate, a narrow pass that opens onto the foothills of Chih-Chuan. From there it's easy going, wide valleys, open fields, and farms all along the Great Wall, until you come to Changan.

"In roughly 50 li after Jade Gate Pass, you'll see a split in the main road, one part leading slightly south. That's the way to the Tun Huang caves, it won't delay you more than a day or two."

"Sounds intriguing," Talima said. They walked into the cool, shade of musky cottonwoods where the Chian caravan was camped. "We cover 250-300 li in a day, Ssu, barring misfortune and formidable terrain. How long will it take us to reach Changan?"

"You are persistent, aren't you, Tam?" Ssu laughed. "All right, let's see, six or seven days. Maybe another day if there's new snow in the pass. Can you really trail all those horses that fast?"

"A week. One week more of freedom!" Talima suddenly began to cry. Tears flowed from the deep well of her misery.

"What's the matter, Tam?" Ssu put her arm around Talima. "Are you afraid? You mustn't be, life at court is exciting. It will be a whole new adventure for you!"

"I suppose so, what's it like, Ssu?"

"Oh, you are to be part of the emperor's household! A concubine or even a wife, perhaps, if you are so fortunate as to birth a son. Are you afraid of losing your virginity? The *play of rain and clouds* can be quite wonderful, I assure you!"

"No, it's not that, it's just that my father needs me. My people need me. And then too, it's Pirjhan—we love each other, and I *must* go back to Burkhan Kaldun with him. I want to be what I've been trained for all my life, to be Chagan, to rule my people wisely by the Great Wolf's Law, true to the Everlasting Sky! I want to be Jhani's wife, to bear his children, and have him by my side the rest of my life. Loving him *is* my life," Talima said, her blue-green eyes awash with tears. "I must make the emperor understand! I cannot be a *hat-and-girdle* town person in Chian! I don't belong there!"

"So, you and this handsome herdsman have perhaps been playing in the rain and clouds already? Is that so?"

"I don't know what you mean."

"Have you allowed his Jade Stalk to enter your Cave of Wonders?"

"If you mean what I think you do, yes."

"Once?'

"Many times."

"We *do* have a problem. You were to be virgin tribute to His Most Illustrious Majesty, were you not?'

"Yes, so he must allow me to leave, don't you see? I'm no longer a virgin. I cannot be a part of the bargain he demanded of my people."

"You Central Asian people are so impractical! My Uighur Prince didn't care a *pi's* worth of silk whether I was virgin or not, so long as the blood-line was pure," mused Ssu. "It's not likely you'll be allowed to leave, you know."

"But I *must*."

"Personal desires don't count for much in court, Tam. Are you with child now?" Ssu turned Talima to face her.

"Oh no! At least, I think not."

"What are you doing to prevent that oh-so-complicating event?"

"I didn't know...is there anything *to* do?" Talima brushed back stray hairs stuck to her tear-streaked cheeks.

"Great Mother! Didn't your mother prepare you for being a woman at all?"

"My mother died when I was very little, not quite three."

"Oh, I'm sorry. No sisters either?"

"No, I was my father's first-born, his heir. He raised me, taught me The Law and hunting and falconry. I sometimes helped the women make felt, but no more than necessary."

"Can you embroider? Do you play the lute or sing? Have you been trained to please a man?"

"No, those skills are not important for an Igren Chagan," Talima answered with pride.

"Oh, my dear, my dear...such an innocent! What are we to do with you?" Ssu comforted Talima, rocking her back and forth as she would a small child.

"Well, first I'm going to show you how *not* to create a child in your belly, my sweeting. That at least is within my power. If you arrive in Changan with Pirjhan's seed ripening within you, I'm fairly sure the hours of your life, and his, will be few and fleeting. When you belong to the emperor, my dear new friend, you must be discreet, lie as necessary...or you will be killed...snuffed out with no more thought than stepping on an ant."

Talima shivered, looked at her new friend in total confusion, "But I would not try to deceive the emperor!"

"Of course not. But sometimes, Tam, you may find that deception is preferable to death."

"But lying with intent to deceive *is* death!"

"In the great luminous palace, lying with intent to deceive is called politics, or possibly, survival," Ssu said. Her melodious voice sounded dry and harsh. "Well, enough of my practical cynicism, my dear. I fear you'll learn all this too soon. Now let's look in my bags together. I want to give you something."

Shih Ssu's saddlebags held things that Talima had never seen before—small porcelain bowls of a pale-green-crackle surface; a bronze mirror backed with silver, set with moonstones, lapis and carnelians, and silk—silk shifts, silk skirts and tunics, long silk scarves, silk and feather headdresses.

She took out a red drawstring bag. "In here you'll find a small sponge that is roughly in the shape of a hat, Tam. There are also herbs to brew. Take about one *liang* of the herbs, three liangs of water, and simmer until the liquid becomes deep purple in color. Then soak the sponge in this brew. Gently push this sponge into your precious gate until you can feel it rest on a little ledge deep within you

"This will keep Pirjhan's many jewels from mating with your substance. Take the sponge out after your lovemaking and refresh it with water before you put it away. But make it anew, each time, before you and Pirjhan decide to sport midst rain and clouds. Do it before you play with any man, actually, unless you wish to bear his child. Now, little one, what are you thinking about so seriously?"

"I think that I have much to learn...and also that I'm most fortunate to have met you here, in this place, at this time. Thank you, Shih Ssu-sha."

Ssu smiled. "Incidentally, how is it that you speak Chian as well as you do?"

"We all learned *caravan Chia* as we grew up, from travelers we traded with. Then too, the emperor's ambassador taught me more before we left home."

"I wondered. This skill, being able to understand the language, will help you in the capital. So that's good, but you know, Talima, your life at court will be much easier if you have family backing. I've been consulting with Li Jho."

"But Ssu, I have family. I'm an Igren!"

"That's not what I mean," Ssu said thoughtfully. "Li Jho is very wise... he has called my attention to the possibility that his vision of the dragon in the lake is a major portent. And if that *is* true...first of all, you will need a Chian family name so that you do not appear powerless. Otherwise, dearling, your life will be miserable."

"How miserable? As the emperor's bride won't I be...? But then, I won't be wed to the emperor, will I?"

"I don't think you even begin to comprehend, Tam! I know what I'll do! I'll ask my parents to adopt you! They'll see this as a way to gain extra merit, I'm sure, when I explain it to them. After all, they're losing one daughter, me. So you can be a Wu family daughter. Sort of a trade, you see?"

"Not exactly, I thought you said your family lived away from the capital."

"Yes, in Tai Yuan, northeast of Changan, but not far. You could follow the Great Wall east an extra day or so, then spend time with my family. Have more suitable clothes made, then take the post road to the Cinnabar Gate, Changan's gate of entry on the north.

"I do believe that would work! That way you could have the protection of the Wu family name. What d'you say, Tam? Would you be willing to stop over in Tai Yuan before you reach the imperial city?"

"I'd have to ask Jhan and Juchi, of course, but if you think it would be wise?"

"I do. That's settled then. I'll write my father with a complete explanation."

"What is *write?*" asked Talima.

"Great Mother! That too? Writing, my innocent, is putting symbols of words onto *paper* with a brush and *ink* so that you can communicate with others. Without regard to time or place. It's talking without sound, over any distance. Persons of merit, of breeding, of education, learn how to write."

"Can you show me what this writing is?"

"Certainly. That's exactly what I plan to do. But first I'll need to grind the ink. Come with me."

Shih Ssu delved back into her saddlebag and came up with some pointed brushes set into bamboo handles. Then she took out a small, hard rectangle with gold designs along its edge that perfumed the air around them with the pungent smell of camphor.

"This is an ink stick, Tam. And this..." she said, showing her a flat ceramic dish stained black in its hollowed end, "...is the grinding stone. Now we'll need some water. Here's a bowl, and this is a roll of paper made from the husks of rice ground into a pulp in water, then flattened and dried."

They walked down to the lake to fill the bowl with water, Ssu explained how ink was made, how one learned to write.

"One character at a time, slowly, turtle, slowly" she laughed. "Sometimes I thought I'd never master the skill. But there's such satisfaction in it, I just kept practicing."

"I wish I could write! It seems like magic though, perhaps it wouldn't be right?"

"There are many kinds of magic, my dear, some are good magic, some not so good, some positively evil. This is *good.* But it, too, can be evil I expect, if used by evil men, I mean."

"Evil men. I have known one evil man, but I don't think he thought he was evil. Maybe no one ever thinks he's evil, just that everyone else is wrong." Talima said. "I hope you don't meet his men on your way to Samarkand!

Shih Ssu concentrated on grinding her ink stick into a powder fine enough for writing. Then she dipped her brush into the thick black ink, paused for a moment, and then, like snakes slithering into their hole, danced a flowing script down the paper.

Fascinated, Talima watched as a determination to learn this wonder was born in her heart.

THE SUMMER DAYS CAME TO A CRASHING CLOSE WHEN A THUNDERSTORM ROLLED, like a playful god's hoop, around the mountain valley.

Shih Ssu's party, realizing that they must make forced marches in order to reach the western mountains before heavy snow, loaded their animals efficiently. For safe traveling, cambric-covered bolts of silks, a dowry of incalculable worth, were buried under packs of food and furs.

Talima, Pirjhan, Juchi and Tulak gathered the banner of horses that had scattered among surrounding hills. Kilar and Faina packed camp for the trip east toward the Jade Gate and Chian.

And then, another dawn, another leave-taking. Moving on once more into the unknown. In the midst of the neighing, braying, jingling confusion, Talima and Shih Ssu stood together. Knowing they would probably never see each other again, they prolonged the moment by trying to give last minute advice about everything that might be useful to the other in her new life ahead. Realizing how futile that was, they laughed.

Talima wore a length of striped silk wrapped around her waist that Ssu had given her. It replaced the one she had worn when she left home, that Mazar Tagh had taken. Merket's talons grasped the sheepskin edge of her gauntlet.

"Ssu, I have a gift for you. One that is dear to me, one who will suffer too much if I take him with me into the city." She held up her arm. The falcon lifted his wings for balance. "Here is Merket, I want you to have him, Shih Ssu, to hunt the mountain meadows of your new home."

Talima transferred Merket to Ssu's arm. She put the tiny, blue hood over his head, tied it securely, then smoothed his feathers for the last time.

"Tam, really? I shall cherish him. He'll remind me of you, and my thoughts will fly the thousands of li between us."

"If you should ever find yourself south of Khotan, near Burkhan Kaldun Mountain, know that Igren Clans will welcome you. And if that should happen, tell them that the daughter of Chagan Tashih Shaymak plans to return."

"I pray it will be so for you, but..."

"No buts, Ssu-sha! I've done more difficult things than this, I'll find a way!" Talima hugged her friend. "Goodbye, there's so many things I still want to ask you, tell you..."

"I know, me too. You have the scroll for my parents?" Ssu held Merket unsteadily. "Go safely, little one."

Kara bugled as she flew onto Talima's shoulder. Talima staggered and almost fell from the weight of her full-grown swan.

"Kara! You're too big for that now! Yes, we're leaving, silly. Here, up onto Bagatur's back. He can hold you more easily." Talima tried to move Kara, but she only nestled her long neck against Talima's, crooning softly against her ear.

"What is it, Kara? Don't you feel well? This isn't a good time to be feeling poorly! 'Sky! I wish you could talk! This is the most affectionate you've been in days! You're usually neck-winding with that other large swan, gliding together across the lake."

Faina rode up. "Tam, Pirjhan says we must leave and would you come now, please?"

"Yes, Faina. I'm coming. But there's something wrong with Kara."

"I think Tam, if you would not mind me saying..."

"Of course not, say it, Faina, whatever it is. What's wrong with her?"

"Kara has a new friend. A person-friend, I mean a man-friend. How d'you say that, Tam?"

"By the Everlasting Sky, Faina! I believe you're right. She has a *mate!* Of course! What will we do?"

Kara answered the question by jumping to the ground. She ran a few steps and then lifted into the air. As she cleared the trees, a large male joined her. Together they flew to the far end of Half Moon Lake where they settled into the water, side by side. Their long-drawn-out, crooning song drifted behind them.

Talima's face was wet with tears as she mounted Bagatur and joined the others. They drove the horses east again onto dry, rolling plains.

16
Snow Leopards: A Stampede: Through The Jade Gate

SEVERAL DAYS PASSED. AS THEY MOVED ALONG THE SILK ROAD, they passed other caravans. Some plodded wearily behind ox-drawn wagons, some lumbered along on heavily loaded camels. The going grew more difficult.

They climbed gorges along flashing, falling streams where the trail was narrow and steep. Bones of animals whitened on the rocks below. They lost one foal over the cliff edge, but it had been sickly before that, so it was a small loss. The Igren horses flowed around and over every obstacle. But the way was more precipitous than they had anticipated and they were forced to slow down. The moon grew fuller as they trailed the horses higher into the mountains.

"Shih Ssu called this the Moon of Hungry Ghosts," Talima said, riding beside Pirjhan as they came into a barren, bouldered valley. "It's beautiful isn't it, Jhan...unreal though."

"Unreal? What's unreal, love?" said Pirjhan. "I was thinking of something else, I'm afraid, something quite real."

"This world of black shadows and silvery light. It's so still and yet every hoofbeat echoes. What d'you suppose ghosts are hungry for?"

"Tengri, Tam, how should I know? Ghosts, hungry or otherwise, are only in that young woman's imagination, not real at all."

"No, Jhani, she said that's what everyone, everyone in Chian, calls it. I don't know, but there do seem to be ghosts, standing in the darkness between all these jagged rocks," Talima shivered involuntarily and moved closer to him. "What else were you thinking of just now?"

Pirjhan turned in the saddle to look at her. "I was thinking of how beautiful you are in the moonlight, my Inanna-Tam. I think maybe my eyes are the hungry ghosts, hungry for you." His laughter laughed back from the mountains around them.

"I'd like to stop at some caves Ssu told me about on the other side of the pass, if you and Juchi wouldn't mind?"

"I don't know, my love. There may be wild tribes roaming the countryside down there. Our horses would be mighty attractive, might just be wiser not to stop, just get to Changan as soon as possible."

"Shih Ssu didn't mention any wild tribes—I can't believe there'll be any trouble we can't handle!"

"Trouble? I'd like to get these horses to Changan safely, then talk to the emperor, and get this business settled before more trouble. We're in so much trouble already, you and I, that I have trouble sleeping at night. What have I done! How can we ever...?"

"Is it sleeping you're interested in now, my fickle lover? A moment ago I thought you might be interested in night of another kind?"

"Don't tease, Tam. You know I want you, to hold you and to love you. Always." His felt cloak glowed blood-red where it lay along his horse's back.

"I do know, but I love to hear you say it." She saw him silhouetted against the night sky, saw his supple strength and her love for him sang its own song in her body.

As they rode, the carved wood of their stirrups bumped against each other. The distance between them dissolved, became a single many-legged shadow in the moonlight as they traveled through the night.

The moon hovered above ragged peaks as the sky began to grow light. The breath of horses and humans plumed out in the frosty air. Pirjhan stood in his stirrups, raised his arm and whistled a long, wavering whistle that signified a halt to the others. They rode to the front of the herd and stopped.

"It's nearly dawn. Time for a fire and chai," Pirjhan said. "Has anyone seen Kilar and Faina?"

"Yes," said Tulak, "they were riding tail most of the night. Seems like those two are most always in the same spot lately. I'll go get them."

"Good. I'll see if I can find something to make a fire with," said Talima.

"Don't go far, not out of sight."

"No, I won't, Jhani, just ahead up there a little way. Where you can see those scraggly little pines. There might be some fallen twigs or branches."

"All right."

Talima unbridled Bagatur and loosened his saddle girth. She walked over rock ledges toward the only trees, watching the ground for dry dung or firewood as she went.

The surrounding mountains were suffused with reflected light from clouds crimson with the approaching dawn. Talima passed a few trees, found nothing, then stopped abruptly. The land dropped away. The mountains ended, the road they traveled zig-zagged down and down onto a luminous plain far below.

She sat and gazed out, knowing that the land down there was Chian. This necessary journey through the night had brought them over the pass to within a few days of their destination.

She saw a flock of blue-gray mountain sheep grazing nearby, their wide horns curved against the sky, a crystalline sky, blue as the color of ice caves. She heard the sheep's throaty bleat as they leaped from crag to crag, feeding on sparse grass and lichens.

A pair of eagles hunted the canyons on either side of where she sat. As she watched them, they soared away from the escarpment, voicing their harsh, exultant cry. She imagined she was one of them…the tips of her wings caressed the updraft, her feathered head turned from side to side searching for movement below. Lost in the moment. The sun poured into her eyes, and all the world flamed.

Small stones rattled around her. Startled, she looked over her shoulder and saw a male sheep leap a chasm and land on the slope behind her, starting a small avalanche of pebbles. Unaware of her presence, he came directly toward her in bone-jolting bounds. He was chased by an animal that Talima had never seen before, a lithe, catlike creature, as big as a month-old colt. Its thick, white fur was spotted with black-petalled flower shapes, and as the leopard-cat ran, its long, tufted tail whipped back and forth for balance.

Both animals ran at top speed, not yet seeing Talima in their path. Closer they plunged. The snow leopard lunged and caught the sheep on his rump. Her huge paws tore out hair and hide, sent slate-colored fluff flying into the air. The sheep veered sidewise sharply and miraculously ran off to safety.

In that instant, the leopard saw Talima, and slid to a stop. They stared at each other, blue eyes absorbed by sun-flare-red eyes. The cat pulled her small, round ears tight against her head, and melted down onto the ledge.

If Talima had not been looking straight at her, she would not have seen the pebbled-snow shape. Neither moved; neither looked away. Even breathing seemed to cease as they regarded each other, not in hostility, but in the stunning recognition of the awesome unknown, incarnate.

Talima heard a mewing sound, faintly on the freshening wind, of a baby crying. She turned to see where it came from. Startled, the leopard jumped and ran. This time ran directly at the men and horses beyond, answering the kitten's cry with a low rumble. Two moon-shadowed cubs pounced on her from behind a boulder. Momentum carried the three of them into the horse herd.

The big cats tumbled against the first of the horses whose shrill neighs alarmed the others. Horses' eyes rolled white with fear, nostrils flared with the smell of leopard. Horses stumbled into each other and struggled for balance.

Hooves scrabbled against stone. Snorting and bucking, they circled in chaos, gaining speed and fear.

Talima saw Juchi, the first to be mounted, charge into the horses, followed by Pirjhan and both the other chapars. They whistled and waved their hats, trying in vain to contain the horses. Faina was struggling to get on her horse.

Talima whistled for Bagatur and ran toward the tumult as fast as possible.

"Faina! Stop!" Talima shouted. "Follow slowly, don't try to help! Stay out of the way!"

Horses streamed past. The sound of their passing reverberated like thunder against the stony hills. She saw Bagatur surge past, Shira by his side, unable to come to her, unable to swim against the full-running tide of horses.

Talima ran, knowing she couldn't stop them. Her breath came in ragged gulps of thin mountain air. She saw the last horseman disappear over the ridge and knew that havoc waited on the other side.

She reached the crest as the wave of horses swept by, the pack animals scrambling along at the rear. Down the precipitous, zigzag trail they poured, a flood of cream and brown creatures flowing down a course that could not contain them. Each turn of the trail betrayed them.

Horses fell like feathers. They lifted slowly into the air and then bounced soundlessly against ledges below, over and over, down and down.

The pressure of bodies behind them, the simple fact of being pressed forward inexorably, kept many of the herd from being swept away. Those that survived streamed onto the high golden plain of Chian.

Talima could see one, two, three horseman down there. Not four. Who was missing? The pain in her side flamed into her heart. *Not Pirjhan! Great Wolf, not Pirjhan, please...* She stumbled, fell, ran on. At every turn, bleeding bodies lay. The farther she went, the higher the pile of mangled horses.

She noticed ragged bits of black-spotted fur flattened on the ground, remnants of the leopards that had begun this run toward death. On and on, down and down, she ran. She heard a high keening sound, but did not realize it was her own voice.

And then, in a mound of dying horses, she saw a boot sticking out.

With strength she had not known she possessed, she rolled bodies off him. But it wasn't Pirjhan. It was Juchi, his arms and legs stuck on at odd angles, still breathing. She gathered his broken body into her arms.

"Juchi! Oh, Juchi my dear old friend." Juchi opened his eyes.

"Talima-sha, little girl," a smile flickered around his wrinkled face like a wreath. "It is enough for me. But for you, you must hold...hold to the highest, as our Bequi said. Now take my reed...keep it and remember me..."

Talima felt sudden release shudder through him and knew he had died. She reached into his arrow case and pulled out the supple reed that Juchi had kept wrapped so carefully ever since Kuriltai. Then Talima held him and rocked him as her tears washed the dust from his familiar face. Memories of her childhood with this man, teacher, storyteller, friend, sang bittersweet melodies in her mind.

That was how Faina found her, still rocking, still holding Juchi. Remembering.

"Tam? Tam, what can I do for you?" Faina said helplessly.

"It's all right, Faina," Talima said. "I'll be all right, It's just, well, I didn't realize how much I loved him and now he's gone and I can't tell him and..."

"He was old, Tam."

"I know, but that doesn't matter. I loved him. He was like another father to me. He was always there for me, whatever happened. He was a part of my life!"

"Your old life, friend. You must go to new life now."

"Oh, Faina! I don't want to. But none of that is important now. We must make Juchi ready for his passage into the Everlasting Sky. Help me, Faina."

Together they carried Juchi off the trail. Talima tore her silk sash into long strips and wrapped them around his body. They brushed rocks and branches from a narrow ledge and laid him down.

They had already covered him with stones when Pirjhan rode up, leading Bagatur.

"Juchi?" he asked quietly. "Can I help?"

"Yes, he died in my arms," said Talima, brushing her hair back with her forearm. "We need a few more large stones...the buzzards are circling already."

"He was a good man. We shall miss him." They finished the stone cairn and stood back. Pirjhan put his arms around both Talima and Faina.

"I'm so relieved, so glad, to see you in one piece, my beloved."

"No gladder than I am, Tam. 'Twas a wild ride, that! We're lucky any of us survived. We lost many horses, only one camel."

"Where is the herd now?"

"I left Tulak and Kilar rounding up stragglers. We lost at least twenty or more, and those that survived are exhausted—most of the horses are down there rolling in the yellow dust."

"Shira?"

"Shira's there. If you're finished here, we need to head down and join them."

"I hate to leave. It's like leaving a part of me, leaving my childhood and memories of home, gone forever. But look, Jhani, before he died he reminded me of what the Bequi taught us, to be strong and hold together, to hold to the highest. I feel we've come a long way since then!"

"Leaving an old friend, leaving the past, is always hard. We do what we have to, the best we know how."

"Yes, thank you, I'm coming." She took the last strip of blue silk and placed one end under a stone on top of Juchi's grave mound where it flickered, a bright flag waving in the wind.

Talima and Faina rode Bagatur, following Pirjhan as he led them down the last mountain pass.

17
The Igren Are Strangers In An Ever-Stranger Land

SHIRA NICKERED TO THEM AS THEY PASSED THROUGH THE REMAINING HERD that grazed peacefully on tall, dry prairie grass. Ahead they saw Tulak and Kilar talking to a fierce-looking man who dwarfed the stocky pony he rode. Pirjhan urged his horse into a canter.

As she and Faina followed, Talima could see that the Igren men all seemed to be talking at once. The stranger sat stolidly, one hand on his reins, the other on a short sword that hung by his side. He wore a knobby helmet and thick leather armor that covered his upper body. His legs were wrapped with padded material and hung straight down without the benefit of stirrups.

"No. We cannot. We must take these horses to the emperor." Pirjhan said.

"I am Emperor Tai Tsung's representative. I am the Commissioner for Receiving Surrender in the West. All tribute from foreigners must be processed at my post before passing into the country."

"Processed? What does that mean? "

"Surrender? Who's surrendering?"

"Who's at war?"

"Barbarians! Do you understand nothing?" He spat into the dust. "You are violating the law and I..."

"Just a minute," Talima interrupted, "we do not know this law you speak of, we have only just come to your country."

"That at least is obvious," the man replied. "The law states clearly that all foreign horses must be branded and marked with the most imperial mark as they enter the country from the west."

"I see, but there must be some other way, for branding all our horses would take a long time and we need to go on, to finish our journey."

"Tam, I'm not sure the man understands what we're saying," Pirjhan said quietly, "but we can't stay here long enough to brand all these animals! We don't have enough supplies left."

"I think you're right. Thank Tengri that I learned as much of his language as I did! He seems to be a person in authority, and we don't want to violate any laws...let me think a minute."

"No exceptions for mon-barbarians!" The official glowered at them and tried to hear what they said, restlessly reining his pony into tight circles.

"Perhaps this might work... sir?" Talima put Faina down and rode toward him. "We are not foreigners going directly to the capital, we are going to Tai Yuan, so that I may be adopted by the Duke and Duchess Wu Shih-kuo. I have here a scroll that will tell you all about it."

She opened her saddlebag, took out the scroll that Shih Ssu had written, untied the ribbon that bound it and leaned out of her saddle to pass it down to the man.

He opened it and studied it for several moments before he cleared his throat and spat again. "The Duke Wu Shih-kuo, eh? I served under him in the war against Silla. This changes things. It says you have safe passage on important, official business, so I suppose I must let you."

"Tam, is that really what it says?" whispered Pirjhan.

"I don't think so, at least that isn't what Shih Ssu told me it said. But he's holding the scroll upside down—I don't think he can read!"

"I will provide you with an escort. To Tai Yuan. Just to be sure you, ah...arrive there." The Commissioner's voice seemed, oddly, more insinuating. "Wait here. My men will come for you." He rode off, sitting with dignity on his absurdly small horse.

"Never underestimate the Chagan's beautiful daughter!" smiled Pirjhan.

"Well, you just never know, do you?" Talima laughed. "Some chai would taste good now, but we've so much to do, I expect we'd better get started. Tulak, could you?"

While they worked to get the herd and the pack animals into traveling condition again, they spoke of Juchi, remembering him with affectionate stories. They knew they'd never know another like him, knew also he was glad to be traveling the high road of the Everlasting Sky, one with the Great Blue Wolf and all Her Immortals.

Realizing that their journey was essentially over, they reminisced on events of the past four months. The difficulties and dangers they had overcome. They keenly felt the trust that grew from shared experience. They were comforted by each other's strengths, drawing closer in spirit. Companions, holding together as the Bequi had shown them that long ago Kuriltai celebration.

In a short while, six men dressed in armor similar to the Commissioner's but wearing short bows rather than a sword, rode over the ridge and joined them.

"Ahatou, Chian-men," Talima and Pirjhan spoke in unison.

"We have been sent to guard you and the horses," one of the men said.

"No, we are to escort you to Tai Yuan," corrected another quickly.

"Good. That should save us from wandering around trying to find our way. Time we could use in other ways."

"If you are ready to travel, we can get a few li down the road before we stop at sundown," they said.

"We'll travel through the night."

"All night? When d'you rest?"

"As we ride."

"Hah, barbarian ways! Well then, two of us will ride at the rear, one on each side of the herd. I and my partner will lead the way. That way you'll be...safe. Follow me!" He turned his pony and headed northeast.

The four Igren bunched up the herd, prodded the camels and moved out after him. A multi-colored river of horses moving over yet another ridge.

Faina, riding ahead, shouted, "Tam! Tam! Kilar! Come and see!"

Talima spurred her horse forward.

"Great Tengri! What is that?" exclaimed Kilar.

"A great stone snake!"

"Chian-men, what is this apparition that we see?" asked Talima, feeling somehow apprehensive and, at the same time, as if she has seen this great stone snake before.

"The Wall?" The soldier looked astonished. "It is The Long Wall, The Great Wall that holds and protects our country from the Mongol dogs."

"What is it made of?"

"Stone and packed earth. You see the battlement there? Soldiers like us are stationed up there to keep watch."

"Against what?"

"Against invasion, naturally. Invasion from the dark hordes of the north. When enemies are sighted, signal fires of a thousand rushes are lit. The next battlement lights their signal fire and so on until the alarm is passed the length of the country within a very short time, I can tell you!"

"Amazing, it's so high! Does it ever end?"

"Not for many hundreds of li. Not until it reaches the eastern sea. Would you like to go up on it? The view is excellent."

"Should we, Jhan? It wouldn't take long."

"Leave the horses, Tam? Should we?"

"I suppose not, but look how far it goes! It winds across the hills and into the sky! I guess we'd better just keep going. We're not going to be able to see those caves either, are we? The ones Shih Ssu told me about?"

"Sorry to disappoint you...maybe on our way back?"

"I know...onward then."

New sights, new sounds. Spurts of yellow dust marked every step along the road that followed the Long Wall.

Where barley had grown in isolated clumps at home, here Talima saw rolling fields of grain ripening in the late summer afternoon. These people lived in oddly shaped houses, square or rectangular, perched on hard earth foundations, timbered and thatched. Igren dwellings were always round. The Chian dwellings were clearly unmovable and she wondered what they did when winter came. Did they just abandon these buildings and set up new ones?

A man scratched the earth's skin with a metal tooth, making the hard earth soft and crumbly. They saw another man drop a wooden bucket into a hole in the ground and draw it forth dripping with water. Then he poured the water down narrow water-paths beside the fields, over and over, creating a stream where none had been before.

Country people worked all over the fields, their bare-bottomed children beside them. Talima couldn't tell if they were men or women as they all dressed alike in loose, natural-colored cotton jackets, patched and padded. They wore flat, straw hats and carried loads on long poles balanced across one shoulder. Dogs of every size and voice barked at them as they passed: red dogs whose shaggy tails curved over their backs, huge mastiffs, and smaller, lean, fast dogs.

They attracted little notice. Once in awhile someone would stop work to stare at them. Once a person waved as he rested beside a heavily loaded, one-wheeled vehicle he'd been pushing. But mostly, they passed through the country as if they were invisible, part of the usual landscape for those who lived there.

Night fires sparkled at intervals atop the Wall. They had ridden far into the night. When they came to an unoccupied corral, the Chian men insisted on making camp. As they fell into an exhausted sleep, squeaks and chirps of unknown birds sang accompaniment to their dreams.

SEVERAL DAYS LATER, THEY CAME INTO A WIDE VALLEY at whose center was a walled city. Inside the wall were thousands upon thousands of the strange, cornered houses. Some even had square windows and wooden doors. Others thrust up into the air, several stories high.

Their escorts stopped outside the gates, for this was Tai Yuan.

"Stop here. I will find pasture for the horses before we arrive at Duke Wu Shih-kuo's estate," the leader said.

While they waited for him to return, they brewed chai and sat drinking it on the hillside overlooking Tai Yuan. Grass was plentiful; the horses ate and rolled in it. Young ones, born on the trail, leaped and skittered about.

"Did you know there would be so many buildings, Jhani?"

"When I was a boy in Persia, there were cities as large as this."

"Their ger are so peculiar. I wonder what they're like inside, where they put the fire without a fire hole. Those roofs look solid. See how they turn up all around the edges...why d'you suppose they do that?"

"I expect we'll have some answers soon."

"Everything is different from what I expected!"

"Most of life is, in my experience."

"You know, I'm, well...a little scared!"

"I never thought I'd hear you say that, Tam. That you were scared. I didn't think you knew what fear was! Anger, yes, but fear?"

"You give me more credit than I deserve, my love! You know better, don't you, Faina? Remember?"

Faina smiled. "You are always brave, my friend."

"Juchi always said that Talima-sha wasn't..." Kilar began.

"Juchi said I wasn't *what?* What did he say, Kilar?"

"Just that you weren't really brave, only stubborn." Even though his face was deeply tanned, they could see him blush. "Stubborn for life, I think he meant. Not just selfish stubborn, but kind of holding-strong-stubborn. When things are bad, that is. You know he loved you, Talima-sha."

"Yes," Talima said quietly, "thank you for reminding me, Kilar."

The Chian soldiers returned. They herded the animals into a large, fenced pasture on the outskirts of the city, took what they thought they might need for a few days in their saddlebags and headed back to the Tai Yuan gates.

Within, buildings on both sides of the streets had wide eaves that curved across, almost touching each other, creating a shady tunnel for people and animals that passed beneath. The Chian soldiers kept up a steady mutter of oaths as they pushed through the mass of people headed toward the city's center.

The Igren marveled at wheelbarrows, whose front wheels were higher than a man's head, that were laden with vegetables or wood from outlying farms. Two-wheeled carts rattled along briskly, sometimes pulled by a man, sometimes by a small, long-maned pony.

"It's market day, you see," the leader explained.

"What is *market?*" asked Talima.

"What is market? You'll see!"

The crowds grew denser, compressed by the narrowness of streets they rode through. Waves of sound, the undulating bird-like murmur of thousands of voices speaking a language they barely understood, filled the air. A dry, dusty wind swirled around them, bearing a bouquet of scents—spicy or sweet, smoky and strange.

They came into a wide-open square, a li wide in all directions. The Igren stood still and simply stared at the vast confusion of goods and people.

"So many! It's like Kuriltai only more so! What are they doing?"

"They're selling what they grow or make. For cash like this," the Chian leader opened a leather pouch that hung on his belt and took out a flat piece of metal marked with characters which Talima recognized as similar to those that Shih Ssu had written.

"But what good are pieces of metal to them?"

"To buy anything they might want, of course." The Chian man was puzzled but polite.

"Can we *buy* these things, too?"

"If you have cash or silk. They'll also trade."

"Trade? That we understand," laughed Pirjhan.

"I didn't know that there could be so many beautiful things to eat," said Talima as they walked along leading their horses. "Tell me what they are, please."

"These," the soldier said, gesturing at each stall as they passed, "are leafy vegetables...broad and bitter-leaf, sweet indigo kohlrabi, palinga spinach.

"And these long, red, yellow and green pods are *fagara*—hot peppers used to preserve meat or abolish coldness in the stomach. Some say they'll also help grow more hair, but I don't know that for a fact," he grinned, rubbing a bald spot on the top of his head.

They passed a group of women who sat on the ground with their legs around wicker baskets filled with small round nuts. Their hands and arms were stained blood-red as they rubbed rough crimson husks from the brown inner nuts that they tossed into smaller baskets. As they worked, they called out melodiously, "Nutmegs! Nutmegs! Fragrant nutmegs!"

The soldier continued to call out Chian names for the wares of each vendor they passed. Small stalls sold costly roots and barks and seeds of ginseng, cinnamon, camphor, cloves and frankincense. Larger stalls were filled with the color and fragrance of flowers Talima had never even dreamed existed...voluptuous peonies and cinnamon-scented wild roses.

The men bought from food stalls and shared with the Igren: sea mullet, salted and dipped in wine, covered with *leaping-fish* sauce; pickled meats; sticky rice balls rolled in sesame seeds, and fruits; persimmons and pomegranates from lands far to the south.

"I've never tasted anything so good!" said Faina, licking pomegranate juice from her fingers.

"How do all these foods get here?" asked Pirjhan.

"Some by post roads, some by river transport."

"There must be a vast network of roads and rivers!"

"Well, they're not natural rivers, y'know, they're canals that connect the empire to the capital."

"Look, Tam! Here are nuts, pistachio nuts, like those I had as a child!"

"Best be careful there, my friend," the soldier laughed, "those nuts will increase your sexual vigor beyond, well beyond what the little lady here might be able to handle!"

"Never mind. Pay them no mind, Tam. That's just an old joke because of the way they look."

"You men are always thinking of...but what are these small creatures, these tiny men and tigers and other sorts of animals here?"

"Those? I'll get some for you. They're *stone-honey* cakes. See this piece of cane? Suck on it. Sweet, isn't it?"

"Delicious!"

"They take sugar cane juice, boil it until it becomes thick, then pour it into molds of many shapes and let it harden, making these stone-honey elephants and lions and tigers. Children love them."

"So do I! Jhani, these are like a whole honeycomb in one mouthful. Here, taste."

"Sweet as you are, little love," he whispered.

"I never want to leave this market day. I want to hold it forever!" said Talima, ignoring him with a smile. "How wonderful to be here, at last."

"But we must go on. To give you into the safety of the Duke Wu Shih-kuo's establishment."

"Sometimes I feel as though I'm always taking leave of where I want to be, always saying goodbye."

"But you can come back to market," said a soldier, "it happens every seven days, different in different seasons, but always here, just the same."

"But we have to go to Changan!"

"The market in Changan is ten times better than this one! There are truly exotic things there...little monkey-men from islands to the south, birds with long blue tails, glass from Hrom, crystalline ices...never-ending wonders! This is nothing. The imperial city draws the best of everything from all the world!" the soldier said.

"Greater than this? Tengri!"

On the other side of the marketplace, streets were wider, eaves did not meet above them even though the buildings were larger. People walked beneath evenly spaced trees. Ornamented walls fronted on the roadside, their gates carved and heavy, hinged with hammered bronze. They stopped before one of these massive gates and pulled the thick, worn cord that hung to one side. Inside they heard a bell ring and the sound of footsteps coming toward them.

A small slot in the gate slid open. Black eyes peered at them. Their escort spoke rapidly, mentioning the name of Duke Wu Shih-kuo several times, gesturing toward the dust-covered, travel-worn Igren. Soon they heard a bolt slide back and the gate swung wide.

"You wait here. I will see if his eminence wishes to receive you." The gate-opener put his hands inside wide, midnight-blue sleeves. His single, long braid swung across his back as he shuffled away.

18
Adoption: Her Tai Yuan Family

"DOES THIS MEAN YOU ARE WU CHAO TSE TSIEN NOW? Tam no more?" asked Faina.

"No, of course not, silly. It's just a name, a mere formality, just a way of saying that I am *sponsored* by a well-known and influential family," said Talima, "rather like my protection of you. Pass me some of those grapes, will you, please? I can't seem to stop eating fruit since we got here, it's so good."

Talima and Faina sat together on a low bench beside a willow-shaded pool. They dropped crumbs for fish—bronze, black and silver—that came to the surface. They were alone in the inner courtyard garden of the Wu family mansion. It was the first quiet hour they had had since their arrival several days before. At first they had felt ill at ease but by now had settled into a comfortable routine within the compound's walls. Although the Duke was away on a hunting trip with the emperor, his wife and family had welcomed them after reading Shih Ssu's scroll.

"Wu Yang-ssu, my new mother-to-be, explained all this to me after the family agreed to adopt me as Ssu requested. Subject to the Duke's approval, of course. But she seemed quite sure he would enjoy the idea. She's really nice, Faina, wants to give us both what she calls "proper clothes" so that we won't look strange when we arrive at the palace, but I told her that I would rather have my own tunic and trousers, so we compromised. She'll have new clothes made for us before we leave, out of silk most likely, but made in the Igren fashion."

"The Lady Wu's clothes are most beautiful though, Tam."

"But would you feel comfortable with sleeves that long, Faina? And with your breasts practically bare? I'd be embarrassed!"

"They're very pretty..."

"We could have *some* Chian clothes I suppose."

A maidservant, carrying a tray of sweet bean cakes and herb tea, came toward them. She wore the customary, long, loose-sleeved dress, with a wide sash wound several times around her waist, tied with an elaborate knot in front. Her black hair was massed into a knot on top of her head and pinned with lacquered sticks.

"Madam requests that you attend upon her," the maid said, "when you have refreshed yourselves."

Talima laughed. "She actually means when we have combed our hair and look more presentable. All right, thank you. We'll go to her quarters within the hour."

"Come in, come in, do! We must teach you how to enter a room, how to bow...so much you must learn, so quickly...while there's yet time." Lady Yang-ssu did not rise. She sat with her daughters and ladies around her, teasing a small dog with a long-handled fly-whisk. Apricot-winged birds twittered in a hanging bamboo cage. From a porcelain dish on the low table beside her, musk-scented smoke drifted into the room.

"'Hatou, Lady Mother, it is a pleasure to see you."

"Come here, sit beside me," she patted a pillow on the reed mat at her feet. "But first, take off those awful dirty boots, *do!* Oh, I'm sorry, dear, I don't mean to offend you, but we simply do not wear our outside shoes *inside* the house!"

"Sorry, as a matter of fact, neither do we. Wear our boots inside I mean. So many things are new, I'm not sure what's right or wrong." Talima looked around at the elaborately dressed women seated nearby.

"Of course not, and that's what we mean to change, don't we?"

The Lady Yang-ssu wore an apron of plain red silk tied beneath her breasts over a blue dress embroidered with multi-colored birds and flowers. Under an outer robe of diaphanous silk, her bare shoulders were visible. The up-curved points of lavender satin slippers showed from under her robe. Her hair was pinned into intricate knots and twined with coral beads and white chrysanthemums. Tiny bells hung from silver hairpins, making a faint melodious tinkle whenever she shook her head or laughed.

The other women's gowns were similar, the colors as brilliant and as varied, Talima thought, as a garden of flowers...jade green, saffron yellow, peach-and-gold stripes and peacock blue. Some of the women wore gold and silver bangle bracelets or necklaces that lay curved on their high bosoms. Over their shoulders, many wore a floor-length, transparent scarf that wafted around them as they moved.

Talima could not keep from staring at one young woman in particular. Small-boned and dark, her lips and cheeks were rouged and her eyes were accented by violet shadows that extended up to painted purple eyebrows shaped like a hawk's wings in flight. A bright yellow, sickle-moon was painted in the center of her forehead.

"I see you are fascinated by my cousin, Jing-ma." Lady Yang-ssu's laugh invited Talima's confidence. "She has just returned home from court, you see, and has brought some of the current fashions with her. I can't hold with these *huang-hsing-yen*, these yellow-moon-mouches! Too extreme for me, although the eyebrows are appealing, don't you think?

"Bring me my make-up box, Jing-ma, let's introduce our new daughter and her handmaiden to the pleasures of rouge and lip-salve! What fun we'll have! You don't mind, do you, Wu Chao?"

"No, no, of course not. If you wish me to."

"It's a pity your hair is so short, my dear. What can we do with it? Such an amazing color, too! I never expected to have a daughter with hair the color of polished copper, I must say! And Faina, with your hair the color of dry straw...we'll have to find a more suitable name for you, too...well, our most illustrious emperor may be intrigued, who knows? Now first let's..."

They whiled away the rest of the day playing with Talima and Faina as if they were new dolls, painting on and rubbing off various make-up designs, combing their hair this way and that, dressing and undressing them in layered silk clothes.

In the midst of good-natured laughter and teasing, in the sweet and easy companionship of women, Talima began to feel happy in a way she had not known before.

LAMPS CREATED POOLS OF LIGHT ON DARK POLISHED WOOD. A three-legged, bronze brazier warmed the cool evening and sprayed occasional sparks onto reed mats that covered the floor.

Classical Chian melodies sang from a bent-necked lute and wether-drum, played on the porch outside the room where the Wu family and guests were gathered.

It was the celebration feast for Talima's adoption. Duke Wu Shi-kuo, having returned that morning from a successful hunt, was in a jovial humor. He sat on cushions at one end of a wide table, beaming over a wine cup at his women and children. According to his rank, he could have been dressed more sumptuously, but he was a plain man, a practical man, and so kept more to the old ways, as his emperor also did—soft black leather house-boots, tight black cap with starched points on either side, dark blue trousers and shirt. His only concession to the festivities was a long silk tunic embroidered from shoulder to hem with four-toed golden dragons and iridescent clouds, belted by a broad band of blue linen studded with carnelian and mutton-fat jade.

Talima felt too tall and shy in her new Chian clothes. She sat between the Duke and his lady, facing his brothers and sons. At tables on either side, concubines, daughters, cousins and the Igren dined. The air was filled with the cloying smoke of incense and the spice-fragrant steam of food. She felt hot, and increasingly queasy, as she listened intently, trying to understand the rapid conversation around her.

"Will harvest be sufficient to meet the grain tax this year?" The Duke asked one of his sons.

"Ample, Father, the rains came at just the right time and the summer was hot."

"I trust you were able to find enough men, after harvest, to substitute for the family's public service?"

"Not completely," said another son. "I sent two of the stronger Turkish slaves hoping they won't be refused."

"But that's not the letter of the law, son. This new triple-tax system of the emperor's, on labor, cloth and grain, is working out well, stabilizing the economy—and prices are certainly down. We must cooperate in whatever ways are required, for the good of all."

"Respectfully, Father, the slaves I sent would be far better at building roads or digging canals than any of our farmhands."

"I'm sure you're right. I depend on you to be right about our tenants. By the way, is that young wife of old Yang still refusing to weave their tax-cloth?"

"She *is* a one! Gives that old man what-for every time he suggests she might sit down at the loom and produce a length of linen so the tax collector will stop griping at him! Besotted by her he is, even though she's on the way to putting him in debt to the merchants for all her shopping sprees!"

"What can we do to help him?"

"I have no idea! He should manage his household better, but..."

"Changing the subject, I see you've returned from Changan, youngest son." The Duke turned to look down the table. "Does this mean you've completed your examinations in the venerable Law of Confucius?"

"Not exactly, father." A young man wearing a be-ribboned tunic and brocaded hat shifted uneasily.

"What does that mean, not exactly?"

"The examinations were so crowded with students from lesser *chous*, other counties of less prestige than ours, that I deemed it wise to wait for another time."

"Another *what?*" the Duke thundered. "You've been in the capital for eight moons! You must pass that examination before you'll be useful to the emperor—or yourself! I find your moral laxness reprehensible. The precepts of Confucius, our great ancestor-teacher are just what you need to set you straight!"

"Now, my dear husband," Lady Yang-ssu interrupted, "this is not the time or place for chastisement, is it? This is a time for celebration, for welcoming a new family member, one that may, indeed, bring merit to our name in the future. It's time for the evening's entertainment, if you will so order, my lord."

"You're quite right." He shook his head as if to clear away unpleasant thoughts. "We will continue this discussion at my office in the morning, immediately after first meal. Now, what charming drama have you arranged for us, my jewel, *The Peacock King?* or *Po-Tuo* perhaps?"

"No, this is a new one. Cousin Jing-ma brought it back with her from Changan. She says it's fagara—that's how these young persons say that something is red hot, you may remember, my dearest lord. She says that an ambassador from Champa taught this classic play to the palace entertainers. It's called *Kalavinka,* named after a divine bird that lives in a Buddhist paradise somewhere in the mountains there. We lack many of their instruments, but we'll make do. If you're ready?"

"Let the play begin!"

Four young boys, trilling in imitation of the celestial kalavinka bird, leaped into the room, turning cartwheels and tumbling between tables. They wore flowered crowns and silken wings and played small cymbals.

Then they stood and mimed the story of an angelic being who flew down to comfort a lovesick maiden, only to have her die of sorrow, abandoned by her lover.

The wether-drum's beat pounded in Talima's head. The lute's song thrummed in her ear. *A whining dissonance, unmusical and interminable,* she thought. The entertainment seemed to go on and on. She longed for the evening to be over, longed for the familiarity of her own things and her own people.

The dancers pretended to cry over the tragic story, comforted each other with extravagant gestures and, accompanied by a rapid clanging of cymbals, cartwheeled around the dining hall. In a final cacophony of horns, cymbals and drums, the dancers disappeared into the night.

Talima gratefully joined in the clapping. Although that too seemed odd, as Igren only clapped in disapproval, snapping their fingers as a sign of appreciation.

"Now a toast to our new daughter, Wu Chao Tse Tien, the luminous one of the family Wu. May she shine in the luminous palace as she does here with us!" The Duke wiped wine from his long mustaches and set the thin porcelain cup down with a resounding thump, not noticing how his wife winced. Empty cups echoed him around the room. House-slaves hurried from dimly lit corners to fill them again.

Talima dutifully drained another cup. She could hear Pirjhan's voice and Faina's, Kilar's and Tulak's. The broad flat sound of their words was welcome contrast to the undulating birdlike rhythms of the Chian language. She felt light-headed and rather dizzy.

It can't be the little amount of wine I've drunk—only half a dozen of these tiny cups. I'm used to kumiss, much more kumiss than this watery but pleasant drink. But my lips feel numb and...

Just then a series of explosions ratcheted the night. Everyone jumped up from the tables. The Wu family shouted and ran outside. Talima shouted in alarm. She tried to stand and found that her legs had gone to sleep. She held onto the table to steady herself.

Showers of light sprayed past the opened doors, lighting the darkest corners. Pirjhan's arm was suddenly around her. He pulled her close and moved outside.

"Come and see, Tam!" he said. "It's amazing! You've never seen anything like it! Fire in the air...but nothing burns!"

"Is it an attack, Jhani? 'Sky, I can hardly stand. What's wrong with me?"

"Just a little drunk, my love. It's all right, I'll hold you."

They came out on the porch as a fountain of red and white stars burst against the sky.

"What is it? How do they do it?"

"There you are, new daughter! Do you like the fireworks in your honor? These are not particularly grand, of course. Out here in the provinces we can't compete with really great fireworks! But we try. What d'you think?"

"I, aahh." Talima felt herself sag against Pirjhan, heard the laughter and floated into a haze of dreams.

Dreaming.... long-remembered dreaming of the great gold and green dragon that she'd ridden in so many dreams before. Surging ever higher on wings that spanned the Everlasting Sky, spiraling above the earth in dreamed stillness, until mountains and rivers and valleys were vague shapes in the clouds below. On and on and on until...

Pirjhan carried her to bed where he tucked her into furs. Then he sang the lullaby they both had sung so many times together since he'd taught it to her on that day so long ago, before the terror of Mazar Tagh, when their bodies had joined in the exhilarating delight of first love.

"Sweet is the sleep of hand-to-hand, sweeter still the sleep of heart-to-heart." He lay down beside her and cradled her head on his shoulder as they fell asleep.

19
SEPARATION

FAR AHEAD, THE CINNABAR GATE GLOWED THROUGH A HAZE of peach-colored dust. Their progress toward this northern gate of Changan had been frustratingly slow. It took all their skill to move the horse herd and pack animals around and through the throngs of other travelers on the South-winding Post Road. A dozen Wu farm slaves accompanied them, but were so inexperienced that they were of little help.

Theirs was not the only caravan. There were Uighur and Turkish traders with tall, fur hats, Sogdians on tasseled camels, Tocharians and Persians. Buddhist monks in tattered orange robes held up their begging bowls to all who passed.

There were farmers pushing enormous wheelbarrows heaped with vegetables and tinkers with their metal ware jangling from carts. Aristocratic ladies, luxuriantly swathed in silks, peeked out from billowing curtains as their sedan chairs swayed along.

Drunken students, their long braid loose on their backs, lurched through more sober groups of Chian citizens bent on business. Musicians, drumming and fluting, loitered on the grassy roadside. An occasional armored rider, plumes streaming out behind his helmet, galloped by, scattering people and chickens and sheep in all directions.

Talima, on Bagatur, cantered up to Pirjhan. "We've got to stop, Jhani! I can't tell what belongs to us and what doesn't! Sky, what a mess! I never thought there were this many people in the whole world! At least not this many who were so different!"

"Agreed. We need to round up for a bit anyway, to give the messenger time to announce our arrival, to send an escort. I can't see taking this herd into the city by ourselves. Tengri! I'm beginning to see the wisdom in branding the herd first. But too late now!"

They moved aside from the main flow of traffic out onto rolling meadows. Mares whickered to their foals and prodded them to graze. Yearlings raced around exuberantly. Many of the horses rolled in the tall grass, kicking their heels in salutation to the sky. The camels kneeled, grumbling, and surveyed the commotion around them with their usual disdain.

While Tulak checked the packs, Kilar started a small fire. Faina unbound a skin from under her horse's belly and poured curdled mare's milk into chai. They drank the hot familiar brew with relief and watched the motley procession flow past them.

"It was kind of the Duke to give us bows after he heard how we'd lost ours in the stampede," Pirjhan said as he unslung a new bow and quiver from his shoulders, laying them on the ground beside him. "I must say it makes me feel a lot better to be armed again, more like myself somehow."

Each of the Igren men had a small horn bow, strengthened with sinews, and a woven-vine quiver lacquered with red and black geometric designs—gifts from the Wu family to their adopted daughter's retainers.

"I thought it interesting," Talima said, "what Mah Yang-ssu said about the bows, how the Chian word for *bow* has a broader meaning."

"A bow is a bow is a bow, no?" grinned Pirjhan.

"Not in Chian! The written character for bow is just like the ones for dragon and for rainbow! So it also means a *vault-the-sky-power* of rain clouds with lightning shooting out."

"Tengri! Didn't know I carried all that on my back, did I now? How about you, Kilar, ready to pierce the rain and clouds with your arrow?"

Kilar, understanding the allusion to lovemaking, blushed and smiled adoringly at Faina.

After some discussion, they decided to spend the night and continue south early the next morning. They curled up together, heads on saddlebags, feet toward the fire, and watched stars wheel overhead.

The last thing Talima saw as she drifted into sleep, was the crescent moon that cradled the Metal Star, the lover's star. The last thing she heard was Pirjhan's voice, low and soft.

He sang Inanna's song, *"As she was shining, bright and dancing, singing praises to the coming of the night... my beloved met me, took her pleasure of me...*Tam, are you asleep? Goodnight, sleep well."

Fog lay in the hollows. Dew-drenched grasses glittered in the first rays of sun that shafted over the hills. The post road was empty. Only the twitter of seed-eating birds broke the silence. Talima sat quietly, savoring the dawn.

How good to be here! Another day begun—filled with promise and a new beginning! Dear Father, I wish you could see me now...we've come so far... I wonder if you knew how far it would be, or how many dangers there would be...I think we've done well, all things considered...I think you'd be proud of me. You'd understand about Pirjhan and me, wouldn't you? Maybe you even meant it to be this way?

She felt the vibration of hoof beats in the earth "Jhani! Kilar! Faina! Tulak! Wake up!"

A dozen men on big-headed, long-maned horses appeared over the rise, galloping to a stop around them. Pirjhan grabbed for his bow as he stood up. Kilar and Tulak stepped quickly beside him, shielding the girls.

"Hai!" A wiry, bow-legged man slid from his horse. "Are you the mon-barbarians with unmarked tribute that we were notified of?"

"We are Igren from the western Ferghana valleys," replied Pirjhan slowly. "And yes, we do bring tribute to the emperor."

"The Most Luminous Son of Heaven is not referred to as a mere emperor, barbarian! Best you learn quickly or..."

"Sorry. I did not mean to offend. I do not know your ways."

"Aye, well, now, " he scratched his scanty beard. "We have a long day's work before us I see. Where are the rest of your men?"

"You see us. There are some farmhands, but they scarcely count for much."

"Three men? And all these horses? I don't believe it!"

"There are five of us, Chian-man."

"Your women? Surely you jest! What can they do except warm your bed at night?"

"Enough!" Talima pushed forward angrily. "Who are you? Who gave you the right to question us? Identify yourselves immediately or I shall require you to leave!"

"Ho now, missy! Slow down, who are *you?*"

Talima tossed her hair back and looked directly into the eyes of the stranger. "I am Talima-sha, heir to Chagan Tashih Shaymak, daughter of the Duke Wu Shih-kuo of Tai Yuan!"

"Are you now? A young she-dragon breathing fire, more like and fire-headed too! Very well, I am His Most Luminous Majesty's Commissioner of the *Horse Corral of the Heavenly Park*, commonly known as Kapi, dragon-rider.

"It is my duty to oversee the disposition and installation of horses in the various pasture *Inspectorates* that belong to the palace. We received word that you were on your way into Changan. We're here to mark and separate your horses into appropriate *hsien*, according to excellence or need, before you pass through the Cinnabar Gate. Is that clear?"

"Clear as boiled yak hair," muttered Talima and then, more loudly, "Thank you, Kapi-sha, I accept your explanation. Explain, please, what is necessary to be done now."

"Hai! First I will inspect your horses and grade them. Then we will separate them into groups that will be sent to the various hsiens—the *Corral of the Flying Yellows* or that of the *Auspicious and Well-Bred,* possibly the hsien-corral of *Tao-tu, the Dragon Decoys.*

"If you have any truly outstanding animals—*Blood-sweating Chargers* or *Precious Whites,* they'll go directly to Heavenly Park, the main *chiu* stables, within the palace walls. There we maintain the best and most beautiful for the exclusive use of His Most Luminous Self or his hunting companions and family."

"Does that mean that we don't give these horses to the emperor himself? That he doesn't even *see* them? How does he know that we met his demand for tribute?"

"First of all, it is one of my responsibilities to *memorialize* the transaction for him, to send a memo in written form to the *Office of Tribute from Mon and Hu Barbarians,* a notice that your tribes have met their quota. Secondly, his Most Luminous Majesty cannot be bothered with trivial details like this. He doesn't need to *see* the horses, only to have them ready when he desires to ride."

"Sky! It gets complicated, doesn't it?"

"Yes," Kapi smiled wryly. "Now, if you're quite satisfied, can we proceed?"

"Certainly," agreed Talima.

"We'll need fires for the branding-irons, won't we?" said Pirjhan.

"I'll get the farmhands busy on that. Tulak, hobble the camels at some distance, will you? Faina, we could use some food soon." He organized the camp quickly.

Pirjhan, Talima and Kilar began to bunch up the horses. The Chian men put up several, small corrals from materials they'd brought with them, and began to funnel a few horses into the first one. There, they were first branded on their right shoulder with the character *kuan* or *official.*

The branded horse passed between Kapi and another man for a quick yet thorough inspection. Kapi then waved the horse to one or the other makeshift corrals for a second branding.

The next brand, on either side of the tail showed the country they came from and the horse's quality, either *flying,* dragon or *wind.* An additional mark on the right cheek showed the work designation, whether it was *sent forth* for those sent to the army or on post-horse duty, or *bestowed* for those given to private persons of privilege.

As the day went on, the sun grew hotter. The smell of singed hair and burning horseflesh hung heavy in the air. Tempers grew short. Dirty, sweaty and tired, Talima and the others looked more ragged and disheveled than they had after weeks on the trail.

"All right, that's the lot of 'em," Kapi slapped dust out of his clothes. "You four take these mares to the Tao-tu pastures. They'll stay there until they foal."

"Not Shira!" said Talima. "Shira stays with me, she's mine!"

"Not now! She belongs to the Imperial tables now."

"No, I really cannot permit that, Kapi-sha. She was given to me by my father, the Great Chagan, to be my personal horse."

"And the one you're riding? That one too?"

"Yes. Two horses. A small thing, really, don't you think, for a woman sent to His Most Luminous Majesty?"

"You can't be responsible for them. You won't be able to care for them."

"But *you* can, and my men can, until we...until they, leave."

"They can't leave right away...they'll be around for quite awhile, long enough for that white mare to drop her foal. I'd like to help, I s'pose it would be all right."

"Wonderful! I knew you'd think of a way! But, just as a matter of curiosity, why are you so sure that our men, that *we,* will stay?"

"The law states that all tribute horses must be looked after by their own grooms for at least the first six moons. Saves a lot of trouble. So, if that's settled, let's get these horses out of here before dark. The camels will go to the auction corrals to be sold to other traders.

"We'll take all the precious whites with us to the Park. The rest of you can trail the remaining horses to the Corral of the Auspicious and Well-bred. You should be there by tomorrow. These horses are especially fine—tall, with slim legs, strong, arched necks and broad backs, visibly stamped with the marks of their divine origin! You can be proud of their breeding."

"We are."

In herds of a hundred or more, the horses went toward their separate destinies. Drained and strangely contented, the Igren, Kapi, and three of his men moved the finest of them all, cross-country, to the Heavenly Park corral, west of the Cinnabar Gate.

They rode slowly, keeping the tired horses close together. As they went, they talked horses, horses they had known and loved, crazy horses, stupid horses, valiant horses. How to train them, how to game them, how to keep them sound and healthy. The talk of horsemen wherever they meet.

By twilight, they turned the remaining herd into an empty corral, part of the extensive maze of corrals and stalls that comprised the Heavenly Park.

Talima was awed by the size of the compound. "There are hundreds and hundreds and hundreds of horses here! What do you do with them all? Why aren't they at pasture? Do you hand-feed them all?"

"Yes, we feed them, though they're rotated to pasture occasionally. Some are here only temporarily, before they're stabled within the palace itself, as many of yours will be, I'll warrant. As to why, imperial necessity's the best answer I can give you, Wu Chao."

"Necessity? What necessity, imperial or otherwise, demands a thousand, a banner, of horses at the ready?" asked Pirjhan.

"Hunting...war...ritual journeys, inspections of outlying chous, gifts to foreign dignitaries."

"Great Tengri! I begin to understand!"

"Yes, there'll be much that's wholly new to you, I'm sure. Tell you what, I like you mon-barbarians...you're all right, I'll put you up in my quarters tonight and tomorrow we'll see what we can do to make a pleasant home for you."

"That will be fine, suit you, Tam?"

"I didn't mean the women!" The color drained from Kapi's face. "The women could not stay with me! They must go directly to the palace. It would mean torture and death for me to keep his Illustrious Majesty's women, even to ride with them like this, except I reckon that no one could tell who they are, dressed like you are, ridin' astride rather than in a litter...oh no, my friend!"

"Just one night? No one would notice."

"Listen, when you enter the Cinnabar Gate, or the Vermilion Gate, or any gate to the palace for that matter, *eyes and ears are everywhere!* Everything that happens is reported within minutes to the Illustrious Chamberlain, who whispers it to the emperor's aides. Aye, you must be very, very careful, my friends!"

"But, if..." Talima objected.

"No ifs, my lady! You and Faina will go to the White Jade Pavilion in the palace...*tonight.* I'll send a groom with you. He'll see that you arrive safely. There is nothing you can say or do to change this, believe me!"

"Better do as he says, little love, we'll work out some other arrangement as soon as we can."

"But Jhani, it's so sudden! I'm not ready! I don't want to leave you or Tulak and Kilar and Bagatur and Shira. You're all I have left!"

"It's only for a little while, Tam. Faina will be with you." He rode closer, leaned out of his saddle, brushed the hair off her forehead and kissed her cheek. "Remember, I always love you."

"And I, you!"

They left the horse corrals and rode to the northern gate. Massive, red-stained timbers, carved from the ground to the giant crossbar above their heads, were silhouetted against the evening sky. Heat haze shimmered along the horizon.

Above the wall loomed the city of Changan, glowing with the light of thousands of lamps. One door of the foot-thick gate was already closed and bolted down. There were few people to be seen because, as Kapi explained, it was almost curfew time and all proper citizens were behind their own walls for the night.

"And those that are not proper citizens know other ways of entering, or leaving, the city," he chuckled.

Their horses' hooves clattered on stone-paved streets that grew wider and wider as they climbed up the hill that led to the palace at its top.

"Are all the streets in Changan as wide as this?" asked Talima.

"No, only the ones from the four gates to the palace grounds. Most are like the little alleys you see over there," explained Kapi.

"I believe this is wide enough for most of my people to stand, shoulder to shoulder, across it! And that's more than 200 souls!"

"Yes, about a quarter of a li, I've been told, but none too wide when the army is marching and the carriages are hurtling by, as well as all the other traffic! You must've seen what it was like when you came down the Post Road?"

"Wild, it was simply wild!"

They came to the top of the hill and dismounted. From where they stood they could look across Changan, the city that stretched for li after li to the east and south and west.

Some areas had buildings of the same height, others contained buildings of several stories high. Dark patterns of tall trees wound through the checkerboard of streets. Shining waterways glistened through the trees.

Far beyond the walls, above the cut-paper shapes of southern mountains, autumn lightning flickered. The air was thick and damp and heavy. As they followed Kapi through a narrow gate into the palace stables, thunder, like a great hoop, rolled around the horizon.

The Igren were amazed—the stables were so enormous. There was a large covered ring at the center of hundreds of box stalls, and behind those were many more pens that held five or six horses each.

"Everything about this place is enormous, bigger than I could've imagined!"

"Yes? You'll get used to it. Here's where you can leave your saddlebags. I'll have yours sent to you tomorrow, Wu Chao, so take just what you'll need tonight."

"You've been most kind, Kapi. I'll not forget."

Talima took pants and another shirt. The new one, from her Tai Yuan mother, was dirty and torn at one shoulder. "Do you have my comb, Faina? All right, I guess we're as ready as we'll ever be."

"Nandi here, will escort you as far as the White Jade Pavilion. Farther he cannot go."

"I'll go with you, Tam," said Pirjhan.

"*Are you mad?* You'll stay right here with me. The less you two are seen together the better. The way you look at each other could be disaster for you both! Go now. Quickly!"

Kapi hustled Talima and Faina down a passageway, out the door. Before she realized it, he and Pirjhan were gone. Kilar and Tulak, Bagatur and Shira, all behind them. A dimly lit hallway ahead.

The little groom hurried them along a dark hall as it twisted and turned through the building's maze. They could hear voices and laughter from behind the walls. Finally, they stepped through a door and out into a garden. Night-blooming water lilies perfumed the air. Somewhere, water gurgled and splashed. Stone lanterns glowed beneath trees whose shadows danced in the wind.

The path ended before a door set into a wall where flowers spilled down from above. Behind the wall, a deep-voiced bell announced them. A small door at the top of the larger one slid open. Black eyes peered out, looked them over, and slid the bolt back.

The musky smell of incense wafted out the opening door. The man who stood there was small and fat and shiny. His clothes shone, his skin shone, his bald head shone. He put his arms into his long sleeves and glared at them impassively.

Nandi, anxious to leave, jabbered at the man, then shooed Talima and Faina through the door. They stooped under the lintel of the door and went inside.

At once, thunder and lightning crashed around them. Wind picked up leaves and dust that pricked their skin. The first large raindrops fell. Grabbing Talima's wrist, the shining man shut the heavy door and slid the bolt home.

20
The White Jade Pavilion

TALIMA AND FAINA AWOKE THE NEXT MORNING IN A DIFFERENT WORLD. A soft, clean, scented world where the sun painted shadows across gauze curtains. Where vivid silk pillows lay in tumbled piles on patterned rugs and small birds sang in gilded bamboo cages.

They were in a large room that opened onto a garden. Slippered servants rustled by, carrying trays.

"I wonder if they'd have some chai," whispered Talima, "I'm famished! Did we eat last night?"

"I can't remember. Where are we, Tam? This be heaven?"

Talima giggled. "No, at least not *my* heaven, Faina. All I know is what Kapi told us, that we were to go to the White Jade Pavilion. That strange little man last night...if I hadn't been so tired I'd have asked where we could find the emperor."

"And then go back to Kilar and Pirjhan, right, Tam?"

"Shhhh, someone's coming."

Two women, one small and slender, the other, tall and muscular, walked briskly toward them. They both wore long, cream-colored robes that were girdled at the waist by a wide, brocaded sash. Even at this early hour their hair was looped in elaborate curls and their faces were carefully painted.

They stopped and looked down at Talima and Faina. With a slight inclination of their heads, they gestured to each other and said, "Lu Mei...Lu Li. Can you understand us when we speak?"

"Yes, yes we can."

"Excellent! Your names?"

"I'm Talima and this is Faina."

The two shivered as if they had tasted something bitter. "Mon-barbarian names! Too bad, but we shall change all that, shan't we, Lu Li?"

"If you prefer," began Talima, "my Chian parents gave me another name—Wu Chao Tse Tsien."

"Now that's much better! Come along, Wu Tse Tien and whatever-your-name is."

"Where are we going?"

"To bathe, of course! You surely don't intend to stay in those filthy clothes, do you?"

"No, we brought clean ones with us."

Lu Mei looked at their bundle of clothes and sniffed, but said nothing. The two turned and walked off, "Follow us!"

They walked down a long hall. The timbers of doors leading from it were painted vermilion, the ceiling, an azure blue. Some women in the rooms they passed were still asleep, some were dressing, others were combing each other's hair.

At the end of the corridor was an empty room in the center of which was a sunken tub, lined with blue-decorated tiles, filled with steaming water.

"All right, undress, girls, and take a good soak. Be sure and wash your hair well. Lu Li will stay and help."

"Do you mean for us to get *into* that pool?" said Talima.

"How else can you bathe, child?"

"But it's *hot!*"

"Mercy! Would you rather it be *cold?*"

"No, it just seems strange to actually get into all that hot water. But if that's the way it's done here!" She shrugged. They began to take off their clothes.

"That's better. I'll be back with robes for you."

"Wait, Lu Mei? I assume you are the emperor's wife? When can we see him? I've urgent business to discuss with him...perhaps after we bathe?"

"Mercy me, oh, deary me, such ignorance! We, Lu Li and I, are only poor servants to His Most Divine Blessedness! We are, Lu Li and myself, Imperial Instructresses to the court ladies, that is all! And as to when you can speak to him in person, I have no idea. At present he's not even here. In the palace, that is. Off on some imperial business, no doubt, in some desperately barbarous place. Holy Mother-Keep-Him-safe! But even if he were here, it's unlikely."

"Why is it unlikely?"

"Why? Why, *I've* never even seen him, up close that is. We don't ever leave the Garden, you see, unless..."

"Unless?"

"Unless one of us is sent for and then..."

"The women in the rooms we passed...do they leave?"

"No, when a person of the court wishes to be entertained, he comes *here*."

"Someone must go out of the garden," said Talima, now standing barefooted, clad only in her shift, "or else you'd never eat."

"Very sensible, Wu Chao. Our eunuchs pass freely throughout the palace in order to procure whatever we might need or desire."

"Was that one of the eunuchs that let us in last night?"

"Must have been, don't you agree, Lu Li? It wasn't either of us and none of our girls are allowed to open the doors."

"And where do they, the eunuchs, live?"

"They live upstairs, with the Coordinator—we rarely see him either, unless it's a problem or a disaster. He has *such* a terrible temper! And when someone is punished, it's just more than we can stand! Isn't that right, Lu Li?"

Lu Li nodded and looked pained. Lu Mei, obviously upset, wrung her hands and turned this way and that as if she would like to run away.

"Really! Quite enough of this conversation! I must be off!" And she left, her hyacinth-edged robe sweeping the floor behind her.

Talima and Faina slowly lowered themselves into the bath.

"Tam, this be so fine!"

"It does feel good, doesn't it? I think I could grow to like it."

"What will we do now, Tam? How will we..."

"I don't know, Faina. I've got to think. There has to be a way, but it may take me a day or two to figure it out."

In a day or two the situation was no better. If anything, it was worse.

Talima thought she was reasonable, she felt it was the only way to get along, to get what she wanted. But no one could answer her questions, no one seemed to care. In every way she could, she complied with what was required of her, meals with the others, baths, attendance at the morning roll call. Every way but one—she steadfastly refused to wear the diaphanous gowns the others wore. She went on wearing her Igren tunics over pants. And Faina, of course, followed her example. With only one change of clothes, it meant that every bath was also clothes washing time. They were laughed at, but it was worth it just to wear something that felt familiar.

Talima asked for her belongings to be brought from the stables as Kapi had promised. Nothing came. She demanded to see the head eunuch, the Imperial Coordinator. Nothing happened.

They were assigned a place of their own, a tiny window-less cubicle in the center of the building. Here they spent hours lying on their bedrolls, endlessly planning, twined around each other, legs over legs, arms beneath each other's head. They found a comfort in their isolation, each remembering and longing for the touch and scent and feel of their nomad lovers.

Days and nights blended into each other. Talima and Faina blended into each other in a wordless loving way.

Lu Mei and Lu Li tried to interest them in doing things that the other women did—playing board games, learning to play one of the many musical instruments, dancing, trying out new ways of using a variety of cosmetics, painting lacquer on their nails. But neither Talima nor Faina were interested enough to try, and the beautiful women who lived in the Garden of Delights saw no reason to befriend the odd mon-barbarian girls.

One morning, when Talima awoke, she was alone. Faina was not in the bedroll beside her. She ran down hall after hall, looking in each room. No Faina. She burst into the garden and collided with Lu Mei.

"Lu Mei, have you seen Faina? I can't find her anywhere! She wasn't with..."

"The Faina-person is fine, Tse Tsien, just fine. You are not to worry. We have taken care of her."

"What do you mean? Where is she?"

"She is...well, by now I expect she is where she belongs. Behind Guild walls."

"What are you talking about? You can't take Faina away!"

"Can't, Tse Tsien? *Can't?*"

"Faina is not a slave to be moved without consent! She is a free person!"

"That is correct. But now she is a free-person-apprentice in the Silk Weaver's Guild. A silk girl, I believe they call them." Lu Mei explained. "It's a wonderful opportunity for a young girl like your friend to learn a useful trade, one that's always in demand. You should be grateful."

"I...should be...*grateful?" Great Everlasting Sky! Grant me patience with this smiling idiot!*

"Now, Tse Tsien, temper, temper! We mustn't be foolish. Lu Li and I only do what's good for you. We saw that it would take you much longer to adjust to your new life here if you and the Faina-girl were together. You have many things to learn and you weren't showing much interest in learning them while you had your little friend. It's simply better this way, you'll see. Besides, she wasn't old enough to be an imperial woman, nor was she...well, good enough."

"But it's wrong! I would never have let you apprentice her! She's in *my* care, not yours! You get her back here immediately, d'you hear?" Talima was screaming at Lu Mei, tears of rage and frustration running down her cheeks.

Other women crowded around them to see what was happening. A few giggled behind their hands. Lu Li pushed her way through them.

"Lu Li, take her to her room," snapped Lu Mei. "We must handle this ourselves, quickly! Before the eunuchs hear and report our new girl to the Coordinator. Hurry!"

"Leave me alone! Don't you touch me!"

Lu Li simply picked her up, kicking and crying, and carried her off.

"You need some time to cool off, missy! You're a smart girl, make it easy on yourself. You'll have a good life here, *if* you behave, Think about it." She dropped her on the floor of her room and went out.

Talima heard a key turn in the lock.

Pirjhan, I need you! Hear me, come to me! Why haven't I heard from you? Where are you?

She cried until she fell asleep.

21
What Of Pirjhan? And Faina ?

PIRJHAN WAS DRUNK. HE KNEW HE WAS DRUNK AND HE WAS GLAD OF IT. Every day he had sent a message to Tam, hoping to see her, pleading for a reply. There had been none, not a whisper. He couldn't understand it.

Not that things were bad. On the contrary, each day was filled with new experiences, new foods and new friends. Life in the imperial stables was good.

Pirjhan poked into every corner of the vast stables. Quartered in roomy stalls were the choicest horses, those the emperor favored most: *Dragon* horses, ewe-necked, tall and powerfully muscled, yellow-grizzled or dappled roan in color, *Tajik* horses, fine-boned, small-bellied, quick and dainty, from sandy lands beyond the sea, and *Blood-sweating Chargers*, massive and invincible in battle. There was even a matched pair of *Fairy* horses from hot lands far to the south. There were so many that after Pirjhan had counted to fifty, ten times, he gave up.

He watched as men trained the horses in large arenas, leading them on a rope, round and round, touching them lightly with a long whip at a voiced command, drilling them to pirouette, jump in place, back and turn instantly. His obvious admiration for the Chian grooms had made him many friends.

He sat with those friends in a noisy tavern, drinking millet wine and telling jokes. The tavern was in one of the few remaining sections of the old city, before the great fire, before the great rebuilding fifty years before. Here, the narrow unpaved streets twisted and turned as if, his new friends told Pirjhan, the fabled one-horned *barlan* had wandered aimlessly in search of a truthful man.

Open gutters on either side stank with a rancid smell of excrement and garbage from hundreds of people who lived and worked in that quarter. Second-story balconies met above the street and formed a dank tunnel where the sun never reached.

It was a merry place despite the squalor. Everyone in the Old Quarter struggled with the same problems: too much cold in winter; too much heat in summer; too little to eat; too many little wood boxes to bury too many dead children, not enough work, not enough pay. They also shared the same joys: drinking the stomach-rotting wines, rice or millet; gambling, betting on the outcome of a game, a horse race or a cock fight; playing with their children; wenching with their wives or a willing prostitute, tale-telling. They enjoyed life when they could and forgot the rest.

Women found Pirjhan exotic and mannerly, considerate and handsome, and they made it quite clear that they would welcome a closer relationship. They stood behind him as he drank and twisted his wavy black hair around their fingers, giggling in their sweet, girlish voices. Some would even curl up in his lap, snuggle their face into his throat and ostentatiously breathe in the horse-incense smell of him.

And so, night after night, he had become quite drunk, intending to remain so until he stopped missing Tam, stopped even thinking about her.

Weeks passed. By day, Pirjhan, assisted by Tulak and Kilar, was busy working with horses. By night he was swept into a dazzling round of pleasures. The stables were the meeting place for a cross-section of men from every social class in the palace. Some of those who rode every day were palace guardsmen—a group of young bachelors who came from many countries.

One of the guards looked enough like Pirjhan to be his twin. He was muscular and broad-shouldered. Tight black curls ringed his head. He, too, came from The Land of Lions and was the son of King Yazdgard III, scion of the Sassanids, Firuz by name. He had come to Chian as his father's emissary several years before. But during his first year there, warring Arab Tajiks had banished the king who had sent word that his son should remain where he was—if he wished to live. Which Firuz did. For life was gaiety, song and dance for him—and Changan was filled with all three.

When he realized he could not return home, Prince Firuz had presented a memorial to the emperor requesting his protection. Tai Tsung sent him an official wallet in which to carry the imperial token, which was in the shape of one-half of a bronze fish. This token assured his safety anywhere in the hegemony of Chian. The emperor then granted Prince Firuz an appointment in his palace guards, with all their perquisites and privileges, for the duration of his stay in Chian, however long that might be.

Firuz and Pirjhan were attracted to each other instantly. They laughed at the same jokes, they sang the same songs, they loved poetry and melons and women. Not necessarily in that order they assured each other, speaking in unison, laughing boisterously.

The guardsmen lived in barracks at one end of the Imperial Polo Park. They frequented a different part of the city than Kapi and the stable hands did. Between the palace and the Eastern Market was the *P'ing-k'ang Quarter*, surrounded by the mansions of court nobles. Broad, quiet streets led past blank walls and massive doors.

Inside the P'ing-k'ang, however, men with enough cash found beautiful women, courtesans skilled in music, dance and flattery. Gaming boards and *bones* were available for gambling. Thousands of lamps made the passage of night hours inconsequential to all revelers. Here, young scholars recited their recent poems to admiring crowds and Sassanian musicians skirled wild melodies for dancing.

Prince Firuz and his friends took Pirjhan to one of their favorite places, a tavern close to the Eastern Canal near the Gate of Spring Brightness. Pirjhan hungered to hear from Talima and chided himself for being a fool. He longed to see her, touch her, hold her, taste the honey of her mouth...and reminded himself that he, a Chagan's horseman, could not begin to compete with noblemen she must be meeting every day in the palace. Resolutely, he closed his mind to those she might be meeting every night as well. He called for wine, more wine, more wine.

IN ANOTHER PART OF CHANGAN, BEHIND TEN-FOOT WALLS, in the Silk Weaver's Guild Quarter, Faina lay in a long, airy dormitory with a dozen other apprentices, trying to sleep. Her body was weary enough, but her mind, released from the tensions of the day's requirements, wandered.

She thought of her life, each event strung together with such rapidity that she had not even noticed, until now, any pattern. She realized that she had just gone along with whatever happened, never objecting, only reacting to circumstance. Simply surviving.

It had never occurred to her before that she could do anything about the direction of her life. But Talima had made her feel like a person of worth, a human being worthy of being loved, not a slave. Tam had shown her how a free person lived and thought and acted. Faina wanted in all ways to be like her, to make her friend proud of her.

She remembered the sleepy strangeness of the night a man had carried her away from the Jade Pavilion. She'd not been sure whether or not she was dreaming, it all seemed so unreal…the quiet, midnight streets where dogs yipped and were silenced as they passed, the thump her body had made on the hard earth as he dropped her inside the gate. Then, picked up by someone else, carried through darkness, pushed onto a pallet in a musty-smelling room, an order barked at her…a command she could not understand but knew, nevertheless, what was meant by it—silence—stay here!

And the days since…awakened before dawn, she and all the girls in her dormitory were herded into a huge inner room that contained row after row of open racks. The shelves of these racks contained trays of fat, white caterpillars.

It was the girls' work to pull out each long tray and feed bunches of dark-green, waxy leaves—from mulberry trees, she was told—to the hungry caterpillars. By the time they had fed those on the topmost shelves, reached by standing on a short ladder, it was time to start over with those trays near the packed-earth floor. Over and over, up and down.

At first, Faina was so fascinated by watching the caterpillars eat that, by the end of the day, she hadn't finished feeding the ones assigned to her. That night and the next morning, she was given only water to drink, nothing at all to eat. She became much faster rapidly.

Each day, a woman came around at mid-morning with a wooden bucket from which she ladled broth into each girl's mug that hung at the edge of her tier of trays. She also passed out sticky rice balls. They did not eat again until the day's end.

Light filtered in through open slits in the roof above their heads, shafts of dust motes highlighted dark heads of other workers, one after another, as the sun passed overhead. Faina's pale hair glowed like a candle in the half-light. It was strangely quiet. The girls were too far apart to talk easily, but they had little to say in the dormitory either. The loudest sounds were the crisp munching sounds of thousands of pearlescent caterpillars and the buzzing of innumerable flies.

Once in awhile the monotony was broken by the arrival of boys who carried wide, wicker baskets heaped with more mulberry leaves.

Faina thought it made no sense whatever. Why would anyone want to feed caterpillars? And even if you did, why not find caterpillars that didn't eat so much? It was a mystery. But she worked deftly and swiftly and was able to finish feeding those assigned to her sooner than anyone else. Some of the others gave her black looks, but the man who walked through on inspection was pleased and patted her head as he passed.

It wasn't really hard, thought Faina as she lay on her bed, just tiresome. She began to wonder if this was what she would have to do the rest of her life. It was not a thought that she welcomed.

What would Tam do if she were here? Would she try to escape? If I could get a message to Tam? Maybe get one of the mulberry-leaf boys to carry word to the pavilion? Tam would surely be trying to find her. Worth a try, Tam could get me out of here if she knew where I was. Yes! Tomorrow I'll see what I can do! Tomorrow I'll talk to one of the boys and perhaps...

She felt so happy at having figured out a plan of her own, that she fell asleep immediately.

As the weeks passed, Faina was astonished at how fast the caterpillars grew. They had been only as long as ten millet seeds, laid end to end, when she began. Now they were three times that length, their ivory skin fat and glossy. And how they ate! Mulberry leaves disappeared by the basketful. The mulberry-leaf boys came twice as often. Faina tried to talk to them in her halting Chian. Most only shook their heads and ran off. But one boy, smaller than the rest, smiled at her.

He was very thin and Faina noticed that he limped by the end of the day. But he was always cheerful, whistling through a gap in his teeth as he shouldered his heavy basket. She began to save bits of her rice ball for him. One day he lingered beside her.

"My name is Faina," she said. "Your name?"

"Ping."

"Ping? No more?"

"Just Ping, my name."

"We are friends, yes?"

"Hai, friends!"

"D'you live behind these walls like me?"

"Sometimes, when the worms grow big, like now when I'm too tired to go home. I sleep here now, until we start over again on new worms."

"When you stay, do they feed you, you and the other boys?"

"No," he grinned, "only worms get fed, not boys."

"But that's not right! Faina will share with you."

"Then you won't have enough to eat."

"I have enough, it's good to share...with a friend." She gave him the sticky bits she'd saved. He nodded his thanks and left, chewing happily. It was a beginning.

The next day, as she was racing to keep up with the voracious caterpillars' demand for food, Faina noticed a strange thing happening. In the midst of their feeding frenzy, the caterpillars stopped eating and began to exude a silvery thread from their bloated bodies.

Ping lowered his basket of leaves and stood beside Faina as she pulled out tray after tray of spinning caterpillars.

None were eating. All were winding themselves with layers of filament, round and round, thicker and thicker, until the caterpillar form itself disappeared into an ovoid shape of gleaming web.

"What's happening?" asked Faina. "Are they dying? Have I done something wrong?"

Ping chuckled. "Naw, they're doin' just what they always do, afore they go to the vats."

"They're supposed to do this winding 'round?"

"Hai!"

"Then what?"

"Then you get new worms to feed, to fatten up until they too, spin cocoons."

"But why?"

"I don't know. It's what we do...feed worms, then take their cocoons to the boiling vats. That's all I know."

"How very strange! Chian men must be mad! Not you, Ping, but why would anyone...?"

The inspector walked down the long aisle. Ping fled. Faina, not knowing what else to do, stood at attention beside her rack.

He stopped to look at a few of her trays as he had done to the others in turn. Before he went on, however, he took Faina by the shoulder and spoke softly, "I've been watching you, new girl, you're quick and careful. When the boys take the trays away, you'll go with them. You'll have other work from now on."

"I'd like to go to Tam, if you could make that be, please."

The inspector stared at her, not understanding what she said. "What is this Tam?"

"Tam is my friend, my best friend."

"Silk-girls do not need a friend. Silk-girls need to work, to obey. Silk-girls need only silk worms. Don't talk to me of friends. You are a lucky silk-girl already, don't be a foolish silk-girl." He walked away, shaking his head, his braid slithering back and forth across his back.

First a bear-girl, now a silk-girl, thought Faina. A not-free-girl, again.

NOW FAINA'S DAYS WERE LONG AND BUSY, BUT NO LONGER AS DIFFICULT as they had been at the beginning. Her quick mind and deft fingers had combined to put her in a position of skill rather than pure drudgery.

She joined other *threaders* on their high stools before dawn each day. They sat in front of flat screens on which were spread, one-thickness only, white cocoons that had been cooked briefly in boiling vats of water, then cooled and dried.

Beginning threaders were taught the skill by unwinding wild silkworm casings whose shorter threads were dun-colored and tougher than the mulberry leaf-eaters Faina had fed previously. She graduated from that job and now enjoyed her status as one of the best threaders, a *silver threader.*

A threader's job was to find the filament of transparent thread outermost on the cocoon, unwind it gently and rewind the opalescent silk onto wooden spindles. When their rack of spindles was filled, they were taken to the spinners' shed next door where two or more filaments were spun into one long continuous thread.

Faina's new position entitled her to better food and a bit more freedom. She was able to go out into the meager courtyard garden at midday where she could see the sky and watch the clouds.

22
A Kitten Shows The Way

NEW SOUNDS, NEW FOODS, NEW SMELLS. TALIMA LIKED SOME, disliked others. It did not matter what caught her attention, her interest was brief before she turned away, sighed and stared off into space, space that was always too cluttered, too confined, to be of any comfort. She ate little and slept a lot. She tried to escape, but there was always someone watching and she was always stopped. At night they locked the door of her room.

Talima watched as the other women spent hours primping, arranging their long hair in elaborate twists and curls, plucking out their natural eyebrows and painting on new ones with blue or purple kohl in shapes they gaily named, *Distant Mountains, Sorrow Brows* or *Moth's Antennae.* Some added a small yellow crescent moon at the center of her forehead, as Wu Jing-ma had done, so long ago, before Talima had come to the White Jade Pavilion.

They played interminable games of *Double Sixes* and *Five Winds*, kneeling on thick rugs, balancing between them the purple sanderswood board whose gold and silver flower designs gleamed beneath transparent tortoise shell. Or they gathered around a *gho* board, inlaid with animals and rosettes of ivory. They prattled and pointed excitedly with their curving polished fingernails when the black and white jade buttons surrounded imagined territory as the patterns of play emerged. They offered to teach Talima how to play these games, but she only shook her head and drifted off to another room.

Older concubines taught dancing, the formal, stylized dance of court entertainers. Talima was required to attend these classes, but she always looked out of place. Her embroidered Igren tunic and belled pants contrasted sharply with the colorful silk robes that the other women wore, robes that she still refused to wear.

Pets were everywhere: tiny long-haired dogs yipped and yapped, long-tailed monkeys leaped and chattered, gaudy parrots screeched and whistled, finches twittered. Braiding melody into this basic cacophony of sound, were the songs of lutes, bamboo flutes and fairy drums. The tinkling laughter of girlish women embellished the daily symphony. Talima felt besieged by these strange sounds. She longed for the silence of mountains and for the open bowl of sky.

Even in the garden, Talima felt stifled by the women. Their perfumes filled the air, settled in scented currents along paths and under trees. The heavy smell of musk, the spicy fragrance of cinnamon, smells of mystery—myrrh and frankincense—competed with subtler scents from flowers. Birds and butterflies seemed confused, unsure of which attractive smell to follow. They fluttered among gliding females as often as they did amidst the flowers.

Most of the women were friendly at first and the imperial instructresses were persistent in their efforts to include her. But Talima declined their invitations to do her hair, change her face or try on different clothes. She refused their offers to teach her how to play the crook-necked lute. Those who noticed were puzzled by her haughty refusals. Some were hurt by her curt answers and icy manner. They felt her disdain and thought her rude. They saw her choose to be alone and thought her arrogant. Except for the few who continued to harbor a grudge against her, she was left alone.

One day, Talima found a scruffy brown kitten hiding in a corner. She had never seen a young cat that close before. Wild cats she had known, mountain lions and panthers, usually hid their young. She picked it up.

"Dear little thing," she whispered into its translucent ear, "you feel lonely too, don't you? Such golden eyes..." She put the kitten on her shoulder where it peered through strands of her hair down on the other animals, safe at last. "I shall call you Takla Makan after the desert we crossed."

Takla Makan became a small brown shadow wherever Talima went. The kitten sat on the edge of the tub and swatted at soap bubbles while she bathed, snuggled beside her at night, reassuring, soft and loved.

Talima spent hours idly stroking its satin fur and crooning remembered melodies. *I don't understand why Pirjhan hasn't answered my messages. I send one every day...not one reply...he can't be that busy, can he, kitten?*

Dreamily, she knew there was a solution to her predicament, but she just couldn't find it in the fog that seemed to envelop her thoughts. She waited to take advantage of circumstances she was sure she'd recognize when the moment appeared.

DAILY LESSONS IN MANNERS AND MORALS OF THE COURT WERE TAUGHT by Lu Mei and Lu Li. Talima was required to attend.

"Correct your character as with an ax..." Lu Mei told them.

"...embellish it with a chisel," Lu Li added. "And remember, ladies, a man is heaven..."

"...and heaven cannot be shirked. Cut away laziness, contain your relationships with courage."

These precepts for Fragrant Pillow Women were time-honored and precise.

Boring...I never knew what that word meant before, but this is boring. Life would be boring if that sort of thing were all you thought of. Man is heaven? Piffle, not very often and not very well! Don't these people do anything worthwhile? Don't they ever ride or hunt...or think about anything except the way they look to others, to a man?

"Yes, indeed, Lu Li speaks truly. If your words are good, men will be responsive to you. If not..."

"...it doesn't matter how sweetly your lute sings or how willowy your dance..."

"...even a devoted bedfellow will shun your company."

Lu Mei finished with satisfaction. "Fulfill your duties..."

"...in all things, calmly and respectfully."

Their litany of correct behavior droned on. The day dragged on. Each day much like the one before.

Days seem endless....how long has it been? A week perhaps? Or more? Seems like forever. I miss Faina, miss Shira and Bagatur...if only I could lie along his back and feel the wind in my hair. Oh how I miss my family, my people, and the mountains. I miss Pirjhan, miss his songs and his laughter, miss most of all being held by him.

I feel cut off from all I know and love. Great Tengri! When will I be able to see the emperor, talk to him? leave this perfumed, trivial world where nothing changes, nothing happens?

Her one constant pleasure was her bath. It stood ready at any hour and was rarely occupied in mid-afternoon, when almost everyone else napped.

Followed as usual by Takla Makan, she slipped down the hall and into the steaming room. She took off her boots and put them beside her folded tunic and pants near the door to keep them from getting wet. Then she sank down slowly into the blue-tiled pool. For a little while she could forget all her frustrations and simply lie in the hot water and breathe the rosemary-scented steam.

She heard muted footsteps coming down the hall and tensed in order to jump out and dress. But no one came in to bathe, so she drifted back down blissfully. As her body relaxed, pleasant memories surfaced. She dreamed and floated, floated and dreamed.

The kitten curled up to sleep in a stripe of sunshine from the garden window. Time passed.

Finally, Talima looked at her water-wrinkled fingers and decided, reluctantly, to get out and get dressed. She splashed around the pool and then stepped out onto the cool floor. She reached for one of the large linen towels that were usually stacked on shelves, but the shelves were empty.

Well, guess I'll just have to drip for a bit and hope my clothes will dry out as I go. "Wake up, Takla Makan, time to leave. But where *are* my clothes? I know I left them right by the door when I came in...maybe the wind?"

But she knew there was never a wind in these still rooms strong enough to blow away a pile of clothes and boots. Besides, the door was shut. But she went to it, to look into the hall, to make sure...

The door was locked. As she looked around, she realized that she and the kitten were the only things in the whole room...no clothes, no towels and only one way out—the window into the garden.

"'Sky! Those footsteps! Someone came and stole my clothes and locked the door...why would *anyone* want to do that, kitten? Well, we'll just climb out the window, won't we? We can get back to our room that way, too...we'll not give them the satisfaction of staying prisoner in here!"

She tucked Takla Makan under her arm and swung her long legs over the windowsill. Her hair dripped, and the kitten's fur stuck to her. They dropped into rose bushes on the other side. Thorns scratched thin, jagged lines in wet skin, ragged lines that rapidly filled with blood.

No one was in the garden. She walked to the nearest door. It, too, was locked. She could see the women clustered inside, peering out at her. Although they covered their mouths with their hands, Talima could hear them tittering. She tried every door that opened onto the inner garden, becoming more and more angry, door by door.

Great Tengri curse them for a pack of fools! How dare they do this to me...I'll never forgive them...never, never!

She ran down one path after another, seeking a way out or a way in. It didn't matter, either would do. The terrified kitten dug its claws into her bare shoulder in order to hang on. She didn't even feel it. She stormed down the garden path, reviling the women, cursing Chian, her life here, the Emperor, her Father...her fury, long-capped, seethed out on anything and anyone who had anything to do with her being here.

This path ended at ivy-covered stairs, stairs Talima had never noticed before. She ran up them and came out on a wide balcony that overlooked the garden. Here, there was an open door. She brushed aside the curtains and walked in.

TALIMA STOOD STILL AS HER EYES ADJUSTED TO THE DIM LIGHT OF THE ROOM in which she found herself. Looking around, she saw that the floor was covered with woven grass mats, the walls were of white plaster framed with wood. A black covered pallet, with three brown pillows placed precisely left, right and center, lay in front of low shallow shelves. A small, polished table stood against one wall, and on it were: A bronze bell shaped like a bowl, its leather-wound striker beside it, a three-legged bronze tripod that held sticks of incense, one of which sent a gray-blue spiral of dry-wood-smell smoke into the air, a blue bowl filled with water, and a small ivory carving of a person seated cross-legged, one slender hand pointing at the floor.

In a recessed arch in the wall she saw a scroll that depicted mountains and trees and a waterfall. In front of the painting stood a slender vase that held a single spray of tiny green-gold orchids. That was all. It was a clean, spare room whose simplicity appealed to Talima.

"Fei...fei...fei! What have we here?" A sonorous, penetrating voice. Talima turned quickly to confront the man who had just entered.

He was not much taller than she, but he seemed mountainous.

His presence filled the room. Filled with concentrated energy held in conscious order, filled with innate power. His grizzled hair and beard hung around his shoulders like a feathered mantle. His feet were small and bare. His skin, the color of strong chai, shone with oil. He wore a floor-sweeping tunic of midnight blue.

"What have we here?" he repeated. "Why are you here...and as naked as a newborn at that? Are you perhaps propitiating the rain gods in this fashion? True, we do need rain, but I hadn't known that anyone nowadays believed in that old magic! Where did you come from? How did you get in? Explain yourself."

"I'll explain myself, as you put it, as soon as you stop asking me questions and give me a chance to say something!" Talima's anger kindled again. "I came from the garden of course. And why? Because those stupid, sniveling, be-cursed women down there stole my clothes and locked me out and..."

"Ah-hmmnn, a spitfire, yes? Slow down. I'll hear the whole story, from the beginning if you please. But first..." he knelt down, lifted the cover of one of his shelves, took out a blue robe and handed it to Talima. "Put this on."

She slid the welcome gown over her head and wrapped its voluminous folds around her. Her anger cooled as the thick cotton warmed her body.

The man called to an unseen servant to bring refreshments, then sat down and motioned her to do the same. "First, your name," he said quietly.

"I am Talima, daughter and heir of Tashih Shaymak, Chagan of the Pamir Igren." She spoke with the pride she always felt when she thought of her people.

"And how did you come to be here?"

"I came with a banner of horses, as tribute to..." She continued to tell the story of their journey to Chian. Somehow, Pirjhan's name was never mentioned—nor her love for him. While she talked, hot tea and small bean cakes were brought.

The man listened intently, watched her steadily. He was an experienced judge of people, of women in particular and he was intrigued by this one. *She is fire and ice...innocent, yet wise beyond her years—intelligent and courageous to the point of stubborn foolishness—and withal, beautiful.... beautiful in a profound, disturbing, sensual way.*

"...and so I'm held prisoner here until I can talk to the emperor and it's been so discouraging and boring and until the emperor returns from wherever he's been and I get to see him, I have nothing to do! Nothing worthwhile, I mean."

"What would you *like* to do?"

"I'd like to learn to *write!*" Talima surprised herself with her answer. But it was true...ever since Shih Ssu had shown her the brushes, ink and paper, she had wanted to take this learning back to her clan.

"Would you now? How unusual for a woman to want to write, hmmnnn. It might be possible."

"Would it really? That would be wonderful! Aaah, what should I call you, please?"

"I am called many things," he smiled, "some good, some not so good. You may call me Zanggi."

"Zanggi? That's a strange name...is that what your father named you?"

"No, but I've nearly forgotten what that was. Zanggi will do. You see, little Spitfire, I, too, come from a land far from Changan, a land I left as a young boy on one of the great Tajik sailing ships, a land know as Kat-Kat-Zanggi—and so the name they call me.

"You've seen the sea? Oh, please tell me what it's like!" she smoothed Takla Makan's drying fur.

"The sea?" He settled back and sipped tea from his iridescent green cup. "The sea is our mother, sustainer of life, always changing, always the same. To know the sea is to fear the sea, but the fear is love also."

"Go on, Zanggi, please go on."

"Fei...fei...fei, enough of these musings. We had best pay attention to what will best serve our father, his most illustrious self, our Emperor Tai Tsung."

"Are you a prisoner here too?"

Zanggi laughed. He held his shaking stomach and laughed. "No, I'm not a prisoner. I'm a most fortunate person, part of the emperor's household, his head eunuch in fact, Coordinator of the *Shuh-mi-Yuan,* the Eunuch's Palace Council, in charge of all the imperial women, wives as well as concubines."

"*You?* You are the dread Coordinator that Lu Mei keeps threatening me with? Why, you're not terrible...I *like* you!"

"Thank you, my dear. But I'm afraid you rather caught me with my guard down...coming in here dressed only in a kitten!" And he began to laugh again, until tears rolled down his dun-colored cheeks. "I am not always so...amiable."

"I wish you would always be, with me...it's so nice to talk with someone sensible," she sighed.

This set the head eunuch off in another gale of laughter. It bubbled up from the depths of his body, spilling over into a pervasive merriment and good will that Talima could not resist.

Sobering, she said, "I don't suppose you meant it...about the writing, I mean, you couldn't really..."

"I think there's a way to set that in motion, yes. Are you an honorable person?"

"Honorable? Certainly, absolutely! I'm an Igren! Why?"

"Because, if I arrange for you to learn how to write, to calligraph... and that means learning to read as well...you'd have to leave the Women's Garden during class-time and I would have to have your word that you would not run away."

"If you can do that, Zanggi, if you can make it possible for me to learn! Oh, that would be so fine! You have my word. I'll not try to run away...I promise."

Zanggi looked at her, his dark eyes taking the measure of her. He made up his mind and clapped his pink-palmed hands together. "Done! This is what you will do. You'll participate in the normal activities of the pavilion in the mornings, but every afternoon, you'll go to the Forest of Pencils to learn to read and write.

"I'll arrange your release with the instructresses...and provide you with an escort the first few days. From then on you're on your own... except that I would like you to give me frequent reports on your progress. Is that clear?"

Without thinking, Talima jumped up and hugged him. "Thank you, Zanggi! Thank you very much!"

"Fei...fei...fei, well, humph...impetuous, too impetuous, Spitfire."

He felt the hard core of his heart warm and melt. *So long, it's been so very long since such sweetness has walked into my life.*

Talima danced around the room. Takla Makan, held at arm's length, legs hanging down, rolled her golden eyes and tried to stand on air.

"Get out of here, both of you! I'll die laughing at this rate, yes, go... take the gown, you need it more than I do...and remember to return in one week.

"But, before you go, I must give you a Chianese name, you'll never find the characters to write your mon-barbarian name, I fear."

"But I have one already...I told you about the Wu family, Shih Ssu's family, adopting me, remember? They gave me a Chianese name—Wu Tse Tsien."

"Ah ha! Splendid! Tse Tsien it is then, Spitfire. Now get along downstairs."

"But I can't get in Zanggi! All the doors are locked against me down there." She grew quiet at the thought of returning to the jeering women.

"Aaaah, we shall go down together then. We will, however, go properly, down the main stairway."

Side by side, they walked the length of the balcony to wide, inner stairs that led down in the Jade Pavilion. Two blue-flame figures descended... one slim and copper-headed, one massive and dark. They came quietly into the hubbub of women who still watched and waited at the door for Talima's return.

They shrieked and moaned when they suddenly saw the Coordinator, fearing his displeasure, then quieted as they recognized who stood beside him.

"Where are your noble instructresses?"

"Here, my lord, here..." said Lu Mei, bowing low.

"...we are," added Lu Li, bending even lower, until her headdress touched the floor.

"Ye-esss, yes..." Zanggi stared at them and waited.

"We didn't know, we didn't..."

"...mean to! It was all in fun—to teach her a lesson."

"So, just so," Zanggi interrupted. "She needs lessons and she shall have them. As *I* choose, *not* you. You are not to hinder her in any way, any of you...do I make myself quite clear?"

As one, they murmured assent.

"I want you to provide this girl with suitable clothes from now on," he stroked his beard and smothered a smile, "and keep her very busy learning whatever you have wit enough to teach her. Lu Mei, Lu Li, come with me. I'll explain what I wish her to do, beginning tomorrow. Tse Tien? In one week."

"Yes, sir, without fail! You have my promise."

"I depend on it." He sailed out, the imperial instructresses tripping along in his wake.

Talima walked into the garden and sat down on a flat stone at the edge of a pond. She switched a twig back and forth for Takla Makan to pounce on and watched a bronze and black fish fan the shadows. She felt at peace for the first time in days. She gazed at the harvest moon—the moon of fulfillment, a flaming orange sphere—as it rose above the garden wall.

This is the opportunity I have waited for…from now on things will be different. Anything is possible now…I feel it with certainty, deep within me…

23
Wu Chao Tse Tsien Learns To Calligraph

ZANGGI SENT ONE OF THE PALACE EUNUCHS TO ESCORT TALIMA to the Imperial Academy. Clad in an appropriate *t'ung-cotton* shift under a sturdy indigo-linen apron, Talima put her hands in her sleeves and ran behind him. The soft soles of her pointed slippers whispered against the slate-paved path. They went through gardens where oddly-shaped trees grew, past small lakes alive with many kinds of ducks and geese and over a wooden half-moon bridge that arched across a sparkling stream.

The Academy, surrounded by a moat, sprawled over several *mou* of an artificial island. Its earth-red tile roofs were alive with the scritch-scritch of birds' feet, its warren of rooms a-buzz with voices.

A clerk at the portal assigned Talima to the studio of Li Chang Chao, master calligrapher and renowned poet. As it was already midday, the master was just ending his lecture.

"Be aware that calligraphy is a dance," he was saying as she entered, "a dance of brush on paper, thick and thin, sun and shadow. Your writing should be like the dance of life itself, full of grace and beauty, symbol of the meaning within."

Talima stood just inside the doorway and listened. Each word bloomed in her mind, fragrance from a garden she longed to know.

"Take your brushes and begin the afternoon's practice. Do not grow weary with practice! Remember, students, you have a thousand bad characters in your fist! The only way to get rid of them is to write them out! Practice, practice, practice! It is our battle cry, our shield and our solace! To work then!"

Talima felt invigorated, eager to begin. But she didn't know how—or where. The broad hall was packed with little slanted tables that stood on tall, carved legs. Brushes hung from a thin rod along the edge of each desk, pencils and other writing paraphernalia stuck out from bamboo cylinders set into the surface. Flat ceramic dishes, stained black as soot, lay beside foot-long polished metal rulers. She didn't know whether to find a desk to stand at, or speak to the instructor first.

That decision was not hers to make, however, for one of the students beckoned her to a large sink on the far wall of the studio. When they got there, he told her what to do. The sink was filled with dirty water containers and odds and ends of cups and bowls. He indicated that she should clean them, then he returned to his desk.

Talima was surprised, but not unhappy. She knew she was only a beginner. It was enough, for today, to be away from the women's garden, to be where writing was taught.

The first few days, she did little else than wash or clean desks. Gradually other tasks were added. She took completed scrolls, carefully coiled and tied, from her studio to others in the building. She got lost, but students always helped her on her way again. She went to the storerooms and brought back wooden boxes filled with camphor-saturated ink sticks, or rolls of soft rice paper for the students. Wherever she went, she took time to look at the writing or painting that students of each classroom worked on.

She stayed longer and later in The Forest of Pencils, as students referred to the Academy. Late one day, when the students had gone, Talima stayed to study their posted practice sheets that curled in long rectangles against the studio wall. She concentrated on each written character, tracing its form in the air with her finger.

The Master is right, it is a dance! She thought, while she watched the rhythm of her finger as it danced out the written characters. She was so absorbed in what she was doing, that she failed to hear Master Li Chang Chao come into the studio, did not realize that he watched her as she pretended to write.

"What are you doing?"

Talima gasped and jumped. "Nothing! I'm not doing anything!"

"You most certainly were doing *something!* What did you think it was?" He sounded amused.

"I was trying to learn, to learn to write," Talima whispered.

"So you want to learn to write, do you?"

"Oh, yes!"

"Well then, what's stopping you?"

"You are, if you please, Master Calligrapher, you are stopping me from learning—by not teaching me."

"By the Three Pure Ones! All right then, I expect I'd better take care of that omission. Get some paper and pens. We'll begin immediately."

Talima could hardly breathe. Quickly she laid paper on a desk.

"What's your name, girl?"

"Talima, sir."

"That's not a decent name…don't you have a good Chian name?"

"I do have a Chian name, it's Wu Chao Tse Tsien."

"Ah-ha, that's better! Best of all, we have something in common—the character *chao*. That's part of my name too, you know. Here is what chao looks like…"

He dipped his brush into the deep end of an ink stone, moved it around for a moment, then brushed the excess ink off on the edge of the dish. He held the brush vertically, between his thumb and straight index finger, poised over the paper. Then, without further hesitation, he made a few rapid lines on the paper.

"Now you try it—like this." He held her hand that held the pen and directed its movement. "Almost…a good beginning. You just need practice. By the way, d'you know what chao stands for?"

"No, I never realized it *had* a meaning." Talima thought her crude strokes looked nothing like the elegant thicks and thins of the character he had written.

"The strokes that make up chao are simplified from the original picture that showed all the celestial bodies of the universe illuminating the Void below, the light of the world shining there for those able to perceive it! Rather wonderful, don't you think, for us to have all that as part of our own names?"

For the first time, Talima was pleased to think of herself as Chao Tse Tsien of the family Wu.

TALIMA SPENT EVERY AFTERNOON THEREAFTER IN THE FOREST OF PENCILS learning to write, listening to the lectures, stories and exhortations of Li Chang Chao. She was intoxicated with the smells and sounds and sights: the smell of camphor as ink sticks were ground and ground into an ever finer powder to make sooty, viscous ink; the rustle of paper and murmur of student voices; the black lines that flowed from her brush and defined the intricate, balanced, white spaces on her practice paper. Every moment was magic, every act one of beauty. All else faded into insignificance.

Many things that had been important before no longer mattered. She wore what Lu Mei gave her without objection, attended pavilion classes during the mornings and paid attention. Focused on the afternoon, she even let the other women teach her how to play "Double Sixes" and found that she enjoyed it enormously. She got doubles so often when she threw the sticks that some accused her of witchcraft. She laughed, but won more often than not, discouraging those of lesser skill.

Lu Mei approved of the change in her charge, which was due, she assured the Imperial Coordinator during her daily report, to her own patience and forbearance. Zanggi nodded but knew better, knew that a girl like Tse Tsien thrived on challenge.

As Talima went to and from the Academy, there was an ever-changing parade of people, stranger, more colorful, more fascinating than she had imagined possible.

They walked, as she did, on Nine Dragon Hill, within the vast, intriguing palace compound, on an autumn day luminous with reflected sunlight from trees aflame with gold and ochre, vermilion and rust.

She stopped on the moon-bridge to watch variegated leaves float by below. She remembered Li Chang Chao's words from his lecture that afternoon.

"Remember, Wu Chao," he had said, "your brush is an extension of your arm—but not your arm alone. It is also an extension of your heart and your mind. For what your heart believes to be true, your mind directs your hand to write. That's why brushwork is often referred to by the character that says *heart's print*, and it looks like this..."

Heart's print...black lines, white spaces, that show the condition of the heart, a truly magic act, writing is. I wish I could show Father...he'd be fascinated! If I get home, I'll be able to teach him, teach our whole clan!

I wonder what my heart's print looks like? Not sad anymore...how odd to feel so happy, when I don't know what's going to happen...when I'm still separated from everything I know and love...

"No, Wu Chao Tse Tsien", she said aloud, "that's no longer true!" She laughed when she realized that, having written it so often, she had begun to think of herself, not as Talima, but as Wu Chao Tse Tsien. She moved off the path as she heard the sound of hooves from behind her.

She first noticed the horse, its mane tied up evenly in small bunches that looked like miniature battlements on the Great Wall. Then she saw how well its rider sat his mount, his back ramrod straight, legs long in the stirrups the way Pirjhan rode. His dark hair was drawn up into a topknot, and his leather breastplate and thigh-protectors were covered by a rippling tunic of scarlet silk, embroidered front and back with a golden dragon that seemed to fly in the wind as he rode.

He reminded her so suddenly, so poignantly of Pirjhan, that she wanted to cry out, to run after him. At the same moment, she recognized the dragons on his tunic. They were the same dragons as those in the dream that had disturbed her sleep so many times.

She also realized that she had been given a measure of freedom now and perhaps, if she were careful, she could locate the imperial stables and find Pirjhan. The idea took root in her mind.

I'll have to allot enough time before or after class to search for the stables. I can't ask directions for fear they'd find out who I really am... and that I rightly belong somewhere else, but somehow I'll manage! Somewhere in this honeycomb of buildings and paths and gardens I'll find him!

Her feet scarcely touched the ground as she ran home. *Tomorrow I'll begin to look...tomorrow!*

24
PIRJHAN MAKES AN ENEMY AND GAINS A PATRON

"YOU SHOULD HAVE SEEN HER, PIRJHAN!" PRINCE FIRUZ TOLD HIS FRIEND that night. "She was smiling and radiant and, by my ancestor's eyes, the most beautiful kitchen wench I've ever seen—just your type!"

"You know I'm not interested in kitchen girls, Firuz, beautiful or otherwise. I'm still in love with my Talima and until I find her, and if she still wants me..."

"Ah, faithfulness, thy name is Pirjhan! All right, I respect this great love you swear on, but I tell you this girl was gorgeous! Red-gold hair blowing around her face, eyes like the sky, and just standing there, smiling as if her life were some marvelous adventure!"

"Did you talk to her?"

"No, and I wish I had. Maybe if I go back there at the same time tomorrow, she might be there again."

"Worth a try, my friend. Meanwhile, do you have any plans for this evening?"

"Forgot to tell you! We're invited to Li Cheng Chien's, the eldest son of the emperor. He's giving one of his grand parties to celebrate the arrival of some new Sassanian musicians. He's crazy for their music, you know. It's just an excuse for a party, really...but he's always generous. D'you want to go?"

"Would it be all right for me to come?"

"Of course, but just to make sure, come up to my room when you're through here."

Later that evening, a pair of clean-shaven men, as alike as two stars in the sky, resplendent in the uniforms of palace guardsmen, walked from the barracks toward the inner palace. Their scarlet capes swirled behind them like tail-feathers and rustled against their knee-high boots. The first frost of autumn whitened dry leaves that littered the path. Prince Firuz and a transformed Pirjhan, beardless and clothed in one of Firuz' uniforms, joined other young men who walked beneath the harvest moon toward Li Cheng Chien's residence.

As they came into the inner courtyard formed by a wing of the palace, bronze braziers that stood around the gardens were just being lit. The fires illumined a scene that astonished Pirjhan.

"Mad! It's quite mad! This looks like the Chagan's camp... like an Igren rendezvous! What're they doing?"

Firuz laughed. "It's one of Cheng Chien's eccentricities, my friend, one of many! He simply believes that westerners have the best of everything. Come and see."

They wandered through paths lined with flowers that surrounded sky-blue tents larger than any Igren ger. Totem flags flew from tall standards beside open doorways. At the center of the courtyard was a huge fire that sent sparks skyward, lighting an enormous, profusely embroidered tent. Seated on piles of furs, under a wolf's head ensign, was a man dressed in Turkish-style baggy trousers and flaring coat. It was Li Cheng Chien, Emperor Tai Tsung's eldest son, entertaining friends.

Firuz led Pirjhan to meet him. "A friend from the west, Sir. You'll find you have a lot in common I think. A better horseman has yet to be born!"

"Your Most Gracious Majesty." Pirjhan bowed.

"Forget that nonsense here! Here we are brothers! Come—eat and drink with me!" Cheng Chien speared a piece of mutton with his curved dagger and chewed off a large bite. He offered the remainder to Pirjhan while he wiped grease from his long mustaches onto his sleeve. "Sit here while the dancers and musicians get ready. Tell me who you are and why you've come to our gala city."

Pirjhan sat down rather self-consciously, but soon was regaling the prince of the imperial realm with stories that made him laugh. Before long, after wine and kumiss, they were arm in arm as Pirjhan taught him chapar trail songs.

"Ho! Firuz! This is a fine fellow you brought tonight. I like him. He says he isn't really a guardsman though and that seems a shame. Remind me to appoint him. Tomorrow. We can't have him wandering around without suitable privileges, can we? We'll see to it...a promise!

"Now tell me what you think is the best way to train a hunting falcon. You must come hunting with us in the north. I'll lend you one of my birds. Ah, here come the musicians!" He jumped up, a bit unsteadily, and clapped for attention.

Guests gathered into an amphitheatre lit by torches. Pirjhan thought he'd grown accustomed to the variety of people and costumes in Changan, but here there were more differences than similarities. One man was dressed in layers of sheer cotton, tied over one shoulder and belted at his waist by silver chains that held up a long, curved sword. Pearls twined across his chest. Another wore a tight-fitting, high-necked, brocaded coat and a turban. Some wore yellow-orange robes or cotton sarongs printed with vivid batik designs.

"Who are these people, Firuz?" whispered Pirjhan as they took their seats.

"They're sons of royal families from a dozen other countries—Silla, Tibet, Karakhoja, Paekche, Koguryo—to name a few. By my ancestor's eyes, there's that notorious Nestorian monk Reuben, I think he calls himself, says he comes from the Roman Emperor Constans the Second, whoever that it is! Some barbarian country far away to the west, I expect."

"Are they hostages?"

"No, they're sent here to be educated in Chian's excellent universities, just as I was. Some like it so well they never leave. It's hard to go back to your own less-civilized country after you've seen and tasted the pleasures of Changan!

"It's exciting, don't you think?" Prince Firuz continued, "living here at the center of things, where all the goods of the known world are ours for a few cash pieces, where new philosophies flow through on a vast river of languages and cultures?"

"Yes, it is exciting, but I wish Tam were here to share it. Are these women also of royal families?"

"Some are daughters or sisters of noble families, some are courtesans who come for the evening. You mustn't be selfish with your attentions, Pirjhan, there's many a lovely lady here who'd be delighted with your company."

Pirjhan's embarrassed laughter rolled over the heads of those in front of him. As if that had been the signal, acrobats in many-colored costumes tumbled onto the stage, cartwheeling, spinning and somersaulting in all directions.

Musicians who circled the stage accompanied them. The percussion group included a great shining gong, several small *wether* drums and a grand drum suspended from a vermilion frame, crowned with carved, gilded flames and carried by dwarves. Prancing musicians who blew flutes, oboes, and mouth organs played the high-pitched melody. A zither and a lute filled in the harmonies.

The acrobats began a complicated juggling routine using flaming torches and then continued juggling balls while they balanced on larger balls or boards or each other. The crowd yelled their enthusiastic approval.

"Where's my new friend? Where's that wild young mountain man?" roared a voice.

"That's Cheng Chien. I think he means you, Pirjhan, you'd better go to him."

"Me? Alone? You come too, Firuz."

"All right, but get going! His imperial princeness doesn't like to wait. You're lucky, Pirjhan. He usually forgets someone instantly. He's not a bad sort...but be careful all the same."

"Make room! Move over!" Cheng Chien said to the courtiers around him. "Sit next to me, you'll be able to see better, and I can better enjoy your amazement. The western prancing dance is about to begin! Watch!"

A dozen boys leaped onto the stage as the acrobats ran off. They wore tight-sleeved Persian shirts and high, peaked caps covered with sparkling beads. Their waists were wrapped with several long belts whose fringed ends fluttered like flags behind them. Lutes and flutes wailed as they crouched and stomped vigorously in a dance equivalent of high-spirited horses.

"How'd you like to ride one of those, eh?" Cheng Chien snorted and slapped Pirjhan's knee.

Pirjhan smiled. He felt oddly uneasy.

Gongs and drums beat a crescendo. The dancing boys pranced off. Torches surrounding the stage were extinguished. There were a few moments of darkness.

Pirjhan felt a moist mustache nuzzle his neck. Startled, he shied away, tried to stand. Just then dozens of fat, red candles were lit. He saw the imperial prince, smiling benignly, gesture for him to sit back down.

In the center of the candles, sitting on embroidered pillows, were four exquisite girls. Purple net shirts hung from their slender shoulders like petals from a flower, silver girdles studded with tiny bells, wrapped the dusky skin of their bellies. They wore conical hats from which long, diaphanous veils billowed like incense around them. A simple melody full of longing and loneliness wavered from panpipe flutes.

Pirjhan sat down. Cheng Chien nodded and smiled. His full lips seemed to caress his large, yellow teeth.

The girls began to move, unwinding toward each other like buds opening before the sun. As they rose, the drums began. Slowly, slowly, they turned, hips circling, bellies undulating. Faster, faster, the drums beat. The audience was silent, held by the spell of their sinuous dance.

Pirjhan scarcely breathed.

"The *Chach* dancers—you like them, my friend?" whispered Cheng Chien. "I could arrange for one of them to come to you tonight. Choose one...she's yours."

"No. That is, thank you, your Highness."

"You needn't mind, Pirjhan. It's my pleasure to give to my friends...a little roll in the rain-and-clouds with one of my dancing girls might whet your appetite for greater pleasures, eh?" He snickered.

The girls shimmied toward them, arms stretched out in supplication. The drumbeat was frenzied. Pirhjhan wanted to reach out and hold the dancer nearest him. He wanted to run away. He began to shake with the intensity of his longing.

At that moment, a dozen explosions thundered. Fireworks shot into the air. Thousands of incandescent stars winked against the night sky and showered down over them.

The crowd roared their excitement. Pirjhan bolted. He ran through the starlit night, back to the familiar safety of the stables.

"WE SHOULD CELEBRATE, PIRJHAN!" FIRUZ PUNCHED HIM PLAYFULLY on the arm. "Today you've found great favor with his Most Luminous Majesty Tai Tsung and doors will open in a way that will amaze you!"

"Favor? I? No, it's the horses that did it, Firuz."

"But they're *your* horses he chose! He's never been known to choose unbranded horses before...did you realize that? This will more than make up for the way you slighted Prince Cheng last night...disappearing without ceremony, Pirjhan, really! You'll need to learn better manners if you wish to survive at court!"

"I'd rather not discuss Prince Cheng, Firuz. There were... circumstances that compelled me to leave. But the horses...they're not mine, actually, they're Igren horses. I only..."

"You only groom them and train them and pamper them. Don't be modest—they're real beauties and Tai Tsung took the ten best for his *personal* use. It's remarkable! Of course, no one could resist them. Their divine origin is stamped in every hair from nostril to tail."

Firuz helped Pirjhan unhalter and brush down each of the horses. As they began feeding them, they saw the emperor, unaccompanied, coming down the dusty passageway. They put down their hayforks, straightened their clothes, slipped dress tunics over their heads and were standing at attention by the time he reached them.

Emperor Tai Tsung was taller than either Pirjhan or Firuz. He was large-boned, wide-shouldered, massive. His beard was thin and tapered, his mustaches waxed and pointed. Only the long sideburns below his tightly wrapped topknot showed any gray hairs. His face was broad and smooth. Deep creases from military campaigns in the sun and wind extended from his slanted obsidian eyes. An old scar crinkled his left cheekbone. As he walked, he hooked his thumbs into his leather belt, emblazoned with gold and jade. It was the only bit of color in the whole of his black eminence.

"Sire!" Both guardsmen bowed deeply.

"Be at ease. I came to see my new horses. Which of you is their groom?"

"I am, Sire."

"Your name, horseman?"

"Pirjhan, Noble Sire," he said, bowing even lower.

"Magnificent animals, Pirjhan! They remind me of lines from a poem written by my cousin, Li Bo, *"...the Horses of Heaven come out of the dens of the Kushanas, backs formed with tiger markings, bones made for dragon wings."* The emperor's smile softened the stern lines of his face. "Indeed, these horses are like the ones he imagined. Are they as stalwart as they look?"

"Absolutely. We trailed them many thousands of li across mountains and desert. Difficult country, as I'm sure Your Most Luminous Majesty is aware. From Igren territory, the Kushanas, as you might say."

"How did they come to be in my stables without being branded? Who neglected his duty?"

"No one was at fault, Sire." Pirjhan spoke briefly of the circumstances of their entrance into Chian, of the stampede and resulting losses, of the letter to the Wu family of Tai Yuan, of Talima and their arrival in Changan.

"We must give them my brand without delay. Tell Kapi to find another groom for the rest of your horses. I want you to concentrate on these ten. Train them well, Pirjhan. Many of my splendid old bayards have fallen in battle. These will replace them."

The emperor tilted his head to one side and smoothed his beard with his left hand. "I shall have their portraits painted. One at a time? Or all together, what do you think? Their names must be carved above their stalls, too. Hmnn, names. Can you remember, exactly, what I tell you?"

"I will write them down, Sire," said Firuz.

"Excellent! Thus will my heirs and all those who come after me, down through the ages, remember these, the horses of my middle years. First, names for the white ones...*Frost Prancing White, Shining Snow Grizzel, Frozen Dew Grizzled* and *Suspended Light Grizzle*. Then, the golden ones—*Wave Plunging Bay* and *Flowing Gold Yellow*. How many is that?"

Tai Tsung looked pleased with his decisions. He went to each horse in turn, caressed its forehead and ears, ran a hand down their forelegs.

"Six—only four more." Pirjhan noticed that although Tai Tsung's hands looked soft and small, they were so large that they easily spanned a horse's ankle.

"Yes, the roans...*Running Rainbow Red, Lightning Darting Red, Sunset Flying Roan* and *Soaring Unicorn Purple*. Perfect, if I do say so! It's like creating a whole new family isn't it? A family more manageable than my human one, I must admit."

"Perfect names, Sire, for perfect horses," said Pirjhan. "Your Majesty, I would not presume, but I wonder if..."

"What's that, Pirjhan?"

"It's just that, since we've come to Changan, my family has, my companions that is, have been separated and I wondered if I could ask you where..."

"Yes? Go on, man, ask!"

"It's Talima, the girl I told you about, the one who was sent to you as tribute along with the banner of horses."

"What about her?"

"Is she all right?"

"I have no idea."

"Hasn't she been with *you* these past moons?"

"I've been in the outlands most of that time, but I'm sure she's been well cared for. Tribute of all kind finds its place in the palace, but I'm rarely aware of, or even told of, its whereabouts. A thousand things—too many things fill my days." He sighed.

"But I need to find her!"

"Do you indeed? Why is she any business of yours now?"

"Because I promised her father to look after her until she was safely wed. I've sent messages, but there's no reply and I fear for her safety. I thought she was with you, you see, but now..."

"Steady, Pirjhan," Firuz cautioned him. "My companion is a man of honor, Most Luminous One. He feels remiss in his duties to his Chagan. Without being sure of his ward's condition, you see. A small thing, really, but important in his eyes."

"I see. Well, if it relieves your mind, Pirjhan, I'll have my equerry make inquiries. You say her name was Talima? I would have noticed a peculiar name like that, seems to me. I'll have someone let you know when she's found."

"Thank you, Sire. I would appreciate knowing, beyond measure, most grateful." Pirjhan bowed deeply so that the emperor could not see his sudden tears.

"Good, that's settled then. I'll soon be gone again, to make inspection in the southern chous till early spring. By the time I return, you'll have these horses proficient in all military maneuvers. I trust you to see to it, Pirjhan. Ask Kapi for whatever you may need, or anything that you need to know about my requirements."

"It shall be done, Your Majesty."

"Splendid!" He went the way he had come—softly, heavily, more as if he were stalking game than striding down his own stables. Yet even the horses lifted their heads and flickered their ears toward him as he passed.

25
A Report to Zanggi and a Polo Game

"WELL, SPITFIRE, HAVE YOU ENJOYED THESE LAST WEEKS?" asked Coordinator Zanggi, as he poured tea into porcelain cups so thin that the pale green color shone through.

"Oh, yes, it's been wonderful!" She replied.

"Do you find Li Chang Chao to be a satisfactory teacher then?"

"Satisfactory? That's not exactly the word I'd use, Zanggi-sha... brilliant is closer to the truth. He knows so much and I'm learning a great deal because he's so inspiring and funny and..."

"Funny?"

"Yes," Talima held up her right hand, "see the ink stains on my fingers? Chan Chao says that they're honorable marks of initiation. He calls them the signs of privilege...black ink flowers that make me a member of The Ancient Order of the Black Chrysanthemum!" As she had promised, she was making a full report on her lessons to Kat Kat Zanggi. The two of them sat on bamboo mats in his light-filled room. Takla Makan wandered back and forth between them, purring loudly. Birds sang in the garden below.

"Thank you for making it possible for me to learn how to write—it's great magic, and I hope to be very good at it as soon as I can."

"There's no hurry now, is there?" He watched her intently, wondering what kind of mischief might be brewing in her agile mind. "A good calligrapher studies for years—a lifetime."

"But I want to learn it *now*, I can't wait, you see..."

"Patience...patience and perseverance, Tse Tsien. Allow yourself time. Curb your restlessness, my dear."

"You sound like Lu Mei, Honorable Coordinator!" The sun shafted through the open doors and haloed the froth of curls around her smiling face.

Zanggi sucked in his breath. *This is one to watch...she'd charm the scales off a dragon...what a beauty...a perfect setting for that jewel of intelligence that burns with such fire within! Assuredly a precious gem for his majesty's crown. She needs polishing though and careful guarding, hmm...*He twisted his clear green jade ring round and round while Talima played with her kitten.

"Zanggi-sha? You've been generous, I realize, but could I ask you for...?

"Anything, ask me anything—although you may not get the answer that you want, you know."

"You're teasing...seriously, can you request an audience with Emperor Tai Tsung for me? I know he's in residence, for his dragon flag is flying over the palace...I've asked Lu Mei a dozen times and nothing ever happens!"

"An audience with his Most Imperial Majesty? Why?"

"I must talk to him, and no one seems to help me—will you?"

"The Emperor's days are crowded with vitally important matters—he has little time for the pleasures of conversing with a pretty girl, Tse Tsien."

"You don't understand—*I* have *vitally important* matters to discuss with him! This isn't an idle whim of one of your garden women—I *must* talk to him and surely you could arrange it, couldn't you—please, Zanggi?"

"Well, I suppose it wouldn't hurt to try...it's most unlikely though. Now don't look so unhappy—it hurts my heart to see you sad—I'll send a memorandum through channels and we'll see what comes back."

"Oh, would you? That's wonderful—how soon might we expect to hear?"

"There could be an answer by your next report, but..."

"A whole week?"

"But you have much to accomplish in that week, every week. Remember your lessons? Now finish your tea and be off with you, I have reports of my own to finish. It's good to see you looking a bit more cheerful than before—be one with your true self until we meet again." He stood and ushered her into the hall that led to the steps down to the pavilion of women.

Talima picked up Takla Makan, satisfied that she had set the wheels in motion that could lead to a resolution of all her problems.

TALIMA DID NOT STAY IN THE ACADEMY AFTER HER CALLIGRAPHY CLASS was dismissed that afternoon. She had overheard some of the foreign students discussing horses and had gleaned enough information from their talk that she thought she could now find the imperial stables.

She struggled into her padded coat as she ran. When she saw that people she passed were staring at her haste, she slowed down to a walk, impatient as always, but less noticeable. She followed the carriage road that wound around the north end of a lake. Ducks and geese of a kind she'd never seen before dabbled in reeds near the shore. Black-necked ivory swans preened farther out.

I wonder if Kara is happy in her new life, if that mate she chose loves her...maybe they have little ones by now...what a child I was when I found Kara...what an innocent child...

Two-wheeled carriages drawn by sleek, high-stepping horses passed her, their riders stood facing forward, the driver flourished a long flexible whip. Some of the fast-moving carriages trailed long banners of white silk streamers behind them in an ostentatious display of wealth. Others seemed content to have a flamboyantly uniformed servant ride alongside.

Talima saw merchants accompanied by slaves who carried goods from all corners of the known world—fragrant aromatics, gaudy little birds, thorny lizards, oddly-shaped fruits. Servants dressed in the gold and blue livery of the palace bustled by her. She turned onto a narrower road that branched north to where she thought the stables ought to be. This road wound through gardens and woodlands where peacocks and spotted deer wandered freely. She could hear the laughter of children and see an occasional couple sitting together beneath the trees. The beauty of the place pervaded her thoughts and she felt more at peace, but even so, hurried on.

Before long she saw the palace compound's wall and remembering the first night that Kapi had brought them into the palace, sensed she was close to the right area. The wall twisted over a slight rise and beyond, she saw the stables. Horses, both led and ridden, were going in and out of the open gate.

She walked directly toward the center of the stables, but before she got there, a stable hand stopped her.

"Hai there, where d'you thing you're goin'? Yer way outa yer way, aren't ya, girl?"

Talima tucked a straggling curl under her kerchief and did not smile. "I have business with Kapi the stable-master."

"The stable-master is it? He doesn't let women into the stable, miss, and besides—he's not here—gone to a relative's funeral. You sure he expects you?"

"Aaah, no, he doesn't exactly expect me, but..."

"Then you'd best get outa here...no place for a kitchen wench!"

"I'm not a kitchen wench! I'm..." She realized that she'd better not say who she really was.

"Well, y'look like one in those clothes."

"Probably, thanks. I'll find another way."

"I'll tell 'im—what's your name?"

"Never mind, it's not important. What's the shortest way to go back to the main palace...aahh, er...the palace kitchens, I mean."

He drew a map in the dirt at their feet. She thanked him and walked away quickly.

I'll be back...but not as a girl...I'll get some other clothes, bind my hair and they'll not notice me...

She slipped through the back door of the White Jade Pavilion at sunset, frustrated but determined.

The next day, carrying a bundle that contained clothes she had convinced one of the serving eunuchs that she needed, Talima stopped in a copse of trees outside the stables. She changed her dark blue skirt and jacket for beige and black print trousers and tunic. She bound her hair with a long cotton scarf, leaving the tasseled ends over her shoulder, then added a small-brimmed helmet on top of that. She left the woods looking like any of the young men who roamed the palace grounds.

When she walked through the stable gates this time, no one noticed her. It became more and more crowded as she got closer to the wide straw-covered arena. It was hard for her to see what was happening there so she ducked under arms and squeezed between men until she reached the central ring.

Foreigners there were dressed in the custom of their respective countries—Sogdia, Silla, India, Burma, Khorastan. All the Chian nobles were dressed as usual in a variety of color-saturated silk tunics. Talima saw a dozen or more horses milling around the far end of the arena. Grooms and stable hands led them past the honored spectators, one at a time, then past a clerk who flipped the disks of an abacus rapidly, writing in a thick journal.

It looks like some sort of an auction...wonder if Pirjhan is here...I don't see his beloved bearded face anywhere.

Not recognizing anyone in the crowd, she nevertheless gasped audibly when she saw the next horses, for she did recognize them—they were Igren horses—some gray, a few spotted and tiger-marked on their backs, a few, perfect-white. She craned her neck, peering between all the broad-shouldered horsemen standing in front of her so that she could see the men handling these horses, but they all seemed like strangers in their guardsmen uniforms.

I wonder if those tall boots they're wearing are really good for riding? How good to be with horses again...but where can Jhani be?

Before long, she caught sight of Tulak and Kilar bringing more horses into the ring. She tried to get near them before they entered, but failed until they were on their way out again.

"Pssst, over here!" They looked at her without smiling and continued after the horses. She ran after them realizing they hadn't recognized her, dressed as she was.

"Hai! Kilar, Tulak! It's me, Talima!"

Both men looked startled then grinned. They beckoned her to join them as they herded the horses back to their stalls. When they were alone, she hugged them both.

"I'm so glad to see you! How are you? Where's Pirjhan?"

"Ah, Talima-sha, we've been that worried about you—where've you been? What've you been doing...why didn't you let us know how you were? Is Faina with you?"

"Didn't you get my messages? I sent one every day, but not one of you ever replied!"

"We never got a single message...did you get ours? Pirjhan-sha sent something almost every day...at least at first, he did."

"No nothing...it must've been Lu Li who...oh, Tulak, it's worse than

I knew! Where *is* Pirjhan?"

"He's been with the first group of Igren horses, here, most of the day...didn't you see him?"

"No, he couldn't have been! I've been watching a long time."

"Where's Faina?" Kilar insisted quietly.

"They took Faina away from me—she's been apprenticed to the Silk Weaver's Guild—whatever that is. I'm so sorry, Kilar, I've tried and tried to get her back, but it just hasn't been possible."

"I'll find her then," Kilar said grimly, "I'll find her no matter where she is...or what they've done to her."

"Of course you will and I'll help however I might be able to...now, exactly where was Pirjhan this afternoon?"

"He was one of the men who brought our horses in...the first ones, the best ones."

"No. There were only palace guardsmen riding herd on those."

"That's right, one of them was Pirjhan-sha. They've made him a guardsman now. He's shaved his beard and cut his hair short and wears those fancy Chian clothes and tears around the city all hours of the night and day with his friends."

"You mean he's gone?"

"Probably, there was nothing more to keep him here today, a shame you missed him, but I have an idea..."

Talima felt small and alone and suddenly empty. "An idea? All right, Tulak, what is it?"

"Most every day some of the guardsmen and nobles get together to play polo—it's the same game as alabolo at home—Pirjhan-sha plays often. Why don't you come tomorrow, dressed as you are, and we'll have Bagatur saddled and ready for you to ride with them!"

"Too risky," Kilar said.

"Great idea! Talima said with renewed hope and enthusiasm. "I'll be here. You're both wonderful...I love you and I have to go now...but I'll see you tomorrow...Pirjhan, too...won't he be surprised?"

26
Together Recklessly

"Come on, Pirjhan, come hunting with us...we'll only be gone six or seven days...it'll do you good to be out of the city for awhile...cheer you up!" Firuz said.

"I can't, Firuz. You go...I must stay with the horses." Pirjhan rubbed oil into new halters for the emperor's chosen horses.

"By my ancestor's eyes! You look as though you'd lost your last friend—and you haven't—look, I'm right here."

"I'm just not very good company right now, Firuz, sorry"

"Look I know why you're melancholy and I don't blame you—when Tai Tsung's equerry told you he couldn't find anyone by the name of Talima registered on the roll of palace women, it was a blow, I admit. But not the end of the world—there's a hundred women for our delight, Pirjhan—stop thinking of her for a little while—hunt, drink, carouse with the rest of us—begin to forget her."

"I can't...I'd just be in the way."

"Nonsense! You're coming—I'll tell Kilar and Tulak to look after these horses until we return. You'll have plenty of time to train them before the emperor returns...come on...I'm not going to let you sit here stewing in your own miserable juices...get your gear together, we leave by the third quarter hour."

Pirjhan shrugged and sighed, "You're probably right...there doesn't seem to be much of anything I can do about her right now...but if I..."

"It's settled then, meet me by the west gate."

Talima scarcely slept that night. Memories of Pirjhan filled her mind, the way his brown eyes looked at her with love and longing, his

laughter, the way he rode—lank and loose in the saddle, his songs and poems. Her body came alive remembering the caress of his rough hands on her skin, his mouth on hers, the smell of his maleness rising, musky, sweet. The soft flesh around her precious gate began to tingle and warm juices from within her body began to flow.

Jhani, soon, we'll be together. Great Everlasting Sky, bring him safely to me...

Takla Makan purred against her as she moved. She stroked the kitten's fur and dreamed of a reunion to come. How it would happen, she wasn't sure. But that it *would* happen, perhaps today, she was completely sure.

Sorrows may endure for the night, she remembered her father saying when she was a little girl, *but joy cometh in the morning! It must be almost morning, even though it's still winter-dark in here.* "Come on, brown kitten, let's go out into the garden."

She dressed in her warm, tree-floss padded clothes, slipped quietly through the sleeping women's quarters and went out into the dawn. Bare, brown rosebush sticks were rimed with gleaming frost, each thorn outlined. The gardens were sere and dark. But on twisted plum branches, small gray and white birds twittered their seed-eating songs. Spiders spread their crystalline webs between thin blades of grass, catching minute rainbows as the sun touched them.

Talima lifted her face to the sun's warmth and saw Zanggi watching her from his balcony. She smiled, nodded and continued to walk the garden's length. The kitten scampered around her feet.

Zanggi met her by the ivy-covered stairs. "Good morning, Wu Chao Tse Tsien, you're up early this morning. "

"I couldn't sleep."

"You aren't ill?"

"No."

"Are your writing classes still satisfactory?"

"Yes, thank you. I'm fine, Honorable Zanggi, just fine."

"I'm glad to hear that, Tse Tsien, for I've something to ask of you. "

"Yes?"

"I've wanted to have some of my master's sayings calligraphed, and I've been waiting for a likely person to come along who could do it well. The honorable Cheng Chao tells me you're an outstanding student, most talented and unusually adept. So it occurred to me that you might be willing to spend some of your mornings..."

"Writing for *you,* Zanggi-sha? I'd like nothing better! But how?"

"I have a writing table, brushes and so forth in my rooms. It would be a simple matter for you to use them. Have you had enough experience with different papers that you have a preference for one or another?"

"I've used less costly mulberry and bamboo papers most often, but real rice paper is elegant, if you thought you could?"

"I can. Certainly. Do you know the wisdom of Lao Tzu, the sage who wrote the *Tao Te Ching?*"

"No, I've never heard him speak that I know of."

"Only his words still live, Tse Tsien, the man himself died many centuries ago. He was of the Li family. Our Most Illustrious Emperor claims him as an ancestor, even built the great Taoist temple the *Hung-fu-ssu,* in his mother's memory. Dedicated it himself, eight years ago."

"And you want me to copy his book?"

Zanggi's laugh startled the birds from the tree branches. "You are young, Tse Tsien, but you do not have enough years to finish such a task! No, my dear Spitfire, I only want you to do a few relatively short sayings, ones most important to me in my practice."

Takla Makan leaped wildly about trying to catch the flying birds. "I'd be honored, Zanggi-sha."

"Shall we begin this morning then?"

"I can still go to The Forest of Pencils, can't I?"

"Fei-fei-fei, I approve your eagerness, Spitfire. Certainly you may."

They went upstairs to the Coordinator's quiet rooms. He talked steadily as he laid out writing materials. "You see, Tse Tsien, in a true sense every Chian person is a Taoist. It is, after all is said and done, a practical way to live...and Chianese are always practical. They are Taoists even though they may claim to follow the teachings of Confucius or the Buddha, because all things depend on the Tao for life."

"What is this Tao, Zanggi-sha?"

"The Tao? Tao is unknowable, the great mystery, a great square without corners, a great voice which forms no words—being without form...the beginning and the end...there is not a single thing without Tao."

"If it is unknowable, how do you know it?"

"A reasonable question, my dear. A man knows the Tao by following *Wu Wei,* the path of right action, the action inherent in his nature. If he is a rock, then it is his nature to be heavy and sedentary. If he is a cloud, it is his nature to appear, disappear and reappear. If a man..."

"What if you're a woman? How then do you experience the Tao?"

Zanggi's laughter shook the walls of his room. "You are always delighting me, Spitfire! Your innocent wisdom is refreshing. A man and a woman are the same in the Tao. There are no differences."

"But you say it's a practical way to live. How can it be everyday practical if you don't recognize the differences between men and women?"

"Because both men and women must be aware of right action in daily life. Lao Tzu urges us to love the earth, love what is profound in our hearts, love faithfulness in our words, love order in government, love competence in handling affairs and love timeliness in our activities. Now, do you find anything there that is not equally true for a man or a woman?"

"No, and much that is similar to our *Yasa*, the great Law of the Igren."

Thoughtfully, she put down the aromatic stick, dipped her thick brush into the viscous ink, wiped the excess off on the edge of the bowl and, with brush poised in the air, said, "The ink is ground, Zanggi, I'm ready to begin. What phrase would you like me to write?"

"I'd like you to write this—There is only Tao."

"'Sky! I haven't been taught the character for Tao!"

"It looks like this..." Zanggi picked up the ink-filled brush and made a few quick forceful strokes.

"Zanggi-sha! That's beautiful!" Her breath rushed out in awe.

"The perfection of beauty." He smiled.

"But if *you* write so well, why do you want *me* to do this for you?"

"Why indeed?" He sat back on his heels and rocked back and forth for a few moments. "I suppose it's because I enjoy your company and also that I know you should be learning more important matters than what Lu Mei and Lu Li can teach you."

"Why?" *Why do I hear the Bequi's voice in my mind? And Ssu's soothsayer's prophesy? Strange...* She shivered.

"Don't you want to learn what I can teach you?"

"I want to learn *everything!* You know that, don't you? I want to taste all that life has to offer! I just wondered why you wanted me to do this one thing, that's all."

"You see, Tse Tsien, I know how important it is for us, people like us, to know and understand, to be aware, consciously aware of the profound inner realities of life.

"When I left home, left Kat-Kat-Zanggi, I knew very little. But I, like you, had a great hunger to learn. I wanted to know how the universe worked and I was not content to believe in the multitude of small-minded gods that my people feared and worshipped.

"Soon after I arrived in Chian, I heard a simple man, a great philosopher, speak on a mountainside one day. He showed me The Way, Wu Wei, the Great Way that I now share with you."

"I see. You know. Zanggi, I've truly missed discussions like this. My father and I often talked of serious matters, of religions and philosophies and law, but since leaving home all my life seems to consist of simply staying alive, of surviving some crisis or other. Takla Makan, you rascal! No! Scat!"

The kitten, fascinated by the sound and motion of Talima's brush, had jumped onto the writing desk. The paper slid from under her claws upsetting the ink dish that flew into the air, and landed upside down on the pale bamboo mats. Ink splattered in all directions spraying the whitewashed walls and Talima with jet-black drops.

"Hai! What a mess! Oh, Zanggi-sha, I'm so sorry! I'll clean it up! She didn't mean to."

"Fei-fei-fei! Was she not following The Way? She was acting in natural cat fashion—pouncing on a small, twitching movement. It might have been a mouse for all she knew. I'll have the wall repainted by the painter whose nature it is to earn his livelihood by painting. There's no need to disturb yourself. But the hour grows late...you must eat and leave for your classes. Thank you for a most entertaining morning, my dear."

"Thank you for everything! You're very good to me." She brushed a kiss onto his smooth cheek and scooped up her trembling kitten.

So this is what it feels like, he thought, to love someone. Smiling, the head eunuch of His Majesty's Palace Secretariat watched her leave.

27
KAO TSUNG IS CURIOUS; ZANGGI'S CALLIGRAPHY

CALLIGRAPHY CLASSES HAD NEVER SEEMED LONG ENOUGH TO TALIMA before, but today every minute seemed to drag on interminably. With hopes of surprising Pirjhan at a polo match, she left class as soon as possible, walked to the woods, changed her clothes, bound her hair, and continued on to the stables. Looking like any other young man, she walked through the gate. Tulak fell into step beside her.

"Hai, Talima-sha," he said quietly, "this way...Kilar and Bagatur are waiting for you."

"Has Pirjhan arrived yet?"

"No, none of the guardsmen are here this afternoon. I don't know where they are. Perhaps they'll come a little later. It's a good thing, really, for you'll have a better chance to play a chukka or two if the regular players aren't there."

"I suppose you're right, Tulak." She saw Bagatur across the yard and whistled.

The sorrel horse pricked up his ears and clattered forward, pulling the reins from Kilar's hands. He raced up to Talima, whickering and nuzzling her excitedly. Heads turned in surprise as passersby wondered what was happening.

"You shouldn't do that, Talima-sha...you mustn't attract notice."

Talima was talking to Bagatur, smoothing his satin coat, scratching him between the ears, blowing in his nostrils, letting him know how much she loved him. "Don't fuss, Tulak, it's wonderful to be back with you all. I've missed you so! Hai, Kilar, have you been able to find the silk weavers' part of town yet?"

"No time, but I will, as soon as I can leave Nine Dragon Hill I'll go down into the city and walk every street if I have to!"

"Do you know where Pirjhan is, Kilar?"

"No, but I don't think he'll be here today, one of his guardsman friends stopped by this morning and asked us to feed the horses that the emperor chose, until he gets back, from wherever they've gone."

"Did he say how long they'd be gone?"

"No, I'm sorry, Talima-sha."

Talima checked Bagatur's cinch as she hid her disappointment. "Now tell me, where is the polo field, and what rules do they play by here?"

"The field is outside the North Gate, in the Hundred Li Park that surrounds the new Jade Flower Palace. Men gather there every day, some play, most watch and drink."

"It gets pretty wild sometimes," warned Kilar.

"They play polo about the same as you did at home. You can't ride across the line of someone going for the ball, can't ride him off, and the last person to strike the ball has the right-of-way."

"Can you hook sticks?"

"Yes, you can, I've been thinking...maybe Bagatur is a bit too tall, Talima-sha, some of the horses they ride here are only twelve or thirteen hands high."

"Ah, but he's fast, Kilar, and turns on a millet seed, as you know. We'll see..."

"I saddled another, smaller horse, just in case you wanted to change mounts, when you got there."

"Good, are we ready then? Let's go, it gets dark early these days."

Leading the fourth horse, they trotted onto the broad thoroughfare that wound down to the Cinnabar Gate.

It was dusk when they passed through the gate again. Talima had played all six chukkas and scored two goals, to the delight of her teammates. She had quickly formed a liaison with one man in particular. They had ridden in almost synchronous movement, hitting the little, bamboo-root ball back and forth between them down the field, effectively shutting out opposing players, scoring alternate goals that had made their team victorious.

That man, riding a dun-colored pony whose flat back was marked by a black ridge of hair, accompanied them. Not much taller than Talima, his thinness belied the force with which he rode and played polo.

"And wh-when you leaned w-way out of your saddle and snicked the ball from right under his horse, I thought he'd have a f-f-fit right there on the field! Where did you learn to ride like that! You ride superbly for one so young!"

"You're kind, Kao Tsung, you're very good yourself!"

"But without your d-d-dash and determination, Tse Tien! You played splendidly...why haven't I m-m-met you before?" Kao Tsung shook his head impatiently, as if he might shake away the stuttering that burdened his speech.

"I, I've only been here a short time." Talima answered.

"Who's your family? Where do you come from?"

"My...my family is the Wu family of Tai Yuan, Kao Tsung."

"That explains it then. I rarely leave the p-palace, but when I do, I usually travel west to our Li ancestor's chou or south by boat along the canals." He spoke now in a kind of singing rhythm.

"That must be interesting, traveling by boat, I mean, I've never done that. We always go on horseback."

"Yes, it's the old saying, 'Horses in the north, boats in the south'. I do hope that you'll play again, any day, every day—we make a great team."

He smiled with such sweetness that Talima was charmed. "Thank you, I'd like to. I'll try. Do you live in the city, Kao Tsung?"

"The city? Why no, I have a place of my own within the palace, naturally."

"By yourself?"

"Just me and my books...there's rather a crowd of them though. Hard to find a p-place to sit sometimes..." he laughed.

"You're a scholar then?"

"You might say so..."

"I'm a student...at the Academy."

"Which one?"

"I didn't know there was more than one...the Forest of Pencils."

"So you're a calligrapher?"

"I'm learning."

"What an admirably modest man you are, Tse Tien, it's refreshing. Most men brag about their accomplishments."

Talima chuckled. "Do you like poetry?"

"I write some, now and then, as one does, but I p-p-prefer history and the study of law."

"You do? I, too, have studied the law."

"Do you have your degree?"

Talima felt she was getting into perilous areas she knew nothing about. "Not yet."

"I'd be pleased to help you study for your examination sometime... I have all the texts, the Regulations, the Code, the Statutes and Ordinances."

"Thank you, but I, aah, I have too much to do just now, perhaps another time?"

"Yes, of course, I didn't mean to be rude, I just thought..."

"It was very good of you, Kao Tsung, I don't think you're rude at all, in fact, you're one of the nicest fellows I've met since I got here."

"Thank you. Most people think I'm a dull stick because I'd rather read than participate in the life at court." He smiled beatifically. "When you can live a life of the mind, through books, all other life seems trivial at best."

"I know what you mean! The people I live with don't seem to have a worthwhile idea in their heads...entertainment is all they ever think of...that, and the way they look!"

"I don't mind that, but I do mind it when they make fun of me for reading! I don't make fun of them for being frivolous... "

"I know, there are so many things I want to learn!"

They dismounted and walked their horses into the stable. Talima handed Bagatur to Tulak. Kao Tsung walked along beside her, back toward the palace, and she began to wonder how she could get away from him to change her clothes.

"It's so easy to talk to you, would you like to come back to my place for a cup of wine?"

"Thank you, no, Kao Tsung. I promised to be somewhere by dark... sorry."

"Will you play tomorrow?"

"Probably, if I can get away. Say, do you by any chance have a book called the *Tao Te Ching?*"

"Yes, certainly, but the *Tao Te Ching?* You are a fascinating mixture, my friend! I'd be glad to bring that tomorrow. Anything else?" He nodded as if pleased with himself.

"I just needed the *Tao Te Ching,* to find some quotes to calligraph."

"Of course. Until tomorrow then."

After that, Talima spent most of each morning in Coordinator Zanggi's room writing for him, early afternoons under the tutelage of Cheng Chao learning to read and write, and, until dusk, playing hard-and-fast polo in the Hundred Li Park. Her friendship with Kao Tsung grew rapidly. It was almost as if she could read his mind, know when he would turn or what strategy he had in mind to carry the ball through the goalposts. It was so exhilarating that Talima didn't mind waiting for Pirjhan's return.

On a morning, a few days later, Talima was concentrating on her brushwork in Zanggi's study. He had a variety of things he wanted her to calligraph, quotes from Lao Tzu and some other poems that he liked.

She was having difficulty with the character for *"greatest skill"*--it didn't dance its thicks and thins the way she knew it should. She tried again, "*...the greatest skill seems to be clumsy* and...'Sky! The greatest skill is definitely eluding me, Zanggi-sha! I'll come back to it. What's the rest of Lao Tzu's quote?"

"And the greatest eloquence seems to stutter." he told her patiently.

Talima laughed.

"You find that amusing, Ts'ien?"

"Yes, I mean, no, it's just...well, you wouldn't understand, Zanggi-sha."

"Try me."

"No, really, it was just a momentary foolishness on my part." *I can't tell him about Kao Tsung and his stuttering, she thought, he'd find out about me playing polo. Funny, but Kao Tsung is eloquent, in his way.*

"I see," Zanggi said slowly. "By the way, I've had all your things removed from your room, Ts'ien."

Sudden fear tingled into her fingers. She felt her chest tighten, felt the old familiar symptoms of asthma taking over her breathing. She held her breath and waited.

"Lu Mei tells me that the other girls wonder about your comings and goings. So in order to maintain harmony in the White Jade Pavilion, I have transferred you to a place on the far side of the garden. It has its own entrance, so you won't have to go past all the others' rooms nor through the main living quarters to come to me or go to the academy."

"That's, that's wonderful!" Talima let her breath sigh out in relief.

"Were you afraid? Of what?"

"A little, I'm never quite sure that I'm not doing or saying something that will give offence. And I never know..."

"You're a clever girl, Ts'ien, you must have realized by now that I have placed you under my protection and my patronage. You have a capacity for life, for learning, that I can foster and use, for the good of my Illustrious Emperor, of course."

"Of course."

"You know, my dear, the ideas you calligraph for me can, if you allow them to, be seeds in your mind that take root and grow to form the flower of a strength and faith that will never desert you, regardless of circumstances. Li Bo, wrote a poem that ended, '...when the heart is a lute thrice tuned, the Way can be attained.' Tune your heart, Wu Chao Tse Tien, concentrate your mind.

"Concentrate your mind. Do not hear what the ear hears, but hear what the heart hears. Listen!"

"You sound like my father again, Zanggi."

"Then he must have loved you dearly, little Spitfire."

28
HAPPY, YET HEEDLESS

AND THEN, AFTER ALL THE WAITING AND UNCERTAINTY, there he was. Simply riding beside her, stirrup to stirrup, as if they'd never been separated.

"Hatou, my beloved Tam."

Talima felt, suddenly, as if she were dissolving, she feared she might simply slide out of her saddle onto the earth right there in Hundred Li Park.

"Jhani! Oh Jhani...you look so different...but just the same...how did you find me?"

"Didn't I tell you during the Buran that I would always find you?"

"I mean...is it so obvious, who I am, dressed like this?"

"To me, yes. I just looked for Bagatur and there you were. Actually, Kilar told me you'd be on your way to play polo about now. Tengri, I've missed you! Why didn't you let me know how you were? I've been worried out of my mind!"

"Why didn't you send *me* a message? I didn't know *what* to think! I've missed you terribly...constantly!"

They spoke in a rush, all at once. Their eyes spoke the only message that mattered. Their senses swam in the current of love that passed between them, washed over them, swept them into a flood of passion, long denied.

"Can we?"

"Yes, let's!"

"The woods grow thicker on the other side of the meadow...it isn't far."

Talima laughed, lifted her reins, leaned forward in the saddle and chirruped to Bagatur. Whoever watched saw only a noble lad on a chestnut stallion and a handsome palace guardsman riding an oddly-marked black and white horse, racing pell-mell away from the polo field.

Reins hanging loose on the ground, the two horses stood in companionable silence, cropping long grass. Little birds twittered and hopped from bare branches. The low sun slanted through trees and created a dried-grass, fragrant nest for lovers. A breeze ruffled the leaves. And, suddenly, Talima could hear only the pounding of her own heart filling her head, a current of desiring flowing through her throat, breasts, belly.

Pirjhan touched her face with his fingertips, smoothed stray hairs back from her forehead. Her skin tingled and she shivered in anticipation. He took off her tight-fitting cap and watched, smiling, as her hair flowed into his hands and around her shoulders. He cupped her head with both hands and, like a falcon, bent his head down over her.

His grass-smoke smell filled her. She yearned for him, a yearning so long denied. She leaned into him, longing for his kiss. Her desire for him, every part of him, flooded her, her passion radiated out around his hard body, surrounding them both with the urgent need to get closer, quickly.

The flowered scent of her, the feel of her soft skin beneath his hands, inflamed him. With raw strength, he pulled her into him and kissed her, his mouth crushing hers. Tasting her only made him want more. He watched as her blue-green eyes clouded over with pleasure. Her moan told him she was his.

With hands too eager, they tore at each other's clothes. Wanting. Needing each other, body, heart, breath, life itself.

Skin to skin, touching her in the way he had hoped for all these long, lonely months spurred him into a frenzy of wanting more and more. What his body screamed at him was so all-consuming that he could scarcely breathe, and he knew that they must go more gently, if only to prolong the moment.

"Tam, my little Tam, easy now, love, here..." They floated to the ground like heavy smoke. He spread his cape in the dappled sunlight and pulled Talima into his arms. He kissed her again, slowly, slowly, as she kindled herself against him.

The hot skin of his body that she had dreamed of for too many nights, sent her senses flaring, and she gave herself completely to his demanding caress.

Moving in the quick, hot dance of loving. Breathing, trembling, as their mouths fed the flame of their consuming need to be inside each other until, as he entered the molten darkness of her body, they became fire...leaping...soaring...incandescent. Her exultant cry echoed into the forest.

Then gently, tenderly, they subsided into the glowing embers of their separate selves. Two again.

"Mmnnn, at last," Pirjhan murmured into Talima's hair. "Never leave me, you are my sun and moon, my life, I know, is not complete without you."

Talima wriggled under him, sighing with contentment. She licked his throat, tiny cat-licks with the tip of her tongue.

"Hai, wench, that tickles!"

"Jhani? I'm getting cold."

"Here, turn over and lie on top of me, I'll wrap us in my cloak. There...better?"

"I think I'll just stay here forever..."

"Forever, yes. I will love you forever. Longer, maybe. What's longer than forever, d'you suppose?"

"Love itself is longer than forever."

They lay together for what seemed like an eon or two. Finally, becoming completely distinct and different beings once more, they unwrapped the tangle of each other and dressed.

The sun was setting. Winter air was quickly cold. The horses' breath plumed against the darkening woods. Birds were quiet and only a lone squirrel chattered at them as they mounted and rode away.

IT WAS NOT POSSIBLE FOR THEM TO MEET EVERY DAY. Pirjhan's duties as guardsman and trainer for the emperor's horses kept him busy. Cheng Chao, Zanggi or Lu Mei claimed most of Talima's time. But they did manage to steal away frequently, making love in unused stalls, in the hay barn, in the woods, wherever they could be alone. They were drawn together irresistibly, heedless of watching eyes, risking their own future for the moment.

It was as if all the moons of frustration and separation had never been.

They were caught up in a whirlwind of romance. Whenever possible, their days were spent in dangerous delights.

POLO GAMES CONTINUED SEVERAL TIMES A WEEK AND THE TRIPLE THREAT OF TALIMA, PIRJHAN, and Kao Tsung proved virtually unbeatable for other teams. Pirjhan was rather unsettled by Talima's friendship with Kao Tsung, but when she chided him for being jealous, he only laughed self-consciously. Kao Tsung, however, intrigued by Talima's curiosity and zest for learning, competed for her attention by discussing things he knew would not interest Pirjhan.

There were also many other things to do, as the palace was alive with possibilities for entertainment.

On windswept park meadows, men and boys flew kites. Some kites, tall as a man, had sharpened knives wound into their tails and kite-strings that slashed and cut anything airborne that crossed them. Other kites, reinforced by bamboo, were wild, darting creatures that seemed to have a life of their own, flying farther into the everlasting sky than eyes could follow.

Talima and Pirjhan flew simple, red-and-blue-striped paper kites that Pirjhan had bought in the market. Kao Tsung sometimes accompanied them, bringing kites he had made which sang as they flew.

"Flying kites," he declared, "has been one of the b-b-best times of my life...until now," he added with a smile. His favorite kite, which he called his *"hawk-lute",* was strung with seven silk strings across a gourd-shaped framework of thin bamboo strips. He also flew *wind-psalteries* and *wind-zithers* and flying *Aeolian harps*, all of which created eerie melodies as they dipped and soared past low-hanging clouds.

As they let out their silken kite lines, Kao Tsung told them the history of kites in Chian. "You see, Tse Tsien," he began, "ever since the aerial cars of the Chi-Kung people, long, long ago, we have used kites for pleasure and for m-m-military purposes...to drop leaflets behind enemy lines or to carry signals over vast distances."

"Who were the Chi-Kung people?" she asked.

"Skills of the Chi-Kung people were truly marvelous! Their land lies north of the I-Pei country of one-armed men. In fact, it is said the Chi-Kung people, too, had only one arm. But their three eyes probably made up for that. They were partly male and p-partly female, you know. By studying the winds, they created and built flying wheels with which they rode along the paths of whirlwinds. Some say they still do!" Kao Tsung's eyes sparkled with enthusiasm.

"Really? How?" Talima let out more line as her kite struggled into the wind.

"They m-made screw-bladed rotors and attached them to the front of their aerial cars. This rotary *wheel* empowered their cars to ascend to great heights and travel along the wind...*'traveling along the hard wind'*, they called it. This was several centuries ago, of course. I myself have never seen them, or their wonderful creations."

"Sounds rather fanciful to me," said Pirjhan.

"Oh no, we know it to be true! There are men in court who experiment constantly to make these same contraptions again. Think what it would mean if one could ride the wind!"

"This sounds like stories I've heard traders tell of carriages drawn by unicorns and bird-headed animals and other mythical beasts," said Talima, doubtfully.

"Shouldn't be confused with f-f-fairy tales like that, Tse Tsien. These *really* existed! It's just that their secrets died with them, even their country is now lost to us."

Talima worried that Kao Tsung might find out who she truly was. As the days passed, even this failed to concern her. Heedless, she was living in a world of realized dreams, oblivious to the whispers around her.

One afternoon, Pirjhan escorted Talima, dressed as a plain town-girl, to a wine-tasting party. She felt shy among the fashionable young men and women. Only Prince Firuz, who was privy to all his friend's secrets, knew who she was and why Pirjhan was so protective of such a simply-gowned girl.

Sometimes, they rode with other guardsmen and their ladies in gaily-painted pony carts drawn by dwarf ponies, bowling merrily along on narrow, paved streets to Grape Park in the south palace grounds.

There, inside a small curved-roof pavilion, bronze braziers blazed. They sat around lacquer tables and were served *mare's teat* grape wine and thimble-sized cakes of intense sweetness. Talima listened to the court gossip, but rarely spoke.

There were also Sassanian concerts, theatrical operas, and

boisterous Turkish-type dances sponsored by Prince Li Cheng. Talima sometimes went with Pirjhan, but they were rowdy affairs and he was not comfortable with her beside him. Talima enjoyed the music that was so much like that of her own people, but was fearful of the Prince's evident displeasure. He made cruel and derisive remarks about Talima in her hearing and insinuated himself physically between her and Pirjhan. She couldn't understand why Prince Li Cheng disliked her when he obviously liked Pirjhan, yet Pirjhan couldn't bring himself to explain his suspicions to her.

THE KINDLY MOON PASSED, THE WHITE MOON WAXED AND WANED. The Emperor had not returned from his inspection tour of the southern chous. Frosty days and nights held them all in thrall.

The Bitter Moon, last of winter moons, hung its crescent above the city on the afternoon Prince Firuz invited them to go to the Western Market.

They let their horses amble through crowded alleys on both sides of which goods and foods from dozens of countries were for sale: fresh fish and lychees from Annam; frankincense and fagara from the Land of Punt; patchouli, gold and elephant tusks from the Tamils of Tenassarim; green-bronze tails of the k'ung sparrow, Bird of Viet whose feathered eyes belied its distant kinship to the mythical Phoenix; ermine tails, leopard skins, and other furs from distant mountains. Talima wanted to feel and touch and taste each wondrous thing.

They passed the Bazaar of Saddlers where leatherworkers cut the shapes of chamois and stags into molded saddles. The clang and ring of heavy hammers on metal deafened them as they went by the ironmonger's stall. Gutted carcasses hung in butchers' shops. The acrid smell of fireworks came from stalls nearby.

Uighur money-lenders, suave and fatuous, surrounded by furniture, slaves and sacred relics they had accepted in trade for cash, plied their usurer's trade in tile-floored counting houses. Lengths of shimmering silk, multi-colored, iridescent, hung over thick bamboo rods in the Bazaar of Silk merchants.

They came out of the silk-seller's shop where Firuz had bought a pi's worth of halcyon-blue silk and presented it to Talima.

"A little something to match the lady's eyes," he explained to

Pirjhan.

"Thank you, Firuz, I've always loved the way silk feels against my skin. Whenever I wear it, I shall remember this day...and good friends!"

"Let's stop for a cup of tea before we start back, shall we?" Firuz asked.

"But not long, I must get back soon." Talima replied. They tied their horses outside a teashop and went inside.

Tea, so recently introduced to Changan from the Sapphire Isle, was fashionable among the young at the palace. Teashops had sprung up like spring flowers through winter snow on every corner of the market. Drinking tea, although expensive, was rapidly becoming a national obsession.

They sat on thick pillows on grass mats around a low, round table and drank hot, amber tea from pale green cups. Deep in conversation, they didn't notice a scar-faced man dressed in Prince Cheng's livery sitting at the next table, watching them as intently as a cat watches a mouse hole.

29
A BABY IS BORN

OBLIVIOUS TO THE TURMOIL SHE WAS CAUSING, UNMINDFUL OF THE DANGER that threatened her, Talima continued to fill her days with exciting pleasures of the palace as well as pleasures with Pirjhan whenever possible.

AS HER BRUSH SWOOPED AND DIPPED LIKE A SWALLOW IN FLIGHT ACROSS THE PAPER, Talima thought...*if only the emperor would return so I could speak with him! It's been more than half a year that we've been here and I haven't managed to talk to him yet! I wonder if he'll see reason and let me go, or if I'll have to...*

Kao Tsung says he must return for the New Year's celebration and that will be soon. The Bitter Moon of spring is almost full and buds are swelling on the trees.

She spread another sheet of paper on her desk and began to calligraph the quote from Chuang-tzu that she planned to give to Zanggi as a surprise. "Life goes on like a galloping horse...each must live according to his nature." The rhythm of her brush strokes echoed the rhythm of a horse's gallop. Time passed.

When finished, she hung her work to dry and washed her brushes. She left The Forest of Pencils at the usual time. She was only a few yards from the gate, however, when Tulak fell into step beside her.

"What are you doing here?" Talima hissed.

"Waiting for you, Talima-sha."

"What's wrong?"

"It's Shira...she's begun to foal!"

"She can't be! She's not due for..." Talima counted the moons on her fingers quickly, "for at least three weeks!"

"I know, but she's laboring, having a hard time. Kilar said I'd better find you and get you to come."

"'Sky! Have you waited long?"

"No, not long. But it will take us awhile to get to her as she's in the barn on the other side of the stables. We should hurry!"

"Pirjhan?"

"I don't know, Talima-sha. No one's seen him in the stables since yesterday."

"I'll be so glad to be home again where it takes five moments to find someone, not five days!"

"Yes, we'll all be glad to be home again. Life is sweeter there."

Home, yes, and yet there's a lot I'll miss of my life here...I've grown accustomed to so many different ways of doing things, of new ideas... days and nights here are a rich tapestry, shining with gold and silks... Igren days are so different, austere, simple, like rough felt.

But we'll bring home all that we've learned, try to give our people some of what we are finding valuable, and yet...I wonder what's happening at home, where the herds are...who sits at my Father's left these days?

When they arrived at the stall where Shira lay, it was dark and quiet. An oil lamp in the corner shone on bare wood walls. Shira's coat shone silver in its flickering light. Talima knelt beside the mare and smoothed her forehead and ears.

"'Hatou, my dear, I see you're impatient for that little one to be born! Now you'll be fine, Beauty, just fine."

Shira began to tremble, moaning suddenly from a great depth within her womb. She lifted her head and rolled her eyes toward Talima as if pleading for help.

"Do you have all that we'll need, Kilar? Cloths, some kumiss, a knife?"

"All here, Talima-sha."

"I wish Juchi were here." Talima said quietly, remembering all the births she had helped him with since she was a little girl.

Talima soothed Shira's flank and tried to see if any of the foal's covering sheath was showing yet. She remembered hours of anticipation while she and Juchi waited, wordlessly wondering all the same questions. Will the foal be strong, well formed and healthy? Will it be a filly or a colt? Will it breathe as it is meant to breathe? Will it nurse willingly?

A longer shudder shook Shira's body, rippling out from her hard, distended belly. A trickle of blood-striated, thick liquid brought with it the foal's first appearance.

Tulak and Kilar knelt beside her. Through the tough, transparent bag they could see thumb-sized hooves pushing outward. Talima grasped the sheathed legs and began to work with the mare's surging contractions, sliding her hands around the emerging baby, smoothing the muscles around its exit.

"Gently, gently, now...steady girl...that's right, easy...easy." Hand over hand, she coaxed the foal toward her, toward the world of wind and rain and long green grasses.

Shira's muscles stood out in ridges along her abdomen, she drew in rasping gulps of air. She and Talima both rested, panting, for a moment before their final effort. Head thrown back, neck stretched long against the hay, Shira pushed with all her being. The nose emerged...the forehead...the whole head...and then, burbling into Talima's arms, the foal itself.

Shira sighed gustily. The foal rested in its shining bag, still part of that other world, not yet initiated into a breathing life. The cord connecting the newly-two pulsed with bright blood. Talima wiped sweat from her forehead with the back of her sleeve. Tulak and Kilar laughed with the joy of birth and handed her the knife.

Talima broke the bag and freed the wobbly, bony, little head. Its felt-colored nostrils sucked in the first, inebriating draught of air, then sneezed explosively. Its soft, pointed hooves scrabbled at the remaining skin that held them. Carefully, Talima stripped away the sack. She saw it was a colt, white with grey muzzle, dappled, perfectly proportioned in the mold of its divine ancestry.

Tulak tied off the coiled cord. "Let your knife bite through that, Talima-sha! Let this laddie stand on his own two feet at last."

Talima cut the cord. Blood of the old life within his mother and of this newly independent life flowed together in an immemorial christening. She poured kumiss over the cut, then wiped down the little body with a kumiss-soaked cloth. The colt trembled, shivering.

Shira shuddered. The purple-blood-filled mass of food that had fed her baby for nearly a year poured out onto the hay. Shira whinnied, lurched to her feet, and prodded the baby with her head, urging him to stand. The colt stood on its spindly legs, weaving unsteadily, falling forward onto his knees, standing again, moving forward out of balance. Gradually he steadied, took his first steps and nuzzled his mother's belly instinctively. Finding a nipple, slurping, then sucking. New life established, strong, continuing...a small male horse who would one day shake the earth with the power of a winged dragon.

Smiling, Talima turned to speak to Kilar. But it wasn't Kilar or Tulak that stood there. It was Pirjhan. Pirjhan with the look of a man from whom all outer skins are stripped, a man who has witnessed truth, transcendent. His dark eyes shone in the lamplight with awe and love.

"I didn't know. I forgot what a capable woman you are," he said.

"I'm glad you're here!"

"I came as soon as I heard. What a fine job you did, Tam. Such a beautiful colt, worthy of its dam and mistress," he smiled tenderly at them both.

Talima put her arms around Pirjhan and laid her head against his shoulder. Together with Shira, they watched the colt indulgently. Shira whickered. They laughed as the colt tried to frolic and fell, spraddle-legged, with a most amazed expression on his face. He scrambled to his feet and charged off in another direction, this time running into a wall before he realized how to stop.

"Our children will be like that, courageous and strong," Pirjhan said as he hugged Talima to his side.

"Our children! I love that, Jhan, our own babies tumbling around our own hearth. Oh, my dearest dear, it will be simply wonderful..." Talima sighed. "You know, I was thinking on the way here today that, all in all, Changan has been good for us. We've learned so many things that will enrich our lives and those of all the Igren when we return."

"Yes," Pirjhan held her close to his side. "Yes, we'll return soon. The compulsory six moons are over and it's time to leave Chian. I admit I'll not be sorry. Somehow I don't feel as if I'm getting on with my life here."

"I know, Kao Tsung says the emperor will return soon, for the New Year's dedication, though why *he* should know this, I'm not sure."

"You don't know, Tam...about Kao Tsung?'

"Know? Know what?"

"Kao Tsung is our luminous majesty's *son*, his second son, to be sure, but in direct line after Prince Li Cheng."

"That awful man? They're *brothers?* I had no idea! Kao Tsung is so nice!"

"Certainly different, at any rate."

"Great everlasting sky! I forgot how late it must be! I'd better fly! I hope no one's noticed!"

"Must you leave? I was hoping we might..."

"I want to stay here with you and Shira and our new baby, but I mustn't. It's as Kapi told us from the very first...there are eyes everywhere! We must be careful a little longer, but hold me, Jhan, for just a minute before I go."

She kissed him and ran out of the stables. The net of night closed around her.

30
Muddy Truth At The Polo Field

IT HAD RAINED FOR DAYS. STEADY SHEETS OF COLD, GREY RAIN; GROUND soaking, root soaking, seed soaking rain. It rained as if winter believed that it could hold the land in its power against all of spring's advances.

But now the day was fair. Cloud streamers feathered a kingfisher-blue sky. The sun was warm and plants speared up through the soggy soil as if by magic.

Talima rode through the Hundred Li Woods. Shining branches of trees that arched above her were nubbled with pale pink buds that seemed about to pop into flower even as she passed beneath. She breathed deeply, reveling in the freshness of fragrant, rain-washed air. She saw that Tai Tsung's dragon emblem, scarlet and gold, flew over the palace, declaring his presence within.

He must have sneaked into the city by night. I didn't hear the customary grand procession...well, this time I'm going to get to him before he leaves again and just...just tell him about Pirjhan and me... make him see reason...that, all things considered, we must go home.

The first chukkas were over. Riders and horses were at rest when she and Bagatur arrived. The polo field was more a quagmire of hoof-churned mud than hard-packed turf. Kao Tsung and Pirjhan, standing by their ponies, were so covered with mud, they were scarcely recognizable.

"Hai there! You're a mess!"

"You will be too, Tse Tsien, play just one chukka and your own mother won't recognize you!" Kao Tsung laughed, teeth gleaming in his mud-streaked face.

"What's our score?"

"We're behind, aren't we, Pirjhan? It's hard to tell, we have several drop-in players today, and it's so soupy out there that the ball gets lost!"

"I thought I had a goal and it was only a hunk of grass balled up... looked just the same as the ball, but it was a roundish lump of *mud!*" Pirjhan shook his head.

"Mind if I take your place for a bit?" said Talima.

"Not at all, you're quite welcome to that mud bath!" answered Pirjhan.

The referee's whistle blew. Talima and Kao Tsung moved out together, joining their two team members. Horses of both teams moved restlessly. Their hooves made sucking sounds as they pulled free of the soggy turf. Talima recognized one of her teammates as well as two of the opposing team as guardsmen she had met before. The other three of both teams were unfamiliar A mounted referee signaled the beginning of the game's second half. The players released their eager mounts.

The field they played on was thirty *chang* long, twenty chang wide, with goal posts two chang apart, wide enough and high enough for three or four horsemen to ride between in the heat of making a goal. Each post was twined 'round with colored silk ribbons whose loose ends at the top, fluttered and spun in a celebratory manner.

At full gallop, the riders criss-crossed the field, leaning out of their saddles in order to get the longest reach with their cane mallets. One chukka, one full turn of the measuring wheel, ended. No goals were scored by either team. Horses and riders rested briefly and went back with renewed speed.

Talima and Kao Tsung played as two halves of one rider, sending the bamboo-root ball whizzing back and forth between them down the field while their teammates guarded their flank with equal vigor.

Kao Tsung controlled the ball as he prepared to send it to Talima. She saw one of the new riders, a powerful competitor, galloping up behind him at an angle certain to intercept his drive. She spurred her horse toward Kao Tsung. The other rider drove his mount between them. His stick tangled with Kao Tsung's and both were thrown off balance momentarily.

Kao Tsung's horse wheeled instinctively to avoid the impending collision. The stranger's horse reared, pawing the air, walking backward on its hind legs in order to carry his rider out of danger. Momentum carried Bagatur into the midst of the melee.

With no clear idea of how it happened, Talima felt herself catapulted through the air. Her mallet flew in one direction, her cap in another. She slid into the mud with a bone-jarring thump. Breathless, she lay still as horses skidded and slipped away from her, splattering her with more mud as they went. Kao Tsung dismounted swiftly, but the rider of the intercepting horse reached her first.

Talima saw his face as he bent over her. There was an old scar on his left cheekbone. He was an older man, a powerful looking man whose look of consternation seemed oddly out of context. She tried to sit up, tried to speak, but could not. He lifted her head out of the mud. Her hair cascaded over his arm, a shining, copper waterfall against his muddy sleeve.

"I...you are not...I mean, I never suspected that you were...*a girl!*" He said, his voice hoarse.

Talima looked beyond his shoulder and saw Kao Tsung staring at her in shocked disbelief.

"We'd better get her to the sidelines. She may be hurt badly." Pirjhan ran up, his face pinched with worry. He knelt beside them, started to put his face beside hers and then, remembering where they were, stopped. "Are you hurt? What can I do?"

"No, no, I'm all right, thank you." Talima said, recovering her voice.

"Thank the Mother of Lightning!" the older gentleman said. "Can you stand then?"

"I think so, but something is wrong with my arm...I can't move it."

Brushing Pirjhan aside, he lifted her as easily as if she had been a child, walked across the field and into the spectator's tent, where he lay her down on the rug.

"Now then, let me see that arm." He rolled up her sleeve and began to touch her skin with great tenderness. "Where does it hurt? Here? Or here? Ah-ha, there it is, I see by your face. It doesn't feel broken, a bad sprain at best, I think. We'll soak it in ice, wrap it...should feel as good as new in time for New Year's!"

"I'm most grateful..." she began.

"For what? For getting unhorsed by me? It is I who am grateful that you're not badly hurt! I must say, young lady, whoever you may be, your horsemanship is first class. I've rarely seen anyone as young as you are play with such skill and mettle! I wish our young noblemen were as good, but I suggest, strongly suggest, that you confine your riding pleasures to the park from now on."

"I don't wish to be rude, sir, but if you approve of my horsemanship, why don't you approve of me playing polo?"

"It isn't done."

"But why? Isn't the ability to play well the criterion by which players are usually admitted to a team? And haven't I demonstrated that ability? Ask Kao Tsung if..."

"Are you disputing my word?"

"No, sir, only your prejudice."

Both Kao Tsung and Pirjhan began to speak at once, "Tse Tsien! You mustn't!"

"Let her speak." The strange gentleman chuckled...a laugh rumbled around his heavy body before it reached his throat. "She has a point. I'll consider it. Meanwhile, I gather that you two are familiar with her, see that she has care for that arm. Tse Tsien then, I'll let you know through your friends here, my decision on whether you may ride to the sticks. Until then, you'd do well to restrict your activities to those more suitable for a young woman of your obvious breeding."

He stood, looked unsmiling at those around them and walked out. Everyone in the tent began to talk immediately.

"Well, you certainly gave us a surprise today, Wu Tse Tsien!" Kao Tsung was angry. "I suppose I should have known but somehow it never occurred to me that you might be...a female! Did you suspect, Pirjhan?"

Pirjhan looked down at her. Talima caught her breath with the beauty of his smile, the love shining through. She hoped it was not apparent to anyone else.

"She certainly had me fooled," stated Pirjhan.

"Do you need us to help you get home?" Kao Tsung asked.

"No, I'll be fine. Kao Tsung, who was that man?"

"The one who rode you down? He's my father, of course, our Most Luminous Majesty, Tai Tsung."

Talima wailed, "*That* was the emperor? The man I've been trying to get close enough to talk to for more than six moons, ever since we came? Why didn't you tell me?"

"I d-didn't know you d-didn't know!" said Kao Tsung, looking bewildered.

"I tried to..." said Pirjhan. "You should leave now, Tsien, before you..."

"Damn and blast! So near! Does he ride here often?"

"Once in awhile, not often. Only when his court duties allow."

"Then I will wait here every day! I *will* speak with him, if not through proper channels, then through improper ones. I will not be stopped by this, this run-around any longer!" She whistled to Bagatur, mounted easily and cantered away.

"Juchi always said she was stubborn. Stubborn for life." Pirjhan said quietly.

"Who's Juchi?" Kao Tsung asked.

"Only an old chapar, an old groom who knew her, a wise old groom," he answered.

With the freedom of being able to go in and out of the Jade Pavilion at will from her own apartment, Talima quickly found a way to meet with Pirjhan often. The palace gardens were a vast world that stretched out in all directions. Hand in hand like children, they explored. At the farthest parts, they felt far away from prying eyes. One day they found a tiny summer house almost completely obscured by ancient hibiscus and honeysuckle vines. It soon became their favorite place to meet.

31
KAT KAT ZANGGI SEES CLARITY AND TERROR

KAT-KAT-ZANGGI DIVIDED THE YARROW STALKS, OVER AND OVER, winnowing out possibilities.

Like the sound of distant thunder that grows louder as a storm approaches, reports of Wu Chao Tse Tsien's activities had grown.

First there was Lu Mei's worry...but she's always fussing about her girls. Then Li Chang Chao's mild complaint surprised me, I must say. He said that his star pupil wasn't spending as much time studying as she had been. Adding to that, Kapi, the stable master, told me some time ago about her dressing up as a lad, riding to the sticks with some of the court's gentlemen, Kao Tsung among them. Well, that's not so bad, a good outlet for her exuberant energies, I think. After all, she practically grew up on horseback...no, that's not why I'm so uneasy. Feels like I've got some insect crawling up my spine.

Several times this winter I received reports of a girl who might have been Tse Tsien, seen in the company of reveling guardsmen at Grape Park and other public places outside the palace grounds...but that's so downright foolish that it seems unlikely...

But I can't ignore the gossip at the Shuh-mi-Yuan Council last night...nor the demand...

Prince Li Cheng's secretary posed a problem to them all—he said that his master found a certain female troublesome. He had asked his secretary to find out who she was and to see to it she did not attend any of his parties henceforth. The secretary's problem was that he'd been unable to find out anything about this girl. He asked his colleagues to look out for a tall girl whose hair curled around her shoulders and glowed with the light of dawn.

I knew then there could be no mistake, it must be Tse Tsien. What could the girl be thinking of? And how, by the Three Pure Ones, had she become mixed up with that wild crowd that surrounded the heir-apparent? I thought she'd have more sense. If she's offended Prince Li Cheng in some way, she's in real trouble...and so, by inference, am I.

She hasn't actually broken her promise though...she hasn't run away. But how in heaven has she been able to find so much mischief in such a short time? What can she be thinking? Not thinking, it sounds like...that quick intelligence and curiosity leading her astray. I must find out more about the men she's been seen with...

I want her to become familiar with suitable aspects of her new life...perhaps to capture the attention of the emperor himself some day...now that would gain merit for us both...but this is craziness.

At least, Zanggi smiled at the thought, *the gecko-lizards have not turned red—those little palace-warders who warn of promiscuity on the part of our Jade Pavilion women. It's probably not true—that they can actually do that, but I find some reassurance in it, at any rate.*

All the reports are adding up to one thing—I must do something quickly to both restrict and protect my ward—while there's still time. Aaaaahh, what would be the right action to take in this delicate, dangerous situation?

Shaking his head from side to side, he sat down to quiet his mind in meditation. When he had finished, while candles burned and incense drifted like languid mist in the pre-dawn light, he brought out his worn *I-Ching* scroll and a bundle of yarrow reeds. He began to voice the question that needed answers from the ancient *Book of Changes.*

"What to do about Wu Chao Tse Tsien, that girl of bright promise? What is the natural action, the right action, to take at this time?" He gathered the yarrow stalks and let them drop onto the mat.

"Old yin in the first line, old yang in the second...changing lines, changing times," he said to himself.

He separated the reeds again in preparation for the third line of the first trigram, took a stalk from the pile on his right and placed it between the ring and little fingers of his left hand, then counted out the small thin sticks remaining. He continued the ritual division of stalks, four by four, adding the number remaining, three times for a line, until he saw the pattern of all six lines.

"The third line...young yin, eight, the fourth line, old yin again, then young yin, and young yang, seven, at the top. The first trigram, then...ah yes, it figures." Zanggi murmured.

"Meng, or Youthful Folly...water below, mountain above...*the spring rising at the foot of the mountain. Inexperienced youth who must overcome the mountain of experience.* "Well, folly is not evil when one is young...

"Six at the beginning"... *Law is the beginning of education—there must be discipline:..but not through restricting the flow of the spring.* "...naturally!

"Nine in the second place"... *One must understand women and give them recognition, consider their follies with chivalry..."* If one can maintain the strength of mind to bear such a burden!" Zanggi's sigh flurried the incense smoke.

"Then, six in the fourth place"...*Entangled folly brings humiliation. Frequently the only means of rescue is for the teacher to leave the young fool to herself and let the humiliation teach its lesson.* "Hard, but appropriate, I expect." He shifted his weight as he gathered up the stalks.

"Let's see now, those changing lines create a new outcome, a different trigram. Old yin becomes young yang and old yang becomes young yin and we have...*Shih Ho, Biting Through!*"

"Fei, fei, fei, I truly wish it weren't so! Here we have thunder and lightning forcibly removing obstacles from nature. A necessary recourse to law and penalties, judgment and punishment, vigorous measures to be taken with the clarity of lightning and the terror of thunder!"

"The only way to strengthen the Law," he read, *"is to make it clear and to make penalties certain and swift, yet it is important to proceed in the right way at the right moment.*

"But I think the moment is not quite yet, I'll allow her folly to continue a bit longer. I wonder which of the men she has been influenced by... some inquiries are in order. And perhaps she'll correct this unfortunate direction before I need to follow the directive of Shih Ho—the biting through. But I must warn her..."

Day dawned imperceptibly. The wind blew bitter cold.

The next morning, Tsien came into his room quietly. Zanggi sat wrapped in a blanket, a silent mountain of a man.

"I've brought you a new..." she began, stopping as Zanggi stood abruptly, towering over her.

"Sit!" he hissed.

"Zanggi? What's wrong?"

"I trusted you and you have betrayed me."

Talima felt his anger settle over her like a shroud.

"From every quarter of the palace, I hear stories of this wanton, flame-headed girl cavorting with wild young guardsmen at Li Cheng's licentious parties...at the stables...even in the town! What are you thinking of, Wu Chao Tse Tsien? Where now is your honor?"

"It's not the way it looks, it's just that..."

"Not? Are you quite *mad* as well as extremely foolish? Have I been so remiss in your education that you are ignorant of the penalties for one of the emperor's women who dares to go out in public?"

"I guess I got carried away. You see it's being so much in love and believing that the emperor will allow me to return, return home, I mean, when he knows. And always knowing freedom before"

"What is this *in love?* In love with *whom?* What man would *dare?* Is there *more* that you have hidden from me?"

With sudden clarity, Talima remembered that she had never shared her love for Pirjhan with Zanggi, never even mentioned his name before.

"Yes," she tossed her hair back, "Pirjhan, one of the Igren horsemen who rode with me—the man I love, the man I *will* marry!"

Zanggi's stillness evaporated like steam from hot tea.

"A...man...you...*love? It is not permitted!"* His face became a grotesque mask like those of stone warriors that guarded the temple gates. His voice like thunder itself.

"You *will* not see this man again! You *will* confine yourself to quarters except for classes at the Forest of Pencils."

"I can't! Don't you see I love him with all my heart! He *is* my life!"

"This lowly horseman *will be the end* of your life! Tse Tsien, listen carefully. You stand at the very edge of a cliff where the slightest whisper will send you to your death. You must protect yourself...or even I may not be able to keep you safe!"

"I'm sorry, I didn't think...I keep waiting to speak to the emperor and he's always away...but when I tell him I'm no longer my father's virgin daughter required as tribute and that my clan needs me, he'll have to let me go, don't you think?"

"Fei, fei, fei, you are too innocent of our laws, even now, after all these months, this past year." He was suddenly saddened. "It can never be—this that you ask. The emperor can never let you go. *I* can never let you go. You have become too precious, too necessary...to me. You *will* do as I say, won't you?

"I'll try but I'm not sure how to..."

"You *must,* Spitfire, you *must!"*

She could hardly breathe. Zanggi's wrathful denunciation of her love, her honor, all that she held dear, blazed a searing path in her mind and heart. *I didn't think I was doing anything wrong, I didn't think of it the way he does, the Chian way ...I thought I was free...I never meant to betray his trust in me...what can I do now? How can I tell Jhani? I must think...figure out a way...*

Zanggi pulled her to her feet. She realized he was trembling as much as she was.

In joined fear and sorrow, they parted, each one planning what must be done.

32
She Makes A Plan

Talima ran down the narrowing garden path and over the half-moon bridge that spanned a brook where petals, like pink snow, had fallen into its rushing current. Then she skipped along the zigzag boardwalk that wove itself over blooming iris on every side. Butterflies basked in the late afternoon sunshine, drying their virgin wings. The path led her into a thick bamboo forest. Green light and the smell of moss enveloped her.

If I'm right, it will change everything. Everything! It's almost a New Year—the first day of spring, the Budding Moon, in just two weeks. Oh, Jhani, I'm coming, my dearest, I'm coming...

Humming, she quickened her step as she came closer to the small summerhouse known as Phoenix Terrace.

Honeysuckle vines hung over the archway of the terrace stairway. As she ran up the stairs, she heard the distant rattle of small firecrackers. *Testing fireworks already, the first explosions for the New Year!* Laughing, breathless, she pushed aside the wooden screen and stepped onto a Persian carpet spread across a small room.

Pirjhan sat cross-legged beneath the open windows, facing the doorway. His head and shoulders outlined by a green glow, his face and hands in shadow. Sunlight poured over him onto the carpet, making its woven birds and flowers seem alive.

Talima was radiant, sun-washed, gilded, as she knelt before him.

He touched her face in awe. "My beauty...you are beauty itself. Great Tengri, you shine like the moon..."

"And you are my sun, beloved."

"Come, let me hold you."

"A moment, Jhani...I want to tell you something...two things, actually, before we…

"All right, but only two. I'm a patient man, but not patient enough for three." He smiled at her, dark eyes half closed, a-dazzle in her reflected light.

"Promise me you won't say anything right away? You won't argue until you've had a chance to think about it?"

"Possibly…"

"Possibly isn't good enough, Jhani! No discussion until later, all right?"

"If that's the only way you'll get on with it, love, I suppose my answer must be yes."

"Good, well, I've decided that we're going home. Soon. Next week maybe, as soon as I can get ready!"

"You've talked to the emperor then?"

"No, and I'm not going to bother about him anymore."

"But, Tam…"

"Ah-ah! You promised! Now for my second thing…" she drew a deep breath, then the words tumbled out. "I think, no, I *know*…that I have happiness within me!"

"I'm not sure I understand…could you mean…could it be? A child? *Our child?"*

"Yes, my dearest love, our baby, our first child! I suspected it by the time Shira foaled, but I wasn't sure until I'd missed my second moon-flow."

"Why, that's *wonderful!* Simply, overwhelmingly wonderful! Oh my Tam, my darling! You have made me so happy, so proud!" He pulled her into his arms and laid her down on the flower-strewn carpet beside him. Slowly, tenderly, he stroked her face, her throat, then pushed aside her collar and felt within to her swelling breasts.

She felt the delicious roughness of his hands, hands that ordinarily commanded and controlled even the most fractious mare. Her senses reeled with his smell—fresh hay and horses and musky maleness. She felt the heat of her precious gate prickle and trembled as the molten shimmer within her answered his caresses.

He bent his head and kissed her, his tongue tickling her lips, before he plunged into her mouth, hoarsely calling to her without words, demanding. He felt her move under him, molding her soft flesh to his hard body, yielding to him. He watched from half-closed eyes as she surrendered herself to him. He heard her small, bird-like sounds as her ecstasy grew.

A floodtide of love swept through her, sweeping away all thought, leaving only the urgency of her need for more of him, everything he had to give. Eyes half-open she saw him watching her and reveled in her power to excite him. Of their own accord, her hips rose up to meet him, inviting his jade stalk into the deepest part of her body.

Together they became
    within-without, the same…
flowing like sun-warmed honey…
    into self-dissolving…soaring….
light…
    of life…of love

Skin smooth and hot against skin. Mouth and tongue…slippery, sweet. Passion melting away mind, leaving one spirit, neither him nor her…one being only.

Until…slowly…time began again.

"I do love thee Tam, you make me feel like fire, burning with love for you. In the first breath of your being, there I am, in you, in love."

"How…I…love *thee!* And I, I feel like the air that rushes into the breath of your fire, creating it anew, making it burn and blow like a comet shaking its long starry tail feathers against the Everlasting Sky."

"Tam?"

"Mmnnn?"

"D'you really think we can leave…just like that?"

She shook herself, willing her awareness back into ordinary reality, still riding the long streaming letdown of their lovemaking. She sat up and rearranged her tunic, pulled up her full trousers, combed her hair back with her fingers.

"I do. But there some things I'll need to do before we go. I want to gather writing materials to take home and some rolls of silk and food for the trail and…"

"How can I help?"

"You can get the horses ready and put together some food for the journey. Tell Kulak and Kilar to get ready to ride…could Firuz cover for you long enough to give us a head start, d'you think?"

Pirjhan jumped up and began to pace. "Yes! By Tengri, it's a good idea! Shouldn't take more than nine or ten days to wind things up…that takes us right up to New Year's...a perfect time to get away as everyone will be extra busy and there'll be noise and commotion everywhere!"

"Oooh, I'm so happy, come dance with me!" In and out of the summerhouse's sunshine and shadows they danced as if they didn't have a care in the world.

"Meet me here in two weeks, Jhani, we can be ready to go by then, or at the very least, *almost* ready...meanwhile, we must be very careful not to do or say anything different from our ordinary routine. We must not attract any more attention than we have already." ***I won't tell him what Zanggi said, it would only worry him and besides, we'll soon be gone...***

Hand in hand, hearts still together, they left the Phoenix Terrace and went into their separate lives, hers to her little house in the Jade Pavilion gardens, he to the imperial stables and the guardsmen's barracks.

The stables were in more than the usual uproar. Grooms and guardsmen strode rapidly through a milling throng of skittish horses. At the center of it all was the black eminence of the emperor, who pointed imperiously at this horse, that horse, choosing mounts for himself and friends.

Pirjhan, Tulak and Kilar led the chosen horses into the ring. "It's a big hunt up in the mountains. Cougar, I'm told. Dangerous sport...I'm almost afraid to let our horses go...but then, there's not much I have to say about it, is there now?" Pirjhan talked with the Igren grooms as each lifted steep-cantled hunting saddles onto the horses' backs.

"Hey you! Head groom!" A shout followed them into the inner stables. A man ran toward them. "His Most Excellent Majesty wants you, Pirjhan!"

"Me? Now?"

"Yes, hurry, he's waiting."

Pirjhan ran back into the arena, bowed to the emperor and saluted. "Yes, Sire?"

"We'll be hunting for a week to ten days, up north. I want you to come with us in case the horses go lame or get hurt, as I know you are capable of remedying both."

"Of course, your Excellency, I'll just be a short time to pack a kit. You said ten days?"

"More or less, as long as the weather holds."

Pirjhan ran back and almost ran into Kilar.

"Kilar, I must go with the emperor, but should be back in ten days. Watch for Talima, tell her what's happened, that I'll meet her as I promised at the Phoenix Terrace in just two weeks. His Majesty will get us back by that time, I'm sure. Meanwhile, you and Tulak must do my share of getting supplies together for our journey, right? See to the horses we'll need. Firuz knows our plans but speak to no one else. And Kilar...be *very, very* careful...tell no one."

33
The Morning Of The World

IT WAS THE MORNING OF THE WORLD AND THE DAWN WAS FILLED WITH PROMISE. Little birds sang mating songs and flew streamers of grass for new nests into blossom-ruffled boughs.

Talima walked across the garden. She walked in beauty. Beauty was around, beneath, above her. Her embroidered slippers whispered as she floated along the winding path. Burbling streams and fountains sang spring songs. No wind blew. The air was still, still.

Flower cups of fragrant dew opened themselves to the sun. Tasting the contents of each open calyx, fuzzy new bees hummed ecstatically. A million minute diamonds sparkled on the tips of grasses. Talima was filled with light, drunk with the joy of being alive. Melodies of fountains, birds, and bees were in harmony. Peace pervaded the garden.

Except in that wing of the palace, Talima looked across flowering shrubs to the two-storied buildings on her left. *There's rarely any peace there from what Kao Tsung tells me. No wonder the poor fellow hides in his books all the time. Pots and pans banging...and listen to that wife of his! She's screaming at her children and servants already and the day's scarcely begun.*

She turned to look at the opposite wing that formed the walled garden and shook her head. *Not a sound there,* she mused, *Prince Li Cheng and all his cohorts are probably still asleep. I could hear Sassanian music far into the night. What a party it must have been!*

Behind her was Tai Tsung's three-storied main palace, his flag hung limply from its brass pole. She had slipped out at dawn while everyone in the Jade Pavilion was still asleep. There was no one to be seen anywhere in the vast palace gardens. She walked along a diagonal path that led across a new-moon-bridge. In the mirrored lake beneath, spotted carp fanned.

Talima's thoughts rambled like the bees that flitted from flower to flower without apparent pattern.

So much has happened in these past weeks! It's almost as if Kao Tsung was relieved to find I was a woman, not a man. He's shared so many of his hopes and dreams with me…he wants only to be a scholar, poor man, and even though he won't be emperor, as he's younger than Li Cheng, he's required to fulfill many royal duties. I don't think he likes the emperor, his father, very much, but I thought he was quite nice, a lot like my father, actually…the same kind of inner strength and competence.

I feel rather competent myself these days. I don't even care whether I have an audience with Tai Tsung or not! I'm going home, regardless!

If I'm right about the baby, we'll be able to get home before it's born. In some ways I feel badly to just disappear after all I've learned here, after giving my word to Zanggi, but I don't see that I have a choice—not really—besides, I'm certainly not needed here. Funny, I didn't realize I could simply go. We'll just pack up, take our own horses, and ride west…be into the mountains before they know we're gone.

Father will be relieved to have me back. He must. I'll tell him how things happened…that we fell in love. That I have not brought dishonor to our clan even if…well, I'll make him understand. Surely he will!

Together…such a wonderful word! We'll be together, always, for the rest of our lives. Oh, my Pirjhan-sha, I love you so!

As a surprise, Talima had practiced some of the skills she'd learned from the Jade Pavilion women. She had lined her eyes with lavender kohl, rouged her lips and lacquered her nails. She had pinned up her hair with tortoise-shell combs. Wayward amber-yellow strands blew across her cheeks. Flowers were knotted in colored ribbons that tied the full sleeves of her hyacinth blue dress. Its transparent fabric molded itself under her breasts. She smiled to herself, knowing Pirjhan had never seen her dressed like this, wanting him to think her beautiful.

She was vividly alive to the bright morning, tingling in anticipation of Pirjhan's touch, insistent yet gentle. Of Pirjhan's mouth, sweet yet demanding. His deep, caressing voice. The incense of his hard body. Pirjhan, waiting even now, she knew, in their rendezvous in the summerhouse at the far end of the garden. Humming, she quickened her step.

Coming into the little clearing where the tile-roofed Phoenix Terrace stood, she walked more quietly. She could see a beloved shape in silhouette, waiting for her in the upstairs window. She stopped to look up, stopped for a moment to simply realize the happiness that waited for her.

I hear footsteps though... is someone with him? I only want a little time alone with him today...so we can make final plans...

Over the seated silhouette, illumined by sunlight pouring through a window on the other side of the room, a mask of fury and retribution appeared...a Kat Kat Zanggi she did not know, eyes bulging, lips drawn back over clenched teeth. An incarnation of the stone warriors that guarded the temple gates. She could not move, could not even speak a warning, mesmerized, watched, as a glittering sword swung its deadly arc up over his head. Silently, without breathing, she watched it curve down, dream down, with the power of lightning...slowly, slowly, splitting down through an eternity of timeless terror.

And then the screaming began, a primal wail from the bottom of her heart erupted in her throat. But before the sound was fully born, she was engulfed in a scarlet fountain...a viscous crimson pulsating fountain that shut out all light, flooded her eyes and filled her nose and mouth with the red smell and bloody taste of life, soundless, a head bouncing strangely, falling...a dead weight on top of her.

And then her scream was truly born. She heard it echo her agony down through an eon of sorrowing time. Pain pierced her like a sword, a sword with a thousand teeth that ripped and tore through her belly, biting through the life so new within her.

Only blood-red darkness pulsed with life. Darkness that engulfed her, obliterating love. Forever. Dark and dead and gone.

As if playing accompaniment to the crescendo of her screams, a fusillade of fireworks crackled in a jubilant shower, adding a strange vivacity to the morning. When the fireworks died down, no sound remained.

In silence, a grieving Zanggi gently gathered her unconscious, blood-soaked body into his arms and walked back toward the palace and out into the New Year.

Book Two

BLACK. DARK. DEAD. THE ENDLESS LITANY CIRCLED. *Blackness. Darkness. Death. No light. No love. No life. Nothing. A long, dark spiral leading nowhere, down and down.*

Scarcely sensate, her young body insisted on continuing its diminished existence. Her listless mind careened back and forth between the colors of life and death. The red of blood that meant death, the black of life she endured. The torrent of blood that had swept away the life of her love now flowed from within her womb carrying away the unborn child created from that love.

34
Coming Back Into The Light

THE MARROW OF TALIMA'S WILL DISSOLVED, leaving a paper-thin, unresponsive husk. Words, inconsequential, unrelated words, penetrated her awareness dimly as from afar.

A deep, dark voice: "I had no choice..."

A light, lilting voice: "She may not survive the shock..."

"The council ordered..."

"Drink this."

Diving down again without volition into the vortex of limitless bleakness, longing for death.

"You will see to it, Mistress Alchemist, that she lives? His Most Luminous Majesty requests..."

"Does he know? About the baby?"

"The emperor need not know that she was pregnant with this child..."

"No one will, Noble Coordinator, no one will. Swallow this, child."

"Wu Chao Tse Tsien..."

"The elixir is ready, Honorable Teacher Feng."

Unrecognizable names, unrecognizable faces, irreconcilable grief. Emptiness. Forgetfulness that fogged the mirror of her mind and made the harrowing pain less distinct. Floating, weightless, will-less.

The days became weeks, the weeks disposed of the Holiday Moon and drifted into the Budding Moon. High holy days came and went. People came and went. Slowly, infinitesimally, her young body began to reassert itself.

Gradually she became more aware of her surroundings, the bed in which she lay, filtered daylight, lamplight at night.

"Wu Chao Tse Tsien, you must drink this." That name again, the only words, the only name that was repeated, day or night.

"How are we feeling today,Wu Chao?" The same cheery, chirping voice.

"Tse Tsien, little Spitfire, rally your spirit, please!" A velvet purr. "How could you betray me—and yourself—with that, that insignificant Igren man? Why did you bring this on yourself? I trusted you, and yet you...but it's over now and no one will ever know your transgressions...for that I give you my word."

And then one morning, she awoke. Simply woke up, whole. Weak. Scoured by the winds of mourning. Barren, windswept plain of person. But alert, alive, aware...and hungry.

She lay and looked at the light through translucent, painted screens that walled her bed. A four-toed dragon that held a gleaming pearl in its claw, gazed at her from the foot of the bed. Birds with wings like flames... *phoenix* was the word that appeared itself in her mind...flew above frilly flowers. *Peony*...the word that popped up...on the panels at her side.

They pleased her, those two words did...*peony...phoenix.* They tasted good on her tongue. But they did not satisfy her hunger.

She moved her hands along her body, feeling the hollow of her belly between the horns of her hipbones, felt the deep ridges of her ribs as they rose and fell with each slow, living breath.

She heard the surrounding stillness. Even her own heart seemed stilled. It was quiet. Not with the still quiet of death, but with the still acceptance of being alive.

Joy, struggle, curiosity, delight, all waited for her, waited for another time. But for today, she was singly, simply aware of life itself, continuing.

She stretched and found that it felt *good.* She tried to sit up, but her bones lay heavy against silken sheets. Her muscles, tissued with disuse, lacked the strength to lift her.

Footsteps whispered against the floor. The shielding screen was folded back. A tiny, bright-eyed face peered in at her.

"Our patient is awake! Good morning, Wu Chao!" It was the cheery, chirpy voice, vaguely remembered.

Wu Chao...I keep hearing that. It must mean me..."Wu Chao?" she asked.

"Yes, yes, yes! And we know our own name today, don't we? Very good! We've brought some good nourishing broth, Wu Chao!" she gestured to a woman who stood beside her.

The broth's aroma wafted toward her. Its smell poured down her nostrils, flooded her mouth and coursed through her body. She trembled. The women lifted her and held the cup to her mouth. It was a drink from heaven, nectar of the gods. She drank it all.

They lowered her down again and inspected her in a satisfied manner. "Well, well, the Son of Heaven will be pleased with our report today! They said it wasn't possible, but we knew she'd come 'round. With our help, of course. Now then, Wu Chao, time to take your med'sin...

"What...is...it?"

"It's Dragon-and-Tiger elixir, dear. Brewed it fresh this morning, I did! Wouldn't leave it to a lesser person, oh no! Only the most superior ingredients to lighten your body and lengthen your life while strengthening your blood. Of course, we tried Tree-Entwining-Dragon-Spout to begin with, to recapture your soul."

Her long green sleeves brushed the bed as she poured earth-colored liquid into a small jade cup. "I always say that you can't improve on the divine Fomes fungus and cinnabar, and when combined with tuckahoe and ginseng, plus a little deer velvet and cardamom, harmonized, of course, with licorice. Well, anyone will come 'round, even when their vital breath organ has been so damaged. Open your mouth, dear, drink it all."

Her small hands fluttered like little moths around Wu Chao.

Maybe....I might be...what is the word? Dreaming? Wondering dreamily, she drifted again into deep and healing sleep. Mistress Feng-hsien-seng, the Court Alchemist-Physician, closed the screens around her patient, gathered up her grass-green skirts and swept out of the room. Her aide pattered along behind her, carrying the pot of night soil.

THE NEXT TIME SHE AWOKE IT WAS NIGHT. Light flickered through the dragon and phoenixes. A lamp burned beside her bed illumining the silhouette of a human on the thin, translucent-stone panels. She heard a voice that droned on with the slow sound of a great gong.

Reading...he is reading, she realized with pleasure. She listened.

"A white horse comes running, two arrows stick up from the empty saddle. So many deaths have come from this fighting! I start to cry…my tears won't stop." The voice stopped. "Aaiieee, 'tis true, all too true…"

Someone else who cries…I wonder who? She heard him clear his throat and begin again.

"Here's *Fighting South of the Ramparts,* one of my favorites, though it may not be suitable to read to a young girl in her condition. Well, she still sleeps and who knows, the sound of words alone may bring her back into this world again. So…'We have pastured our horses in Himalayan snows…we're the emperor's armies growing old, getting gray…ten thousand miles from home.'"

He read on. Her attention wandered, receding, advancing, like waves on the shore. The swelling dark sucked her under again. And again, her awareness bobbed to the surface to hear the words, to try to make sense of the words she heard, "…the sword's a stinking thing a wise man will use as seldom as he can."

"Li-Bo, dear cousin, you *do* understand the life of a warrior. You truly understand! By the blood of a five-toed dragon, I will cease these everlasting wars that go on and on and suck the life's blood of my people! I will unite this far-flung country of mine! I *must.* But I need *time*. Enough time and wisdom, gods help me!"

His low voice was only a murmur as he spoke, but he was so close on the other side of the screen, that she heard him clearly.

She felt his sorrow and his resolve, strong and masculine against the emptiness inside her. He sounded now like the word, *father.* She felt as if she might hold his hand and comfort them both. She pushed against the folded screen, which opened easily, and saw him sitting there beside her. A rush of new words filled her mind. *He looks like a black mountain. Solid, massive, safe, unmovable by the wildest storm…*

His topknot, wound with starched, black gauze, was pinned at the center by a clear white-jade hairpin. His black silk kimono hung loosely over baggy black pants. His face was weatherworn and an old scar creased his left cheekbone. As he turned toward her, he held his place with the be-ringed forefinger of his right hand, on the scroll book he had been reading.

"So, little broken bird, Wu Chao Tse Tsien, you are awake at last." He smiled so gently that his moustaches scarcely moved. "When they told me of your tragedy, falling down, all crumpled onto that huge boulder outside the Phoenix Terrace…wounded times, wounded affairs, wounded hearts…I just kept on hoping that your fiery spirit that I encountered on the polo field, would not burn out. Not just yet!"

"I don't know…what happened?"

"You don't need to know. Just rest and get well. You've had a difficult time, but you'll be all right now. Don't try to remember the pain. Just live for the moment, for now." He brushed wisps of hair from her forehead. It felt curiously comforting. She smelled the clean grass smell of him. Her tears, held at bay for so many weeks, flowed down onto his gnarled hands.

"There, there, little one, you're a gallant young creature and you have that fighting spirit I so admire, besides…" he took her thin cool hands in his, "besides, I've enjoyed these hours here with you when I couldn't sleep…a rare, quiet time for me.

"Now go back to sleep. Build your strength. I'll leave you now but I'll be back tomorrow night. Sleep well, little phoenix bird."

35
The Peony Moon and Stories

Days slid by like water over smooth stones. She was bathed and dressed. She slept and ate. Nights had a different rhythm. He sat beside her on the bed-bench and read poetry or told stories, some true, some myth, ancient news and current history.

Days were unreal, inconsequential. She floated through them dreamlessly. The nights were vivid lamp-lit islands where her mind explored intriguing shores of thought and bathed in the springs of a new adventure, where she tasted fruits from the tree of knowledge and wandered along companionable paths with an extraordinary man.

She held her energies in waiting for these nights, patiently allowing all the ministrations of her numerous attendants. They told her that it was now the Sleepy Moon, when the world gathered energy unto itself in order to burst forth in the riotous life of summer. She slept away the days.

One night, she asked him his name. "Mistress Feng calls you Luminous Illustrious, but that seems too long for ordinary conversation, so what should I call you, if you please, Sire?"

"You could call me by my family name, Li Shih-min of course, no? And you don't like Tai Tsung either? So...how shall it be between us?"

"Would just plain Sire be acceptable?"

"Ha! I'm not your sire, but I wouldn't mind siring a filly like you. Very well, it will do.

"You know, when I was young, we had a horse, one of the blood-sweaters—don't see many of them anymore, bred too often with the dish-faced Tajiks, I suppose—whose coloring was similar to yours. We called her Peach-flower Cherpadh. Worth thirty pi of silk. Lord, she was a pretty little thing!"

"What was your life like, Sire, when you were young? What did you do when you were my age?"

"When I was your age? Back beyond belief, you mean?" he teased. "Much like the life of any noble family, even today...hunting, swordplay, falconry. When I was young I was fond of archery. I once had ten excellent bows made for me that I thought would last me through a young man's wars.

"And you know, Peach-flower, recently I showed them to a bowmaker who told me that all were of poor quality! A foolish but honest thing to say to one's emperor, don't you think? When I asked him why, he replied—I'll never forget it...'If the heart of the wood is not straight, then their arteries and veins are all bad. Although the bows are strong, when you shoot, the arrows will not fly true.'" He stroked his mustache with his fingertips.

"And I realized what a profound statement that was. That if the heart is not straight—the heart of a nation, of the law, a family, a man, even a child—then all that circulates out from that center is bad, and its course cannot be true.

"Of course, I also realized that even in this—the judgment about weapons with which I'd pacified an empire—my discrimination was insufficient. How much more unlikely that I can ever know all that's necessary to govern the affairs of an empire! Therefore, I rely on talented men and trust that they're honorable."

"I seem to remember someone else saying something like that once. It was...oh! It was my *Father!"* Without quite knowing why, she began to cry. "He was telling me about a man he admired...a man who...I don't remember...but, ohhhhh!"

White-hot pain crackled through her body. Her back arched in agony. Her screams leaped against the walls, a flying ululation that consumed all other sound.

Tai Tsung moved swiftly. He knelt on the bed and pulled her into his arms, rocked her feather-light body back and forth, back and forth, murmuring soothing melodies into her hair. Finally, her screams subsided into sobs and, after awhile, stilled into occasional sniffles, and she lay quietly, held securely in his arms.

He smoothed her tear-soaked hair, "There, there, tell me all about it, my child."

In incoherent rushes, she told him, and herself, pieces of what she could remember...about her Igren life, grief on leaving her home and family, the long trail, Mazar Tagh, a banner of horses, imprisoned with other concubines, The Forest of Pencils, polo and Kao Tsung, and Pirjhan, forever lost. So much, so incomplete, so empty.

What will I do? How shall I live? Where can I go? How did it happen? What did Zanggi...?

Overcome by the weight of memories, steeped in resurrected sorrow, confused and desolate, she cried for a world lost, and began to know, to deeply sense, the part she herself had played in losing it.

"Ah, Peach-flower, the pattern of your life becomes clear. My heart is heavy. Clearly, your life, the life of that bright being known as Talima has been consumed by the triple fires of fate and circumstance and the self-serving decisions of others, myself included. But I didn't know. I didn't realize how that might be.

"You deserve a chance to build a new life of your own." *Will you be strong enough, resolute enough, lucky enough to persevere in this regard, I wonder? I must think of ways to make it possible.* The emperor smiled and patted her slender hand with his gnarled, rein-hardened hand.

First of all the emperor moved her into his own residence, the newly completed Jade Flower Palace, which stood beneath the cliff by the Cinnabar Gate, facing south and east into the Chian sun.

There, in a suite of rooms directly across a red-pillared hall from his own, Tai Tsung arranged for her to live. It was furnished in the old-fashioned way: low lacquer tables surrounded by pillows stuffed with tree floss, called kaipok; polished, dark-wood storage cabinets; a silk-curtained bed whose folding walls were thin-cut ivory, with thick rugs woven in the far reaches of empire. A pawlonia-wood harp stood in one corner.

Gilded pillars held up vermilion rafters that curved gracefully outward into deep eaves where glass wind-bells hung, whispering songs to the wind. The walls were painted with scenes of men and women sporting together beneath lacy trees or beside pools where languid carp swam. Tall windows decorated with bits of colored glass and sparkling mica opened onto a balcony that overlooked a fountain.

"It's a plain room," he said, tucking her into bed. "Not luxurious in the modern fashion. But I find it comfortable. I trust you will, too."

A large brown cat leaped onto her chest and began purring ecstatically. "Takla Makan'! You sweetheart! Thank you, Sire! How wonderful to have my kitty here. How thoughtful you are!"

"To tell the truth, it was Kat Kat Zanggi who suggested it."

"Zanggi!" her face grew white. Her body slumped back against the pillows. "A killer! He...he took his life...he betrayed me! He must be punished!"

"It's not surprising that you feel that way, but I want you to listen to me very carefully. Kat Kat Zanggi is an admirable man, an honorable man. In every way, he adheres to the highest code of right conduct. His loyalty to me and to my *Chen-kuan* reign, the reign of *True Vision* that is the dream I have for my country, is without question.

"Zanggi had no choice. He gave his oath to abide by our laws. The law does not allow for White Jade women to form other relationships. As he saw it, he was protecting my interests, protecting *you*, Tsien, from being defiled, from possibly conceiving a child that would be unacceptable, dishonoring all involved. In addition to that, he is the Head Secretary of the Eunuch's Council, which has complete authority to deal with internal affairs. They voted to eliminate this source of disharmony that you were a part of in the palace. And I must say that I'm personally grateful they did not choose to eliminate *you*."

She stroked her cat thoughtfully. "So, you're telling me I should forgive him?"

"I'm asking you to look at it from *his* point of view. From his perspective, what he did was not a crime, it was the *only* correct course of action. Think about it. You know him. I think you also know that he loves you."

She was silent for a long time. Tai Tsung waited.

Sighing, she said, "Everything seems to be itself and its opposite. What I thought I knew I think I don't know. It's like starting all over, like going down a trail for the thousandth time and finding that it's not the same at all."

"There are times like that all through life. They are times of growth, of going beyond the person you were before and becoming more deeply human, more compassionate."

"Is it always this full of pain?

"Not always. But often. Usually, in fact." He watched her absorb this, then smiled as he saw her straighten her back and lift her head. "You'll do, you have the blood of dragons in your veins."

"Tell him then, tell Zanggi to come and see me. I will listen to what he has to say."

"Your wish is my command, Lady."

"'Sky, I didn't mean it that way, Sire, forgive me, it's just that I cannot bear..."

Tai Tsung threw back his head, slapped his thigh and chuckled. "It's all right, I'm not offended." He clapped his hands. Servants entered carrying trays laden with small dishes.

"I thought we'd celebrate the beginning of your new life with some special treats that might tempt you to eat." As he lifted the cover from each dish, he named its contents. "Let's see, here are dumpling flowers, wine-marinated carp, shoats in garlic sauce, some black, forest mushrooms—wonderful wild smoky flavor—and a flagon of mare's teat wine.

"Then we have *snow babies.* Have you ever eaten snow babies, Tsien, made from frog's legs and ground beans? No? You'll like them. And, yes, persimmons, lychees and dried apricots. I told them to make some—here it is—camphor ice cream for dessert!"

"What is *ice cream?*"

"Milk and rice powder, with various flavorings, whipped and frozen in the ice-rooms below the palace. I thought it might intrigue you. What would you like to try first?"

"The ice cream please, how do they make ice in the rooms below the palace?"

"They don't make it there, they only store it there. Ice is brought, covered with straw, by cart from the far northern chous. See those large fans overhead? They work by mechanical rotating chains, pulled below. In summer, they circulate cold air from the ice rooms and cool the palace. Sometimes, we use ice like this to make other iced foods and drinks. In olden times they were fond of carving ice into shapes of fantastic birds and animals as serving bowls for feasts."

"Ice cream is strange, strange and delicious, it makes the back of my throat ache."

"Eat more slowly then. Watch that kitten!"

"Takla Makan! She likes the ice cream, too!"

"How would you like to visit the stables sometime soon? Do you feel strong enough?"

A flood of vivid memories. "Yes...I don't know, I'll try. Could we see Shira and her colt? Could we go tomorrow?" She wiped cream from the kitten's whiskers.

"Shira, the mare you brought, she's foaled?"

"A healthy colt, silver-dappled, as many of our horses are. He'll grow to be as great as the ones you chose at auction, Sire. Maybe greater, for Bagatur was his sire." She chuckled.

"You know a great deal about horses and their breeding, don't you?"

"Horses were my life."

"In other ways, horses are my life, too."

"How?"

"Horses are the military preparedness of the state," he sipped his wine. "If heaven takes this preparedness away, the state will totter and fall."

"Is that why you require so many horses as tribute?"

"It takes hundreds of thousands of horses to mount an army, Peach-flower. And I keep five standing armies at all times, one for each corner of the empire and one in readiness here in Changan."

She bit into an orange persimmon and sucked the juice from under its skin. "I see. It's wrong, you know."

"What? Wrong to tax vassal states for the horses I need to protect them?"

"No. Wrong to equate human beings with animals, regardless of that animal's nobility."

"What are you talking about? When have I ever done that?"

"I'm talking about the other tribute you exact from border states. The tribute of a virgin daughter, like me, ripped from all that I loved, sent on a hazardous journey of many thousand li, and in the end, ignored, fed and clothed, part of a herd of other maidens, none of whom you care enough about to even see. *That* is what's wrong! It's barbaric, unworthy of a civilization like yours, Son of Heaven. Have you ever *considered,* even for a moment, what it's like for that virgin girl? And her family? How much heartbreak you create?"

"I will admit that it never occurred to me."

"You asked me to understand Zanggi from *his* viewpoint. I ask you to look at this situation, and this law, from *mine.*"

"Very well," he said quietly. "That's fair. I had considered it an honor, actually, but you've shown me its dark side. I appreciate your boldness, Tsien. I need to have someone who tells me the truth."

"That I will always do. What can *you* do, Sire, to put an end to this human tribute?"

"I'll see. We've been revising the Code of Law for five years now. You're right. Women are not horses or parrots or trade goods or chattel. I'll instruct my advisors to remove this requirement. Will that satisfy you?" He smiled and began to cover their empty dishes.

In the time it had taken to eat a meal, she had accomplished one of the things she'd wanted to do ever since that far distant day of decisions with Pirjhan at Half-Moon Lake.

But she no longer knew what to do with the victory. Talima and her dreams were gone; Wu Chao Tse Tsien's future was unknown. The Peony Moon, full moon of midsummer, shone on her face.

Now, what now is right, for me? Tomorrow, tomorrow I'll walk to the stables one step at a time, one tomorrow at a time, just the way that Zanggi showed me, so long ago, when I hardly understood. Well, who knows, tomorrow might bring...something wonderful...and then...

36
Batu Arrives: Zanggi Becomes A Ghost

ALMOST TWO YEARS. BEGINNING THE THIRD SUMMER since my "black time"...how swiftly it's passed...

I feel like a small, round pebble that fate picked up at random and flipped into another dimension. And yet I remember that other world, her world, Talima's world, so clearly.

Down one side of the painting, her ink-filled brush flew like a flock of birds darting out of the forest. As she wrote, she murmured the poem that took shape on the paper...

'I'm a peach tree,
deep in a gorge, flowering,
smiling and nodding to no one.'

His Most Luminous Majesty's "Peach-flower" actually—and, as a flower cannot bloom without its stem and root, I do not exist separately from him, at his side always as his trusted left arm.

You were the moon in my sky, Pirjhan. Now I revolve around the sun, the Son of Heaven. She smiled and sighed as she calligraphed the last line with a movement like that of a frightened snake disappearing into the grass...

'My thoughts don't stop
they are the stream...
they flow
they follow you
forever...'

I wish there were a better character for forever. Forever is not just a long time, it's also yearning for a brighter future, longing for a beloved past. Forever is really a remembering, before it's happened.

She rested her brush on its tourmaline holder, rocked back on her heels and stood up. She picked up her *chop,* the stone cylinder carved with the characters of her name, Wu Chao Tse Tsien, and pushed one end of it into a jar of camphor-fragrant vermilion paste. Then, with her head cocked to one side, she inspected her work. Having decided the best place for her signature, she pressed the end of the chop firmly onto the rice paper's lower right hand corner.

There, I hope Sire will be pleased...both our birthdays on the same date of the Lotus Moon. I'll be twenty-one, he'll be fifty-one. I wonder if he has a special present for me. Last year's was so wonderful it would be hard to match though—my own sedan chair, lacquered in blue and painted with phoenixes! Lady Wang was so rude when I crossed her path the other day. How she glared! Kao Tsung says not to mind Lady Wang's unpleasantness, that his wife simply has a jealous disposition. Dear Kao Tsung, even though we don't get to partner on the polo field as often as we'd like any more, we do have grand conversations together.

Fans overhead sang a steady, fa-la-lumph, fa-la-lumph, as they cooled her room, circulating cold air from the ice rooms below. She washed ink from her thick brush, then went to the window that looked down on a garden below. She watched one of the Jade Pavilion women sitting there and wondered whether she was happy or sad, remembering her own tempestuous months as one of them.

A SERVING WOMAN WALKED QUIETLY AS SHE CAME INTO THE ROOM. "Please pardon this unworthy person, Mistress, for interrupting you at your work." She bowed her head over folded hands. "But I must deliver a message to you without delay."

"I wish you wouldn't bow, Su O, it makes me feel ancient. What's your message?"

"It's from His Most Illustrious Luminous, Mistress—and I'll try to remember about the bowing."

"His Majesty? Quickly, Su O, tell me."

"He requests your presence, Mistress, some matter of a foreign barbarian, I believe, although this humble person has not seen such a one and would be afraid of his evil eye, in any case, but..."

"Oh, for heaven's sake, do be quiet, Su O. Where is His Majesty?"

"If I'm quiet, I cannot deliver the message, can I? I believe it was the imperial stables that he mentioned, although it might be…no, it was the stables, I'm sure, but I'm sure he would not want you to soil your pretty feet in a stable…"

"Thank you, Su O," Tse Tsien interrupted. *Really! The woman is impossible, I shouldn't let her maunderings bother me I know, but…*

"A groomsman awaits with your horse, Mistress, though why you should be expected to venture outside on such a hot day is too…"

She means well, Tse Tsien reminded herself. "If there is nothing else, Su O, you may leave me. I must change."

Stripping off the arm shields and apron that protected her gown from ink spatters, she scrubbed ink and red-orange paste from her hands, unable as usual to erase the *black chrysanthemum* ink-stain from her middle finger. Then she went into her dressing room, took off her linen shift and put on a fitted, ankle-length tunic of pale peach silk that was open on each side to reveal violet trousers over purple boots. As she ran out of the room, she tucked her hair up into a high, curved cap embroidered with pearl dragonflies.

A barbarian? Su O didn't say whether it was a hu-barbarian from the south or a mon-barbarian from the west. I wonder if it could be someone from…

Bagatur, standing quietly in the shade of the palace, whickered softly to her. She vaulted onto his back and nodded thanks to the waiting groom. The clatter of their cantering hooves along stone-paved streets joined the summer song of cicadas.

"IT'S UP TO HER. I'LL NOT MAKE THAT DECISION FOR HER. I can appreciate the validity of your claim, my friend, but we shall have to wait and hear what she has to say." The emperor, looking like an ordinary noble in his simple black tunic and full pants, stood as always, feet apart, thumbs hooked into his wide, jewel-studded belt.

The man standing beside him was tall and angular. His yolk-yellow hair swept the shoulders of his embroidered felt tunic. Blue eyes shone like gemstones in his lean, weathered face.

"Here she comes!" Tai Tsung smiled. His face grew softer as he watched Tse Tsien ride toward them.

"And still riding that wild calf Bagatur, I see!" the man said.

Both horsemen rode to a stop. Tse Tsien tossed her reins to the groom and slid to the stable courtyard.

"Blessings on you, Sire," she greeted him. "You wanted me?"

Tai Tsung was silent, watching her.

She turned to greet the stranger, "And blessings to...Batu? Can this possibly be you? My Uncle Batu? Here?"

Batu swooped her up in his arms and proceeded to prance around the stable yard. His laughter bounced off the cobblestones, causing busy grooms to stare.

"What—how did you—when? " Questions tumbled over each other as she tried to catch her breath. "Put me down, you great wolf!"

"Here, let me look at you. A fully-grown woman! And passing fair at that! It would make my brother's heart glad to see you."

"Oh, Batu, how is the Chagan? And my brothers? Tell me everything."

"As impatient as ever! How do you manage, Your Majesty?"

Tai Tsung smiled. "Your noble uncle has newly come to our city, Tse Tsien. I suggest that we leave the stables for a cooler—and less public—place. Some refreshments perhaps?

"Of course, it's just such a surprise! I was forgetting, or rather, remembering...so much." Her voice trailed off as memories of home and her childhood flooded in. "Would you like to bathe and change first, Batu?"

"We stopped outside the city this morning, Tam, or are you Tse Tsien now? Unless the perfume of horses is displeasing to either of you, I'll stay the way I am."

"Good, I have a hundred questions!" She took the arm of each man as they walked back to the central palace.

They sat on tasselled pillows on a raised, blue-tiled platform under trailing willow trees. Frilled iris reflected in a pond where large goldfish fanned the shadowed sunlight. Servants glided around them, serving tea and trays of small, colored cakes and spiced nuts. A musician played simple melodies on a curve-necked lute.

"Take me home? To Ferghana Valley? To Father?" She felt suddenly chilled. Her breath came unevenly and her hands trembled, causing ice to tinkle against the thin Turkish glass that held her tea. She looked up to see Tai Tsung observing her intently. "I don't know. I'm not sure. What do you think, Sire?"

"I think," said Tai Tsung, "that no decisions should be made in haste or with undue emotion. We should see that your noble uncle tastes a few of the many pleasures that our capital has to offer, don't you think, Peach-flower? Before he returns?"

"Yes, yes of course. Kapi the stablemaster told me that all of the Igren that came with me—except, except the one who was killed, were gone, gone back home, he thought, with Prince Firuz, when he went away, perhaps as far as Persia itself. Kilar? Tulak? Have you seen them? Did any others of our family return here with the horses this time, with you, Batu?" She asked, longing clear in her voice. "There must be others, do you all have a place to stay? D'you think, Sire...?"

"My chamberlain will make all necessary arrangements. They would stay with the horses in any case for the required six moons. Here, Batu," he said, taking a ring set with clear green jade from the brocaded purse that hung on his belt, "Here is a ring for you to wear while you are in Chian. It guarantees its wearer safe passage and respect."

"Your Most Luminous Majesty, I'm grateful for your favor," Batu bowed over the low table between them.

Tai Tsung nodded with pleasure as he saw Tse Tsien's radiant smile shine on them both. "I'll soon leave the city again, I must re-dedicate the Great Canal east of Loyang. It will be a leisurely journey of six hundred li, more or less. Perhaps, Chagan's-brother-Batu, you'd care to accompany us? You'd be able to experience more of Chian—and it will be refreshing to be away from the capital during the summer heat. I'm sure Tse Tsien would be glad of your company."

"Oh, Sire, I know that plans have been made for this touring procession, but if I'm to leave for home, perhaps I shouldn't?

"Have you made your decision then?" Tai Tsung asked with quiet intensity.

"No, not really, but I always thought I would go home, you know, it's what I've planned to do since I left!"

"Ah, yes. But is the Ferghana Valley still your home? Are you the same person you were when you made that resolution more than three years ago?"

"No, I'm not, but I feel as though my first loyalty is to be there. To be my father's heir as I was trained to be, even though there must have been changes."

Batu's attention went back and forth between them as if he were watching the shifting action of an alabolo game.

"We're all growing older," Tai Tsung sighed. "I did not mean to belittle your responsibilities to your people. I only wanted you to think of who you are now. Where your duties and loyalties are *now.* Not yesterday, not when you were a child."

"I see your point, Most Illustrious Mentor. I need time to think."

"The eastward journey would give you that, my dear. You've not left the palace for more than two years. It would be good for your soul, as well."

Batu was allotted a suite of rooms in the House for Foreign Envoys, engendering the muted jealousy of wealthy diplomats from Persia and Sassania who looked on him as a mere barbarian.

Ceiling fans circulated ice-cooled breezes providing the only movement of air, the only relief from the afternoon's oppressive heat. Takla Makan had stretched herself out as far as possible and lay limply over a brocaded pillow, her paws twitching in dreams. Tse Tsien, wearing a gauze cotton shift, stood in the doorway of the balcony as Kat Kat Zanggi came into the room.

"Good afternoon, Lady," he nodded his head but left his hands within the wide sleeves of his midnight blue robe. "You asked to see me?"

"I *summoned* you, yes, Zanggi."

He looked up in surprise. "Ah, yes, well, it's been many moons since we talked. I see you're well again?"

"I am well, no thanks to you, Zanggi. But it's not me nor my past that I wish to discuss today. I called you to enlist your help in finding my friend, Faina." She leaned against the wooden pillar and gazed into the garden below. " I have been unable to locate a friend of mine. Her name is Faina, although that may have changed, of course. The only thing I've been able to find out is that, after she was taken from the first silk dormitory that they took her to when she was spirited away from me, she was sent to one of the many silk villages outside the city—and that's been difficult to trace. You have eyes and ears everywhere. I want to know which silk village she's been taken to and how I can get her back."

"You have never given me the opportunity to explain why I…"

"And I have no intention of doing so, Zanggi. His Most Illustrious Majesty told me that your intentions at that time were honorable. I have had to accept that this may be true. From your viewpoint, that is."

"You are a pure flame, Wu Chao Tse Tsien, I have known that from the first moment when you burst into my room wearing only that brown kitten—who is now full grown and indolent." Zanggi moved toward her, smiling, gesturing with his small, smooth hands. "I remember thinking, at first, that you were a sorceress dancing naked to bring the rains as in the old days."

"Don't you try to charm me!"

"Would you have me be other than my true nature?"

"No, yes, of course not! Stop trying to change the subject, you wily old fox." She stamped her foot and moved swiftly across the room.

"It is *exactly* the subject that I wish to discuss, myself as subject to the Law and to his Most Luminous Majesty. You as subject to those same principles. Could we not, as educated people, take this time to resolve our differences? I miss you, Spitfire."

"Very well, sit here," she said ungraciously, gesturing to a low carved table. "It is still extremely painful to remember."

"It is my hope that, with understanding, you may be relieved from the pain of anger at least," Zanggi settled himself on a cushion, lifting his robe over his knees for coolness. "Nothing, of course, except time, can alleviate your grief. For that I am most deeply sorry."

"Why? Why did you destroy my happiness? I trusted you. I thought you were my friend!"

"I was. I *am* your friend, perhaps the most trustworthy one you have in this vast intrigue of court life. May I?" he began to pour iced tea into both their glasses. "I don't know how much you have learned, in the past year and a half, of our worldly law, our *Tang Code of Law* that is, so I shall start at the beginning, yes?"

She remembered her father telling her to always start at the beginning, "Go on."

"In ancient times, the former wise kings of Chian imitated the models suspended in the heavens, using them to aid in government and to help transform the people, to check violence and prevent licentiousness, you see. This was in the time of the revered Yellow Emperor, and in his most worthy *Book of Rites* he states, 'If one of the relatives of the Prince commits a capital crime, the Inspector of Fields is charged with... decapitating or strangling him.'

"Continue," she said, scarcely able to breathe from the sudden pain in her chest, the feeling that there wasn't air enough.

"I am in the position, in these more enlightened times, of being the prince's, or the emperor's, Inspector of Fields." Zanggi spoke slowly, watching her. "A crime was about to be committed. As I learned later—had already been committed—and had created a child from that liaison. I recognized this as an illicit sexual act between a common guardsman, with no mourning rights whatsoever, to one of the royal concubines—a treason to the emperor! Even though that girl had not been visited by anyone in court, she had willfully chosen her own mate.

"By the Three Pure Ones! It was puzzling on one hand—clear on the other! I had grown to love you, Spitfire. You were under my protection and I foresaw a bright future for you...for *us*. There were those in court who would have imposed the strictest punishment...penal servitude and life exile would not be too harsh for what you did—for illicit sex is a Depravity and therefore one of the Ten Abominations you see."

"I had no idea! I didn't realize it was wrong—even though you tried to tell me, I know, because what Pirjhan and I had together seemed right and natural."

"Perhaps in the place you come from, it would have been, but here it was a capital offense against the emperor himself! As his concubine, you were only in a position of fourth mourning and so I was able to take matters in my own hands without the interference of a judge. But it was hard, little one, hard.

"You were—are—the purest dragon-spirit-person these old eyes have ever seen. I wanted to save you, give you life. Here, where there is real opportunity for you to be of influence, maybe even power, a force for the truest values, a fearless light against the darkness of evil and intrigue and wrong thinking that afflicts our times! I had no choice." He finished quietly and settled back.

"No choice." She murmured. "That phrase seems to prowl through my life, again and again. What...what happened to the rest of our men... what happened to his body?"

"The palace guards, I'm told, took care of his body, and all of your Igren friends fled when news of the execution and your disappearance—as you continued in that kind of coma—spread throughout the palace, so we could not punish them as accessories. Afterward, the whole incident was a matter for Deliberation, of course. But since the emperor chose not to punish you, nothing more was said. There was, naturally, much gossip, but only your physician, Mistress Feng, and myself know the true extent of this misalliance. But the secret of your miscarriage is safe with us, I assure you, my dear."

"You know, Zanggi, it's odd how something, anything probably, can be itself and its opposite depending on where you stand. Listening to you now I hear superior judgment and right action, courage and resolution. And yet, to me, it has been an act of the most evil and cruel nature."

She looked across the table at this soft, dark, mountain of a man, saw him from a new perspective. And, taking a deep breath, she forgave him. The churning anger and pain of past injustices slipped away. In the first lightness of spirit she had felt for what seemed a lifetime, she wept quietly.

Zanggi was beside her instantly. He cradled her in his arms and rocked back and forth, "Fei-fei-fei, there, there, yes, we will do, you and I—the beautiful and talented Wu Tse Tsien and her faithful ghost."

Through her tears, Tse Tsien began to smile, "You are the least ghostlike creature I can imagine, Kat Kat Zanggi!"

"Perhaps so, so, yes." A wide smile transformed his smooth face. "But your devoted ghost in all things, nevertheless. There will be many times, my dear, when you will need my large shadow to protect you."

"From whom?" she said, wiping away tears with the back of her hands, "I am with the emperor himself!"

"Just so. And therefore the target of jealous and ambitious men—and women like the Lady Wang—those who resent your growing influence and the fact that you are so close to the emperor."

"I? I have no influence, no status. I only listen."

"I'm told that you sit behind a screen, behind the throne of His Majesty, on court days. Is this true?"

"Yes, he wants me to become familiar with all aspects of the government. He says I need to become more educated in Chian ways so that I can better understand what he's trying to do and what the problems are."

"And do you then discuss what you observe from behind your screen, with the emperor?"

"Not really, it's much the same role I played with my father. You see, I've been given this ability to hear the truth behind anyone's talk, the actuality of their thinking, not what their words obscure. And so, as with my father, I'm able to tell my emperor the true feelings behind flowery and flattering speeches of those around him." She shrugged and turned her palms up. "It's a small gift."

"Oho! A small gift indeed! More precious than jade to a ruler, Tse Tsien! A treasure. Yes, how interesting." Zanggi stood abruptly and retied the cord that held his robe against his ample belly. "Well now, a friend of yours is missing, my lady?"

Wu Tse Tsien stood also, went to the door and pulled the plaited cord that would summon a servant. "Faina, yes. This is how it happened." She told him what she knew, which was very little, then said, to a bowing servant, "More tea and honey cakes, please.

"It's particularly important that I find her soon, Zanggi, because we're leaving on an eastern tour with the emperor and when I get back—well, I may be leaving Chian at that time."

"What do you mean, leaving Chian?" His large girth belied the swiftness with which he turned to her.

"My uncle has come to take me home. It's what I've always believed I'd be able to do sometime."

"But you can't! Not now—not who you are now! You'd never be satisfied to be a country hill person, a nomad woman again, would you?"

"That's a question I ask myself, ghost. I don't know, yet." She looked out the open door to the sky beyond, stained a sulphurous yellow from river dust and sunset heat. "I feel the pull of duty and love in both directions—returning, or staying. His Majesty says it must be my free decision. I came against my will, so, if I stay it must be willingly."

"When you examine your heart, you'll see that the choice is already made, Tse Tsien."

"Do you know something I don't?"

"No, Mistress, but I know *you*. I'll send my eyes into the countryside, offer a reward for information and report to you when they find your silk-girl friend." He bowed low and moved toward the hall, seeming to float across the polished floor.

"Her *name* is—was—Faina, Zanggi. She's a person with a *name,* not a silk-girl!"

"I meant no offense, Spitfire. They were only words."

"Words are important. They color thoughts. Please be more careful in the future—if you would be my good ghost."

"You have my word." Zanggi smiled again, shifted his shoulders as if settling a yoke across them, and left.

TSIEN RAN DOWN THE LONG HALL, AND BURST INTO HER OWN ROOMS. "Su-O, come quickly, please, Kao Tsung will be here any moment to play our daily gho game, I took too long with Zanggi. You must help me change...Su-O?"

Tsien looked swiftly around the room. Her maidservant was not to be seen. There was only Takla Makan, curled up on her bed.

"Su-O! 'Sky, this is not the time for games, I need you. Now!"

Silence.

"Where can she be?" Tse Tsien was exasperated as she unwrapped the wide celadon-green sash from her dark blue silk gown and dropped it on the floor.

A slight sound came from the balcony. A sound borne in by the early summer breeze, the cry of a nestling at night. Quickly, she went to look. There, curled up on the tile floor, was Su-O, looking for all the world as if she'd fallen asleep.

Wu Tsien bent down and touched her. Su's eyelids fluttered. She looked up in a hazy way, mewing like a lost kitten. Tsien leaned closer until her hair, unbound, spilled over Su O's face.

"What is it, Su? This is no time for a nap, what are you up to?"

"Oh, Mist'ess...ju...ju...juju...bee."

"Jujube? You want a piece of my jujube candy at a time like this? What *is* the matter with you?"

"Ju...ju...bee" Like smoke, her whisper sifted from her froth-covered mouth, her back arced, she shuddered then, shuddered with her whole body and was silent.

Tse Tsien picked up Su's head and shoulders and listened for her breath. Heard nothing. She felt no rise and fall of breast, no trembling, no movement, no life at all. "Su-O! Great Tengri! She's dying!"

She tried to lift her, to take her inside, but could not. At that moment, with a rustle of his stiff skirts, Kao Tsung walked into the room.

Tsien stood up, her arms limp at her sides, her whole body shaking uncontrollably as shock flooded her completely.

"Kao Tsung, it's Su-O. I don't know what happened. I just got here and she was...and I didn't realize she was...and now she's gone, and..."

Kao Tsung knelt down, felt the maidservant's pulse, shook his head, picked up her body and laid it on the bed.

"She's g-gone, Tsien, her spirit's flown away." Kao Tsung said simply. He walked over and put his arms around her.

She was enveloped by the dry, resin smell of camphor. His warmth and strength was at once surprising and familiar to her. For a few moments, she drank in this sweetness, then, sighing, stepped away.

"Was she ill?" he asked.

"No, never. It's so strange, Kao Tsung, look at the color of her lips—grayish, violet—and there's foamy stuff at the edges of her mouth. And when she saw me, she kept saying something that sounded like *jujube!* What do you suppose she meant?"

"Jujubes? Aren't those your favorite little candies?"

"Yes, there's always a dish of them here on my dressing table. Well, no, they're gone! Perhaps Su O ate them and tried to tell me she was sorry?"

"I think she was trying to tell you something infinitely more serious, dear heart," Kao Tsung looked worried as he stroked his small goatee. "She bears the fleeting symptoms of ku-poisoning...the frothing, darkly-colored lips, the arched back...symptoms that would have disappeared very soon and no one would have known, had you not come when you did."

"But why would anyone wish to poison Su O? It makes no sense!"

"True. It was not Su O they wanted to kill, Tsien, it was *you,"* Kao Tsung held her hand in both of his. "Poison has always been," he went on thoughtfully, "a woman's weapon."

"But why? Why would anyone want to kill me? I've not harmed anyone!"

"Ah, but that's not so, my dear, you are seen with my father at many public events. You just haven't noticed the jealous looks sent your way by other court ladies. Even my wife, particularly my wife, I think. You have made enemies. We must find a way to protect you, I'll ask father what to do."

"Oh, no! Please don't bother His Majesty, he's been working so hard lately. It would only be one more worry," she tapped a front tooth with the curved, lacquered nail of her right forefinger. "Let me think...yes, he'll do, he'll be the best in dealing with this. I'll send for Kat Kat-Zanggi again. He has eyes everywhere. He'll know just how to handle this and besides, he's anxious to win favor with me."

"Y-e-s," Kao said slowly, "if you think so, he probably is. But my dear, you must promise me that you will never, never be alone from now on! You are too vulnerable, too noticeable, and I might add, too beautiful."

Tse Tsien looked at him as if seeing him for the first time, seeing him as an attractive man, a man for whom she had great respect and with whom she shared a love for stars and flying kites, for games and books and knowledge. He became not just a polo partner, but a man she could imagine loving.

37
FAINA'S CHALLENGES AND PLEASURES IN KUO

"TO THINK THERE WAS A TIME WHEN PERSIMMONS SEEMED LIKE FOOD OF THE GODS!" Faina said to herself as she bit into a persimmon, sipping at the juice before it dripped. Her small, white teeth nipped at the orange-red skin.

"And now persimmons are practically all there is to eat, at least until the worms grow large enough to tolerate the smoke of a fire to cook with. What I wouldn't give for a bowl of hot steamed millet! Well, by the Lotus Moon perhaps, a few more weeks, there'll be peaches and Persian melons in the gardens."

Faina, her lemon-yellow hair bound up in her customary turban, walked barefoot along a dusty country road in the first light of morning. Each step in the soft, alluvial dirt added more fine powder to the sulphurous haze that hung over the land. On either side of her, lines of persimmon trees marched across high, rolling plains as far as one could see. Ripening fruit—of the fire, lotus and millstone varieties—hung like jewels in the dark green trees. A farmer, pushing a high-wheeled plough down the rows of trees, lifted his head and smiled as she passed.

As the sun spread its promise of sullen, midsummer heat across the horizon, she turned back toward the village and the day's work ahead. Her thoughts were not on the morning's beauty. They were listing things to get done.

As she walked, her thin fingers touched each other, numbering each item to be remembered. *I must inventory the number of sacks of cocoons ready for the spinner—find out if the missing murex dyes have been found—make sure that the spinning mistress's demands for better quarters have been met satisfactorily and check on her requests for gold leaf to wrap thread for a new kind of brocade, and if there's time enough—make sure that mulberry leaf supplies are adequate for the newly-hatching Superior Silver-crystal worms—and then change clothes and report to the village Guildmaster before he gets impatient and irritable as he did last month! Aaiiee! Too much for one day! I must hurry!*

In the still air, red strips of paper, calligraphed with prayers, hung limply from tree branches. Not even the movement of her passing caused them to move.

Surely there'll be time to run out to the gardens before dark. I want to see if Camel has been able to grow that new mulberry with so many more edible leaves per branch. It would be more efficient...be honest, my girl, that's just a good excuse to see Camel, isn't it? Well, we'll see...

As Faina walked through Kuo's eastern gate, she could hear the thunk and rattle of looms already at work. She turned into a twisting alleyway that ran behind large warehouses that served as repositories of supplies sent from other towns. Inside, in orderly heaps, shining in the dim light, lay thousands of lumpy sacks filled with boiled and dried silk cocoons.

She came out into a large courtyard open to the sky, where lines hung with lengths of still dripping dyed silk, crisscrossed the space between three-storied buildings that surrounded the large courtyard.

It's like walking into a rainbow, she thought for the thousandth time. Delight slowed her pace. She stopped at the first large vat. Arms of the women tending the first copper cauldron were dyed as deep a yellow as the silk they stirred.

"Hai, you are well? You have enough yellow-crocus powder? Yes? Good." Faina said, moving on through cobalt blues, spring greens and magenta hues of kettles, cloth and women, until she came at last to the far side of the courtyard. There the women were standing around, gossiping and giggling.

"Well, I guess I don't need to ask if the murex shell dye arrived...how many days have you been idle?"

"Only yesterday and now today, Coordinating Mistress!"

"'Sky! D'you think I can't see? Your arms are person-colored, not purple! So. At least a week, I'd wager. Why didn't you get word to me sooner? We've a large order to fill for the flagmaker. The Dragon Boat

Festival is coming up soon and, in addition to Grand Canal boats, every little river skiff will be flying some sort of flag!"

"We didn't think..."

"I know, it's not your job. To think. What will the Guildmaster say? Well, until I locate those shells, you girls help with the vermilion vats. I'll be back tomorrow."

She ducked under a line of silks and into another alley that wound a circuitous route around a high wall in the center of Kuo. Faina had never been allowed on the other side of that wall. Only the Baron of Kuo, his family and retainers passed between the stout wooden doors. Loiterers and little children lingered around the gates, waiting for an entourage of privileged folk to come or go, for they sometimes threw bits of cash into the soft dust for them to scramble after.

Faina scarcely noticed them as she hurried by. But *she* was noticed. And followed. Like a trained dog, a nondescript man left the gate. A silent shadow, he fell in behind her.

Faina came to the main market square where even at this early hour, men and women were buying and selling. As Kuo was a post-road town, the market was larger and more varied than the population would have merited ordinarily. Faina threaded her way between laden camels and donkeys and tall-wheeled wheelbarrows.

A fisherman, his yoked baskets filled with tame cormorants on one side, their catch from the river far below on the other, swung his pole sideways in order to miss her. And in so doing, came around just in time to hit her follower a glancing blow on his head. The man fell beneath a stand heavy with tubers and gourds that tumbled over him.

Faina hurried on, slowing only when a pungent smell caught her attention. She stopped beside a traveler who was seated on a rug with his wares in front of him. Joints of bamboo, standing at attention like rows of tubular guards, held *dragon brain* aromatic camphor crystals of Baros, from far southern seas.

The aroma enveloped and beguiled Faina's senses.

"A pinch of auspicious dragon-brain to add to the pretty maiden's love-seed?"

"I can't. I have nothing much of worth."

"No suitors? That's hard to believe of one with hair like the sun! Yang feng, you need to cure evil vapors in your heart perhaps?"

"I have only a bit of silk."

"Yes? How much?" The trader looked up eagerly.

"Only half a *man's-day length,* but it's from one of the best guilds. Would that be enough to buy a little dragon's brain?" Faina replied, not betraying any particular of the silk's origin.

"For you, pretty one?" the man smiled, teeth white in his dark, wind-toughened face, "I suppose I could manage that. Since trading is slow this morning."

He took a bit of paper from his bag, sprinkled half a handful of the precious Baros camphor into it, gave it a twist and passed it to Faina.

She, in turn, pulled some red silk, almost as long as her arm, from her sleeve, and gave it to him. She tucked her purchase into her other sleeve, smiled and walked away.

Her smile left the traveling man dreaming of pillow delights and cool nights as he sat in the hot dust of Kuo's marketplace.

SUMMER LIGHTNING FLICKERED ITS EMPTY THREAT AGAINST A CINNABAR SKY as twilight spread itself across the land. As Faina walked, she unwound her hair and let the evening breeze ruffle through it. Slowly, savoring the end of the day's heat and activities, she crossed an arched bridge, looked down into the pool below and saw a man, bent over, standing in the shallows. She stopped to watch him.

The water around him was stained black-blue like the tattered ends of his shirt and rolled-up sleeves. His grey hair was braided in one thin pigtail that lay in a curve around the hump between his broad shoulders. He whistled a merry melody through his teeth as he took dripping seedlings from a wooden bucket and plunged them deep into the water.

"Camel? What're you doing down there?" Faina asked.

"Faina? Well, you see I'm experimenting with these lotus plants. Do come down here so I don't have to crane my neck to see you, it's not good for my old bones."

"You aren't old, Camel." She replied. "And I'm not going to come down there and ruin my skirt with whatever it is you've put in the water. What is it, anyway?"

"Indigo. It's indigo. And I've soaked the seeds and let them sprout in the dye. Now don't ask why, as I'm sure you're about to, Miss Curiosity. I'm trying to develop a *blue* lotus flower for His Majesty's garden…and this may just do it."

"I've never seen a blue lotus, Camel,"

"No. Neither has anyone else, but there are stories of blue lotus blooming on a great river east of Samarkand. I saw a painting of one that the baron had been given, up at the house, and I said to myself, Camel Kuo, you can do that," he straightened and stretched his back. "So that's what I'm doing. What are *you* doing, eh?"

"I came to see *you.*" Faina said simply.

"And I'm glad you did…missed you this past week, I did."

"It's been so hot, and I've had such a lot of things to do!"

"And you're a wonderfully responsible young woman. Not surprising the guildmaster loads so much of his work onto your slender shoulders." He emptied the buckets and sloshed up onto the path. "Come, let's go sit in the garden and have a cup of tea together."

"*Real* tea, Camel?"

"Real tea, dear one, with the first of my rose-cheeked peaches this year. But you mustn't tell anyone…there aren't enough to send to the court yet. They mustn't know that I enjoy the first fruits myself. With a special friend, that is," he smiled down at her.

"Oh, Camel, dear Camel, you make me happy."

"Do I now? That's good. I'd like to always make you happy, fairy-girl. I could feed you on peaches and moonbeams and mother-of-pearl until you were immortal…like me!" His laughter spilled out of his chest like spring water. Faina's laughter joined his.

Rejoicing in each other's company, they walked into the evening, arms intertwined.

38
A Hsun Chou Royal Progress: A River God And Camel Kuo

"PROGRESS? THEY CALL THIS SNAIL'S PACE, PROGRESS?" Batu grumbled. "I made more progress crawling around my mother's ger!"

"No, Batu, this isn't just going somewhere, this is *A Progress, a hsun-shou—hsun* meaning, "to follow a road"—*shou,* "to shepherd". Literally, the king goes along the roads to guard and shepherd his people on behalf of heaven, you see," Tse Tsien moved Bagatur closer to her uncle's horse so he'd be able to hear her without shouting over the cacophony around them.

Kao Tsung, riding on her other side, chimed in, "It w-w-wouldn't do to hurry our p-p-progress too quickly. Hurrying would only lead the p-people to fear some calamity, going quickly would deny them the chance of merit—for not having had ample time to observe, and possibly have audience with, the Son of Heaven."

"And all these people and animals and carriages, Tam…er, Tsien! There are tens of hundreds and that's not including the groups of musicians and acrobats and Tengri knows who-all that I'm not even aware of! Altogether we must cover this post road for thirty li or more!"

"I know, but this is actually only a small portion of the court—the essentials, so to speak." She smiled at his incredulous expression.

Batu, Kao Tsung, and Tse Tsien rode at the end of a full complement of palace guardsmen well to the front of the winding, motley cavalcade. Behind them, carried in ornate sedan chairs, came men of the three central ministries: the Secretariat, the Chancellery and the Department of State Affairs—forty-five men in all, accompanied by their advisors, aides and secretaries. Slaves, who carried the rippling tall, triangular flags that identified each group, marched alongside.

Following them were musicians and acrobats turning occasional cartwheels or flips on the hard-packed dirt. The sound of wether drums, cymbals and spinning spindles of bells, created a holiday mood. Because it was summer, the joyful color of red predominated wherever possible in the clothes and flags, saddle blankets and bridles of those in the parade.

Next, the officer in charge of imperial carriages led undulating lines of sweepers, purifiers and fan bearers. The sweepers brushed unworthy detritus from the path of the emperor, swept the way clean and pristine from coarse material matter dropped by animals, plants or other persons. The purifiers, uniformly yellow from head to toe, broadcast powdered turmeric from bags slung across their shoulders, thereby intensifying and purifying the color of the citron-yellow road they traveled toward Loyang.

Then came standard bearers, six in all, two men on small horses harnessed with a framework between them which held the imperial scarlet and gold vertical flag, twenty *ch'ih* in height, embroidered with a writhing dragon that grasped real pearls in its five-toed claws. Two foot bearers on either side carried slightly smaller flags of the emperor's family lineage.

Several rows of men marched with round, vermilion fans, wider than a tall man's arm span, waving them in unison. Then, four lines of four men, signifying the four directions of power, came carrying enormous fans made from k'ung sparrow tails whose "eyes" glowed purple, viridian and ultramarine in the sun.

The squared-off tops of the magic-eyed fans were held no higher than the base of a wide platform they preceded. This palanquin, carried by a *true number* of nine stalwart men on each side, was covered with gold leaf, carpeted with rare cherry-red carpets from Serindia, and shaded by enormous, tiered and frilled umbrellas. Be-ribboned posts at each corner held his majesty's jessed and hooded hunting falcons.

In the center, under the largest umbrella, His Most Luminous Majesty Tai Tsung, sat on satin cushions of a carved, red sanderswood chair. Around him, several dark-skinned dwarfs, dressed in the Turkish style of baggy satin pants and embroidered vests, waved ostrich plume fans incessantly and ineffectively. Two young women, dark hair arranged in intricate swirls and braids, sat behind them and played soothing melodies on lute and harp.

Eight more fan bearers, then a restless group of young people, dressed in the manner of half a dozen countries, accompanied the bawdy crown prince Li Cheng Chien, directly behind Tai Tsung's palanquin. Occasionally one of them would canter his horse forward for a few minutes, then drop back. They were noisy, using the procession as an excuse for drinking and roistering, ignoring the Code of Moderation laid down by Confucius.

A few dozen sedan chairs and litters, silken curtains maintaining the modesty of the wives and concubines within, lurched along. Young children, their black eyes avid with curiosity, peered out at the passing countryside from the safety of their mothers' swaying boudoirs.

More guardsmen, servants, cooks and supplicants followed. Extra horses, camels, mules and donkeys, laden with heavy packs of supplies, were herded along together. A straggling contingent of a few hundred soldiers brought up the rear.

Flags of many colors and shapes flew at intervals along the whole column so that countrymen from the distance of many li could watch the procession as it wound its stately way in and out of hills along the high escarpment of the Huang-ho River.

Tse Tsien and her alert companions left the procession and rode across fields of blowing wheat to the cliff edge of a deep gorge. Far below, the Huang-ho frothed, a roiling, ochre-colored current racing seaward between rock walls into which tow-paths had been cut.

Below them, they saw a line of about a dozen men, yoked together by bamboo and hemp cables, struggling along the narrow tow-path as they strained to pull a barge, heavily loaded with salt, upstream.

As they watched, one of the ant-sized men stumbled and fell over the edge. The other men fell into disarray, apparently unable to regain their balance or pull him back. Like dominos tied to a string, one by one they flew off the rock ledge and floated silently, down and down. The barge, loosed from its earth-tether, increased its speed backward. Long poles sprouted from its sides. Tilting wildly in the rapids, it caromed against canyon walls and past boulders until it vanished from their sight around a bend in the river.

"All life is fleeting, is it not, Kao Tsung?" Tsien turned to him, her eyes bright with tears. "This river pass is Changan's curse and its blessing. A curse because of the extreme difficulty of transporting goods and produce into the capital—a blessing because it's a natural barrier that protects the city from invaders. At least it has done so, my tutors tell me, in past, more warlike, dynasties.

"You've really been absorbed by this life and this country, haven't you, Talima-sha?"

"Tse Tsien," she corrected absently, turning Bagatur back to the procession.

"Of c-course she has!" Kao Tsung sputtered, "Tsien is a fine student, you know, and my father has filled her hours with state political affairs. He, like I, find it comforting to talk to one-without-political-status, a person who has no outside allegiances to speak of." He smiled and patted her arm as if in reassurance.

Batu looked surprised, but said nothing.

Riding back into the procession, they noticed a cloud of billowing dust caused by a heavy, country carriage rattling toward them, followed by men on mules and horseback.

"Looks like a local lord is coming for an audience, Batu. I'd better ask if the emperor wants me, but in any case, I've some work to finish for him before we reach Loyang. You'll be all right? Kao Tsung, will you please see that my uncle enjoys the afternoon? There are a few mon-barbarians from the west I think by their dress, in the prince's retinue. But be careful, Batu, Li Cheng Chien is powerful, and nasty."

The two men watched her ride away. From the back, with her hair hidden beneath a broad-brimmed hat, she looked like any of the noble ladies, except for the way she rode.

"I should see to my duties also, I'm sorry," Kao Tsung excused himself and rode off.

Batu rode on thoughtfully, enjoying the solitary quiet after weeks of being in the midst of new friends, new scenes, new ideas and the hulaballoo within the palace as preparations were made for this ponderous, majestic *huan-shou.*

"How quiet, how sure of herself my young niece has become," he murmured to himself. His horse's ears pricked up. "The loss of Pirjhan seems to have crystallized something in her...there's a certain hardness there beneath her vulnerability. I wonder what kind of changes she'll make in our lives when she comes home. My brother's grown much older...almost as if she took part of his strength with her when she left. Jalco's a good man though. He's earned the approval of most of the cup-companions...will he willingly relinquish his place at the Chagan's side to his half-sister if she returns? I wonder..."

FIRES BURNED BENEATH HANGING KETTLES IN THE HASTILY ERECTED CAMP. Flags now flew in front of silken tents that sheltered those within from the harsh afternoon sun. A large octagonal cover, embroidered with dragons and phoenixes, provided shade for Emperor Tai Tsung and his cabinet ministers to sit, according to rank, in chairs of varying heights and colors.

Opposite them, the local lord, his magistrate, town chief and town treasurer sat on mats. Low tables had magically appeared on which trays of sweetmeats, jujubes, sticky buns and tea were spread out—a gift of welcome from the village to His Gracious Luminosity. Three bolts of colored silk and one of taffeta lay on the rug.

More villagers, holding the horses, stood in the sun beside their liege lord's carriage. Some of these were elder citizens wearing wide, conical straw hats. One was a black-robed Taoist priest, another, a tall hunchback who held the bridle of a white mule.

Batu rode into the camp, gave his horse to a passing groom and joined the group of guardsmen standing near the makeshift audience hall. He saw Tse Tsien, dressed in formal court silks, sitting well back from the royal chair.

The emperor was speaking, "So, Baron Kuo, what is the state of your town this year? Your people are industrious? Happy? Your revenues better than last quarter?"

Bowing deeply, the baron replied, "Generally speaking, the people of the town of Kuo are productive and happy, Gracious Majesty. I am proud to report that we have produced more and finer silk than ever before. But our revenues are inadequate, I'm told."

"And why is that, Treasurer of Kuo? Why inadequate?" asked the emperor.

"We are poor, Great Luminous One, because of the River God."

"The River God? Explain."

"Well, actually, it's the *marriage* of the River God that impoverishes us each year."

"Mother of Lightning! Are you still practicing that ancient ritual? I didn't know anyone in this enlightened age indulged in that outworn custom!" The emperor spoke bluntly.

"If I may speak?" said the magistrate and, at the emperor's nod, continued in a rather high, sing-song voice, "It has been our immemorial right to collect extra taxes to finance the *necessary* sacrifice to our great Huang-ho—so that the River God, in his anger at not having a wife to sweeten his lonely days, there at the bottom of his watery kingdom, does not cause the water to overflow its banks and drown us all! Then, too, the maiden selected as his bride must be dressed beautifully, fed well, catered to for a whole week before we release her raft to the River God. And all that costs a great deal of cash, you see, and..."

"The point, Magistrate, the point of your story?"

"Well, we collect a great many taxes," he whined, "but it's not enough to do..." he gestured to his two civic companions, "what we would *like* to do, and therefore we have to levy more taxes and the people don't like that very well, and so we thought..."

"Yes, you thought?"

"We thought Your Majesty might remit our village taxes this year, so that we might...not be so poor!" He finished triumphantly.

"Why don't you just stop this superstitious practice?"

"Oh, we couldn't do *that!"* "The River God would send a flood!" "It's never been done!" A chorus of objections came from the village headmen. The baron shrugged his shoulders in mock helplessness.

"I think it unlikely that the River God, or any other god to tell the truth, could cause the waters to rise over these cliffs," murmured Tai Tsung. "But since you are unwilling or unable to discontinue this custom, I will personally attend the next 'wedding' in your village and see what I can bring about in the way of an equitable solution. Until then, this quarter's taxes will be half of the usual levy. Make a note, Secretary."

"Wonderful, Most Brilliant of Monarchs! We will tell the sorceresses. They'll be most pleased!"

"Sorceresses, too—will wonders never cease! What other business do we have today, Baron? Crimes to be adjudicated? Rewards to outstanding citizens for acts of heroism or diligence?"

"It's been quiet in Kuo since your representative was last here. No crimes to speak of, or at any rate none serious enough to require your attention. But I have a man with me today who has served the empire in a most auspicious way. I'm not learned in his field and might be inaccurate, so I'd like to have him tell you of his work in his own words. May I call him forward?"

"Please do."

"Camel? Camel Kuo, His Most Luminous Eminence would hear of your experiments." The baron beckoned to the waiting hunchback. "Most Illustrious Lord, this is your Official Gardener of the Forest, Camel Kuo."

Camel Kuo carried a basket of rosy-cheeked fruit in his large hands. He knelt, touching his forehead on the rug as he held the fruit out before him. The emperor clapped his hands. Camel Kuo sat back on his heels.

"What is this you have for us?"

"Fruits of the earth for Your Most Divine Power," he said, "These are peaches, Most Noble Sir, peaches from our own trees, not those that arrive, half dried from months of travel across the great desert between us and their native land. These are like the peaches from Samarkand, grown right here in Kuo!" Camel's smile was that of a fond father for his favorite child.

"Indeed! How was this accomplished?"

"A year or two ago, I asked a trader to bring me limbs from the tree that bears peaches. He did, and I grafted them to our hardiest persimmon trees. They flourished. And this spring, they flowered. Here are the first fruits, in time to honor Your Majestic Presence. I have an idea, too, how we might improve the yield of wheat in adjoining farms. I've been growing some in controlled conditions with good results and I'd like to know if any blue lotus flowers have been brought into the court recently because I..."Camel rambled on enthusiastically as the emperor and his ministers listened with interest. Here was a man who dreamed—and all his contrivances were for life rather than for personal gain.

"Marvelous! Quite an admirable treasure you have, Baron! I'm impressed by his accomplishments as well as his aspirations. A most unusual man! He shall be rewarded." The emperor opened the bag that hung from his belt and removed a ring set with lapis lazuli and pearls. "This blue stone came from the land close to where your peaches came from, Camel of Kuo, it's a talisman of my respect and pleasure in what you have done, of who you are, actually.

"Now, Baron, have we concluded our business? I see that a modest meal has been readied while we spoke. Let's adjourn to the dining pavilion, shall we?"

One of the emperor's servants caught up with Camel Kuo and engaged him in conversation as they walked. "You seem like a clever man," he began.

"Clever? No." Camel replied.

"Well, at any rate, a knowledgeable man. I'd like to ask you something—would you by any chance, know of a young girl with hair the color of sunshine, who lives in your village?"

"Why do you ask?"

"Oh, no particular reason, but there'd be money in it if you should happen on her and send me a message. My name's Pei."

"Who wants to know? Who would pay?"

"I can't tell you that, old man. I'll pay—that's all you need to know."

"No girl of Kuo has hair like sunshine." Camel looked worried.

"No? Well, do yourself a favor, Camel, ask around. Her name is Faina and somebody important is looking for her."

"I know of no one *born* in our village, by that name." Camel answered quietly.

"Just remember, she's worth money to you, and remember me, Pei." He called over his shoulder as he turned to join friends.

"I'll remember." A troubled Camel mounted his mule and rode back to Kuo alone.

39
TELLING STORIES, DRAGONS AND DREAMING

"I'M SORRY TO SEE YOU LIKE THIS, PEACH FLOWER," said Tai Tsung, "What do you think brought on the asthma this time?" The emperor rode Scarlet Cherpadh beside her during this quiet country section of their trip, a welcome change from village ceremonials. Silk ribbons of imperial yellow, plaited into his horse's mane and tail, rippled as they rode along in the midst of the winding cortege.

"The dust…or the cool wind, Sire. I'm sorry…to trouble you." Tsien spoke in short bursts as her ragged breathing allowed.

"You've been taking your medicine, haven't you?" He leaned over and brushed stray hairs back from her forehead. "Was the cardamom fresh? Not the black, local cardamom, but white, or even bastard cardamom from Java?"

"I really…don't know…I just take…what…Mistress Feng gives me… I'm sure she adds ground ginger though, for it…burns my tongue." Her voice trailed off into the rattle of her breathing. She rode hunched over, head down into the cold wind.

"Well, that's good, for ginger opens all internal passages. I wonder if she included orpiment and ginseng? Those superior drugs would build your strength.

"The wind was even worse yesterday…I thought at the time you might be better off in a sedan chair. I'm most concerned to see you like this, dear child. Would it help if we made camp early today?"

"Thank you, Sire…I'm quite content…riding a sedan chair…would only make me…feel worse."

"Dust everywhere—the early morning rain was welcome. But I can still feel dust between my teeth. I'll grind them down to stumps at this rate!"

Tse Tsien smiled at the idea.

"You laugh! While our Mistress Feng is concocting that vile, but effective, brew of hers—deer's velvet, fagara pepper and ephedra, I believe—I'll try to take your mind away with stories, as we used to, remember?"

"Oh, Sire…t'would be…lovely, but…"

"No buts, young lady. Now, shall we begin at the beginning of the world?"

Tse Tsien smiled, but did not reply as she was concentrating on drawing breath into her lungs, slowly, evenly, desperately.

"In the beginning," Tai Tsung stroked his pointed beard with his right hand, "P'an Kuo came into being with complete understanding of the knowledge necessary to put the universe in order. As he floated around in space, he collected enormous blocks of granite from which he intended to hew the Sun, the Moon, the Stars, and the Planets. Now this was a rather tall order even for P'an Ku! So He called to Chaos. The Black Warrior Tortoise came forth. Next, the Azure Dragon flew to His side, and lastly the third, but by no means least of the great supernatural beings, the Phoenix or Vermilion Bird, came forth. Then the work began."

He turned to look at her. "As P'an Kuo and the other three labored, some say for eighteen thousand years, the earth, in its great green-and-gold glory, spread out vastly. The heavens, in all *their* splendor, arched above, complete with clouds and wind and rainbows. But the heavens were without light and the earth was flat and barren."

"Like the…desert we crossed… the Takla Makan," she murmured.

"Yes, like that great sand sea," he agreed. "Now while P'an Kuo was laboring, he was growing. He grew nine ch'ih a day until his work was done. Then he died and his death completed the universe. As his soul migrated from bright air into fecund darkness, he became his opposite. He became *her,* the Compassionate Mother. The complementary forces of yang and yin came into existence. And this completion began the motion between them that enriches us to this day.

"Now while this was happening," the emperor continued, "the Tortoise, the Dragon, and the Phoenix were creating all the swimming and flying and grazing creatures within their own bodies. When the world was ready, all the animals and birds and reptiles and insects were born from these great three."

"What about...men and women...and children?"

"We are all children of the Great Mother, the Mother of Lightning that you have no doubt heard me appeal to at times, possibly inappropriately." He leaned over and rubbed between her shoulders. "Any better?"

"Not yet"

A servant ran up beside them carrying a wrapped pot and small porcelain bowl. He bowed very low and passed it to the emperor.

"Ah, good. Here's that infusion that our illustrious court physician has made for you. A wicked smell, I know, sweet one," he said, pouring a steaming cupful. "Here you are, drink it down, all of it."

Tsien grimaced as she sipped the inky liquid. She finished it and passed the cup back.

"That should make it better soon. Now, where were we?"

"People."

"The best part. In the body of P'an Kuo, there lived parasites. When he died, these same parasites were penetrated by the wind's vital seed, its *ch'i* -and from this union were born human beings!"

She sighed. "Tell me please...of the phoenix."

"The Phoenix is Empress of Birds, the most honored of all the feathered ones. Her long tail sweeps the world. As she flies you can hear the music her feathers make, the music of the spheres, rather like the breathy sound of reed pipes or flutes, I imagine."

"I wish...to fly like that...like Phoenix...I *will* fly...I *am* Phoenix!" She tossed her head and sat a little straighter in the saddle.

Tai Tsung smiled and said, "Such strong metal you are—like Venus, the grand silver metal star! You've become that last star of morning, first of the evening—my Venus, my *Nahid*. I wish my sons had half your mettle."

"I can begin to breathe again! Thank you for sending for Mistress Feng...she's worked her miracles again. How good the earth smells!" Her smile was as sudden sunshine breaking through clouds.

"You gladden this old warrior's heart, Flower. But it's not *magic* that Mistress Feng practices. That would be a Depravity, subject to the laws governing any of the Ten Abominations. No, she simply demonstrates her superior medical knowledge."

"I'm not sure that I care *how* she does it, only that it works."

"No, no! The ends do not justify the means, Tsien—if the means are against the Tao." He chided gently. "But I'm glad you're feeling more yourself. Now, I see your uncle coming to inquire after you, so I'll go to confer with the Honorable Wei Cheng as he requested. I sometimes wonder if the power of an emperor is worth the bondage to one's responsibilities—but then, this is the life I've been given, and I have no choice, really." He put his arm across her shoulder briefly, then wheeled his red-roan stallion and rode away.

"Hatou, Talima-sha!" greeted Batu as he reined in beside her. "You're looking pleased with the day!"

"Hatou, Batu. Just pleased to be part of it, not struggling for breath."

"I don't remember you as having the breathing sickness—is this something new?"

"It began during my *black time*...after Pirjhan's death. At first it wasn't too bad, or it was a small part of my difficulties. But now, if I'm ill or tired, or if air is thick with dust as it was before the rain yesterday, it gets much worse. But it's no great matter. What have you been doing?"

"Not much. I've played a few games of gho and *six winds*—lost the pocketful of cash the chamberlain gave me!" He chuckled. "But I listened in on an interesting audience the emperor had with some headmen of a town we passed."

"Yes, that was a troublesome problem, wasn't it? Well, by the time we reach Loyang, it will be time for the Dragon Boat Festival. I know you'll enjoy that."

"What happens?"

"I've never been to one, but I'm told there are races up and down the canal, fireworks and parties—a popular festival. It will be a time for the emperor and local officials to work together."

"I was riding with some of Prince Cheng's friends when you and His Majesty were together. You were so deeply absorbed in each other, you probably didn't notice, but there were many in this long cavalcade that sent black looks your way. You should be more careful, my brother's daughter, not to inspire jealousy from these hat-and-girdle folk."

"'Sky, Batu! We were only telling stories!"

"It looked like more than stories. It looked like..."

"Don't be silly, Batu, he was just trying to take my mind off my sickness until the medicine took effect. The emperor and I are like a beloved teacher and loyal student. We are *never* intimate."

"Don't be cross with me! I only thought it was worth a warning."

Batu changed the subject abruptly. "Can you tell me why dragons are so important? Seems to me that dragons are a part of any and every thing in Chian!"

"Ah, dragons!" She drank from the skin flask she carried and offered it to Batu. "There are so many kinds. The first dragon was the Azure Dragon who corresponds with our Everlasting Sky." Her voice assumed a measured, story-teller's rhythm, "It is said, that with the coming of spring, the Azure Dragon emerges from all the waters of the earth. You can hear its voice rumbling in the hurricane that scatters old leaves in the forests, quickening the earth for growth. This dragon's breath comes from its mouth as clouds or sometimes as fire or water.

"There are nine different dragons." She counted off on her fingers. *"Lung* dragons live in the sky, have beards that grow from a pearl on their chins and are supposed to be deaf—probably from hearing the thunder of their voices too close!"

Batu smiled indulgently.

"The *li* species are hornless and live in the ocean. The *chaio* live in mountains and marshes."

"D'you believe dragons are real?"

"Yes, I do. For instance, if the Dragon Keeper isn't consulted as to the whereabouts of dragon-path underground energy fields and a building is erected that blocks that flow...disasters occur! It even happened to the emperor—he had to tear down a nearly completed palace outside Changan just because a keeper had misread the signs! That keeper was rightly strangled as I recall." She shook her head and patted Shira's withers.

"Some people even believe that amber is caused from drops of dragon's blood that fall on sand—but that's known to be untrue. The most fascinating thing about dragons is their variety. *Chao-feng* loves danger—its likeness is carved on the eaves of temples, to do battle with and ward off, evil spirits. *Pi-kan* is a fierce and quarrelsome, one-horned dragon, carved on prison gates because it loves to defend the law. *Ch'iu-niu* loves music, so is carved on musical instruments. There are thousands of craftsmen, Batu, who carve only dragons their whole life!

"River dragon, *Pi-hsi,* is fond of literature, so he's found on stone tablets, memorials and scrolls. If any dragon symbolizes the emperor, it's five-toed and carries the Pearl of Wisdom in one claw.

"Then there's *Pa-hsia*, who can support heavy weights, so he's carved at the base of stone monuments. *Chih-wen* is fond of water, so you'll find him on bridges or on the roofs of buildings to guard against fire, and *P'u-lao* is carved on the tops of gongs and bells because he's had so much practice calling loudly to his sea-companion, the whale." She laughed.

"You'll see dragons a-plenty, Batu, when the Dragon Boat Festivals are held later this summer! There'll be dragon boat races and plays—so much dragon-ness that you could pick your teeth with their claws!"

They rode through the day, telling stories to each other, remembering other times in another land.

It rained again that night and Wu Chao Tse Tsien dreamed her dragon dream for the first time in many years.

But this time, as she flew through the Everlasting Sky on that great beast's back, it was not exhilarating. It was terrifying. This time, the dream was more intense, the colors more vivid, the sky more vast, the rarified air harder to breathe. This time, the dragon, in its slow-moving way, turned its head around, gold scales smoothly sliding along its arched neck and—cold fire blazing from emerald eyes into her heart—*looked* at her.

And that made all the difference.

40
CONVERSATIONS: A CLEVER PLAN: PRINCE CHENG IS OUTRAGEOUS

AT FIRST LIGHT, WU TSE TSIEN LEANED ON THE AFT RAILING of the royal barge, idly watching the eddies and swirls of muddy water in their wake. She heard the soldiers chanting as they hauled the unwieldy boat along the broad canal.

She breathed deeply, gratefully, of the rain-washed air as she thought of the past few days. They had come into Loyang at night so that greeting ceremonies could be kept to a minimum before they settled into their quarters on the royal barge.

And a good thing, too, for the rains have begun, and a more bedraggled group of people would be hard to imagine. No one could have guessed we were the imperial court!

Sinuous mist danced across the surface of the water, dissolving into the first rays of sunlight. Azure kingfishers, the color of a summer's sky, flashed by. Black-winged cormorants were at work for their masters, dipping and diving after fish.

On the shore, carved-stone willow trees, impervious to change, stood side by side with pliant, real willows. Granite, rectangular stairs, embellished with ivy and watercress, worn down in the middle from centuries of sandaled feet, led up the banks to small, thatched-roof homes.

She waved to a small child, who sat in the doorway of one such dwelling. He wore only a carefully patched shirt and a merry smile as he threw grain to red and white chickens on the grey stone steps.

The deck on which she stood was three stories high off the water, just beneath the fourth and highest level, which housed Emperor Tai Tsung alone. Alone, that is, with the addition of his physician, his personal secretary, the Earl of Shaanxi, Fang Hsuan-ling, and several dozen almost invisible servants.

Advisors to the emperor, the dukes, Wei Cheng, Wang Kuei and Chang-san Wu-chi, with their families, as well as Kao Tsung, who had left his quarrelsome wife and children back at the palace; Prince Cheng Chien, as heir, with his favorite concubines, were assigned the most luxurious suites on this third level.

The emperor had been kind enough to invite Duke Wu Shih-kuo and his wife, Wu Chao Tse Tsien's Tai Yuan parents, on this excursion, reminding all and sundry of her notable, First Surname connections. Although their quarters were appropriately smaller, as befitted a country noble, they still were on the third level, and that was a significant honor in itself.

On the first and second decks, palace guards, musicians, lesser ministers, and court functionaries shared much smaller rooms. Servants were crowded below decks on tiered bunks. The rest of the entourage, and the entire kitchen, were housed on four smaller vessels.

Festivities had continued late the night before despite a torrential downpour. Paper lanterns hung drunkenly under dripping, upturned eaves. The court still slept. Tsien's guards still huddled sleepily at her door. Even raucous village roosters failed to rouse the sleeping populace of this floating palace.

She felt a shower of pale pink peony petals drift over her and looked up to see where they had come from. Tai Tsung smiled down at her and, with his finger to his lips, gestured for silence. He threw the peony stems overboard and beckoned for her to join him.

"Dawn always makes me feel like a boy again," he greeted her as she climbed the wide curving staircase that led to the top deck. "As if anything were possible in this best of worlds. Good morning!"

"Good morning, Sire. I enjoyed my early morning shower!" She smiled mischievously and clasped his outstretched hand with both of her own.

"Peony petals...long life and felicity, Peach Flower. May they ever be yours." He led the way aft again, where they sat on pillowed wicker chairs. "My joints feel the damp this morning."

"But you are well?"

"Oh yes, but when you have as many old battle scars as I have, when you've ridden your body as hard as I have for so many years, so many campaigns, well, it has a right to complain." He rubbed his right knee gently with the palm of his hand. "You never *feel* old, you know, or at least I never have. Only my face in the mirror looks more wrinkled."

"My father said things like that."

"You miss him very much, don't you?"

"I've been thinking of him more lately "

"Have you decided to return to your homeland?"

"No, I don't know why it's so hard. My life there, another world. My father must be getting old though, and my half-brother may not be..."

Tai Tsung sighed and shifted in his chair as if to stand in stirrups and find a more comfortable position in his customary saddle. "Yes, those are considerations of the head of state...who will carry on as you see yourself grow older?"

"But *you* are not old, you have more energy than all the rest of us! You'll reign forever!"

"Hardly," he smiled, and looked out over the city roofs to violet silhouettes of mountains against a brightening sky. "I've never really minded the idea of getting older. After all, that's a process that begins at birth, but I do mind the idea of *being* old. It's the lack of control, I suppose, or the death of dreams. I do so love life, Flower. I love righteousness, also, and if I can't have both, I'll choose righteousness—and that means securing the happiness of my people. Look there below us, see that woman and her children?"

From a shallow raft at the water's edge, a woman, wooden spoon in hand, looked up at the sky and watched as the sun rose over barren hills. Frayed, bamboo mats tied over long poles held fishing nets and river-washed clothes. A partly sunken skiff alongside held bundles of firewood and dozens of downy ducklings.

The woman's back was bent as if she were old, but her face was unlined. Her hair was long and thick. She had stopped to watch the dawn, to listen to the dabbling of ducks, then returned to finish spooning hot millet cereal into bowls that lay before her on scrubbed, wooden boards. Seven barefoot children waited patiently for their breakfast and watched the royal barge glide by.

"The simplicity of that woman's life is perfect, perfect." He sighed, patted Tsien's shoulder affectionately and sat down. "That is the harmony we, as rulers, must protect. Ever since those disastrous battles in Koguryo last year, I've felt death nearer. Felt her chilly breath on my neck." He shivered and shook his head as if to shake away an unwanted presence. "No more wars. We cannot continue to spill the blood of our wealth, our men, on foreign soil. We're united the length and breadth of the land. Now I must, I *will* secure the blessings of heaven for my people in order to perpetuate hsien chou, my True Vision."

"Will you perform the grand Feng and Shan ritual?"

"Fang Hsun-ling and Wang Kuei have again urged me to do so. It seems to be the right time, unlike those previous years that I felt unworthy to engage in such solemn rites. After all, who am I to thrust out my belly in front of the whole village?" The heavy silk of his robe rippled over his belly as he laughed.

"It would indeed be memorable. Only three or four emperors, since The Beginning, have attempted it. It's really the most effective way I can think of to acknowledge the many blessings that heaven and earth have showered on this Tang Dynasty—a way to repay the gods. But my most trusted advisors advise against it."

"Why?"

"Financial considerations mostly. The treasury is in a rather desperate state. The Feng and Shan would further dangerously deplete our reserves apparently—with not enough cash for the large jade tablets, much less the necessary new palaces."

"But, Sire!" She poured pale fragrant tea into his cup. "I see so much wealth! The crops are plentiful, the people productive. I see only balance and harmony. How could there be an economic problem?"

"To begin with, the Koguryo war was far more costly than we'd anticipated. Then there are the ongoing monumental expenses of maintaining troops along our borders, so many thousands of li from the capital—and Hrom's yearly gold payment for the silk they bought has been delayed, or lost, somewhere on the long Silk Road."

The royal barge continued to move majestically along the canal, pulled along by uniformed men. Small boats sculled rapidly out of the way. Rafts, piled with produce and propelled by long sweeps, maneuvered awkwardly to one side.

"In addition, revenues from household taxes have declined," he continued. "The registry shows many millions fewer households than five years ago. I suspect that local officials are simply not doing an adequate job of recording in their chous. Something must be done. As with most things, the cause of this problem is a multiple one, and like a many-headed dog, when you cut off one head, two more grow in its place."

"I have an idea—foolish, possibly, and I hesitate to propose it to Your Majesty."

"My dear, you would not believe how many preposterous ideas I hear in any one day—as many as a dozen before breakfast sometimes! Tell me."

"I thought we might sell imperial stable dung to farmers—for fertilizer. There's so much of it. I've seen hundreds of cartloads of it just dumped on the wild ground outside the city."

"Sell horse manure? What an unusual idea. Not one that anyone has proposed heretofore." Tai Tsung stroked his short beard and suppressed a smile. "Actually, it *might* be a source of revenue, a reliable one, certainly! Kapi, the stable master must conduct a survey of its feasibility. Thank you, that's the first practical suggestion I've been given.

"Now come, would you give this old warrior some happiness? Would you comb my hair, make it presentable for the day? No one does it quite as nicely as you do."

She blushed with pleasure. The peace of the misty morning drifted into the quiet room as Wu Tse Tsien softly, silently, combed, smoothed and braided the emperor's jet-black hair. *It's a small thing, really, but I do so love being close to him. I wish sometimes, I wish we could just go on like this forever, floating along, with no cares, no duties, no fears.*

"There you are, Sire! You're looking very proper!"

"I hear people stirring down below, I suppose we'd best be about the business of the day." Tai Tsung looked up at the sky, then stiffened his shoulders, stood up, and stretched.

"I promised my lady mother that I'd go with her to the baths this morning. She'll expect me to have a complete toilette and she does *not* like to be kept waiting!" She walked toward the door, then turned, "Excuse me, may I leave?"

"Go, go! Begone!" He clapped his hands. Three servants, thinking they had been summoned, appeared as if formed from the morning mist.

Dozens of empty sedan chairs lay in tilted profusion outside the wide, arched gate of the Loyang Baths. Their former occupants were inside the pavilion, either strolling through the maze of gardens, drinking tea on shaded porches or bathing in pools formed by natural hot springs. The hard-working men who had carried their sedan chairs to the outskirts of the city, lounged along the wall, telling stories, sleeping, often passing a long-stemmed pipe between themselves. Smoke wafted up through overhanging willows.

Wu Chao Tse Tsien, and her adoptive mother, Wu Yang-ssu, lifted their layered skirts as they stepped over the entrance stones into the welcome cool of the bathhouse. They could hear the sounds of children's laughter and the chatter of women's voices that echoed the murmur of nesting doves. On the far side of the great welcome hall, musicians played lilting melodies on flutes and lutes.

Through open, columned doorways, they could see children frolicking amongst the flowers. Little boys played at being warriors, riding stuffed horses, sparring with stick swords. Little girls played ring games and giggled as they swung on swings. Their mothers glided nearby like so many bright-winged butterflies, the trains of their diaphanous skirts sweeping the ground behind them.

"Daughter," sighed the Lady Wu Yang-ssu, "I'm so glad to get off that boat! What a pleasure to feel good solid earth under my feet! I tell you, boats are fine for fisher folk, but its seems to me an affectation to load everyone, and every *thing* onto a moving platform the size of a village!"

"I'm enjoying it," Tsien said, "it's simpler in many ways than life in Changan. And His Majesty needs the rest."

"That's all very well...I can see that might be an advantage... for him. But the amenities are poor, you'll admit."

Tsien smiled, thinking of the elaborate rooms, dozens of servants, exquisite meals and all the luxuries of their life on the Grand Canal barges. "I'm sure it's easier for you at home, in Tai Yuan, Lady Mother. Would you care for tea first or shall we go directly to the baths?"

"A blessed bath first, Tsien, tea later." She gestured imperiously to servants who bowed and went before them.

Ushered into changing rooms, they were given cotton wraps. They joined others walking along stone paths toward the steaming baths.

It was a somnolent and peaceful place. Large bamboo conduits poured water of varying temperatures from hot springs on the hill into tiled baths in which a dozen women could bathe. Some of the baths were cool and shallow. Mothers with very young children lay in these, suckling their babies, or swooshing the tepid water over their babies' golden bodies. The pools closest to where the springs poured out of the earth were hot enough to cook an egg. Only the most seasoned bathers attempted these. Wooden buckets of cooling water stood waiting.

Most of the women used the middling-hot, middle-sized pools. Wu Yang-ssu and her daughter chose one of these and let their robes fall to the floor where they were scooped up immediately and carried off.

Incense in long-legged bronze braziers, sent smoky fragrance into the air, but it was not strong enough to entirely mask the strong sulphur smell of the steaming pools.

"That smell seems strangely familiar, somehow," mused Tsien, as they slowly lowered their bodies into the hot water. "I can't remember why, but it makes me uneasy. Do you mind it, Lady Mother?"

"That rotten egg smell? No, it's not *too* strong."

Suddenly Talima *did* remember. She remembered being carried by Mazar Tagh past the boiling mud fields...the smell of rotten eggs, the terror and desperation of that time.

"Daughter! What is it? You are suddenly white as snow! Is anything wrong?"

There in the safety and comfort of these luxurious baths, Tse Tsien relived that experience. The memory, long held in locked silence, poured out in words. Finally, her words slowed.

"I wasn't sure whether or not I could do it, Mother. But I did, and Pirjhan, my Jhani." She began to cry as if there were no end to grief.

Yang-ssu held her and rocked her in the warm water just as other women rocked their babies in other pools.

A large, heavily veiled figure walked past them and stepped into the next bath without disrobing. Seconds later, several young women who had been in that pool, leaped out shrieking and pointing behind them. Eunuch guards came to investigate the commotion.

They looked into the water and saw nothing unusual except for the person who remained clothed—unusual in itself. Gradually the women stopped screaming and told the guards that they had been poked and pinched in their most private places right there in the bath! That it must have been that terrible old woman still sitting there!

The eunuchs politely asked that person, now the only one left in the bath, if she would please remove her veil and answer the accusations.

At that, the bather boiled out of the bath, tore off the concealing robe and began to laugh—a deep, male laugh. Complete chaos erupted. Women screamed, scrambled out of the baths and gathered their children as they tried to run across slick stones. For the bather was, quite definitely, a virile man, his manhood at attention as his belly jounced above it.

The eunuchs swarmed around him and half lifted him from the wet floor as they tried to hustle him away. His laughter turned instantly to rage. His face contorted, turned purple. Like a wounded bull he swung on the guards, knocked several into the huddled women, others into the hot water. His long mustaches flung drops of water off their tips. His eyes, under dark, scowling brows, blazed.

"Whores! Miscreants! Daughters of dogs! It was only a bit of fun. You should be honored that I, Prince Cheng, was interested in any of you!" He spat and staggered drunkenly toward the inner gate that led back to the men's baths. "Shit will be heaped on the graves of your ancestors. I'll see to it! You'll never..."

The eunuchs trailed after him, not knowing exactly what to do. When the crown prince violated women's privacy, created a public disturbance and was drunk and abusive as well, what rules applied?

"That is the noble crown prince?" Yang-ssu gasped.

"I'm afraid so," Tse Tsien replied. "He's not what you would call a *moderate* man."

"If he were *my* son, I'd have him flogged!" Yang-ssu said with tight-lipped asperity.

"Well, it's true that he often violates many of the rules of good conduct, but His Majesty feels that he'll grow out of his willful ways...in time"

"But he's *not a child.* He must be more than three decades at least!"

"Yes, something will have to change, I expect, before the emperor will feel comfortable turning the empire over to his son's violent mercies." She sighed as if the weight of these decisions were her own to bear.

"What about the second son, can't he...?"

"Kao Tsung? He's a sweet man, and intelligent, but he's just not interested in governing. He prefers books or polo. He spends nights with his eye glued to a telescope, living in the stars and planets that are more real to him, he says, than all the politics of court. He claims that his studies of astronomy give him power over man and nature, so why should he trouble himself with this petty world?"

"Gracious! I thought there were penalties against the study of astronomy as being a sort of black magic!"

"Only for the common folk, Lady Mother. Those restrictions don't apply to superior persons. But no, Kao Tsung wouldn't be a strong ruler. Essentially, he's a weak man, indecisive, though I'm very fond of him."

"Who does that leave for the succession?"

"Back to Prince Cheng. It's a problem."

"Couldn't His Majesty appoint one of Kao Tsung's sons by first wife Lady Wang, with one of his own advisors as regent?"

"That's a possibility. But he says that Lady Wang is too ambitious already, that her family is too numerous, too grasping. He fears she would connive to usurp all powers into her clan if a son of hers were to become emperor. The ministers are really divided on the subject, each one urging His Majesty to take a different course, usually dependent on their own family ties, unfortunately."

Four other women joined them in the bath at that moment, so confidential talk of state concerns turned to matters of purely feminine interest—food and fashions, men and children.

41
A Blue Lotus: Faina And Camel: Batu Hears A Newcomer

IN KUO, THE GARDEN WAS SWEET WITH THE SCENT OF NIGHT-BLOOMING FLOWERS. The full moon's radiance created a different world of strange shapes and mysterious shadows. Birds and beasts slept quietly in the trees, undisturbed by the two humans below.

Faina and Camel Kuo sat beneath a pippala tree beside a pool in which lotus buds gleamed in the moonlight.

"I love seeing you like this,"said Camel as he lifted strands of her hair, letting it float down over her shoulders. "Faerie girl, you look as though you were made of moonbeams."

"I love the lotus." Faina trailed her work-worn fingers in the pond, drawing circles around flat lotus leaves. "Before they open they look like little hands raised in prayer."

"They suit you, my dear. Pure and beautiful. But wait till my blue lotus blooms! That will be a flower worthy of you!" He turned the emperor's lapis ring round and round on his lean brown finger. "Faina, are you sure you haven't been followed these past weeks? No strangers asking questions around the village? I'm still worried."

"Now, Camel, we've gone over this a dozen times. Why should anyone be hunting me? I've done nothing wrong. I know you didn't like that procurer who traveled with the emperor's party, but that doesn't mean that he was set on some evil plan or even that I was the person he looked for, does it?"

"Perhaps not, perhaps I was mistaken—I just had a feeling. Well, let's not spoil this evening with things that may not be real. I have a treat for you, Little One." He moved sideways so as to keep from turning his misshapen back toward her. He opened a wooden box that stood in the tree's shadow and took out a yellow melon. With two quick strokes of his gardening knife, he cut a slice and passed it to Faina as if making an offering to the goddess herself.

"Sweet melon for my sweet heart," he said with unaccustomed boldness.

She bit into the melon. "It's *cold!*"

"Yes, it's been in the ice bin here since morning. D'you like it?" His high cheekbones glowed as he smiled at her.

"Oh, Camel, you're so good to me! No one has ever been so good to me, except my friend, Tam, of course. I wish you'd known her. I wish I knew what happened to her. It's been three summers since I last had word. She couldn't even find me now! How unexpected are the roads we travel. I never thought I'd end up here. How did you come to be in Kuo, Camel?"

"It's not a particularly interesting story, fairy-girl."

"But I'd like to know, to know you better."

"Well then, how did I come to be here? I suppose," he said slowly, "you could say that I came to be here because I know how to listen."

"Camel! No one gets to be the official gardener of his Illustrious Majesty's forest just by listening!"

"Yes, they do, at least *I* did. You see, I was the eighth son of my family, a country family of Jun-chou, east of here, many li along the Great Canal. We weren't rich, neither were we poor."

"Weren't there any girls in your family?" Faina interrupted.

"My father didn't believe in being burdened with girl-children. Each time my mother birthed one—and there were many—my father either drowned them or sold them to a *gai-shan* house. He was a hard man—but practical. I think, over time it broke my mother's spirit to be so poorly thought of that innocent babies of her sex were thrown away."

"That was a terrible thing for your father to do!"

"No, it was the *usual* thing for him to do. Girls must have dowries in order to be married and they can't work as hard on the farm. Can't officially serve to build roads or maintain canals or any of the ways to earn tax credits. I'm not saying that's right, mind you, I'm just saying that's the way it was. Still is, mostly. So, where was I?"

"You were the eighth *son.*" Faina prompted grimly.

"Yes. Well, I was little—and not very strong. Nobody much noticed me—thought I wouldn't live to grow up, probably. So I had a lot of lonely time to sit and listen. I listened to the birds' continuous conversations about food. I listened to the bees' conversations with each other about where the best nectar could be found. I heard what the trees said as the wind passed through their branches and how plants cried when they needed water. Didn't know for years that everyone couldn't hear the same as me.

"First thing you know, I was out there tryin'to help those plants and those birds get what they needed—that I thought everybody else was just too busy to give 'em! And how they did respond! Just grew and grew! The next thing I know, folks was comin' around asking me how I did it. Years passed. One day, quite a while ago now, you would've been a tiny girl, one of the emperor's men came to our village. He was an inspector of work on the Grand Canal. I remember he called the canal, *The Bridle on the Dragons*. The canals do connect and harness, so to speak, all the great rivers of our country. Another slice of melon? My throat's bone dry with all this talk—sure I'm not tiring you?"

"Yes, I mean, yes to more melon. No, I'm not tired. I like listening to your rumbly voice."

"Well, if you like my melons and like my voice, you might—just maybe *might*—like me a little, too?"

"I like you more than a little, dear Camel. Do go on." She reached over and patted his knee timidly.

"Good," he said with satisfaction and wiped his mouth with the back of his sleeve. "That inspector looked 'round and walked 'round and talked to a lot of folks—he was a noticin' kind of man—and first thing you know, he was asking me a lot of questions about what I thought about growing things. He said the emperor needed a man like me to work in the gardens and forests he was putting together of plants that sea traders and silk traders brought back to him from all over the world.

"I thought about leaving my family and it didn't seem to me I'd be missed. I thought about leaving that farming village, of the peasants there who till with fire and hoe with water—how they're in want all day and starved at night, burdened by taxes they'll not be able to pay, obliged to sell their daughters and even sons sometimes! And I said to myself if the emperor can use a man like me to make this world more beautiful, I was sure enough in favor of it! So that's how I came to be here...and I'm still listening."

"And you do make the world more beautiful, Camel."

"Some folks think I do it just to make up for my own ugliness." He said, smiling.

"Then they're folks who don't recognize true beauty." She reached over his shoulder and rubbed the hump on his back. He flinched.

"No! Don't touch me there!"

"It's all right, I don't find you ugly. You're *good.* Every part of you is good, even your back." Faina caressed his weathered face. "Why did you never marry, Camel?"

"Oh, but I did."

"Where's your wife, then?"

"We were young. She was wild and wanton, always buying great quantities of things we didn't need and couldn't afford. She wouldn't listen—paid no attention to her mother-in-law even—though in some ways I don't blame her. It wasn't an easy life for a young girl. We finally divorced each other and she went away with a riverboat man."

"No children?"

"No children...and that's the sad part. For me. Not for her, I guess."

"I want children."

"You do?"

"I want girl children and boy children. I want to love and be loved!" Faina said, throwing her arms out wide as if to gather the moonlit world into her own body. "I want to walk in a garden and hold hands with the man I love as we grow old together."

"I'm too old already."

"You're not too old for me, Camel."

The moon gleamed in their eyes. Reflections from ripples on the water flittered across their faces.

As naturally as if it had been planned, he took her in his arms and stood up. His head bumped an overhanging branch and they laughed together.

"Fairy-girl, I've loved you since the moment I saw you many moons ago. But I never thought you could..."

"And I thought I'd never get you to notice me!" Faina sighed happily as she snuggled her mouth against his throat.

Gracefully, he carried her along the dappled paths. The garden seemed to float in their wake. He reached the garden gate and put her down. Tenderly, he turned her slight shoulders in his large hands and bent to kiss her.

"It is enough for me, for tonight," he told her softly. "I will take you back to your own room in town. And I will dream of nights to come...if you'll have me?"

"Oh, Camel, d'you mean?" She leaned against his chest and listened to the beat of his heart.

"Will you complete my life? Will you be my wife? I know that I'm not the most..."

She reached up and put her fingers on his lips. "Shhh, my dearest dear, my strong, sweet dragon-man, yes! Yes and forever yes!"

He leaned over and lifted the gate latch. They went out of the garden, holding together so closely that even the searching moonlight could not shine between them. As one shadow, they walked back down the road to Kuo.

"I KNOW IT SEEMS INADMISSIBLE, TSE TSIEN, AS YOU SAY, "TO BURDEN THE FESTIVITIES with somber legal matters. But this trial must be heard. An infraction of any one of the Ten Abominations must be dealt with quickly. There won't be any days free of taboo now until Harvest Moon—and that's too long to wait." As he spoke, Tao Tsung strode the length of his stateroom restlessly.

"We must schedule the trial tomorrow and I regret that it will keep us from participating in the whole festival, but there it is. Service to the people before the purely pleasurable. I have no choice."

"Of course, what would you have me do?" Tse Tsien sat at her low desk, writing informal directives.

"Be there. Listen. See all that I see, hear all that I hear. Remember." He rubbed an almond-shaped piece of translucent violet jade between the fingers of his left hand as he paced.

"The memos to the Honorable Chang-sun and Fang Hsuan-ling are finished. Will you stamp them or shall I?"

"You stamp them." He took his deeply carved imperial seal from the pocket which hung from his waist and passed it to her.

She pushed the end into a small jar of cinnabar paste, poised it above her calligraphy and pressed it down with a thump. "There, I'll have it sent to the ministers immediately."

"Splendid. The trial can begin by first light tomorrow. Now leave me,

I've a dozen other things to do before then."

Tse Tsien bowed low and glided out of the room.

As she set in motion the emperor's plans, she was aware of all the other preparations being made for the Dragon Boat Festival.

The canal, at its widest point here at Pien Chou where Huang Ho River waters joined it, was thronged with boats. Racing boats gathered, jostled for favorable positions, occasionally colliding, their occupants shouting and cursing with holiday good humor. There were small skiffs with one man on a long sculling oar, *fast crab* rowing boats with eight to twelve pairs of young men on the oars, and narrow *scrambling dragons* manned by sixty to seventy oarsmen. Each boat had been made to look like a dragon. The largest had a carved dragon head and scales. Some of the wooden dragon heads were inset with precious stones for eyes.

Then there were spectator boats: family barges that carried the life and livestock of whole families, or little ferryboats for a half-dozen persons plus a pig and chickens.

It was an award of merit to be invited aboard the floating palaces of the aristocracy. Officials and their families crowded the rails, gossiping and drinking the emperor's fine grape wine, betting on their favorite boats for the upcoming races, making it difficult for Tse Tsien to pass through easily.

On land, doorposts and windows were decorated with bunches of artemisia and sweet flag tied together—a tradition from days of propitiating the Goddess of Good Harvest during the rainy season. Gaudy bits of flags flapped. Long, streaming flags hung from tall posts and treetops. Kites of many shapes were tethered into the wind.

Food stalls sprang up on the canal banks. Children recklessly rolled their hoops through the revelers.

Long before dusk, firecrackers ratcheted and spat and crackled along the ground. Dray animals bucked and bolted in alarm, upsetting one-wheeled carts that sold fruits and crafts from the country. Good-natured pandemonium reigned supreme.

VIVID SUNSET COLORS HAD BEGUN TO STAIN THE WATER as Batu came from below onto the high foredeck of the emperor's barge. He'd had the freedom to ride and explore Pien-chou and the surrounding countryside all day, a welcome change for a nomad horseman from the confinement of court life. He was at ease, curious and watchful.

He watched as the emperor sat on his traveling throne, the one that folded when its wooden pegs were pulled, surrounded by fifty or more of his closest court companions and advisors. Each was dressed in the hot colors of summer—scarlet, vermilion, peach, mauve, purple, apricot and rose.

Batu and Tsien had spent the afternoon gossiping and joking together as she was being dressed. He asked her why the Dragon Boat Festival was celebrated and she told him that it was in honor of a famous statesman who had come from Pien-chou itself.

"What did he do?"

"Well, first of all he was well-loved by all the people because of his fairness and attention to their needs. But after he was falsely accused of wrongdoing by a petty prince, and as a protest against corrupt conditions in the court of those days—several hundred years ago I believe it was—he committed suicide by drowning himself in the Milo River. The townspeople didn't know what he intended, so they tried to save him. Then they sent out search parties to look for him when he disappeared but they couldn't even find his body. They wanted to give him an honorable burial.

"So they went home and made lots of little rice cakes, wrapped in leaves, called *tsung.* They decorated their boats as river dragons and, with flags flying and gongs drumming, they raced to the spot where he had been last seen. All the tsung were thrown into the water as a sacrifice to his noble spirit.

"They do the same today. Boats of all sizes and dragon-shapes race to see who'll be the first to reach a designated spot in whichever river or canal is near their town. It's a holiday celebrated throughout the empire, but grandest here in Pien-chou, the statesman's home town.

"I think it may be melded with the older ritual of sacrifice to river gods, rites that used to be observed in order to bring rain and make a bountiful harvest. Today our large storage granaries make us less vulnerable to those lean, dry years. But since this is the beginning of the rainy season, it seems logical that there's some connection."

Batu nodded, realizing that his niece's interest in and grasp of this civilization was much broader than his own would ever be.

Batu lounged back against a cabin wall and watched the noblemen and women assemble. He was curious, storing up impressions to take home. For the first time since he had arrived, the emperor was wearing his crown—a wide band of gilded silver on which raised dragons chased balls of fire—opals and pearls of wisdom around his head. Tiny carvings of ivory and jade hung from the emperor's voluminous silk underskirts. Over these, several wide-sleeved robes of imperial yellow and orange, bordered with gold-dipped threads, layered one on top of the other. A small ivory seal box, carved in the shape of a turtle, hung on a black silk cord from the large jade button of his tunic.

Tai Tsung sat quietly. It was the quiet of a hunting mountain lion, taut and watchful, in command. The emperor's ministers and secretaries, too, were watchful. But they were watchful of him, his needs, responses, and mood.

Most of all, Batu's attention was taken up by the elaborately dressed women. The court women were dressed in slightly more feminine versions of the emperor's own ceremonial robes. They wore their most fashionable make-up—blue and mauve-colored eyebrows, tiny black shapes of moons and stars pasted on their painted foreheads and cheeks.

Their hairdos must have taken hours, Batu thought, *Tam's certainly had! Her maids had been stiffening her red-gold hair with rice broth and twisting it into elaborate convolutions the whole time we talked this afternoon. Here she comes...*

Her tiara, made of silver, formed intertwining branches of shining filigree from which dangled fruits and flowers carved from rubies, pearls, and midnight-blue cat's-eyes that tinkled merrily as she moved to the first rank behind the emperor. Sour-faced men made room for her.

Well, Talima-sha has as much right as anyone to stand behind the emperor! Wasn't she a ruler in her own right? Her own country? What a brilliant, shining star of a chagan she'll be! Soon we'll go home. How different that celebration will be from this one!

Emperor Tai Tsung stood, raised his imperial baton and lowered it decisively, opening the festival. On the instant, fireworks coruscated into the sky, showering the shouting thousands with flickering lights and cold fire. Cheers of the multitude echoed from surrounding hills.

On the broad canal, drums began a regular beat while gongs took up the measure. Rowers pulled on their oars. The dragon boats began to move, steadily increasing their stroke at command of drum and gongs' insistence until they seemed like giant water insects.

Waxed-paper lanterns hung on the boats. On land, stone lanterns pooled light under willow trees where lovers lounged. Bright-colored paper lanterns swung from trees and eaves in the welcome cool of an evening breeze. It had not yet begun to rain.

The five-day holiday was officially begun as it had begun for more than three hundred years on the fifth day of the fifth month, this Lotus-moon-month.

Batu ran down the gangplank onto shore and was swallowed up in the laughing crowd that surged along the waterfront.

The tavern that Batu entered was not the lowest of the low. Cheap wine and willing red-lipped wenches were what he sought this night. In the *Garden of Four Virtues*, he knew he'd found them both.

The tavern-keeper's bare belly shone with sweat as he poured wine into small cups on the bar, told stories and kept an eye on his customers. Young girls from as faraway as Silla or Turfan, dressed in provocatively sheer chemises, took drinks to men sitting at small tables.

Batu strode across the earthen floor and sat down in the back near the stage where he could watch everything. A slight girl, whose raven-wing hair hung loose to her ankles, waited for him to choose between rice or millet wine. He picked the clear amber brew of millet, left a bit of cash in its place and smiled at her invitingly. She shook her head.

Well, there's plenty of time, time to choose the best of the evening for you, my fine chapar. Patience. He settled back to enjoy whatever the night might bring.

Foreigners from many countries frequented this tavern. There were a group of black Malays, quite drunk already, a half dozen rough and rowdy Tocharian herdsmen, some nearly-naked Chams and a few richly-dressed Sassanian Persians, who drank in arrogant isolation.

Onstage, two thin young men dressed in shabby approximation of court dress, began to recite. Some patrons listened, others continued conversations in a variety of languages.

"I will recite a *Song of the Endless Past,*" one poet began, *"A thousand years drift with the wind...the ocean's sand changes to rock...the fish's froth blows down the bridge of Ch'in."*

Arms around each other's shoulders, both finished in unison... *"Bronze pillars melt in the course of the years...empty brightness floats far on the waves."*

Batu snapped his fingers and gave vent to the Igren's wavering howl of appreciation. All heads turned to look at him. In some embarrassment, he pretended not to notice.

At that moment, the swinging door slammed open. Several men burst in. The man in the center, whose blonde head rose well above the dark ones surrounding him, shouted into the sudden quiet. "I heard that Igren yell clear down the alley! Who made it? Where is he?"

Batu signaled the newcomer who pushed through the crowd like a tawny hawk harried by crows.

"Tengri! It's the chagan's brother himself! Batu-sha, don't you know me?" He thumped Batu's back enthusiastically.

"I don't think so."

"I'm Juchi, son of Juchi, grandson of the great Juchi! You must know me!"

"Juchi's grandson? You were but a stripling lad the last time I saw you! What're you doing here?"

Juchi waved his companions away. "It's a long story. Am I glad to find you—someone I can talk to in this too crowded, too crazy country! I need a drink."

Batu beckoned to the vendors that waited near the bar. "When did you arrive?"

"Now. Today. They told me the emperor would be here but they didn't say *you* were with him, what luck! I've just come through the Tien Shans with an urgent message for Talima-sha from the chagan. D'you know where she is, Batu? Nobody in Changan seemed to know anything about her."

"No, our Talima is not recognized by this world, Juchi. Here she is known only as Wu Chao Tse Tsien, confidante and companion to His Most Illustrious Illuminated."

"How do I get to her?" Juchi drained the whole glass of beer.

"I can arrange it, but not tonight. Tengri, not tomorrow either—or at least not until after this trial she's been working on. What's your news from home? It's been more than six moons since I left."

"You haven't heard?"

"Heard what?" Batu asked, sensing bad news.

Juchi spoke rapidly. Batu listened with an increasingly worried frown. Together they discussed problems and possibilities far into the night.

Outside, summer rain was pouring down over tiled roofs into overflowing sewers, creating a muddy quagmire of the narrow alley.

"Where's your horse, Juchi? Have you lodging for the night? If not, come with me."

"I left my horses at a stable outside town, but that seems like a far, wet way to go tonight. I'd be grateful, countryman. Great Tengri! How do these Chian folk manage in this beastly wet weather?"

Heads bent under their short capes, Batu and Juchi sloshed and slid downhill toward the docks.

42
A BEETLE COLLECTOR AND A WOMAN'S POISON

THE RAINS BEGAN IN EARNEST. THE SUSURRATION OF RAIN FALLING INTO WATER woke Wu Chao Tse Tsien early. Wanting to smell the morning, she threw on a wrapper, wound a wide sash around her waist and stepped out of her stateroom onto the deck. Pale gray sound enveloped her senses like tree floss. She leaned over the railing and looked out at the steady, all pervasive rain.

Dense dark clouds hovered. Circles of raindrops rippled into each other endlessly. Curtains of rain obscured mountains and the town. Raining, raining, rain—ducks' weather—ducks diving and dabbling and talking, in their element. Nesting birds warbled in the shower, their melodies and the rain's dripped indiscriminately from every twig and housetop.

A soft, summer rain, she thought—*but not the perfect weather for boat races. How wonderful a rain like this would be, shining down over Burkhan Kaldun—and how rare. Like a miracle of water falling from the Everlasting Sky. Here in Chian, only another day of summer rain, inconvenient at times. I'll remember rain like this when I'm home again. I'll miss it.*

Regretfully, she turned and went below to get ready for a long day in court. The haunting cry of the first street vendor followed her inside.

THE RECEPTION HALL WAS ALREADY CROWDED. Palace guardsmen in full regalia stood at every door, blocking the entrance to casual onlookers. Air inside the long room was thick with heat and moisture. Outside, despite the continuing drizzle, boats raced in preliminary contests while drums beat and spectators cheered their favorites.

At one end of the audience hall, Emperor Tai Tsung sat on a raised dais, flanked by his most intimate and trusted ministers.

On his left were the chief minister, vice-president of the Department of State Affairs, Chang-sun Wu-chi, whose erect military bearing inspired younger men even though his hair and beard were thin and grizzled, and Wen-te, brother of Tai Tsung's consort, dead these many years, who was an ascetic, never married, the Confucian conscience of the court.

On his right, vice-president of the Board of Civil Offices, advisor and secretary, Fang Hsuan-ling stood. His broad face looked as if he were perpetually about to smile. His skills were legendary. It was whispered that he could write an edict for the emperor that was perfectly composed even in the first draft, that his memory was without match for its precise recall of events. He had passed the Sui shin-shih examination at age seventeen, the highest in his class, and had served the Chen Kuan *True Vision* Dynasty faithfully ever since.

Both men were old friends, old campaigners. Both had been among the initial conspirators who planned the Hsuan-wu Gate coup that had made Tai Tsung emperor nearly twenty years before.

Between them, and separating those in attendance, was a runner of scarlet silk, one chang wide, that lay the length of the hall. Town officials and dignitaries stood on one side, court officials on the other. Far in the back, villagers, petitioners, advocates and prisoners crowded together.

Wu Tse Tsien, dressed sedately in a dark blue, small-waisted gown whose high, stiff collar curved around her cheeks, sat to one side behind the emperor's throne. On either side, giant kung-sparrow fans feathered the humid air, bringing only momentary relief to those in their immediate vicinity.

The black-robed Chief Magistrate of Pien Chou and his five assistants, their arms full of petitions and reports, came forward. In a sonorous, trained voice, intoning flowery, highly flattering phrases, he began to read from the scrolls he carried. He made formal requests of His Luminous Illustrious Majesty to have compassion for lesser beings, to pardon minor crimes or to reduce penal sentences, as well as itemized reports of grain stored, roads built and waterways dredged and repaired. All of which was part of the local administrator's responsibilities, but which was routinely presented for the emperor's approval whenever he was on tour.

The official could, and did, adhere to the strictest principles of justice, but he was not allowed to distribute largesse to the general populace, as the emperor might choose to do, nor could he adjudicate cases of *superior* nature—a capital crime involving the Ten Abominations, or one committed by a person of higher rank than himself.

Tai Tsung listened with his usual intensity, leaning forward as if to hear more clearly. Only his stone-black eyes moved, flicking over the entire crowd of people, pausing now and then on one particular person's face.

As the last request—a petition to remit the taxes of some deserving elderly and handicapped citizens—was read, he sat back and put his hands inside his sleeves.

"The ruler depends on the state," he said. "And the state depends on its people. We would encourage harmony between these factions and happiness for the people. If this year's taxes are as oppressive to some as the Most Honorable Magistrate feels, we will forgive them—for oppressing the people to make them serve the ruler, is like someone cutting off his own flesh to fill his stomach. The stomach is filled, but the body is injured. The ruler is wealthy but the state is destroyed."

Everyone sighed and turned to look at each other in pleasure at hearing the Son of Heaven's wisdom spoken in their humble presence.

"Distribute grain and silk to the people who wait outside," he commanded, signaling an end to petitions.

Men gathered up piles of silk squares and small bags of grain that had been prepared in anticipation of this moment. They made their way through the hall, onto the deck, across the gangplank and down to the eager people on the dock, passing out grain and silk as they went.

A majority of those in the hall followed, leaving it less than half full. Now the serious business of the morning could begin—the trial of Pao Heng, Commissioner of Commercial Argosies. He was accused of Depravity, specifically of Sorcery, in the preparation of *ku poison* which was believed to have killed his brother, Pao Chi, a musician and poet.

The Commissioner for Crimes Against the State, whose flowing robes swirled around his portly body, bowed to the floor before the emperor, straightened up with difficulty, and began to recite the ritual admonition of *Shih-o,* The Ten Abominations.

"Shih-o are the most serious of those offenses that come within the Five Punishments. They injure morality and destroy ceremony. We hold the following heinous acts so reprehensible that they comprise a danger to the emperor or the state. These are: one, Plotting Rebellion; two, Plotting Great Sedition; three, Plotting Treason; four, Contumacy; five, Depravity; six, Great Irreverence; seven, Lack of Filial Piety; eight, Discord; nine, Unrighteousness; and ten, Incest.

"Since we are only concerned, today, with the Fifth Abomination—Depravity—it is the only one of whose particular nature I will refresh your memories. The sub-commentary says that this article describes those who are cruel and malicious and who turn their backs on morality. Therefore it is called Depravity."

A thunderous bump as a small boat collided with the barge's hull, reminded the court of merrier matters taking place outside.

He continued, unperturbed, "There are only two commentaries appended to this article. The first states that Depravity means to kill three members of a single household who have not committed a capital crime, or to dismember someone.

"The second commentary, the one we deal with in this case, states that the offense also includes the making or keeping of Ku poison, or Sorcery. This means to prepare the poison oneself, to keep it, or to give it to others with the intent of causing the victim pain and death.

"Know you all, that Pao Heng is accused of this most abominable crime—that of preparing and administering ku poison in order to cause the death of his brother, Pao Chi. Bailiff, bring forth the prisoner."

A slight, wiry man came before the emperor and prostrated himself. His beard was short and well trimmed. He wore a robe of pale silk over green underskirts that were lavishly embroidered with flowers and flying creatures. He lifted his head on command and looked into the emperor's eyes.

Tai Tsung smiled slightly at his boldness. "So. You have been involved in sorcery, Pao Heng? Your own—or others?"

"Not mine own. I may speak now, Most Egregious Marvelous?"

"Later, after we have heard the whole story. Patience, Pao Heng. We will hear the witnesses first."

Pao Heng backed up and took his place beside two guardsmen and a pretty young woman.

"Why do you bring a woman into this court?" demanded the emperor.

"Most Illustrious and Gracious Sir, she is my wife, Li Mei, and figures in my defense, if it pleases you."

"Wives may conceal a crime without committing one themselves, if their husband is at fault."

"We are advised of that, oh Great Star, but since she is of superior birth to me, indeed is a distant cousin in your majesty's own Li clan, it is thought, by this most troubled and unworthy servant, that her word would be of some influence."

"Very well, proceed, Magistrate."

"Our first witness is Pien-chou's honored physician who will report on Pao Chi's death agony."

Tse Tsien shifted her position and prepared herself mentally to memorize each succeeding testimony.

"I was called to the house of our Commissioner of Commercial Argosies last week at sundown. It's a beautiful house, built around a garden that was in full bloom and..."

"Move along, Physician."

"What? Yes, of course. As I was saying, I arrived at Pao Heng's house to find that his younger brother, a rascally, no-good fellow, you understand—handsome, a ladies' man I suspect, but not what you'd call a truly *reliable* or productive citizen..."

"Will you please get on with it, Honored Physician!" the magistrate said testily. "You can't keep His Majesty waiting with your rambling!"

"Sorry, sorry—where was I? Well, Pao Chi was writhing on the floor when I got there. His body was swollen and blue-purplish in color, all his pulses were wildly erratic—sweating profusely, he was—frothing at the mouth, having trouble breathing due to the fact that his throat was closing rapidly. Classic ku poisoning, classic. Really satisfactory when symptoms are so perfect. Makes diagnosis simple."

"Was this the cause of his death in your opinion?"

"Absolutely! His breath just rattled along for a while, maybe an hour or two. His body went into spasms and pouf! He was gone—clean as a fish!"

"Thank you, Physician," the Magistrate said patiently. "Next witness? This man is a pharmacologist of some reputation, Your Majesty."

"I have been asked to elucidate on the nature and preparation of ku poison," he began, in a quiet voice. "Ku poison is an efficacious poison prepared over time. It used to be considered black magic, *tsao-tao or 'way-of-the-left'* I believe, but we now know differently.

"It is general knowledge that the ku beetle is poisonous, mildly so. If a person collects a jar full of ku beetles, they will sting each other, kill each other until only one is left. The poison contained in the remaining one is highly concentrated. This poison, of remaining beetles from several dozen jars full of the same insect, can be collected and combined. Thus, with malice and forethought, the means to an end is achieved. Ku poison can be administered in a variety of ways, usually in highly-spiced food, as its taste is strongly bitter." He ended abruptly, bowed and returned to his place.

"Next, the accuser, Fu-nan, secretary to the accused."

A fat man with a ferret-like face bowed and looked around, beaming with his own importance. "I have worked with the commission for many years. I record and check on shipments of exotics that come up the waterways and post roads from distant places. Such beautiful things that pass through my hands! And I have been scrupulously honest at all times, I assure you. Nothing—not a *Chu-lai* bird in a golden cage or a pygmy cow, not dwarves or books or sculptures from India or jewels from Lion Country—not even the most delicate fruits from the Pearl Islands or a pentachromatic carpet in which all the birds of the world were woven! I have seen such marvels in our business! And never a one stuck to my fingers! Not that some of these things didn't find their way into *some* people's homes, some who will be nameless." He rubbed his hands together, over and over.

"But I'm sure Your Most Omnipotent Luminousness knows all about these things that only seem marvelous to such a one as I?" He looked up under plucked eyebrows and smiled slyly.

"Get on with it, Secretary. Why do you think your commissioner prepared ku poison?"

"Oh, did I say that?" He glanced nervously across to where Pao Heng stood. "I only said that he seemed very interested in beetles, collecting them and examining them, and well, he *is* a young man to be burdened by so much responsibility. Not a more experienced person like myself, for instance. I know that his brother tried him sorely, always hanging around his house while he was at work, singing and laughing with Li Mei. So I thought, when the brother died so unfortunately...I mean it seemed reasonable to suppose..."

"That Pao Heng had poisoned him?" prompted the magistrate.

"Yes, exactly," he nodded.

"You may return to your place, Fu-nan. Your Majesty, there are at least a dozen witnesses here who would like to express their respect for the moral integrity of Pao Heng. They will claim him to be a most upright and virtuous man, perhaps a bit too emotional and ebullient at times, but with outstanding merit both in the community and in overseeing the import and transport of foreign goods through this chou to the capital."

"You have interrogated these witnesses, Magistrate?" Chang-sun Wu-chi asked.

"At length, Most Great One, they seem truthful to me."

"In order to expedite this hearing, we will accept your judgment, Magistrate. Let us hear the story from the accused."

Pao Heng knelt, forehead to the floor, before he spoke, "Most Revered Emperor, Wise Ministers, Honored Magistrates, friends, I am most grateful for this opportunity to clear my name of false slander. My wife is with child and it would be detrimental to her health and that of our unborn son to have this cloud hovering over us. I was raised as a gentleman, one who was imbued at my honored father's knee with the gentle virtues. He taught me that a gentleman has no use for jealousy, envy, slander or flattery, and that personal wealth was an invitation to danger." He spoke in a pleasant voice. "I think today, that he is still showing me these lessons for, although I'm not wealthy, neither I nor my family are in want. Yet I'm in a dangerous position, am I not?

"I think that the relationship between me and my brother needs explaining," Pao Heng rocked back on his heels and cleared his throat. "Brothers come from the same origin and are consequently of the same spirit, even though they are separate in form. While Pao Chi and I were little, we tagged along with the same parents, ate at the same table and wore each other's clothes. In school, we studied the same subjects and knew the same people. Even when one of us got in trouble, we loved each other.

"This situation gradually changed as we grew up and our goals changed. He was primarily interested in music and living a pleasurable life. I went into trade and applied myself to my work. A few years ago, Li-Mei consented to become my wife," he looked over to her and smiled. "We began to build a household and a place in the community here in Pien-chou. The love and respect that my brother and I bore each other suffered some deterioration. I was impatient with what I considered his follies. He badgered me about my stuffiness, as he called it. But we were never enemies.

"You weren't jealous of the time he spent with your wife?"

"Not really, I trust my wife." He smiled at her. "I would never harm someone I loved, Honored Sir! Jealousy eats at the innards of those consumed by its greed."

"Your secretary observed you collecting insects, Pao Heng. Why did you do this?"

The emperor leaned forward as if the minister's question was critical to his own understanding.

"It may seem foolish, Most Honored Sir," Pao Heng shrugged his shoulders, "but I have always been fascinated with bugs and beetles and butterflies, flying things of all sorts. I've made a collection of them, over the years, observed their life cycles, mating and egg-laying and dying."

"I didn't know that insects laid eggs! D'you mean like chickens?" the emperor laughed. Everyone laughed with him. The tension of the morning evaporated.

"We digress, Pao Heng, but I'm most interested in your collection. Perhaps sometime, you could show it to me?"

"It would be of inestimable honor, Your Most Gracious Majesty."

"Splendid. Now, you wanted your wife to testify, is that right? Do you have anything more to add?"

"Only that I am innocent."

"We shall decide that presently. Meanwhile, let's hear from Li-Mei."

Li-Mei gathered her skirts and came forward, stepping in the swaying, small-footed way of the highborn, until she stood beside her husband. Her lavender, high-collared gown was tied in the back with a wide, knotted sash. Tiny silver bells hung from ivory hairpins in her hair that coiled in braided loops over her ears. Although she had obviously taken great care with her appearance, the long, sweltering morning had wilted her.

She made a deep curtsy. Her bird-like voice was scarcely audible. "Most Luminous Majesty, I asked my honored husband if I might give testimony today. I have prayed that I would know the right thing to do. My illustrious father always said that I should not bother the gods with too many prayers, but I pray you all for your understanding.

"You see," she lifted her chin, "first of all, my husband's brother, Pao Chi, never in any way, betrayed his brother's trust. We were friendly companions. That is all. My husband's secretary, Fu-nan, is another matter..."

"What do you mean, Mei?" Pao Heng turned to her.

"I mean that Fu-nan has, on several occasions, said suggestive things to me, of sexual nature, and touched me in a way most repellent."

"That's a lie! She's a lying..." The fat little man bounced to his feet, waving his arms.

"Why didn't you tell me, Mei?" Pao Heng cried.

"I never wish to trouble you, husband, nor cause discord in your work. I thought I could keep away from him," Li Mei looked up at her husband, her face glowing with love.

"The story is complete." The emperor sighed, twisting his jade piece round and round. "We will deliberate, my ministers and magistrates and I."

"Clear the hall! Clear the hall!" the magistrate ordered as the voice of the crowd swelled in anger against Fu-nan. "Guardsmen, open the doors, but hold the accused and his accuser."

The emperor whispered to Tse Tsien, "Send for tea and sweet cakes, Tsien. This won't take long to sort out."

"I THINK IT'S ODD," CHANG-SUN WU-CHI SAID, STROKING HIS WISPY, GREY BEARD, "that we have here a case involving three men, when ku poisoning is notorious for being a woman's crime."

"That's true, the Code so designates it. Well, Fu-nan is a yin sort of man—and only the dark side of yin—not its strength," added Fang Hsun-li.

"That's something we should probably change, in the new revision of the Code," said Tai Tsung. "Will you make a note of that, Tsien?"

The three men sat together in the emperor's aft cabin. Through the open windows, a slight wind ruffled the water below. Boats raced on the far shore. As the rain had stopped, it was refreshingly quiet. Fan bearers and servants moved without calling attention to their presence. Tse Tsien knelt to prepare tea in translucent cups, whipping it into a pale green froth with a bamboo whisk.

"With regard to ku poison, Article 28 states," Fang Hsun-li began. "Making and keeping ku poison falls within what is intolerable, and women who do so are expelled to the frontiers of the empire. In point of fact, however, in recent years punishment for the criminal herself, not including her family, has been strangulation, or decapitation in particularly offensive cases."

"Which is less barbarous than in olden times, when such violation was punished by boiling in oil—for commoners only, of course. A hideously drawn-out death, I believe," remarked Chang-sun. "Where are we in this ugly tangle?"

"First we must decide on the validity of the accusations against Pao Heng. Next we must know whether you believe that he collected the poison? And then, whether or not he administered it, thereby causing his brother's death."

As Tse Tien handed the emperor his tea, he put his ringed hand on her sleeve, bending his head toward hers as if giving an order. What he murmured, however, was, "Tell me, who was lying?"

"Fu-nan, Sire, Fu-nan only." Head down, she whispered back.

He nodded with satisfaction, then, "How say you, my able ministers?"

"It appears that Pao Heng is a moral man, an educated man. His character is that of a gentleman who possesses all the gentle virtues. Therefore, I do not think the charges against him *can* be valid," Chang-sun stated.

"I concur, though not necessarily for the same reasons," said Fang.

"I agree." said the emperor. "That being unanimous, how do you feel about the actual making of the poison?"

"He *could* have, but I believe him when he says he did not, that collecting flying things was only a leisure interest," said Chang. "Which leaves us with the distinctly unpleasant alternative that Fu-nan has falsely accused him for purposes of his own."

"Imagine! Jealousy toward a superior official! D'you suppose he expected to be given Pao Heng's job as Commissioner of Commercial Argosies? He must be crazed." Fang sputtered. "And making advances to his wife as well! He might confess if he thought it would reduce his punishment."

"I'm not inclined to reduce his punishment. Rather it should be *increased* as a strong warning against the moral laxness of lying and jealousy," the emperor said quietly. "Particularly since this is an offense of an inferior against a superior, not only the man himself, but his fifth-rank wife—a heinous crime, subject to the severest penalty.

"Do we know if Fu-nan has a family?"

"He does," the emperor replied. "As the family of one who falsely accuses are punished the same as any criminal's family would be, they will be exiled 2000 li and all their goods and property returned to the state."

"His children are very young I'm told, perhaps they could stay here? Be raised in another household? Trained in the way a twig should grow and thereby be redeemed from his base influence?" Fang suggested. "You, yourself, emperor, have said on several occasions that a good carpenter rejects no worthy material."

"I, a *carpenter,* old friend?"

"Have you forgotten? I well remember that long edict I drafted for you, early in your reign. Shall I refresh your memory?"

"I rather think you must. I'm listening." He sat back, sipped his tea and gazed out into the rain-white sky.

"You said, I wrote, 'The enlightened ruler employs men in the manner of a skilled carpenter. If the wood is straight, he uses it for the shaft of a cart. If it is crooked, he uses it for a wheel. If it is long, he uses it as a roof-beam, if short, as a rafter. No matter whether crooked or straight, long or short, each has something which can be utilized.' Now, could not these children be useful wood, Enlightened Ruler?"

"You old rascal," the emperor chuckled. "You are wise and I appreciate your advice. So be it. The children will be adopted by parents who have never known the principals in this case and I rather think they should be removed to another city."

"One thing, Shih-min," Chang-sun said, using the emperor's family name, "we have not yet settled Pao-chi's murder. D'you think that Fu-nan had the wit to do it?"

"Wit? Half enough is good enough, in this case!" retorted Fang Hsun-li. "Of course he did it."

They nodded agreement.

"We have no choice. He must pay the harshest penalty—for he was a despicable opportunist. He thought to get rid of both brothers, gain a position, and a woman, by the left-hand path of sorcery. Such wickedness! Such unrighteousness! Such total lack of virtue, it saddens me to see it." The emperor stood abruptly. "Let's have an end to this affair. Tse Tsien, will you notify the magistrate that our deliberations are complete, that we're ready to pronounce judgment?"

As she left, Tsien could hear Chang-sun, the old Confucian, saying in his dry, thin voice, "Folly, Shih-min, to trust that girl so far. Women belong in the home, not in council. They're lovely decorations to one's life, but as intimates in the affairs of state?"

She could hear the beginning of the emperor's rejoinder, "Nonsense, Tse Tsien is..." as she stepped outside. The showers had abated. Sunlight streamed into a newly-washed world. She wondered where Batu was and what he'd been doing since yesterday.

43
BATU RESCUES: PRINCE CHENG GOES TOO FAR

BATU AND JUCHI WERE HAVING A SPLENDID TIME. They had discovered that they fascinated girls. Thin girls, plump girls, merry girls, maiden girls all giggled at their great height and long yellow hair. They flirted in a fashion that neither Igren had ever experienced before. The two men had become quite drunk on the adulation as well as the deceptively strong millet beer.

They were part of a crowd that had gathered to watch noblemen and guardsmen ready themselves, their hawks and dogs, for a hunt in the foothills outside town.

Dogs yelped and bayed. Gyrfalcons and hawks—*white rabbit goshawks, skylark-yellow, red-spot-engouted,* and *Fang-shan white* —turned their heads under silken hoods and stretched their pointed wings. Gaily caparisoned horses charged about, pawing at the ground, shying nervously at the unaccustomed crowds and sounds. Only the heads of peasants could be seen here and there in the tall meadow grass where they'd been stationed to flush the game—pheasant, quail, hares, and foxes.

"Look at those birds, Batu! I've never seen so many hunting falcons! There were never that many, even at Kuriltai!"

"Damned undisciplined bunch of horses though." Batu nudged his countryman. "Give me an Igren horse and I'd show up the lot of them."

The girls around them smiled at each other. One lissome girl took hold of Batu's arm in a possessive way. He looked down at her and grinned.

"We could get my horses, they're not far from here," offered Juchi.

"We're not invited. And one thing I've learned is that Chian aristocrats are sticklers for protocol. Everything's got to be proper."

"Well then, let's get invited!"

"You go, Juchi-lad, I've just found something more interesting for today." Batu tucked the girl's arm under his and patted her small hand. As he did so, he noticed that she wore ivory nail guards over her long, lacquered nails and he realized that she was no ordinary country wench. Alarm bells chimed warningly in his mind, but he ignored them.

"I beg your pardon," a stranger beside them said. "Did I understand you correctly when you said you wished to ride in the prince's hunt?"

"You speak Igren?"

"A little, I trade through your country on my route from Sassania."

"You could get us invited?"

"I have the honor of an invitation from Prince Cheng, but, since I'm no horseman and do not care for hunting..."

"Tengri! I'll do it, you're sure, Batu?"

"Absolutely, ride, Young Wolf!"

"I'll get my horse and be back before they leave," Juchi called over his shoulder. "Where shall I meet you?"

"I'll wait for you near the hunt coordinator's post," the stranger shouted back. "And I'll bid you good hunting, Igren." He nodded to Batu and wandered off into the crowd.

"Is Igren your name?" The girl asked Batu shyly.

Batu's good humor bubbled over, "No, my name's Batu, Batu Shaymak, an Igren from the Pamir Mountains, thousands of li west of here along the Great Silk Road."

"I have heard of this Silk Road—a trade route to barbarian lands, no?" Her voice was like the trilling of a small meadow bird's.

"Yes, but you still haven't answered my question."

"I'm so sorry. What was your question, barbarian Batu?"

"You think I've forgotten? Because I've been drinking? You underestimate my drinking capacity. Who are you?"

"You mean, who am I today?" She smiled mischievously.

"By the Everlasting Sky, wench! Yes, today, yesterday, tomorrow!"

"Well, I'm not sure...I seem to be changing all the time."

"But you *do* have a name? Must I guess?" They became completely absorbed in each other.

"A name is really nothing, you may call me what you wish, Batu."

"Lady of Mystery, I wonder why? Well, if that's your game, little one, I'll give you a name—Merket—d'you like it?"

"M- e r- k e t," she said slowly, as if tasting a strange, new food. "What does it mean?"

"Merket, in my language, means falcon, a small, graceful, sharp-witted bird. Rather like you, I think." Batu looked first at the hawks and falcons held by waiting huntsmen and then down at the pretty girl on his arm.

"I like it!" she laughed. To Batu, her laughter sounded like silver bells on the wind.

The hunt gathered. Men collected their prancing horses and took hoods off their hunting birds. They milled around at one end of the meadow, careful not to infringe on Prince Cheng and his party who were in front of all the others. The sun, shafting through scudding, dark clouds, was summer afternoon hot.

Batu and Merket, engrossed in the exciting world of intimacy that enveloped them, walked slowly into the meadow, unaware that they were crossing the hunt's path. The long grass, marshy from the yesterday's rain, soon soaked their feet.

"My slippers!" she cried. "They'll be ruined!"

Without a moment's hesitation, Batu swept her up in his arms. "There, now you'll stay dry, my little falcon!"

"Put me down, do, Batu! It's not proper to..."

"One more moment. I'll carry you to that hillock over there where you'll be able to..."

He strode through the wet grass carrying her as easily as he had carried his golden eagle at home.

Prince Cheng, surrounded by his usual rowdy companions, watched Batu's progress across the field in front of him with disbelief. "Isn't that Hsu Ching-tsung's youngest filly?" he asked. "What does that barbarian think he's doing...being familiar with a lady of the court!"

"She *is* the minister's daughter, Noble Prince, but I doubt he means her harm, shall I?" replied a rider next to him.

"Who said anything about *harm*? She's a pretty little thing, isn't she? Why hasn't she been invited to my parties?"

"She's not been considered old enough by her family, I believe."

"Time to break her out of that cocoon, eh? She can ride behind me. I need something soft to cushion my backside. Get her."

As an arrow shot from a bow, the prince's man cantered after Batu. In seconds he reached them and jumped down from his horse. "I'll take the girl," he said.

"What do you mean?"

"I'll take the girl," he said, more belligerently, "Prince Cheng will have her ride with him."

"Please, Batu, don't let him take me! I've been warned about the prince and his peculiar ways!" She wound her arms around Batu's neck and clung to him for safety.

"Merket belongs with me. We're only going to that little hill over there." Batu kept walking.

"Listen, barbarian, she's Chian, get your clumsy hands off her. Put her down. She *will* come with me. It's the express command of His Most Peerless Self!"

Three more of the prince's men rode up, surrounding them.

"Get - out - of - my - way!" Batu growled, lowering his head.

One man hit the back of his knees. Another hit his head. He sagged to the ground. The other two grabbed the struggling girl and threw her up onto one of their horses. They kicked the partially conscious Batu and, with systematic thoroughness, whipped him with their quirts, then leaped astride their horses and rode back to their waiting prince.

"Pass her to me. Hai, there, girl, a tasty morsel indeed!" Prince Cheng licked his full lips.

They rode up beside him and tried to transfer the girl to the prince's horse. In a fury, she bit and kicked away from them. The prince smiled, watching her struggle. She fell between the horses and began to run. Fast as a hare before foxes, she darted away, screaming for help.

Batu staggered to his feet and lurched in her direction. The meadow wavered and swam before his eyes. He could see her, he could hear her, he knew he could not reach her. Focused only on her, he was not aware at first of the faraway horseman galloping toward them. He did, however, hear a wild, wind-raw yell, and recognized it as an Igren hunting call. The energy it sent into his blood allowed him to lift his head and ululate in answer. For several moments, as the world seemed to hold its breath, that horseman, moving in time-stopping rhythm across the fields, held the only meaning for him anywhere.

Batu recognized an Igren horse, recognized the flying colored tassels of its bridle, knew it could be none other than Juchi. Juchi returning, asking no questions, reacting only to his friend's need, Juchi, reining up beside him, pushing him up onto the wide rump of his horse.

"The girl! We must get the girl!" Batu breathed.

Juchi whirled and raced toward her. They caught up with her while the prince's men were still a short distance behind her. Juchi leaned far out of the saddle and scooped her up. Juchi whispered a familiar signal to his horse and they shot away—the girl holding onto him and Batu, bloody, beaten, with his arms around her. As they ran into the twisting alleyways of Pien Chou, the other horsemen lost sight of them and disappeared. Finally free of pursuit, Juchi slowed their pace and walked back along the yellow, turgid river.

After the first rush of relief, they examined the predicament they were in—guests in a foreign land who had undoubtedly offended its crown prince. And further, made off with a girl whom they learned now was the youngest daughter of a senior minister, president of the Board of Rites.

Batu realized the gravity of their situation but could not make his mind function well enough to work out a solution. They plodded along. One thing he *did* know was that this girl, whose real name was Hsu Wen-chi, had become incredibly precious to him.

They left the river and rode through the narrow streets of Pien-chou, still crowded with festival celebrants. Firecrackers popped and spat from balconies and courtyards.

Juchi dismounted and led his lathered horse down to the canal. They arrived back at the royal barges as twilight reflected burning color across the sheen of placid water. They took Wen-chi to the boat where her family was staying.

"When may I see you again, Merket? Do you mind if I call you that?" asked Batu.

"No, I like it very much, Batu," she said, looking down at the ground, "I would like to be with you again. You'll be all right? You're not badly hurt?"

"Not badly, I'll be a little ragged tomorrow, perhaps," Batu was having trouble standing. "May I call on you?"

"I'll ask my father...I must hurry! They'll wonder where I've been!" She reached out and touched Batu's arm with tenderness, as if testing whether he were real. "Thank you for rescuing me. I'll tell my father what *you* did and what Prince Cheng did, also!"

"If I hadn't been such a fool you would not have needed rescuing," said Batu.

Juchi cleared his throat, "I think you'd better go, Wen-chi, we're attracting attention. I must care for Batu."

"Yes, goodbye, Batu," she turned away quickly and ran up the gangplank.

Batu sighed, swung into the saddle and slumped over the pommel as Juchi hurried him away.

"I'M SORRY TO MAKE YOU GO OUT AGAIN TONIGHT, BATU," Tse Tien said as they walked along the dock. "But when they told me what had happened to you...well, I think His Majesty should deal with this situation as soon as possible." Batu walked beside her without his usual forceful stride.

She had burst into his quarters just as the physician had finished treating his lacerations and bruises. She watched him give Batu a willow extract that alleviated pain and apply herbal poultices to the lacerations where he'd been whipped.

"I don't like to trouble, His Eminence. I'm not sure this is such a good idea, Tam."

"Nonsense, you're not at fault, Batu! Prince Cheng consistently violates the rights of others, consistently breaks the moral code of superior men. His actions have troubled the emperor increasingly, and it's obvious that something must be done about it. For him to attack a guest is unthinkable!"

"It's a small matter."

"A small matter tonight, but by tomorrow? Who knows what Prince Cheng will do? No, the Tao teaches us to deal with things in the state of not-yet-being. To avoid a problem before it gets to be a worse one. So we must tell His Majesty tonight."

"Who taught you that? I don't remember that as being part of our Igren law."

"Not Igren, not law exactly. Who taught me? A wise, but ruthless man, Kat Kat Zanggi by name."

"Strange name..."

"Strange man. I used to think he was my friend. Now he's my obedient ghost. Here we are, I'll send up a request to be admitted."

"Will the emperor be awake this late?"

She laughed. "Awake? We sometimes wonder if he ever sleeps! It's the reason he has us all sleep so close to him. When he gets an idea in the middle of the night, he wants to discuss it and take action immediately."

She led the way up three flights of ornate stairs to the emperor's suite. His valet announced them.

The emperor met them with outstretched hands. "My dear, an emergency? Are you all right?"

"I'm fine, Sire, it's Batu..."

"Holy Mother! I perceive! What happened to you, uncle of Wu Tse Tsien? Here, sit down."

"I don't wish to trouble your..."

"Trouble? Looks to me as though you're the one who's troubled. Who did this to you? How did it happen?"

Batu told him, in quick terse sentences, of watching the hunt, of the girl, of Prince Cheng's men, of the beating, and of the prince's attempt to abduct the girl against her will.

"My son grows intolerable," Tai Tsung murmured. "I shall call him to account tomorrow morning, I'll have to send him back to Changan. He'll destroy the people's faith in the dynasty at this rate. Go on, Batu, what happened to the girl? Who is she? Did you ever find out?"

"As a matter of fact, Most Illustrious, she's the daughter of your minister, Hsu-Ching-tsung."

"My old Szechuan friend? This puts Cheng's behavior in an even worse light, if he knew. Go on."

"I'm not too clear on exactly what happened, Noble Sir, but the first thing I knew, Juchi was there helping me onto his horse and then we picked up Merket, er, Wen-chi, that is, and rode away before they could catch us."

"Juchi?" Tse Tsien exclaimed. "You didn't mention a Juchi before... what d'you mean, Batu?"

"Son of Juchi, grandson of the Juchi who left with you," Batu explained.

"Where is he? When did he...?"

"He arrived in town last night and happened into me at a tavern. As a matter of fact, he'd been trying to find *you!* Tengri, Talima-sha! I forgot, how *could* I!"

"How could you *what,* Batu? You're shaking, Uncle, what in high heaven is the matter?"

"Oh my dear, Juchi had ridden straight through from the Pamirs, from the Chagan, to tell you..."

"News from home? From *Father?* How wonderful!"

"Talima-sha, the news he brings is not wonderful...and not from your father." He put his hand on hers. "Your father, the great Sha-Chagan Tashih Shaymak, my beloved brother, has passed over into the Everlasting Sky."

"Father? *Dead?* No, you said the Chagan sent a message?"

"The Chagan, yes. Your brother Jalco, is Chagan now. It was he who sent Juchi to tell you."

"I must go home!"

"Didn't you hear me, Tam? Juchi had his instructions from *the Chagan*—Jalco Shaymak—who will have been leader of the Igren for more than three moons now. He sent word that you would be welcomed back *on the condition* that you did not question his leadership. Come back as an ordinary woman of the clan with no special privileges and no..."

"My people don't want me? They've forgotten me? I have no home to return to? Father gone...all, gone?" She seemed to shrink, as if the armature on which her self was wound had been suddenly broken.

Batu looked across at the emperor. Their eyes met. The emperor nodded and walked toward her. She turned and started for the door. His large body blocked her way. He held her as the tears began.

"What will I do? What will become of me?" She cried into his broad chest.

"There now, you have all that you had when you woke this morning, all that you need."

"But it all seems so different now!" she wailed.

"Then you must look at it differently." He wiped her tears with his large handkerchief and sat down with her on his lap. "Now listen to me. Pay attention. You have the right to grieve for your great loss, Peach Flower. But nothing gives you the right to pity yourself. A warrior, my dear, does not have self pity."

"But what will I do? Where can I go?"

"You can do what you have been doing. Stay here in Chian, with me.

That can't be too great a burden for your young shoulders, can it?" He smiled at her indulgently.

"Oh no, I didn't mean that!"

"You must have realized how dearly I hold you, the talented daughter I never had, how much I rely on you, more so than I should, possibly. This is your home now, if you'll make it so."

"I'll have to think. I need time."

"Time is what you'll have, lord knows—the obligatory twenty seven moons for mourning—before the final death rites of your father," said the emperor sadly. "And nothing festive for you during that time, no music even. The court will miss you, but there it is."

"I don't understand."

"I'm only reminding you of the mandatory mourning period, my dear, of the time set aside to honor one's parent, to remember him in whatever ways—poetry or calligraphy or whatever things you do—that will keep his name and person in your mind and in your heart."

She jumped up and began to pace like a caged mountain lion. "That's not the way *we* mourn, how Igren mourn!" She shook her head vehemently. "Father will always be in my heart. I loved him. He loved me. That love doesn't die when the body goes, when the *sudde*, the spirit-life of my father, transfers into another form!"

Batu tried to calm her, but she twisted loose from him and continued her restless pacing.

"You see, Your Majesty, what Tam means, what Tse Tsien means is that," Batu began, "we believe that when a man dies, his spirit resides as a potent force in some particular place or thing. But, other than venerating that shall-not-be-named power, the man is not spoken of again...at least not aloud. We continue with life as before. The man who dies would not want it otherwise, would he?"

"I see. But if Tse Tsien does not honor her father, does not mourn him in the proscribed manner, she will be liable for three year's penal servitude, Batu! She has no choice!"

"I *will not* dishonor my father because of a Chian law, a law that is contrary to our law. I will choose. There must be a way!" She wiped tears away impatiently.

"There may be. I wonder...Batu, who knows of this?"

"Only those of us in this room, Majesty and Juchi, of course."

"No one else?"

"Who would I tell?"

"Yes..." The emperor stroked his pointed beard thoughtfully. "We should be able to accommodate this conflict of customs if we're careful. As far as anyone in the court knows, Wu Tse Tsien, you are the daughter of Duke Wu Shih Kuo. His family has adopted you. And this father is very much alive, right here in fact. Yes, it may be possible. I could enlist his aid and that of your adopted mother. It might be wise to remind the court that you are the legitimate daughter of an illustrious Tai Yuan family, in order to strengthen your position, you see."

He looked up, watching her face for a reaction. "Would you permit a small feast in honor of your Chian family? In a week or two, when we get back to the palace in Loyang, after we leave the boat?"

She smiled and stopped pacing. "I can do that," she replied. "I'll be ready by then."

"Splendid! Then we're agreed. You have time to mourn in *your* way and the harmony of the court will not be disturbed. I have always maintained that you have the heart of a warrior, Tse Tsien."

"Batu? D'you think that you and Juchi, Kilar and the rest, might stay here with me?"

Batu, the image of Wen-chi's raven black hair still more real in his mind than Talima's amber hair, said, "I think we'd like to stay—for many reasons."

"The palace guard always needs good men." Tai Tsung smiled.

Tse Tsien stood on tiptoe and kissed his cheek. "You make it very easy for me, Sire. I'll not fail you in any way. Ever."

"You never have." He said quietly. "Now run along. You both need some sleep. Tomorrow I'll speak with the duke on behalf of his daughter. And I'll confront my son with his evil ways, as well as atoning to my minister for the insult to his daughter. Good night." He sighed and turned back to his desk as they backed from the room.

The night was cool and fragrant. A sickle moon hung low over distant mountains.

"You can get back to your quarters safely, Batu?"

"You'll be all right, Talima-sha?"

"Yes."

"May the Blue Wolf bring you comfort."

"Good night."

44
THE EMPEROR DECIDES: FAINA HAS A GOOD IDEA

WHEN THEY WOKE NEXT MORNING, THE ROYAL BARGES WERE ALREADY UNDER WAY, hauled along the towpath by platoons of red-capped soldiers, following the river east, back to Loyang.

Prince Cheng was summoned out of bed before anyone other than his father had stirred. Although no one else was present during their meeting, it was observed that servants still trembled, hours later, from hearing the emperor's wrath.

"You wanton cockerel! Get out...and take all your vicious friends with you!" were the only words, thundering from the half open door, that were actually heard. The prince and his friends left summarily, conducted back to the capital by a contingent of armed palace guards.

Peace pervaded the court, its only concerns were the ordinary business of summer. Feasts and frivolity danced the measure of their days. The Dragon Moon waned, the Lotus Moon ascended, and with it, a complete cessation of the rainy season.

Music and wine filled the short nights. It was a drifting, somnolent time, a time made for lovers. Batu made a formal call on Wen-chi's father and received permission to keep company with his daughter. In fact, Batu so impressed the minister that he was heard bragging to his colleagues about the fine man "...a man from the far west, not too far from my home in Szechuan with connections in court" who was keeping company with his youngest daughter.

Thereafter, Batu and his Merket were always seen together, whether in the merry company of the younger set, betting on matches of fighting geese, cock fights or horse races, or sitting in a quiet corner while she taught him Chian games, Gho or Four Winds, and he taught her his, *Wari*—and how to kiss.

One simmering afternoon, even the emperor relaxed from his habitual diligence. He and Tse Tsien reclined against pillows on either side of a polished, pauwlonia-wood table. They were playing Double Sixes on his small traveling board of purple sanderswood. It was hot enough for the wood to release its fragrance of roses that drifted into the space between them. Languid melodies, played on a five-stringed lute, hung in the humid air. Ostrich plume fans moved slowly, scarcely affecting the room's temperature -stifling within, unbearable without.

"It's certainly peaceful around here without my perfidious son," the emperor commented as he threw the sticks for another round of play. "It's a puzzle to me where he went wrong. For years I thought it must be his tutors. I finally banished them, but that changed nothing. Aha, doubles again! You'll never catch me now!" His counter triumphantly tapped its way around the board like a dancer picking its way between the gold and silver flowers inlaid in the translucent tortoise-shell top of the board.

"I'm thinking of changing the succession from Li Cheng to Kao Tsung," he said, as if speaking to himself.

"Would he be able to…?" She left the question unfinished as she tried to figure out a winning strategy.

"Not as he is today, he's too much the scholar, too little a leader, head in the stars instead of the empire. But he could learn, he could learn," he watched her move.

"Lady Wang would certainly be enchanted to be yin-concubine to the crown prince!"

"An ambitious woman from an ambitious family! If I could only find another wife for my son that could help him, encourage him, support him. Well, there's time," the emperor concluded as he moved two of his counters into a blocking position against her. "Care to bet on this game?"

"Only a fool would bet against *you,* Sire," she laughed.

In Kuo, weeks went by in much the same manner as they had for centuries. Farmers tilled their fields behind slow-moving oxen. Fishermen flung their nets in shining arcs over the silted river. Silk workers spun and dyed and wove. Only the individual players changed.

Faina knew her role well. As Spinning Mistress, she had been busy, but with her promotion to second assistant to the Supervisor of the Colors of Heaven, she was doubly so. She was seen, her sunny hair streaming down her back, by townspeople in every quarter as she flitted from one compound to another, coordinating production between the spinners and dyers and settling differences between workers. Her duties also required her to keep track of supplies and to ensure the color intensity and quality of silk that came from the dyers' vats.

She was dismayed to learn that she was penalized a *p'i* of silk, a length of cloth as wide as the length of her two feet, almost eight times her height, for any small mistake she made. Three p'i, a day's wages, for a greater omission. She had become very efficient, very quickly. Personal time became almost nonexistent. Yet she found a few hours, mostly late at night, to join Camel in the quiet peace of his gardens in the comfort of his loving arms.

One day, Faina and her supervisors met with the pigment merchants, traders of dyes and minerals from far countries. It was an amiable, protracted business, a time for trading gossip and stories as well as dyestuffs. Present were tradesmen from Cambodia with gambodge or *hen yellow*, from Annam with purple *lac,* from Ferghana and Kabudhan, with precious blue kohl—even a man from the far south who brought *gibbon's blood*, the truest of crimsons.

"I've heard that gibbon's blood comes from the dew that forms on meadows in those mighty mountains of mon-country to westward," said the lac tradesman. "The same country that the blood-sweating horses come from. At least that's the same color they use in their woolen rugs."

"I think there can be no doubt that it's blood from a gibbon, whatever that is," said a third trader. "Gibbons are supposed to be able to understand human speech...easy to catch, apparently, as they're addicted to wine.

"Whether the dye comes from gibbons or mountain dew, it's the best and we've been using only inferior *unicorn gutta* and *sapan* too long now. Name your price, merchant," said Eldest Supervisor.

"Six p'i for one *ta-liang.*" The bargaining began.

Six p'i of silk for only one ta-liang! Faina sucked in her breath. *Two days' wages for dye I could hold in the hollow of my hand? I had no idea that anything could cost so much!*

"Four, for two." the supervisor countered.

"Five, for two, and done is done," the merchant finished quickly.

"Agreed. How much d'you have?" asked the Kuo Supervisor.

"Twice-ten *chin*, more or less, enough to last you a few months, at least."

"We'll take it then. Faina, see that he gets a fair payment of silk. Now, how about you, lac merchant? How much of a bargain can I talk you into today?" She asked, obviously enjoying the whole process.

Faina left them, her mind filled with confusion as she tried to figure out just how much silk would be a fair payment. As she ran, she counted on her fingers and murmured out loud. "Let's see, there are ten-plus-six ta-liang in one chin, so if there are twice-ten chin of gibbon's blood, there are...'Sky, there must be an easier way to figure! I'll start the other way 'round...five ch'ih is...oh, dear!"

She snapped a twig off a willow tree and squatted down. The sun beat down on her, outlining the blades of her shoulders under the thin chemise she wore. She scratched a line in the dust for each ta-liang, crossed the number when it reached ten, and started over again. Having finally figured out that she would need to order eight times ten-tens' p'i of silk to be delivered to the gibbon's blood merchant, she jumped up and ran toward the alley of warehouses.

Eight times ten-tens, she reminded herself, eight times ten-tens for roughly six or seven bucketsful of dye? And much of that gets thrown away at the end, it's too wasteful!

As she set about arranging for the silk's delivery and the precious dye's storage, she was busy thinking. She had in mind the sludge left in the bottom of the vats after dyeing...bright blues, mauve, deep yellows, and all the shades of red, never saturated enough to dye cloth again...but strong enough to color the skin of the women's arms who dyed the silk.

That's it! That's the answer! I remember the emperor's concubines in the White Jade Pavilio...their saffron beauty- marks that rubbed off so easily... their rouged cheeks, blue and mauve-shadowed eyes...they had to grind and sieve all those minerals into powder before they could use them to make up their faces. It took hours! What if the dregs of dye could be dried and packaged in some way?

As she hurried through the market she saw, as if in answer to her thoughts, the wares of a Persian merchant spread on woven saddlebags beside his camel—small hand-blown bottles, narrow-necked and graceful, some with handles, all a pale, mottled blue-green glass through which the sun gleamed.

Perfect! We could sell cosmetics to ladies of the court! Aristocratic women all over the empire would follow the fashion and then...

We could give the colors new names, names like gibbon-nimbus-rouge or flowery-mountain-kohl, sperm-of-gold perhaps or lakka-lavender. They'd be so beautiful to look at in those little glass bottles!

The first opportunity she had to discuss the idea with her superior did not come until later in the day. By that time, she'd worked out all the particulars. She felt sure that the supervisor would see profit in her plan.

She could not anticipate, nor even dream, how that ambitious woman would appropriate her plan while turning Faina's life inside out.

45
A TRAVELER BRINGS JOY: KAO TSUNG SINGS

BY THE TIME THE EMPEROR AND HIS ENTOURAGE LEFT THE BOATS and settled into the Loyang palace, preparations were well under way for a grand feast to be given in honor of the family of Wu Tse Tsien's Yuan family, that of Duke Wu Shih-kuo.

Meanwhile, a fast messenger pelted down the Post Road from Changan and brought a message from the pilgrim-traveler, Hsuan Tsung. He'd been gone on a journey of fifteen years and now requested an immediate audience with the emperor. So the celebration would be a reception for him as well. Thousands of servants and merchants and entertainers thronged the palace halls.

Batu, in company with seven-times-ten honor guards, seven being the auspicious number for Hsuan Tsung's arrival, waited outside the South Gate.

Dragons, embroidered with gold-dipped thread on their short scarlet capes, glowed in the late summer wind as if alive. They watched the moving plume of pale yellow dust as a procession came toward them. When they saw the tall banners of an imperial troop, they knew it must be Hsuan Tsung and they made ready, lining the road on both sides to greet him.

Hsuan Tsung, his long mustaches blowing back over his shoulders, rode up between them. Hatless, he wore an orange robe tied simply with an unadorned length of woven hemp. Only his knee-high, dark red felt riding boots were decorated. As he passed each guardsman, he nodded and gestured with one hand. He was a tall, hungry-looking man who sat his horse with almost military bearing. Yet he seemed, in some fundamental way, like a man at peace.

The troop proceeded into Loyang, the ancient city of a million souls, and into the busy southern market. They made their way through streets crowded with people, some carrying produce in baskets on long poles over their shoulders or in wheeled-barrows with fully battened sails, servants bustling by on errands, and merchants from faraway countries with unfamiliar wares. Carriages and sedan chairs of the privileged bolted through the throng. Stalls along city streets sold porcelains and damasks, fruits and flowers, medicines and exotic furs. Loyang, known as the *Godly Metropolis* boasted temples devoted to the worship of many gods.

They rode from the bustling market place into the quieter streets that widened uphill to the sprawling palace. Horns and cymbals announced them as they came toward the main audience hall where twelve ranks of guards stood at attention. Swordsmen, halberdiers, lancers and archers stood under their identifying banners on which symbols of valor were embroidered or appliquéd...leopards and lions, unicorns and hawks. Their dress capes, each in the distinctive colors of their command, swirled in the dry wind, echoing the flutter of parrot and pheasant feathers that flew from their flags.

The guardsmen gave their horses to waiting grooms and walked with Hsuan Tsung through the heavy inner gate. Within, five troops of household guards stood. Four wore purple shirts and capes decorated with tail feathers of the Manchurian snow pheasant while the fifth wore tabards of sea-blue taffeta embroidered with the figures of wild horses. All carried staves and wore short swords at their belts. The softer sounds of lutes and flutes met them in the Great Hall at the end of which sat the emperor, surrounded by colorfully dressed men and women of his court.

The guards melted into the throng. Hsuan Tsung proceeded alone, a scarlet silk-wrapped bundle held out high before him. He bowed low before his emperor, then knelt and with head on the floor, offered up his gift.

"Most Luminous Illustrious, your humble servant begs you to accept this small gift from India, where I studied for so many years in your service."

The emperor gestured to his Officer of Protocol, who took the thin rectangle from Hsuan Tsung.

"Rise, Hsuan Tsung," he said, unwrapping the bundle, letting cloth unwind onto the floor at his feet. "What is this? We have heard that India is the wealthiest of nations. I send you away for fifteen years to study the geography and customs, products and politics of central Asia, and you bring me a pile of bark with indecipherable scribbles on them?"

"With all its material wealth, Peerless Son of Heaven, India's greatest treasure, to my mind, is its wisdom." Hsuan Tsung spoke with quiet assurance. "So, my greatest gift, but not the only one, to the greatest ruler, is the great wisdom embodied in that pile of bark, one of only six hundred, which you hold in your hands."

"Mother of Heaven! What is it?"

"It is the *Prajna Paramitra Sutra* of the Yogacharya School. We'd call it *Fa-hsiang*, one of the major teachings from a master teacher, the Buddha himself. I have in mind to translate it from the Sanskrit for your Most August Majesty."

"So? And why should that interest us?"

"The Buddha teaches how to live purely, how to understand one's place in the universal pattern, how to live in peace. I knew this would interest *you*, Majesty."

"Indeed! Well, we should set aside some time for a longer discussion. But I notice wan looks on the faces of some of my friends here that tells me it's time to go into the dining hall and the rest of the evening's festivities. Shall we?"

Hsuan Tsung bowed and stepped away, silent as he left the Great Hall.

From across the room, Prince Kao Tsung came to Tse Tsien's side. "Greetings, Tsien," he smiled, "I've missed you!"

"Greetings to you, Kao Tsung, I've missed you too. It's been a long time since you left us at the river during Dragon Boat Festival. So much has happened!"

They made a handsome couple, both slender, of the same height, one so dark, the other so fair. Her hair was wound into intricate spirals, his into a tight topknot. He wore several robes in varying shades of turquoise silk. She wore a ruffled, small-waisted dress, printed with scarlet and blue pomegranates, one that left her breasts almost bare to the tips of her nipples.

He leaned closer and whispered, "I may have an amazing surprise for you soon. I think I've discovered a new heavenly body! And I want to name it for you."

Tsien whispered back, "Tsun! You're not stammering, how come?"

"I never stutter when I'm whispering...or singing either, haven't you noticed?"

"I've never heard you sing...do you?"

"Now and then, the *Clear Stream* or some other popular tune. You know how those tunes stick in your head."

Courtiers nodded to each other, seeing the two whispering together, as if their actions were of significance.

"Do you understand my discovery? I believe I'll be able to verify it soon. A few more clear nights' sightings!"

"You know that I'm ignorant of astronomy, dear Tsun. A good thing, considering the stiff penalties for someone other than you royal *men* who study the heavens!"

"I forgot about that. But you, Tsien, you're different," he whispered as they found their seats.

The emperor, his friends, counselors, ministers, courtiers and their ladies, reclined around low tables. The *Emperor's Tongue,* stood behind him, his long chopsticks at the ready to try each and every dish served his lord, armed with the sure knowledge that the ivory in his chopsticks would turn instantly black in reaction to whatever poisons his tongue might not discern quickly enough.

Hundreds of servants in constantly changing lines served course after course of delicacies carefully planned by countless cooks to meet the essential *five flavors* balance. The feast began with astringent, health-giving myrlobans, continued with striped fish in *leaping sauce*, deer tongues from northern Kansu, *Venus clams* from the Shantung coast, and sugar crabs from the Yangtze River. Steamed shoots dipped in summer garlic, *white flower snake*, goose eggs and a Divine Formes mushroom pate´, roast duck tinctured with hot *fagara* and salt, were followed by fresh lychees and loquats, rushed along the roads from far south Ling-nan. There were dried oysters, mountains of white rice, fresh rose-colored melons and, since it was the season, baskets of glowing persimmons. Varieties of real wine—rice, ginger or grape—filled carafes.

"Good evening, daughter," the duke greeted Tse Tsien with a smile. "You're looking radiant tonight!"

"Thank you, Most Honorable Father. It's wonderful for me to have you and all the Tai Yuan family here." She realized, as she said it, how much she truly did enjoy the company of her adopted family. "It's been so good to be with you these past weeks. I see you all much too seldom."

"The very situation I was talking to my good wife about today. I'd hoped to consult with you before, but..."

Ceiling fans turned overhead, fanning cooled air over the diners, blending the smells of food and perfumes and incense into a dizzying potpourri of scents. Trays were heaped with stone honey in the shapes of little men, tigers, elephants and lions, and Persian cakes, made from rice powder boiled in milk.

For the emperor's table only, there was a small basket of the rare golden peaches originally from Samarkand, now grown by Camel Kuo. Their twig ends sealed with wax, this precious fruit lay in baskets lined with bamboo leaves to lessen the shock of traveling from Kuo to the palace.

"Will you come to my quarters after dinner so I can show you my star maps, Tse Tsien?" Kao Tsung leaned across the table.

"I'm not sure I can, but I'll try."

A gong called the court to attention, the Provost of Feasts stood, cleared his throat importantly and intoned, "His Most Luminous Illustrious has asked me to make the following announcement—please compose a poem in celebration of this night, this season, this place, to honor the noble Duke Shih-kuo and his family, as well as the remarkable emissary, Hsuan Tsung. Following the entertainment you will each recite your poetry for our enjoyment."

An excited chatter filled the hall.

"Most Illustrious," the duke said to the emperor, seated at his left. "As you give us great honor tonight, I am going to presume on your graciousness to..."

"Li-shih Min will do, sir," the emperor admonished. "What small thing can I do for you?"

"It's concerning our daughter, Wu Tse Tsien," the duke glanced at his wife, who nodded encouragement. "It might be difficult, as she is obviously important to you, but I wonder if you would be willing to let her leave the capital for the rest of the year, to be with us in Tai Yuan. I have urgent need of a competent secretary, but more than that, we've grown to love her and would like to bring her home with us."

"Has she agreed?" Tai Tsung spoke quietly.

"No, I've not had a chance to discuss this with her, but I thought..."

"Tse Tsien? Have you an answer to the good duke's request?"

"No, I..." she looked around like a startled deer, first at the emperor, then Kao Tsung. "I would like to think about it, if I may. It's very good of you, and I'm deeply honored."

"Very well then, we'll postpone decisions until later." The emperor looked at her hard and long, picked up a persimmon and bit into it so forcefully that red-orange juice squirted out, dripping down over his hand.

Into the wide arena below the dining tables, silk-clad acrobats flipped and twirled beside a dozen high-stepping horses whose manes were twined with silken threads, whose hooves had been gilded. Their gold-emblazoned saddles were topped with unicorn heads and phoenix wings.

Batu and Tse Tsien exchanged glances across the hall, for they recognized Igren horses, although they'd never seen any dressed quite like this before. Their amazement increased as the horses began to perform. They tossed their heads and swished their tails as they took mincing steps from side to side in time to the *ch'ing pei ch'u,* the *Song of the Overturned Cup.* Then they pirouetted through intersecting patterns. Tumblers vaulted over them onto tiers of benches held high by muscular men wearing leopard loincloths.

The music changed as palace girls in diaphanous Turkish costumes glided sinuously into the arena, playing the eight-faced thunder drums carried by dwarves. The drums' deep thunder sounded, the horses followed, responding fluently to the beat. As the crescendo began, more dancing girls gave each horse a cup filled with wine. The horses took the cups in their mouths and lay down with riders still on their backs. Then they scrambled to their feet, returned the cup with the wine still in it and pranced away, their bodies curving around a tight circle. As drums pounded and cymbals clashed, they stood up on their hind legs and pawed the air triumphantly before cantering out of the ring.

Into the now empty arena came a small boy dressed simply in baggy white pants. He played a bamboo flute whose shrill sound pierced the scented air. A gasp went up from hundreds of throats as they saw the gigantic animal that followed him. Great ears fanning, great trunk waving, an elephant walked in with heavy grace. It was painted all over with cerise, white, and yellow designs of symbols and flowers. On the elephant's back, a platform with decorated seats was strapped. At each of the four corners of this *howdah* stood an archer, his bow at the ready. Seated cross-legged in the center was Hsuan Tsung himself.

The boy stood to one side as the elephant knelt before the emperor, then raised its trunk in a screaming, rafter-rattling salute.

The emperor laughed delightedly. "Well, I've heard of these marvelous beasts before, but I've never actually seen one, Hsuan Tsung. No wonder the P'an P'an kings use elephants to wage their wars! Who wouldn't surrender before a whole army of these giants!" He stepped down from his throne and stood looking up, assessing the might of this animal as a military tool.

"Would you like a ride, Most Gracious Illuminated?" said Hsuan Tsung. He gestured to the boy, who played a different tune. The elephant curved its trunk onto the floor beside the emperor.

"I certainly would! How do I get up there?"

At a second musical command from the boy, the elephant picked up the astonished emperor and lifted him under the tasseled roof where Hsuan Tsang sat smiling.

"Splendid! Simply splendid!" Tai Tsung exclaimed, looking down at all the upturned faces. "You have earned my gratitude, traveler. Will this grand beast carry us both for awhile?"

"Aye, and ten more if need be."

They circled the hall several times until the elephant lowered them to the dais again. Torchlight flickered. Another round of wine was served.

"It's time to hear poetry," the emperor announced. "Wang Wei, will you begin?"

Wang Wei, a rotund, jolly looking man, stood and smiled as if at a private joke. "Mine's not long, Sire, but it may amuse us...'If I hear, sir, you've been nibbling cinnabar powder...'"

Most of the audience recognized that he was poking fun at alchemists who believed that eating cinnabar, the stone of longevity, would allow them to join the band of immortals. His poem completed, he sat down to general laughter.

Tu Fu declared himself ready. "This is a poem I call, 'In the city I meet a friend and we spend the night eating and drinking'...rather like we're doing tonight" His voice droned on, through simple-sounding lines."'...and why is life so full of goodbyes?'"

"Very good!" said the jovial emperor. "Now, how about our young lady of honor, have you a poem, Wu Chao Tse Tsien?"

"Yes, I fear it's not amusing, however, it's 'I watch the green leaves turn to red.'"

"Poetry reflects all feelings, my dear," he encouraged her.

"This is simply, A Love Song." She began in a low voice, "'My thoughts are many and tumultuous', and ended with "'If you do not believe I have wept... constantly since that time...open my wardrobe case...and examine my pomegranate flower dress."

She sank back down, strangely troubled.

"Lovely!" "Such melancholy!" Were comments she heard.

"I'm ready," said Li Bo. He rose slowly, towering over everyone in the room, looking more like a wrestler than a poet. "This is a poem entitled, *My Trip in a Dream to the Lady of Heaven Mountain.*

"Hear! Hear!" Several people called out.

"I believe it to be as much a poem of what's yet to come as it is of what's already past." In a sonorous voice he read his long poem. "From space I could hear the Rooster of Heaven. Bears grumbling, dragons humming, fountains rumbling..."

Tse Tien's thoughts drifted. *Just when I thought that life would go on just as it was, it changes! What would it be like, I wonder....to be part of a family again?*

Li Bo continued. "Rainbows are her clothing...her horses are the wind...the Lady Within the Clouds appears...all things swirl as she descends."

How full of possibilities the world is! I'd miss the emperor terribly though, we've grown so close...and I know he needs me, but....

Lines of Li Bo's poem called themselves to her attention. "Tigers strumming zithers...coaches phoenix drawn...the immortals now assemble...gone are the mists of a moment ago...ten thousand affairs out of the past are a stream flowing on."

Ending, Li Bo took a dozen bows as everyone cheered.

Tse Tsien felt the words of Li Bo's poetry sink into her heart like drops of fire. She didn't understand why they hurt so much, what cord of her heart they had plucked. She was not even aware of the next poets who spoke their lines.

Then she heard Kao Tsung begin to sing, *Narcissus by the River* "We have drunk wine and discussed literature. Our hearts have beat together with the same emotions. Softly we sing together the old song..."

He looked across the tables to her, oblivious of the knowing stares around him. She smiled at him, and for the first time heard...that he loved her.

As from a great distance, she watched as the emperor awarded prizes. She knew she should do something, but felt in such turmoil, she could not. Excusing herself, she walked quickly out into the cool night where no one could see that sudden tears had made her purple eye paint drip down over the red and blue pomegrantes of her gown.

She looked up and saw the full moon circled 'round by a double rainbow, felt that it was a sign from her father, a symbol of his presence. She stumbled, unseeing, into the garden.

46
A PRINCE IS PROPHESIED

SHE SAT DOWN ON A STONE GARDEN BENCH BESIDE THE TALL CLEPSYDRA-CLOCK and watched its dragon-headed siphons spit a thin, luminous thread of water into the shadowed, flower-shaped container beneath. The hiss and gurgle of water was a small, comforting sound. She felt her skin soak up the moonlight.

Something, some movement, some sound, made her realize, after a timeless time, that she was not alone. What she had thought was a shadow in the shape of a man was, in reality, a man sitting in the shadows. At the moment she recognized this, the shadow said, "Good evening, Lady Wu, I hope I did not startle you." His voice flowed reassuringly. "I was lost in the moonlight when you came."

"I know, I, too..."

"I sometimes think that the moon gives us strength, a different kind of strength from that of the sun, a way to wash away the dark places within us. As necessary as sunlight, perhaps."

"Do I know you?" she whispered. *How does he know me? He seems to answer my thoughts...*

"I am Hsuan Tsung, I saw you earlier at the grand feast."

His robe shimmered like a pale sun as he sat beside her in the moonlight. A fragrant, smoke-spice smell of frankincense enclosed her in his presence.

"Perhaps I can help you understand your true self, to better understand your grief and confusion?" he said.

Tse Tsien drew in her breath sharply, "How did you know? Who told you?"

"No one told me. It was evident, to one who knows how to see."

Jade pipes tipped water into the next reservoir with a gentle *ping!*

that sounded, in their clarity, like the man's words themselves.

"Are you homesick? For I see by your hair and your eyes that you come from the Pamirs, a countryside I traveled through many moons ago."

"Did you pass by Burkhan Kaldun? Did you see my people, the Igren? The clan of Chagan Tashih Shaymak?" She said excitedly, called from reverie by the thought that this man might bring more news.

"As a matter of fact, I did. They were wonderfully hospitable. I stayed with them as they moved up into summer pasture for some weeks while my leg healed from a fall I took going through the high pass."

"And you saw him, saw the Chagan?"

"I saw the old Chagan laid to rest, yes. His was a peaceful passing. His people were well pleased with their new Chagan. Why do you ask?"

Suddenly she remembered to be cautious, "It has been a long time since I left. I just wondered."

"Why do you sorrow so?"

"It's just, well, Li-Bo's poem tonight, many of the poems, in fact, made me feel so alone. You see, when I was little, there in the mountain valleys, everything was perfect. It was a paradise." She paused and looked up at the moon. "Now I have lost paradise...forever it seems."

"Ah, *ch'an* students never lose paradise! Or so my master says."

"Is that the Buddha that you told His Majesty about?"

"Even so."

"I don't understand what you just said—about paradise."

"I will be honored to help you understand, Princess."

"Thank you, but I'm not a princess."

"No? I think that you are, although you may not have realized it yet. Well, maybe not a princess, more likely a prince. I'll tell you something interesting, if you'd care to listen?"

As she said nothing, he continued, "You were near enough to see the sutras that I gave the emperor, weren't you? In the north of India where I lived, there are many such, stored in boxes, tens of tens of them in rows half a li long.

"One that I happened to read was the *Mahamegha sutra*, we'd say *Ta-yun-ching*, an unimportant sutra compared to the *Prajna-Paramitra,* but interesting nonetheless for it's a prophecy written almost seven hundred years ago."

"It can't be of much use today then, can it?" She said, becoming interested in spite of her self.

"Ah, but it can! Because it tells of the coming of a great ruler in Chian—a *woman* who will emerge as the ruler of an empire to which all nations will submit. This woman would be an incarnation of Maitreya, the future Buddha, all wisdom, all compassion, omnipotent." He reached over and held both her hands in his lean, thin ones. "The sutra, dear Wu ChaoTse Tsien, names this person, prophesies that her name will be the Prince of Wu. So you see..."

"You think this Wu prince is *me?* That's not possible!"

"I think it is, yes. I don't believe there can be any other interpretation. I saw you tonight, felt the power of your presence, heard your mind—and in a sudden flash, I *knew!*"

"No! You must be mistaken! I can't! I don't want to be a prince, nor emperor, nor any such thing. I'm not..." she shook her head from side to side, finding no way to turn that she had not been before. Her whole body began to shake from the storm deep within her.

Hsuan Tsung waited until she stopped trembling. "There, there, you know we cannot escape our karma, our destiny. I didn't mean to add to your burdens. You must know you're not alone, you are part of the universe...integral with it."

She was calm as if time had stopped. Weary, deep in her bones. Only sorrow and a longing for sleep remained. She sighed and stood up. "Thank you, Hsuan Tsung, but I can't seem to absorb any more words tonight..."

"Of course, Maitreya, go to your bed. But remember, He is always with you."

"He?" She glanced again at the lunar halo, incandescent rainbow of remembrance. Without another word, she turned away and went into the palace.

TSE TSIEN FELT THE NEED TO BE ALONE, A NEED TO FINALLY FACE THE GRIEF that clutched at and bound her heart.

It's not that I didn't know father would die, it's just that I've been so busy, just surviving, these past years and I always knew he was there for me...but now, that great eagle has flown from my life forever.

She shivered as if the shafts of moonlight that silvered her room were currents of icy air from off the mountains.

I wish I could hear your voice, Father...I shall miss it so. Your voice has always been the sound of home...where now is my home?

She warmed her hands over the fire that burned in the standing brazier.

Now I must be truly Chian, a Wu family daughter, but you will always be a part of me...all that we shared, all that you taught me will continue...

Memories, acute aching memories possessed her. She curled up on her bed. Her body fell blessedly asleep, while her dreaming soul took wings...

FLYING WESTWARD, RETRACING THE ROAD SHE HAD COME BY, over mountains and dunes, past lakes and streams and high desert and finally over the vast green valleys of the Pamirs in early summer...

Below, she saw the ice-blue slopes of Burkhan Kaldun, saw the Jun and Barun Rivers flowing, left and right, into the valley, saw many domed ger of The People clustered in family groups as far as the eye could see, heard the mourning wail of Igren's throats, ten times ten times ten strong, that filled their mountain cup with sorrow, heard their voices chant the Song of the Dead Leader . . .

"In the time of grass thou didst nourish me, O my Chagan!
In the winter's wind thou didst warm me, O my Chagan!
Thou wert my hearth's keeper and the water
from life's stream, O my Chagan!
Now is the hearthstone, like thy body, cold.
Now is the water gone from that sweet lake
whereby I sat and the shade gone
from the garden wherein I dwelt, O my Chagan!"

As a falcon dives, plummeting from the heights, Talima's spirit speared down with unerring aim to the casket that lay in state before the great council ger. She hovered. It seemed both strange and natural to see Tashih Shaymak laying there, his vital, heavy body inert, his grey cat's eyes forever closed.

She watched as the Bequi, dressed in her ceremonial white furs, danced her shuffle-dance around and around. She heard her keening cry, "The strong stone is broken! The eagle that once flew before us has fallen. Where now, Great Wolf, where now, shall his sudde dwell? Where now his spirit-power living ever? Speak now, Blue Wolf Mother-of-us-all—show us where to look. Give us this blessing, let this strong spirit remain with us! Give us a sign before the sudde of this great Chagan ascends into the Everlasting Sky, to be lost to us forever from the earth."

She saw, with her green-flecked, golden hawk's eyes...the nine-yak-tail standard that stood at the head of the casket, saw the white, wooden falcon at its crest, saw its outspread wings slowly rise and fall as if flexing its wings, preparing to fly into the crisp, mountain air, into the Everlasting Sky they were created from. And she knew it for the sign... knew that the Great Wolf, in her infinite wisdom, had allowed the spirit-force, the sudde, of Tashih Shaymak to remain with his people for all time, watching over them from the eyes of the white falcon. And she saw that it was good.

As if that were the signal to proceed, the Igren gathered to accompany the casket across a meadow and along the trail that led to ancestral mounds on the river. Talima's hawk-flight followed them. Opposite her mother's grave, opposite the stone statue she remembered as Tengri's wife, they stopped under a lacy tamarisk tree.

There, in a hollowed out space between the roots of this evergreen tree, a miniature wooden ger had been built. They put Tashih Shaymak's body inside it, set him upright, facing south. His wives and sisters laid his bows and arrows and embroidered saddle blanket in his lap. Children placed dishes of meat, mare's milk, or millet around his body. The bones of his favorite horses, purified by fire, were laid in front of him by his Cup Companions.

Then the grave was closed. One by one, Igren walked by. Each one threw a handful of dust over the memory of their past. The new Chagan, Jalco Shaymak, came forward carrying the nine-yak-tail standard on which the white falcon flew with renewed spirit. He tamped the raw earth nine times, then turned, and walked away. The people followed him. They flowed back down the hill to the rest of their lives.

Talima-falcon lifted into the air, distancing herself, rising higher, ever higher. She saw below her, in the haze of sunset, her father's remaining brothers mount their horses and ride back and forth before the tamarisk until all traces of the grave and its contents were obliterated, pounded smooth under the horses' hooves. Only then, their wind-raw ululation winding out against the hills, did they leave, dropping down into the valley like heavy hunting birds.

She looked up and up and ever farther up into the Everlasting Sky.

With a deep, heart-shuddering scree-ee-ee! she soared, alone, wingtips touching the eternal, cerulean blue that was her home.

Released from grief, the girl once known as Talima, slept.

The emperor's procession wound its way westward. Campfires cast flickering shadows against silken tents during cool nights. Sunshine and cloud shadows chased each other across ripening grain fields during long days of traveling. The animals, rested from their sojourn of three moons in Loyang, stepped along at a lively pace. Even the elephants and pack camels were content to be on the move.

Military troops and couriers dashed back and forth over the crowded road, bringing news, reports, and memorials for the emperor to deal with, taking his commands back to Changan. He and his ministers held close colloquy, determining the affairs of the far-flung empire as they rode. They did not tarry long in any one place, for Tai Tsung had remembered his promise to be in Kuo for the Wedding of the River God in order to arrange some sort of relief from the excessive taxes the old sorceresses demanded. The emperor was sure that the money raised, ostensibly to finance that ancient ritual, probably ended up in the pockets of those same sorceresses. He meant to find a way to stop the practice without creating trouble from those who still believed in them.

As they traveled, the court women played games and visited each other's palanquins with their children. Some palace girls rode horseback, but to avoid stares from vulgar peasants, wore a *"mi-li"*, a thin, cotton veil that entirely enveloped them from their heads to their ankles. When Batu was not paying court to Merket, he rode or gambled with Juchi and other guardsmen.

Tse Tsien, her hair pinned up under a flat-brimmed hat, wearing a silk version of the full-legged Igren pants tucked into her wine-red, knee-high boots, rode between her watchful bodyguards. Her Wu family mother and father had bid her an affectionate farewell and ridden north to Tai Yuan, urging her to come home as soon as possible. The duke promised all sorts of pleasures—polo, parties and an active part in the organization of their many farms.

Tse Tsien was simply glad to be riding Shira back to the familiar routine in Changan with no plans or expectations of the future. Just moving on under the endless blue arch of the Everlasting Sky.

47
SORCERESSES AND A RIVER GOD'S WIFE

FAINA FELT AS IF SHE FLOATED EFFORTLESSLY THROUGH THE LONG BUSY DAYS. An early autumn haze swathed the hills in a golden aura, a pale reflection of the glow in her heart. She had accepted Camel's marriage offer and her thoughts these days were all on plans for their wedding.

Never before, never in my whole life, have I looked forward to anything! Oh, maybe a feast or a holiday, but never to life itself! Dear Camel, how wonderful it will be, just the two of us until—until the babies come!

She gave a little skip and danced between the noisy looms. She was a ray of sunshine in the cavernous weaving shed. The weavers looked up and smiled, happy for her happiness.

One old crone, the eldest of all the weavers, who had watched Faina with particular intensity, put down her shuttle as if a decision had been made. She left the shed nodding and mumbling to herself.

The same old woman, surrounded by six wrinkled crones, came out of the supervisor's office as Faina went in to make her report.

Odd, thought Faina, *those bright-eyed old busybodies...I wonder what they're doing here...probably pestering Supervisor with gossip about some wrongdoer...not my concern, however.*

"Come in, sit you down." the supervisor greeted her with unaccustomed warmth. "My, it's a fine day, is it not?"

"Yes it is, Honorable One, have our plans progressed? Have you heard from the capital?"

"I'm sure I don't know what you mean, Faina."

"You know—my idea to sell our leftover dye powders as cosmetics that you said you'd help me with. You must remember!"

"Well, I can tell you it *has* met with some interest on the part of a few influential eunuchs in the White Jade Pavilion."

Faina clapped her hands. "I knew it! A perfect market for them! When do we begin to bottle them?"

"Not so fast, Faina. There are other more important—and exciting—bits of business to absorb your time! A great honor, it is! You shall be remembered and praised!"

"I? For what, Honorable One? I've done nothing."

"True. Not yet, that is. But you *will!*" She covered a gap-toothed smile with her gnarled hand. "You saw the delegation leaving? Just as you arrived?"

"Those old hens? Cackling and scratching? Yes, I saw them, why?"

"Faina, you shock me! Those women are the most learned and august sorcerers of the eastern Huang Ho valley! You should be more careful how you speak of them—or they might..."

"If they're friends of yours, Supervisor, I apologize."

"I accept your apologies, Faina, particularly in light of the information they shared with me. I've had a small part in helping them to their decision." She smoothed her eyebrows carefully with the middle finger of her left hand. "Yes, they're getting ready to announce the name of the girl they've chosen to honor this year as the river god's *bride!* Isn't that thrilling?"

"I suppose so, if it matters to you, M'am." Faina was impatient, wanting to give her week's report so that she could be on her way to the gardens and Camel.

"It will matter to you too, yes it will!" She tittered uncharacteristically, "Because you see, they have chosen *you!* Now what do you think of that?"

"Chosen *me?* As the river god's bride? What does that mean? I have too much to do as it is, Honorable Supervisor."

"Never you mind all that now! All your work will be done by someone else beginning tomorrow. Aren't you thrilled?"

"Not really. I'd rather not, if you please, Ma'm."

"It's out of my hands, Faina. You have no choice. Don't be a fool...any other girl would simply *leap* at the chance to be the god's bride...make the best of it, my girl!"

Faina sighed...*first a bear girl, then a silk girl, now a river god's bride? When does it ever stop?* "All right, what do I have to do?"

"Do? All you have to do is loll about all day in lovely, expensive silk clothes made especially for you, eat marvelous foods, drink the best wines—and you'll be waited on hand and foot. Until the wedding."

"And then?"

"Then you'll ride through the village on your bridal raft, adored by all, until it's set afloat on the river! Doesn't that sound wonderful?"

"How long do I have to stay on this floating raft?"

"How long? Well, we don't know that, *exactly*, do we?" she said brightly.

"Roughly how long, Supervisor?" Faina shivered with the sudden chill of apprehension.

"Until the river god accepts you as his bride, of course."

"And how does he do this?"

"We don't really know that either. You see, no one has ever come back to tell us… "

"Are you telling me that whoever rides that river raft never returns? *Drowns* in the river?" She jumped to her feet.

"I don't think you should pay too much attention to that aspect of the celebration, Faina. You would appear selfish in so doing, would you not? It's so important to the whole chou that the god be well satisfied. After all, that's why *we,* why the sorceresses choose the prettiest girl to please him. As his bride, you'll be of great service to your community and we'll be forever grateful to you for averting floods that an unhappy god would visit upon us otherwise!"

Faina turned and ran from the room, demons of fear and anger and hopelessness nipping at her skirts. She ran out of town down the long road to the gardens. *Camel,* she told herself, *Camel will know what to do.*

But Camel did not know what to do. He knew the power of the sorceresses, denied officially, yet awesomely real to the great majority of country people. He was completely at a loss to know what to do or whom to go to. The baron? In past dealings with him, Camel had found him far more involved in the social life of the capital and its parties than he was with his town's problems. Besides, this would not look like a problem to most, it would look like a solution to the vagaries of the river they all depended on. He was sure of one thing, however, he was sure that he would entreat the Earth Dragons themselves in order to protect Faina, the girl that had brought springtime into his life.

All he could do, for the time being, was to hold her, dry her tears, reassure her that all would be well, even though he wasn't sure of that himself. Meanwhile, he had a week while Faina was made ready for her tragic role, one short week to work a miracle.

With a burdened heart, he reluctantly sent her back to Kuo at dawn.

Faina hoped to slip into her room unnoticed. But that was not to be, she realized the instant she entered the street where she lived. Garlands of silk flowers festooned doorways on which were pinned sprays of herbs. Flags, indolent in the morning air, hung from every rooftop. A village drummer sat on the central well-mound, bouncing a beat that kept the workers keeping time.

She hesitated, unsure of which way to go. A little boy began to run past her, stopped, and his face lit up as he shouted, "Here she is! Our bride has come!"

All activity stopped, all faces turned toward her. They clustered around her closely, then melted aside to let the sorceresses walk through the tunnel of their bodies to greet Faina. She stood immobile. Her feet grew into the ground. Her heart scarcely beat. Her breath was ragged like that of a trapped woodland creature.

Singing ancient hymns of jubilation, they lifted her onto the strongest man's shoulders and bore her to her own door. Within, the halls and rooms were lined with fresh flowers. On bamboo mats, persimmons and grapes glowed blood-orange and jade-green in sunbeams that filtered through waxed-paper windows. Bolts of gleaming silk stood against the wall, waiting for the seamstress' skills. Rosemary, sweet basil, and dried peach petals floated on cauldrons of hot water, scenting the steamy air.

The seven sorceresses stood in a semi-circle in the center of her room. They passed a two-handled bronze cup between them, each one adding a pinch of powder taken from within her wide sleeves. They pressed in around Faina and gave her the cup, gesturing for her to drink.

"No, you don't understand," Faina finally found her voice. "This is all a mistake. I don't want to be part of your celebration. You must not choose me, there are other girls who are more beautiful...I'm already promised to someone, a *real* someone! Please, listen!"

"You are the chosen one." They said in unison. "You will be silent now and clear your mind."

Faina stamped her foot in exasperation. "No! I will *not* be quiet and

I will *not* be the river god's bride!"

"Bind her. But first, the sacrament." Several of the surprisingly strong crones held her, putting the cup to her lips. One held her nose, another stroked her throat so that she was obliged to swallow the bitter liquid until the cup was empty. Quickly then, they tied a twisted, white silk scarf across her mouth and around her head, effectively silencing her.

Then they moved quite briskly. They took off their own outer robes, pushed up the sleeves of their chemises and, without another word, stripped Faina and unbound her hair, which fell, a rippling waterfall, down her thin back.

She stood naked while they inspected her like hens eyeing a strange not-quite-dead bug. Their heads were cocked to one side, bobbing up and down as they walked around her. Faina heard someone giggle, and realized with a start that it was herself. *There's nothing to laugh at*, she chided—and giggled again. A seductive languor flowed through her. She found that it felt good to be bathed and scrubbed and rubbed by soft old hands.

Feeling Faina's muscles finally relax beneath their hands, they smiled a toothless smile and removed the cloth that bound her mouth.

After they had cleansed her to their satisfaction. They dried her and rubbed sweet-smelling oil into her body. One sorceress knelt in front of her and, spreading Faina's legs, began cutting off the springy fuzz of her pubic hair until the gentle curve of her Venus mound was bare. Another one poked her gnarled forefinger into the soft lips of her vagina, probing into the moist flesh to ascertain that her *gatekeeper of paradise,* the rubbery shield of her hymen, was still intact—that she was indeed a virgin, worthy of the god they served.

Lastly, they settled a diaphanous silk shift over her head and led her to the pallet they'd prepared. They took turns tempting her with small morsels of exotic foods, foods that few villagers saw in a lifetime. They offered her one tray heaped with tiny, sticky cakes sprinkled with smoky-tasting sugar slivers, more often than any of the others. Soon Faina lay back in weightless wonder, lost in a dreaming world of fascinating splendor that sang in her blood.

One after the other, the strong, quavering voices of the old women sang a litany, "That's right, dearie, eat and dream today…for tomorrow you fast…only to drink the dreaming drink…while we purify your soul of its base desires…for the remainder of your earthbound life…until you'll be a shining star of purity…to save us all from the river god's power to destroy. Sleep now. Dream."

48
JUSTICE

"WAKEN, WAKEN, LADY!" HER MAIDSERVANT KNOCKED on the translucent sides of Wu Tse Tsien's bed. "The sun is high... well past cock's crow and it's time that honest folks were about the business of the day!"

"Go 'way." A voice murmured sleepily from within the shaded bed. "Went to bed too late—too much talk—too much wine—need more sleep."

"Be that as it may—and may is might or rather *must* in this case. His Most Luminous Majesty has sent for you." Mai-li said cheerily as she opened curtained windows, poured water into a large porcelain bowl and bustled about.

Tse Tsien swung her long legs over the edge of the bed and sat there for a moment, stretching her body awake before she reached for a robe. "Sire's sent for me? Hurry! Brush my hair. Lay out my dress, I'll not bathe this morning—just lay out a dress, any dress—I'll cover it with that purple kimono, the one with blue kingfisher's feathers. He likes that one."

"Heavens, Mistress! His Majesty didn't say right *now!* He said when you could. A great lady can't go out half done, now can she? Here's your nice bath now and mercy me, I almost forgot!"

"Mai-li, half done is better than un-done. I'll be old before I'm thirty, listening to you!"

"You'll never be old, my Lady, you'll be one of the immortals." She squeezed warm soapy water through a large sponge and began to bathe Tse Tsien where she stood in the warmth of a shaft of sunlight.

"I wonder what he wants...'Sky, the man turns out more work overnight than most of us do in a day! He must've finished a rough draft of the edict he plans to post in Kuo today. This silly festival is taking up too much of his energy. He looked tired last night, listening to our fatuous host, the baron."

"Not silly at all, Lady, the festival I mean and that's what I almost forgot, I mean that's what I wanted to remember to tell you. As I walked around the market this morning...it was still early, mind, and you still asleep... couldn't help thinking that this was a dear little town to get so heated up about an imaginary wedding—to an imaginary old god, at that! That's what I was telling myself and my basket was getting heavy with all the lovely fruit I bought for My Lady...have some for your first meal, *do.*"

Tse Tsien scarcely listened to her, aware only of the babbling sound of her own mind. She was planning the day ahead and wondering how she could get all the calligraphy done that the emperor requested, much less all that he'd add before the ceremonies tomorrow.

"And so I thought to myself, since you weren't needing me, Lady, that I'd just go down to the river and see this *bride* for myself. I walked down to where her fancy little place was set up on the river and there she was, asleep as I thought at the time but now I'm not so sure. Anyway I was that amazed, Lady!" She brushed her mistress's hair, coiling it onto the top of her head.

"When I saw her I thought 'twas *you*—sort of another you. I mean the girl who lay on that raft, surrounded by flowers...and my, they were beautiful...but so was she. She looked somehow so like you, my Lady, that I lost my breath for a minute and just stood there like a big fish out of water! 'Twas her hair! So unusual! Whiter than yours, more yellow-like and not so reddish, but so lovely, fanned out like that around her sweet little face and I thought you'd ought to see her...that you might want to, I mean, My Lady. Enough like your sister she looked..."

"I absolutely forbid you to utter even one more word! I can't think!" Then, seeing the woman's face crumple into old wrinkles and her dark eyes film with tears, "I'm sorry, I don't mean to hurt your feelings, Mei, but you do go on so! Now, quietly please, help me with my face, nothing elaborate today for we haven't time, I must see what the emperor needs."

All day, in the midst of conferences, hearing the emperor and his ministers debate policy, listening to reports from local Kuo officials on the harvest, on the census, deliberating, writing, Tse Tsien was aware of something niggling at the back of her conscious mind. Something forgotten? Something not done?

She had no time to give the feeling her full attention until she was again in her bed.

It feels good to be horizontal. Now what was it?

Her thoughts felt around her brain like a tongue feeling for a loose tooth. Finally, in obedience to her search, the words popped into her mind "*...enough like your sister she looked...so like you...her hair! More yellow...*"

In a flash, she remembered Zanggi telling her that Faina had been sent to a silk village. And Kuo was a renowned silk village. Her intuition nudged her. She knew somehow that this girl must be Faina. Where had she been? By the river...Mei-li said, asleep on a raft on the river? No, a little house...where? She reached overhead and pulled the bell rope that would summon Mei-li.

Stumbling into her slippers, sleep-slow, virtually inarticulate in response to her mistress's excited questioning, Mei-li came.

From her mumbled replies, Tse Tsien quickly learned all that her servant knew about the yellow-haired girl, the chosen bride for the symbolic wedding to take place tomorrow.

No, not tomorrow, today! It'll be dawn before long. I'll wait until light, then I'll see if it's really Faina, and if so...what might be possible. Whatever's necessary.

"Wake me at first light without fail, d'you hear me? And I'll need Shira as soon as I'm up. Send someone to the stables."

"Now, my Lady? It's the middle of the night."

"I know that, you great ninny. Send someone *now,* so there'll be no delay in the morning. Now let me sleep the few hours there are left."

The first cock was coaxing light from the sky, as Tse Tsien swung onto Shira's back. Thin blue smoke from last night's fires spiraled into fresh morning air. Shira's hooves clattered on the cobblestones as they rode through empty streets down to the Huang Ho River.

She saw the nuptial raft anchored close to shore. It was a flower bedecked bower rocking gently in the wash of pointed-bow fishing boats that passed. Rag-tag guards, a variety of knives stuck in their sashes, stood talking together at the end of the dock.

They're a tough-looking lot, but jolly, they're probably proud to be doing what they're doing, however...

On the floating pavilion, she could see three sleeping girls curled up around a beautifully clad girl with flaxen hair.

It's true. After all this time, it is Faina! I've found her at last! Now, how do I get her out of this predicament?

Into her mind came the image of a ragged dirty Faina, standing beside stinking, steaming springs, holding up her skinny arms to be swept onto Bagatur's back and away from Mazar Tagh's terror.

I could charge down there on Shira, swim across and get her... but what a disturbance that would create! Sire would not be pleased if all his teaching were in vain. So. Slowly, turtle, slowly...how to accomplish a rescue without upsetting the natural balance of things?

She smoothed Shira's dappled coat and sat still looking down on the river below. Its sleepy, muddy current flowed smoothly on. Saffron-colored loess-land in watery suspension rushed along, obscuring the teaming life within its banks.

Yes, that should work...if Sire agrees. It's worth a try. There's not much time!

She turned Shira and cantered back to the center of town and through the walled enclosure of the baron's household complex where they were staying.

She threw her reins to a waiting groom and ran toward the emperor's suite. She found him sitting alone in the courtyard, breaking the night's fast with tea and his favorite steamed buns stuffed with dates and nuts.

"I hope you are well this morning, Sire?" She bowed and sat down on a cushion opposite him.

"Splendidly, thank you. You're breathless, what've you been up to so early in the day?"

She reminded him of the search for her friend Faina and how Kat Kat Zanggi's men had tried to find her without any success. Then she told him of what she'd seen that morning.

"I remembered one of the myths you told me, those long ago days when I was so ill, the one about Ho Hsien-ku, the girl that ate moonbeams and mother-of-pearl and became a fairy, d'you remember?"

"Ah, yes, and after that, ate a supernatural peach, became immortal and lived happily ever after?" He smiled. "As I remember, she always carried an impossibly blue lotus."

"That's the one! You see, Faina *looks* like a fairy girl that ate moonbeams and mother-of-pearl...so that set me to thinking. Now I'm aware that you want to break the bitter hold of these sorceresses...have you been successful in finding an appropriate way to discredit them? Of stopping this absurd wedding ritual?"

"I still have hopes of doing so, although I've not been able to see my way clear to getting rid of them gracefully enough that their followers don't get their dander up and cause trouble. It's difficult you see, to actually do away with those old crones without making them martyrs. Tea, my dear?"

"Yes, please. I was thinking..."

"Mother of Heaven! Again? We're in trouble now!" He teased.

She smiled and continued, "I want to free my friend Faina and you want to free our people from burdensome taxes as well as restoring economic balance in the chou. I think I know how...a way of using the nature of their superstitions to accomplish both objectives."

A servant set an additional cup on the table and Tai Tsung poured fragrant green tea into it. "Here you are...have a steamed bun. We've another busy day ahead of us. Now go on, Tsien, I'm listening."

IT WAS A BUSY DAY, TOO, FOR THE SEVEN SORCERESSES. It would be their day of glory, this year greater than any before due to the sublime presence of the emperor himself.

Shortly after Tse Tsien rode away, as the last rooster proclaimed the morning, the seven crones stepped out of special sedan chairs lent by the baron and walked proudly down the dock. In truth, they could have walked no other way, for each wizened old woman had the most elaborate arrangement of hair, feathers, flowers, twisted silk cords and borrowed carved ivory hairpins that she could manage. The combination of headdresses and voluminous ceremonial robes on their shrunken bodies made them look like a procession of little girls playing dress-up in their mother's clothes.

The village guards, however, knew their real power and bowed deeply as they approached. Then they pulled, hand over hand, on the hemp rope attached to the raft, bringing it alongside the dock so the seven could step aboard.

On the raft, girl attendants propped up a groggy Faina against a pile of tree-floss pillows and began to chant, swinging small brass censers back and forth over her inert body. The smoke of incense blended with the scent of flowers and the stench of river sewage.

Although the wedding was not scheduled until midday, it was not long before the riverbanks began to fill with people. Villagers brought woven mats and baskets of food to establish a place as close as possible to the platform that was reserved for aristocrats, the emperor and his court.

On the crowded riverbank, children played. Little boys rode stick horses heedlessly across tolerant grownups' legs. Little girls played ring games. Babies rolled and tumbled and slept. Vendors sang the delights of the food they had for sale—fresh mussels, chicken bits in hot fagara sauce, stone honey cakes, and sweet melons.

At midday, in a blare of trumpets and tatoo of drums, the emperor and all the town officials arrived and took their places on the platform. While they settled themselves, the guards were struggling to subdue a hunchback man they caught trying to board the raft where only women were allowed.

"Crazy!" "Must be mad!" "It's just that strange old humpback." "What d'you suppose he thought he was doing? Taking the River God's bride for himself?" "Probably drunk." The waiting crowd jeered. The guards finally clubbed the man and dragged him away before his irreverent behavior could spoil the solemn festivities.

On a platform where flags flew from tall bamboo poles, the emperor, Tse Tsien, and a dozen ministers were seated. Kuo's magistrate and town elders filled seats not already occupied by the baron and his cronies. Before endless speeches began, Tai Tsung broke precedent by commanding that the god's bride be presented to him immediately.

The command passed from official to official, finally reaching the sorceresses. They put their heads together and began talking very fast "It's never been done...she is purified and must not be polluted by leaving the *Penance Hall* where she lives this day!" They dared not ask the emperor to come to them but they plainly did not know what to do.

Tai Tsung, seeing their confusion, stepped off the platform and strode down the dock, Tse Tsien at his side. Everyone watched this unusual development. The emperor stood looking down at the floating shell. He stared hard and long at the languid girl surrounded by flowers and haughty old women. Then he turned, smiled at Tse Tien by his side, and murmured, "Shall we begin?" She nodded.

"What?" He thundered, "is this some sort of rude joke that you think to play on your long-suffering emperor?"

Dismay and consternation were plain on the faces of all those within hearing.

"Do you dare the wrath of the Gods of Heaven by this blasphemy? Or are you simply too ignorant to know better?"

The seven old crones, suddenly stripped of their ascendant role, looked pinched and drawn. Town officials swarmed off the platform, running as fast as their trailing robes allowed, to prostrate themselves along the dock.

"What is wrong, Most Luminous Illustrious? What has happened to anger you, Glory of Glories?" the magistrate intoned fearfully.

"Wrong? Who is responsible for choosing *this* girl, for choosing Ho Hsien-ku herself as bride for the river god? Don't you people realize that he will never accept, *cannot* take an immortal into his watery realm?"

Each looked at the person nearest as if to see the blame fixed there. "An *Immortal,* Son of Heaven? Who?"

"I see, it's only ignorance. Then you are forgiven. But we will have to do something rather quickly, I fear, to placate the waiting river!" He glowered at the sorceresses. "Was it you? *You* who chose this girl? I see by the way you try to hide behind each other that it must be true. I will assume, in respect for your years, that you were not aware that this girl is one of the Eight Immortals, though how you could have overlooked this obvious fact judging by her hair alone, that she has eaten moonbeams and mother-of-pearl, just as our wise old stories tell us...you surely remember? Come here. We'll decide together what must be done."

The seven struggled with their terror and climbed up off the raft to stand, shaking, before the Son of Heaven. Thousands of onlookers, unable to hear, wondered what was happening.

"First of all, we must notify the god that there will be a slight delay, perhaps a day or two, while we find a more suitable bride for him. Since each of you professes to be on intimate terms with him, as you speak *for* him in all these matters, I suggest that one or more of you hie yourselves off to notify him. You know the way to his palace, I presume?"

Each of the seven looked around at the officials and the watching village and realized that her honor as a sorceress, her very life was at stake here, that she had no choice but to go...and go quickly.

Only one crone dared to speak, "But Your Gracious Majesty, the river god is known to live in the part of his kingdom where the water boils over great stones before it spills over the cascade below. It might be better if..."

"Splendid! I knew you'd know the way, little sister. Don't let us keep you. Will you go alone?" He summoned one of the guards to bring a small boat. "Never fear, if you don't return soon, I'll send someone else to seek you."

The first old woman grabbed two others and with an iron grip, pulled them along beside her into the skiff.

"Make it swift, sisters! Don't keep him wondering!" He turned to the magistrate. "You will inform the populace of this misunderstanding, Magistrate?"

"Indeed, Most Gracious Illuminated! And may I say that I, for one, questioned their choice from the very start. You know women—you can't trust them for the simplest thing, can you? And although my part is very small, I..." Seeing the emperor's frown, his words died and he backed off the dock. Followed by aides, he went into the crowd to announce the news and regain his authority.

"Wu Chao Tse Tsien?"

"At your service, Gracious Lord," she stepped forward.

"I want you to take Ho Hsien-ku to a place more fitting for an immortal fairy. Your quarters, perhaps? Until we can leave for Changan." He spoke loudly so that no one could have any doubt of his intentions, nor their reason.

Then he called several of his guardsmen. They lifted Faina from the raft onto the dock as if she *were* a barely incarnate moonbeam. Led by Tse Tsien, they walked back through the parting crowd. Gently, they laid Faina on the waiting palanquin. Bearers carried her away to safety.

After three quarter hours had sounded from the town clepsydra, the emperor said to the remaining sorceresses, "I see that you grow restless with desire to see the river god for yourselves. You want to share in your sisters' glory, am I not correct? Bring another skiff for these worthies, townsman, they have an important piece of work to do for us today!"

Plainly enjoying being the center of attention, the remaining four sorceresses nimbly climbed aboard and were set drifting on the river.

Two more quarter hours passed. Nothing happened. No one returned from the river.

"Now," said the emperor, "I understand that you, Magistrate, and at least one of your Kuo elders have helped the sorceresses, have been enthusiastic participants in this ceremony. If it's as you say, that we can't depend on women for anything important, even to deliver a simple message competently, then..." He spoke softly, rubbing a jade piece between his fingers. "It is advisable, imperative even, to be certain that the river god be informed of the delay in his wedding, wouldn't you agree?"

They dumbly agreed.

"Yes. Will you, Magistrate and you, Elder Yu Shih-nan, undertake this important mission?"

The magistrate bowed his head respectfully and looked at the river roiling below. His bowed shoulders showed his resignation.

Yu Shih-nan said, "Most Glorious Son of Heaven, perhaps we should wait awhile...to see if the women return by themselves. Then they could tell us whether the message had been properly delivered. Don't you think that would be a good idea?"

"That is thoughtful of you, Elder," said the emperor with ominous intensity, "You would not want to pass up the opportunity that you have so generously offered to mere girls, year after year, the privilege of conversing with the river god yourself, would you?"

"Yes, you must represent us! Tell the river god, man to man, that we're sorry...that we'll send someone to him very soon," the other elders urged.

Understanding that they had no choice, the magistrate and the elder set forth to add their strength of purpose to that of the seven sorceresses. Realizing that the usual wedding celebration would not take place that day, the villagers drifted away.

Tai Tsung sat patiently, waiting with the rest of the town dignitaries for the messengers' return.

"They must be having a grand time down there, but we must be sure. What shall we do now, Baron? Do you wish to proceed with this festival? Perhaps *you* should go and see if you can find the others?"

The baron's plump face became greasy with sweat. He prostrated himself, knocking his head against the ground so hard that he bloodied his forehead.

"Lord of the Cosmos, do not send me! We'll wait to continue the wedding...wait until *all* the messengers return...even if it should take forever!"

Tai Tsung smiled graciously, “Rise, Baron, since the river god has evidently decided to keep our messengers as his permanent guests, there’s really no need for you to go just yet. It’s time that we moved on to other things. I bid you good day.” He hooked his thumbs into his black sash and marched off between his guardsmen.

The subdued and silent Kuo officials hurried along in his wake as the changeless river continued its silent journey to the sea, sweeping the uninhabited flower-laden raft to its inevitable destiny.

One person remained where he had been thrown, under the platform. Camel Kuo awoke with a painful head and a desolate heart.

49
The Emperor Proposes

ANOTHER NEW YEAR—AND LATE THIS YEAR. THE HOLIDAY MOON GONE, the Budding Moon nearly full, one of the last mornings before firecrackers batter our peace for days! I've never gotten used to that shattering sound. How still it is, only the birds trilling their delight. Me, too. I'm happier than I thought possible—content is perhaps a better word. How many times I've walked this path since that morning when I went to meet my love, my Pirjhan... seems such a long time ago. Another lifetime, another person, even.

She had awakened early, eager to see what the day would bring. Spring winds, blowing through gauze curtains, called her to come out and taste again the morning of the world.

She wandered along garden paths that led north, away from the palace, and lingered by a pool where carp—poppy-orange, black and silver—fanned the bottom. Mirrored on the surface of the water was the incandescent disc of the moon that hung above the horizon as if reluctant to leave this world for another. She leaned over and looked into the pool. She saw her own face reflected there, haloed by the blue-shadowed moon. It was the face of a stranger. *Inanna, he used to call me. Hail to Inanna, first daughter of the moon, he'd sing...* She stirred the water's surface with her fingertips and watched her face dissolve into ripples as the fish swam up to investigate.

When Pirjhan was killed, I thought my world had ended. In a way it had. Now I have a new life, a new family—two families, actually, one here, one in Tai Yuan.

She stood up just as the sun erupted above the palace wing on her right...*the wing that Crown Prince Cheng used to have before the emperor could no longer stand his violent excesses, and exiled him to*

Ling-nan for the rest of his life. Three thousand li away seems hardly far enough!

She shivered and walked along with her hands tucked into the trailing sleeves of her violet gown. *And now Kao Tsung is the crown prince. Lady Wang still complains—her ambition is never satisfied, but how hard Kao tries! How hard it is for him. Dear man, he only really comes alive with his books or in a polo game…how obsessed he is with that comet he's discovered! I must ask him why he believes that this particular comet portends a woman ruler for Chian…a Prince of Wu just as the pilgrim prophesied.*

And there's Batu, so involved with his new life, his sweetheart and her family. They've been good to him—I wonder if they've consulted an astrologer for their wedding date yet, I must ask him, he's bound to be at the polo field this afternoon. I think I'll try out Shira's colt for the runoff games today—he's almost a three-year-old now and ready to ride, I'm told.

It's interesting…some parts of my past life are gone—my Jhani, old Juchi—some are still a part of my present life—Bagatur and Shira, Faina. Who could have imagined, in that ugly village of Mazar Tagh's, that we'd be living in the Chian palace together!

Now, with Camel living in the head gardener's cottage close by, Faina is happier than I've ever seen her.

She startled a pair of nesting ducks that flew over her head near enough that their wingtips flicked her hair.

Faina, my immortal Ho Hsien-ku, what a jewel she is. She certainly keeps my personal household humming efficiently! I was afraid silly old Mei-li might be jealous when we brought Faina home but, after the first weeks, she was as proud of Faina as if she were her own daughter. And it's so wonderful to have a friend, one I've known so long, that I can talk to about anything, even foolish small things.

Then there's Hsuan Tsang…I treasure the long, peaceful hours we spend together, discussing the meaning of life, here and hereafter, learning the Buddha's teaching, as he insists it will be useful to the Prince of Wu…foolish notion. He says there's no contradiction between his teaching and other ways of thought in the Tao, or even my early Igren upbringing. Makes it easy for me.

I've even made peace with my good ghost, Zanggi, who keeps me informed about tricks and threats from the family of Kao Tsung's wife.

Yes, it's all rather easy right now. . .ominously so, if I think about it...

She watched a k'ung sparrow swagger across in front of her, his tail spread in its regal fan, the eyes in each feather shifting from blue to green to purple in the morning sunlight.

What a wonderful cape your feathers would make, you elegant bird! Sometimes I wish I had all your eyes so that I could see into the future...

I have such a satisfying life, really . . .why do I feel more and more alone? Alone isn't necessarily lonely, but I sometimes feel as if I were only an observer in my own life, watching it unfold by its own volition. That's not how I planned to live. I intended to be in control of my life, and yet...

I wonder what I'll be doing by this time next New Year's Day... and the next? Probably about the same as I'm doing now...calligraphing, helping to rewrite the Code of Law, playing polo, learning, thinking, the emperor's shadow in these as in all things.

'Sky! The sun's getting high, I'd better get back, he'll be looking for me.

She ran along familiar paths back to the main palace, her sheer skirts flying behind her.

AND INDEED, HE WAS LOOKING FOR HER. Or rather, dozens of servants were, at his bidding. The first to see her, as she came into the Great Hall, hurried to her and told her in a breathless, self-important way, that the emperor wanted her and that they'd been looking for her since dawn and everyone was afraid that something terrible had happened to her and would she please hurry?

"I'll be along as soon as I change and..." Tse Tsien began.

"No, Noble Mistress! His Most Luminous Majesty said you must come as soon as we found you—and that was a long time ago! Please don't keep him waiting any longer!"

"Very well, then I'll go as I am."

The servant looked relieved. Tse Tsien smiled as she walked away. *They think he's such an ogre! Yet they love him.*

She entered his room, bowed and said, "You wanted me, Sire?"

"There you are Peach Flower! I do have something urgent to discuss with you. I've been up all night thinking and now, before the business of the day takes over, I want *you* to start thinking. By the way, you look lovely with your hair down like that. Why don't you wear it that way more often, instead of hidden, all tucked up into one of those hats or turbans that you affect?"

"You know perfectly well why not," she smiled, "for it was you who suggested that I'd be less noticeable if my hair wasn't in evidence, remember? My *blazing hair* was the term you used, I think."

"So I did. Well, that's still true, but I like to see it this way once in awhile when we're alone together. It's such a glory, have some tea?"

"Thank you." She sat on large cushions by his side.

"This is not what I wished to talk about. Your health...it is good these days? No severe breathing problems?"

"Not really, I just need to avoid dust storms...emotional storms too. I get a little short of breath sometimes, but nothing serious, why?"

"Are you happy here? Do you still long for your Pamir Mountain valleys? If you were given a choice, what would you *like* your life to be?" He sat back and looked at her intently.

"Interesting that you should ask that this morning for I've been thinking of those things myself. Am I happy? I'm not sure I know what happiness is, or rather that I would recognize it if I were. I was happy as a child, but now that childish things are behind me, I'm not so sure. My Tai Yuan family has been urging me often and vehemently, to come live with them, to share their peaceful country life, and it sounds as though I might be helpful to the duke.

"I don't really long to be anywhere but here." She sipped her tea thoughtfully. "Tai Yuan might be a wonderful life...but Changan is my home, here with you and my other friends. "

"It pleases me to hear this. I thought I knew your heart—that you no longer yearned to return to your birthplace—but I wanted to make sure. You see, Flower, I am old and increasingly concerned with the welfare and continuance of this empire I have built."

"Sire! You're not *old*...just *experienced.* You told me so yourself!"

"That was years ago, I'm afraid," he countered dryly. "But now my body aches from old battle wounds, my memory fails me on occasion, the shallow well of my patience is often dry and I weary of the human condition. One more thing—do you have plans that I may not be aware of, plans for a husband and hearth of your own?"

"There is no one, Sire, in my life like that. Any more." Her voice was strong in its conviction. "I am content to remain as I am."

"A more peaceable way to live, I'm sure, all things considered. I had two sons for whom I had great hopes. One son was so violent and strong, flouted damn near every one of the Ten Abominations! So headstrong and immoral that I had to banish him forever. The other son is a stammering weakling, a scholar and fine horseman, yes, but weak...and worse, uninterested in politics or power!"

"But Kao Tsung tries hard. He's a good man."

"Good yes, but not good enough to rule, either wisely or well." He shook his head like an old lion annoyed by flies. "Now if either of my misbegotten offspring had half the wit, half the fire, half the good sense and capabilities that you have, my dear, I'd be a happy man. But they don't. I owe Tashih Shaymak a great debt. Somehow he was able to do what I failed in...raising a child well. Perhaps if I had spent more time at home and less on the march with my armies...hai, it's too late for these thoughts!"

"The chagan, my father, was a great man, a wise man, it's true."

"I didn't mean to get maudlin on you, my dear, take it as just one more sign of senility." He smiled and touched her hand. "So here's my proposition—and I don't want an answer, mind you, I just want you to consider it for awhile, as long as necessary."

"And you will be impatient until I give you that answer...right?" Her smile was an attempt to lighten his mood.

"True. Now, my idea is this, it came to me this morning as I watched the moon set. Let me backtrack a bit," he pulled his jade piece out of his sleeve and rubbed it thoughtfully. "You are dear to me, Tse Tsien. I love you as the daughter I never had, as the son I *wish* I had. I also realize that your position here is precarious at best. When I'm gone, you'll have no position, no protector, here in court."

"Kao Tsung is my friend," she reminded him quietly.

"Yes, but he doesn't pay attention. And there are many in this vast compound...petty men and women who are jealous of you, would try to see you killed or at least discredited, were it not for my presence, were it not for the fact that I *do* pay attention. You must be officially protected if you stay in Changan. That's *one* of my concerns, a large one, but not the greatest.

"As you know, since before you were born, the greatest, all-consuming passion of my life has been creating, adding to, consolidating and governing this great empire." He spread out his spatulate hands, palms up. "It's the birth of a glorious dream, my True Vision reign, the first reign that history will view, if I'm not utterly undone, as one of the greatest of all time—the T'ang Dynasty.

For a few moments he sat still, gazing into an inward distance. Tse Tsien waited.

"I have able ministers and secretaries. The government is running as smoothly as any government will. But a government this size cannot be run by committee. Perhaps no government can be effective unless there is a strong person at the head who bears the splendid yoke of kingship, who accepts the use of power and the consequent personal alienation and agony—the one who is, ultimately and inevitably, *responsible.*

"As things now stand, I have no one who can be that person. Except... you, Tse Tsien. And I cannot name you my heir. Every Confucian in the land would cry havoc! A woman's place is in the bedroom and the nursery as far as they're concerned."

The incense clock between them spiraled its smoky way through time.

"If, instead of being my concubine, my companion, in truth," he smiled, "you were my son's *wife,* it might be possible to accomplish a solution to both my besetting problems.

"But Kao Tsung already has a wife—the Lady Wang!"

"There is no law that says he cannot have more than one. I've discussed it with him and he's willing. More than willing...he's very fond of you. You must have realized that by now. I don't for a moment," he hurried on, "expect that you and my son would share the same bed, only the same quarters, the same life. If you were married to Kao Tsung, you would be protected by all the laws of the land, written and unwritten."

"I don't see how that would protect the empire though, Sire."

"That's the beauty of it! My son has no interest, nor talent, for governing. But you *do!* You, as his wife, could stay by his side at all times, at all public times that is. You could sit behind the carved screen that stands behind the throne...see all, hear all, and tell him what to say and what to do! No one would ever know the difference! They might suspect if they knew Kao Tsung, but they'd never be able to prove a thing! You, in all practical respects, would govern.

"I'm asking you, Wu Chao Tse Tsien, to be emperor in all but name when I die, the Prince of Wu fulfilling your destiny—and an ancient prophecy."

"Hsun Tsung has been talking to you!"

"Of course. A wise man, I believe.

"You do me too much honor, Sire, I don't know what to say."

"Honor be damned. It's as much a curse and you know it! But I'm a selfish old man and I'll do anything, even sacrifice your life, Flower, to see that this dynasty continues on the course I've set. Of course, you don't know what to say...you'd be a fool if you did. All I ask is that you give the idea some thought.

"I want you to understand fully that this is a *request,* not a command. I will not coerce you in any way. You will always have my love, regardless of what you do. I would never, as much as I'd like to, never say that you *must* do this, that you had no choice.

"You *do* have the choice. And a hard one it is. Make no mistake, if you do this, you will give up a personal life for the rest of your days. You will be flattered by some and vilified by many. You will find it necessary to do things that hurt you deeply. And love, in all its common beautiful ways, will not be yours.

"Think about it. I'll wait for, and abide by, your decision. For I do love and respect you." He stood, held her close for a moment, then walked with her to the door. "Now go."

50
CHOOSING: THE FACE OF THE DRAGON

SHE LEFT THE EMPEROR AND CROSSED THE HALL TO HER OWN ROOM, throwing her dress on the floor as she went. Takla Makan stretched her brown, supple body and purred a welcome to her mistress.

"Mei-li? Anybody? I need you! Now!"

The quiet, orderly room was suddenly alive with servants, waiting for her rapid orders. "Send for Bagatur. Where are my riding clothes? Braid my hair, no, not that fancy way, just fast! Fill my drinking skin with cold water. If anyone asks for me, tell them—oh, tell them anything you please. No, I don't know when I'll get back, so don't worry about me, I'll be all right. I just need to get out of the city. Now *move!*"

Out the great Southern Gate she rode as if dragons were in hot pursuit, their fiery breath licking at Bagatur's hooves. Up into the greening hills she went at a steady, mile-devouring canter. Small rodents popped up briefly from their holes, then dived underground to avoid being trampled. She rode as she had when she was a girl, her red-gold braids streaming out behind her, until she and Bagatur left the city and its civilization far behind them.

Cares and confusions, doubts and decisions, all dwindled into nothing. No thoughts, no plans, no expectations. Simply alive under the Everlasting Sky, moving on into the unknown, trusting in the rightness of the natural world. Only then did she slow Bagatur's joyous, surging gallop. They wandered then, in a desultory fashion, throughout the afternoon.

A fretful wind whirled through canyons and over ridges. Dark clouds scudded overhead, carrying their burden of rain to its final destiny in some other place. She could see grey shafts of falling rain in a dozen spots around her, but none fell where she rode. They climbed until they came to a stream that rushed and burbled through rushes and watercress and woodland flowers. She unbridled Bagatur. They both drank. He waded in the shallows. She lay on her stomach on the bank, cupping the cool water in her hands.

She tossed a handful of oats from her saddlebags into the water as an offering to the kelets that she had believed in as a child.

"But now?" She spoke aloud. "What do I believe in now? It seemed so simple then, didn't it, Bagatur? Simply to live under the sky of the universe, to know what was right and what was wrong and what one should do, and how to do it. But now? Who am I now? Am I Talima or Tam or Wu Chao or Spitfire or Tse Tsien or Peach Flower? Would you know me, Bagatur, if you'd never seen me before?

She fondled his ears. He whickered in response and bunted her with his head.

"Yes, I suppose you would at that. What d'you think I should do, old friend?" Her thoughts rambled on...

As fine as it might be to live in Tai Yuan with those good and kind people who have given me their surname...I know I cannot...it feels too much like running away.

Am I wise enough? Mature enough? Capable enough to do as His Majesty asks? He seems to think so, but I don't know...some days I'd probably do all right... but others? I've seen how the politics of the court work... formidable! Could I wend my way through that maze? I would have strong and able supporters, my guardsmen, Faina, Zanggi, I suppose...but in the end, I'd be alone. Hsuan Tsung says we are never truly alone, but...

When Sire gave me my beautiful hand mirror, he said something I didn't understand at the time—I was only looking at the sun-speckled amber inlaid on its back, I guess. He said that when I had doubts, as I doubtless would, about whether or not I could do something, I should look in the mirror and see the woman that he sees. Does he know me better than I know myself?

"You know, Bagatur, there could be no turning back! Once begun, once the commitment was made, I could never do less, *be* less, than everything I'm capable of—all my heart and soul and breath and beliefs and understanding—all that I was and am and ever will be. *Everything!"*

She slipped the bridle over his head again, put her foot in the stirrup and swung into the saddle. They continued on. Finally, they came to a high place where she could see an endless pattern of valleys and foothills that rose into mauve mountains, jagged shards of mountains that chimed like great bells against the windy sky.

She dropped the reins, crossed her arms on the pommel, loosed her boots from the stirrups, leaned forward on Bagatur's neck and gazed toward the far mountains as if they held the answers she sought.

Her eyes became unfocused and she felt her whole being lift into the sky. Her spirit's wings felt the horizon. She saw the yellow land below, felt its majesty and the overpowering sweetness of life—and fell in love with it all...above, below, between. A part of it. Never separate again. The glory of the Everlasting Sky, the strength of mountains, the joy of knowing...all, all of it her own, her self.

As sudden as sunlight shafts through grey clouds, she made her decision...*I'll do as Tai Tsung asks so that his vision can live after he dies. I'll marry Kao Tsung and help him to be the best emperor I know how. It won't be easy, but it is the right action. Governing the kingdom from behind a latticed screen is not how I thought my life would turn out...unable to be recognized officially...there will be long hours and loneliness, I know. Unlike his father, Kao Tsung understands little of what's important or practical when it comes to governing... and I'll have only my own wisdom and experience to rely on.*

Her decision was made, but the pain in her heart abruptly pierced her as she turned away, resolutely, from the great loves of her past. *Will this feel like a leftover life? Can I build a life all over again?*

Doubts crept in. Uncertainties shook her resolve. *But, oh, what high purpose it could be! What a joy to put all I've learned into securing a better life for all the people of Chian—to actually plan and influence the course of events! It might be a barren life...but it would be a useful and honorable one.* She shook her shoulders as if settling a burden on them, took a deep breath, and smiled.

Wu Chao Tse Tien watched as the lengthening shadow of her horse and his rider undulated along the hills, keeping pace beside her. Heart-weary yet exultant, she was riding home, truly home—to Changan.

She rode through the wide city gates at twilight as a light rain began to fall. Spring rain, like a scarf of shimmering gray silk, shone the roof tiles and silvered the road that led uphill. She licked the sweet taste of rain and decision from her lips. *The rain smells of beginnings*, she thought.

For the last time as a private individual, she slipped unnoticed into the palace.

THAT NIGHT, SHE DREAMED HER DRAGON DREAM AGAIN. But it was not the same. *This time, as they climbed the air on gold-speckled wings and flashed through constellations of time, and on, and up into the starry universe of the Everlasting Sky…this time, the dragon turned its twin-horned head, and looked at her…*

Its comet-colored voice, like cymbals clashing, called her name. A violet, singing sea pounded within their joined hearts. Green fire, drawn from the veins of the earth itself, flickered from its jade eyes, piercing the innermost soul of her being.

This time, for the first time, with a shock of recognition, she saw… that the face of the dragon…was her own.

Book Three

SHE WOKE HAZILY, NOT SURE OF WHERE SHE WAS, *the sense of something momentous, something ended, something begun, filled her with stillness and satisfaction. She opened her eyes to the morning. The Everlasting Sky, rose-tinged with the rising sun, promised blue skies ahead. She stretched, feeling her body alive and lithe against silk sheets.*

51
Promises

Today, yes, today I'll talk to Sire, then spend the rest of the day calligraphing, to celebrate the future...mmnnn, and then, perhaps I'll...

A flurry of feet ran down the hall, fists pounded on her door, voices hushed but urgent called to her.

"Yes? What is it?"

"It's His Majesty!"

"Please, Mistress, come now!"

Faina, her hair flying, burst into the room unceremoniously. "Come quickly, Tam, er, Tse Tsien—it's His Majesty. He's taken ill, very ill, and calling for you. Don't bother to dress, here's a kimono..."

Instantly alert, Tsien floated the orange kimono around her body and cinched its sash. She ran out of her room and across the hall, through the emperor's outer rooms onto the balcony beyond, where guardsmen and servants milled in confusion.

Tai Tsung lay in the midst of broken pots and flowers where he had fallen. A small pool of drying blood beneath his head told the story. Conscious, but breathing hard, he looked up at her as she knelt beside him.

"Oh my dear! What happened? Are you all right? What can I do?"

"Better now...not sure of what happened, just felt pain like a knife-thrust in my chest, down my shield arm...couldn't breathe...and then nothing, till now." His words were a whisper; Tsien bent closer, her unbound hair tenting their faces together.

"Make them all leave...I must ask you..."

"Faina, get Mistress Feng immediately. Bring her here. Guards, help me get His Majesty onto cushions so he can rest more easily. Someone bring us water, grape wine and rice cakes. The rest of you, go!" She ordered.

Several guardsmen lifted the emperor as easily as if he'd been a sleeping child, carried him inside and laid him into a nest of tasseled pillows. Tsien sank down beside him, picked up his hand and caressed it with both of hers.

Tai Tsung let a long sigh hiss out into the sudden quiet. "Well, I had a premonition this sort of thing was waiting for me."

"You'll be all right, you've just been working too hard, worrying too much."

"No, I'm dying. Oh, not just yet perhaps, but soon. I must know, Flower, have you thought about my proposition? Have you made a decision?"

"Yes, yes I have...made a decision, my dear father-friend." She hesitated, smiled at him, and patted his hand. "I will do as you ask. I will marry Kao Tsung and see to it that your True Vision will continue on."

"Aaahhh, you have given my heart new strength."

She thought his smile was the sweetest she had ever known and was glad that she was the cause of it.

"So. We must act quickly before other factions gather to block this alliance between you two. I will talk with my son, an autumn wedding is auspicious I feel sure...bring that master schemer, my secretary Kat Kat Zanggi to me...we must line up support for these nuptials."

"But, Sire, I think you should be calm and rest now...all these arrangements can wait."

"No. They cannot. There may not be enough time and you must be made safe before I..."

Mistress Feng, followed by her maidservants bearing trays of bottled liquids and packets of nostrums, came in and curtsied deeply.

"Now, Most Illustrious Luminous, what have we here? Could you please tell me how you fell, where it hurts, all the details, so that I will be better able to prescribe for your renewed health? First, let me feel your pulses." She took his left hand by the wrist and touched it lightly with her long fingers, then turned to speak to Tse Tsien in an urgent whisper. "I would like to send for the most honorable Sun Simao, a celebrated physician whose specialty is in alarums of this sort. I've heard that he is in retreat at a monastery just north of Loyang, one where the martial arts are practiced...Kat Kat Zanggi will know...can you send a runner immediately?"

Tse Tsien, eyes wide with fear, shook her head and gestured to Faina. "Go quickly, get Zanggi to come here. Now."

"Can you lift your arm for me, Emperor? Good. And now your throat—I'll have to open this collar, Majesty. Hmmnnn, so." She shook her head.

"What? What can you feel, Mistress Feng?" Tsien asked anxiously, hoping for consolation.

"Not good, Tse Tsien, a weak pulse in all three major places, I'm sorry to say. But, until Sun Simao arrives, we'll do our best to fix that with some fine old Fomes and fagara tincture, won't we?" She pushed up the long sleeves of her apple-green gown and began slowly to measure both ingredients into a tiny celadon cup. "Lie still, Your Majesty, for a bit longer."

"I am not ungrateful for your ministrations, Mistress Feng, but I do wish you'd get on with it." Tai Tsung shook himself as if to shake off his weakness. "I have much to do...Tse Tsien, will you bring Kao Tsung here?"

"May I dress first, Sire?"

"Certainly...I have a feeling that Mistress Feng needs more time. So, hurry back...or rather, come as soon as you can. We have a celebration to plan...a quiet one perhaps. We'll see."

Leaving Tse Tsien's rooms, Kat Kat Zanggi blew in with the wind, his robes in a most unusual state of disarray. He bowed low, lifted his head at the emperor's command and sank down on the floor beside the divan where the emperor lay.

"The Lady Wang. My son's wife. Will she object to her husband taking another wife, d'you think? Will she rally her powerful Wang family against it?" Without preamble, Tai Tsung asked for the information he wanted.

"May I speak without fear of retribution, Majesty? These are perilous seas you ask me to sail upon."

"No one else is in this room, Zanggi, you may speak freely, for I am sure you are aware of all that goes on with the women in this sprawling palace."

"Fei...fei...fei, I am grateful for your confidence in this humble person, Majesty." He settled his robes more exactly in front of him, cleared his throat, sniffed and said, "The Lady Wang is a calculating woman who thrives on intrigue. Her tentacles reach out into every section of the city. She seems to be familiar with the lowest elements from dark alleys, for they visit her chambers in the dark of night. Quick to anger, she is ambitious...and ambitious women, men too, for that matter, can be, and often are, completely unscrupulous in the ways they conceive to bring about desired ends."

"Hmmnn, not a reassuring report."

"All that being said, her reactions may be modified or intensified depending on the woman Kao Tsung would be marrying...whether it were a matter of state only...how high a status this woman's family is... and therefore how much a threat to Lady Wang's dreams of succession for her son." He brought out a silk handkerchief from his sleeve and wiped his forehead. "Aaahh, may I be advised who the Crown Prince has chosen?"

"I see no reason why not," the emperor said before he drank. "It's someone you know well, I think...Wu Chao Tse Tsien."

Kat Kat Zanggi stiffened, breathed in with a slow hissing sound. Little bronze bells that hung from the eaves caught the gusting wind and answered each other's melodies.

"My son did not choose her. I have. She is necessary to me and has agreed to this union."

"Fei...fei...fei..." Zanggi sighed and was silent.

"I have in mind to adjourn to Loyang sooner than usual in order to hold the wedding there. I'd like to look on those mountains, breathe that clear air...I'll rely on you, Old Schemer, as I have so many times in the past, to assure the safety of Tse Tsien and her people before and during the event. Will you have enough qualified men to guard her?"

"Perhaps not, not enough in these delicate and difficult, times," Zanggi replied. "We shall have need for an unusual mix of extraordinary defensive skills as well as the ability to blend into the court in a plausible way, hmmnnn, do you think...?"

"I see that your mind is traveling the same route as mine own." The emperor templed his fingertips and smiled. "I remember how those men tipped the balance in my favor against Wang Shichong, before I become emperor, when I was just plain Li Shimin, a warrior fighting for his dream. Yes, Shaolin, the Shaolin fighting monks. Send for them."

Kat Kat Zanggi smiled, bowed and, backing away from the emperor's couch, left swiftly.

52
A Royal Wedding Is Planned

"I HAVEN'T BEEN HERE SINCE THE TIME MY YUAN MOTHER AND I BATHED—the time Prince Li Cheng was so abominable…I wonder if the jungles of Annam have been kind to him, in exile…" Tse Tsien stepped into the steaming bath. Faina, more slowly, dropped her towel, and gingerly followed her. Palms rattled in the breeze above them.

"Oooohhh…this is heaven, for true!" Faina sighed as the hot spring water swirled around her.

"Faina, my dear, do I see a little change in weight lately? Have you and Camel been sporting in the rain and clouds again?" Tse Tsien teased, swishing her arms around her body.

Faina's cheeks turned redder than the steam would warrant, and she smiled with that listening-inside smile that newly pregnant women have. "Yes, Tam, I mean Tse Tsien—I'm sorry but I have trouble remembering—yes, I have happiness within me—I've missed four moon flows now."

"Oh my dear, that pleases me so much—that you are happy—that you and Camel have found each other."

"Perhaps you and Second Son will make this kind of happiness, after the wedding?" Faina asked impetuously.

Tse Tsein's quick laughter echoed the bubbling waters in which they lay, creamy bodies suspended in green dark water. "Faina! Well, maybe so, but Mistress Feng has warned that I may not be able to conceive—complications from the Black Time, she says. But I would so love to have a baby…"

"I'll share mine with you," Faina volunteered quickly, her long hair spread like a halo around her head in the water.

"You are the best of friends, Faina, think how long we've come together, how far from that awful village of Mazar Tagh's…" The smell of rotten eggs wafted around them now as it had then. And suddenly, the anguish of that time, of watching Pirjhan grow weak, of being captive, the hopelessness and then the resolve, came back to her again and filled her mind.

"D'you ever have dreams of that time?" Faina asked.

"No, not any more. I try not to look back—it's so painful. And yet... even now, especially now perhaps, I remember...the joy of being in love...just looking up at Pirjhan, seeing him smile at me, feeling his arms around me, holding me close—the good times like pearls on the string of my memory...when I allow it. Long hours when we rode together, the Buran and how Kara demanded more food all the time, silly little swan... the cave when, for the first time he...when we were captured...oh Faina, it seems like such a long time ago. When I was in love and all the world seemed full of promise."

Faina listened quietly, smiling at this woman she had admired for so long, remembering the wild ride out of the Tagh's village, under a winged blanket of calling swans. The sulfur smell was strong in her head. "You were magnificent, my friend," she said simply.

Birds twittered and rustled in the palms above them, hanging bells conversed with the wind, voices of other bathers murmured in the distance. But all seemed still, just the same.

"I was so young, only a girl really—I've become someone else I think, many years older and more experienced...wiser, I hope, thanks to all that I've learned here. But oh, d'you suppose I'll *ever* know such sweetness again?" Tse Tsien sighed, brushed back her wet hair and took a deep breath. "My father gone, Juchi gone, Pirjhan...aaahhh, sometimes I ache for them." The springs hissed around her, hotter than before. "Well, all I can do now is go on, one step at a time—slowly, turtle, slowly, as Zanggi often tells me. That reminds me...Zanggi asked me to get your help in a matter of some urgency..."

"Anything." Faina sat up straighter.

"He is worried that some of the royal women, Lady Wang and her family in particular, may not be reconciled to having me as Kao Tsung's wife, that they might, oh, I don't know, try something along the lines of Ssu's poisoning from the jujubes a few months ago. Although the person who did that has never been identified, the fact that poison was used, a woman's crime Zanggi called it, and so he says to stay alert." She pulled herself onto the edge of the pool to cool off.

"He says that you must listen, Faina, and listen well, to whispers and gossip that you may hear as you go about your days in and out of the inner palace corridors. If you hear anything unusual or strange to you, you should tell either of us. Even though Ssu died, I've never thought it was evil aimed at *me,* you know. I'm just too inconsequential and besides, my family does not threaten hers in any way that I'm aware of. Zanggi's an old fuss-budget, I think, but I said I'd ask you."

"Of course I will," Faina slid deeper into the warm water. "Actually, yesterday, I overheard two of the guardsmen talking about some skilled fighters that have, evidently, been sent for already. They seemed to believe these warriors were magicians of some sort that could walk on water, fly through the air or vanish on the spot altogether!"

"Really? Sire mentioned some monks whom he had sent for, ones from a monastery to the north, near Loyang...I wonder if it could be the same Shaolin monastery where the physician, Sun Simao was located?" Tse Tsien dabbled her feet in the warm water before she slid back in with a splash. "These warrior monks, Sire said, fought with him many years ago, before he became emperor, but he didn't say anything about *magicians.* These are times of chaos, though, as we get ready to move to Loyang, and if a group of Taoist monks would add some stability to this seething culture, it would be wonderful. Well, we'll soon see, I expect... let's leave the baths, Faina, I'm turning into a wrinkled, dried-up old apricot."

They stood, stepped onto sun-warmed stones, wrapped lengths of thick cotton around their bodies and went toward the bathhouse to change.

THIS TURNED OUT TO BE THE LAST ORDINARY DAY THAT EITHER OF THEM HAD for the next tumultuous weeks as the palace gathered itself for the move, 675 li to the north, to Loyang and the approaching wedding.

The court astrologers were consulted. A date in the autumn *was* deemed auspicious. Several disagreed, claiming that the spring equinox with its promise of fruition was better. All the dates were set before the emperor. Without more discussion, he proclaimed an early fall date for the wedding of his second son Kao Tsung and Wu Chao Tse Tsien.

"The sooner the better," he was heard to remark, "I could wish it even sooner, I feel my time grows short."

Cooks and costumers, jewelers and tradesmen of every sort, were commanded to be ready for the festivities within six weeks, a scarce fortnight after they arrived at Loyang. Organized chaos ensued. Runners, carrying the news of a royal wedding were dispatched along canals and rivers, into the foothills, across the plains, throughout the vast land.

Alerted to the seeming inevitability of this marriage, the Wang sisters met in secret to discuss ways of ensuring that no new heirs to the peacock throne would be born.

53
Soldier's Heart

"AAAHH, IT FEELS GOOD TO BE MOVING ON," Tse Tsien shifted in her saddle to talk with Sun Simao, as they rode beside the royal litter in which the emperor rested.

"I think you're better adjusted to these long days in the saddle than I am," Sun replied with a grimace. "My body is happier walking… haven't ridden this much since I was a much younger man."

Tse Tsien laughed, "Yes, I suppose it would be hard for someone not brought up as I was…half my life on an Igren horse…"

"Is that your stallion's name?"

"No, his name is the same as his grandsire, Bagatur…different in color, but the same temperament…" she said quietly, then reached forward and smoothed her horse's sunny mane that waved over his pearl-white withers. "This Bagatur has been trained in all the ways our men have known since time began although, in this case, my uncle Batou, as Head of the Imperial Stables, trained him personally since I didn't have enough time."

"His Majesty keeps you very busy, doesn't he? I mean, I've noticed you sitting behind him, so silent, so alert, both in formal court hearings and even during his council meetings."

"Yes, the emperor works long hours for his people, for his vision of right action." A constant wind off the broad yellow plain blew Tse Tsien's hair from under her turban, whipping her face with long, shining strands. "Sun Simao, in your experience as a physician, what can we expect for the emperor? Do you think that the *Mai Men Dong* medicine that you're giving him will make him well again?"

"Well, that's not mine to say, Wu Tsien. The emperor, as you must realize, suffers from *soldier's heart*, which is always fatal, although some live a long time even so. The *ophiogon* I've been giving him is a strong herb for his yin deficiency... it nourishes the heart and moistens lungs, which should help with the cough that's been worrying him lately.

"At Shaolin, we had several older monks—some may have fought with His Majesty—suffering from the same weakness. Nothing can make him truly well, Tse Tsien. His soldier's heart may weaken gradually or he may fly away with the intake of a breath. Only the Tao that contains us all, knows."

A sudden premonition rippled through her, and she shivered, even though the sun was hot. *Tai Tsung is dying...I can't imagine what Chian will do without him, what my life at court will be like without him—he's been such a powerful force in my life all these years. A father, a teacher...how good he's been to me...no one else realizes...*

"I think we should keep this solution of nitro on hand at all times, just in case." Sun Simao urged his horse forward until they were stirrup to stirrup, and took a small vial of clear yellow, oily liquid from his belt sash. "If you notice that His Most Illustrious is having trouble breathing, possibly groaning or indicating pain, get him to swallow some of this. It should help in an emergency."

"I hope I'll never have to use it, but thank you." She took the vial and placed it carefully inside the lining of her shoulder bag. They rode on silently, listening, looking.

Around them, and as far as they could see, were riders on many-colored horses—hundreds of guardsmen, scarlet and purple capes fluttering—on both sides, close in. And farther out into the farming countryside, occasional black-clad riders on dark horses, evidence of the infusion of a few of the mysterious Shaolin monks. Dust from the fast passage of Kao Tsung and his palace guards who rode ahead to make the Loyang palace ready for the emperor's presence, settled in fine sandy layers on everyone.

Far ahead were the slender, vertical banners heralding the emperor's procession, followed by drummers, cymbals and hand-held zithers, making music that lent a merry sound to the tiring, relentless pace toward Loyang. Then came the broad platform on which a small, pagoda-shaped room had been built to house the emperor. Embroidered dragons writhed on curtains that rippled in the boisterous wind. Inside, Tai Tsung rested and dreamed peacefully, ignoring all the sounds coming to him from outside—feeling safe as the murmured conversation of Tse Tsien and Sun Simao continued.

Relatives of the emperor, wives, concubines and excited children followed his ornate, gilded litter. Behind them were large crowds of servants and their families, either in wagons or riding mules. At night, cooking fires were lit under bulbous copper pots for stews scooped into cups for all except the palace personnel themselves, who had their own cooks, up ahead.

At Tse Tsien's insistence, Faina rode Shira, now a gentle old mare, who plodded along placidly. Camel trudged along beside her, making sure nothing happened to his *fairy girl* and their unborn child. Around them were a babble of voices and languages from court followers from a dozen other countries: red hat Christian monks from Hrom; curly-bearded Sassanian merchants; men of Zoroastrian faith in deep philosophical conversation with Hindu and Buddhist monks.

"Are you comfortable, my dear?" asked Camel, reaching up to hold his wife's hand.

"Not particularly *comfortable* I'd have to say," Faina smiled down at him. "But very happy to be with you, with everyone on this important move. I just hope that the great physician, Sun Simao, will be successful in making the emperor well, so he'll be fit enough to lead Tsien's wedding ceremony."

"Does the emperor know?"

"Know what?"

"Know how ill he is?"

"Tse Tsien says he is very aware, but that we are not to talk about it because it's not general knowledge—and not wise for everyone to know now, best to not know as long as possible. "

Everywhere the procession went, crowds of villagers stood along the road to greet them, holding up their babies for blessings: a wave from the emperor perhaps, bits of cash, or small squares of multi-colored silk to use as trade in the marketplace.

After the first week of traveling, the travelers began to see, through the haze of distance, the mountains that surrounded Loyang on the north: jagged lines of lavender through the valley mists, only a few days' journey away.

At twilight, Tse Tsien sat beside the emperor to entertain him with the gossip of the day, with stories or poetry she had read, or with a song from her childhood that always seemed almost foreign to her now.

"D'you remember, a dozen years ago, Tse Tsien, in your Black Time, the poem I told you?" He brushed back grey hairs that wind was pulling out from his topknot.

"I'm afraid that my memory of that time is foggy, but I do seem to remember one about being ten thousand miles from home...it made me so sad then...does that remind you?"

"Ah yes, *Fighting South of the Ramparts*... I was just remembering that one...let's see...*we have pastured our horses in Himalayan snows...we're the Emperor's armies growing old, getting gray...ten thousand miles from home*...is that the one you meant? I must say I can identify with these words...growing old, getting gray."

"Yes! That's it!" With her forefinger, she smoothed the veins on his weathered hand absentmindedly. "Sire...since that time, you've always been so kind to me...I want you to know how grateful I am for all you have gifted me with—not only material wealth, but your trust and your wisdom. I feel so blessed by these. When I first came, in such agony at leaving my home and all those I loved, I was angry and hurt for so long, believing you to be some sort of evil man. And now look at us—best friends, best teacher and student. Ever. Little could I have known how deeply I would learn to care for you and Chian."

"Can you know, Flower, how it gladdens *my* heart to hear you say that? You have become the central jewel in my crown, the one person I can rely on, in any circumstance, to hear the truth and then act on it, with discretion and wisdom." A sudden breeze parted the concealing curtains and he looked out, seeing far ahead. "So many people out there, all needing, all expecting something good from me, from this True Vision government of mine."

"I know, Sire." Single-hearted, Tse Tsien's affection for the emperor spilled over as tears ran down her cheeks.

"Come, come, Peach Flower, *crying?* Have I hurt you in any way?"

"No, I'm just overwhelmed with loving you." She sniffled and bent her head to use the end of her long sleeve to wipe away her tears.

"May it always be so, my dear," he reached over and pulled her into his arms, rested his cheek on her head, and held her. Held her close and strong and sweet.

The acrid smell of him, of ginseng and strong tea filled her nose. The fresh scent of her, of meadow grass and horses made him smile.

For this moment, time stood still, transparent to each of them in the fierce clear light of realization of what they meant to each other, of who they were, together.

54
Sun Simao Tells Of Shaolin: Sisters' Fury

FIRST LIGHT BEFORE DAWN OF THE LAST CAMP, only one li from Loyang, found Tse Tsien, deep in thought, wandering through fog that lay in the valleys, smudging out the foothills, with only the higher peaks scratching at the sky. Startled, she chirped like the sound of a waking bird by a man emerging in front of her,

"I'm sorry," Sun Simao's bell-like voice sounded. "I saw someone out here and rose to see who it was...I didn't mean to frighten you—aren't you sleeping well?"

"Not well, S'mao, I'm so worried about the emperor's health... and apprehensive of all the ceremonial rigmarole ahead of us."

"Well, it won't be long now, when will the caravan get underway?"

"It's the same here as it was in my childhood...the horses and men don't move out until it's light enough to see the lines on the palm of your hand. You'll notice increased activity here shortly," she smiled at him even though he could not fully see her face. "Makes sense, don't you think?"

"Yes, not much use before that, I suppose. At Shaolin, though, we usually began training, teachers and students, well before dawn, all year. And in the winter, in the mountains, it was mighty cold."

"What was this *training* that you speak of?"

"You've not heard of our stringent training then? Young boys, four to ten years old, come to live at the monastery for about three years—after that, they can see their parents only on official holidays, a total of about one month a year. At 5:30, the big gong is rung and there's chaos as the boys scramble for class. For an hour and a half there's high-speed and strength conditioning—running up 1000 stairs, short sprints followed by hopping on left foot, then right, until the summit is reached at Bodhidharma's cave."

"Who is Bodhidharma?"

"He's not with us now, passed on about two hundred years ago. He was the son of King Suganches, the 28th successor of Buddha and adept at both Hatha and Raja yoga in India. Came to Shaolin and found the monks all spindly and weak from too much sitting, too little exercise. So, he set in motion the hard, relentless training of mind, body, and spirit that's carried on to this day.

"Later in life, he meditated in front of a wall in the mountains, in a tiny cave for nine years—so long that the sun burned the outline of his shadow onto the stone wall. After the boys reach this cave, they start down again, doing press-ups every hundred stairs. When they get back, they break the night's fast with *Ba Bao Jou,* eight objects soup; *Yao Tiao*, a deep fried dough, *Don Fu Noir*, a milk made overnight from soy beans, noodles and rice. Then, at nine o'clock, there's stretching training: splits, lying on your back while another presses down the legs and arms, all repeated many times—and this is on stone-hard ground mind you. Lunch, then a rest before more training. This time with forms of acrobatics—forward and backward somersaults in the air, flic-flacs, jumped cartwheels, and weapons—*guns*, long sticks and *dao,* swords, or *bian,* whips.

"You mean they train all day, every day?"

"Only six days a week, while in between training there are classes in reading, history, and some time each day, meditation on the *Eight-fold Path,* of course."

"Astonishing! Can young children keep up this pace?"

"Strangely, it's easier for those supple young bodies than it is for those who, as I did, enter the monastery as an adult. It's cruel hard, at first, to remake your body, but as Bodhidharma himself claimed, this training is meant 'to enhance health, energize internal organs, and steel muscles'. And it decidedly does, producing *kung fu* men known as *iron, wrapped in cotton.* Unbeatable in hand-to-hand combat."

"Are there many monks who begin their training later?"

"Quite a few, Tsien, for the monastery is a totally isolated sanctuary for men who, for many reasons, need a base, a home, a new way of living. Being part of Shaolin allows one to be profoundly, completely, part of a brotherhood outside from any other part of society. "

Deep in conversation, they had not noticed the sun coming up until its warmth spread across their shoulders. Daylight also brought a group of horsemen riding out in welcome from Loyang, among them, Kao Tsung. He reined up beside his father's platform, dismounted, and formally requested an audience. Then disappeared behind the concealing curtains.

Tse Tsien hurried over to her own tent, to get ready for the procession into Loyang. She changed from comfortable riding clothes—long pantaloons, short jacket and soft boots—to ceremonial clothes—layers of silk petticoats, a pocketed tunic with long-flowing sleeves, a wide flowered sash tying it all together, and pointed brocaded slippers. She bound her hair up under an embroidered turban, Sassanian style, picked up a painted fan and went to pay her morning respects to the emperor.

She found him speaking to Kao Tsung with fierce intensity while his son simply nodded now and then.

"Hatou, Most Illustrious and Second Son," Tsien greeted as she curtsied to them both.

"Ah, Tsien, just when I wanted you," Tai Tsung said, "Make room for her, son, here between us."

"Yes, T-ts-tsien, wu-w-we have been t-t-t-aw,"Kao Tsung shook his head in frustration over his stutter. "Discussing plans."

"I have told my son that I wish for you both to lead us all into the city, to ride side by side," Tai Tsung went on, "so that my intentions are clear to all who witness this progression—that you two are . . ."

"But . . ." Tsien began.

"No buts, Tsien. I feel that we must bring attention to this union that is about to take place. And there can be no better way than to let the people see you together in this ceremonial way, right now. Get them prepared, so to speak."

"Well then, my friend, " Tsien said, rather breathlessly before turning to Kao Tsung, "are you ready to be seen and known as partners?"

Kao Tsung did not try to speak. He picked up her hand and brushed her palm with a kiss. His brown eyes were warm with love.

Sky! How interesting...just when I thought I knew the direction for the rest of my life...poof, it changes! Just when you think you're going down this straight path, it switches direction...what a crooked path my life has been! And now, Kao seems delighted to be my husband even though I never thought to marry anyone. But, as usual, Sire has the interests of his True Vision paramount in all his decisions...well, we'll see how it goes, one step at a time.

She flung open the curtains and jumped down into the soft alluvial dust, whistling for Bagatur the Second.

As the wide tumult of wheeled vehicles, litters, horses, carts, animals and people wound up the last hill into Loyang, Lady Wang, flanked by her sisters, was carried along. Her litter bearers, three on each side were beginning to struggle for balance because Lady Wang kept switching sides, leaning way out through the curtains on her right, then to the left, in order to whisper first to one sister then the other.

"It's an outrage!" She spat.

"A disgrace!" Her sister agreed.

"How do they dare flaunt themselves in public by riding in front of us all?" She shrilled.

"It's a wonder the emperor doesn't whip them for such audacity."

"They say he's impotent before her..."

"No! She must be a witch..."

Lady Ssu-sui Wang withdrew, fueling the fire of her fury.

"Her Wu family is not even listed in the Record of Aristocratic Families!"

"How dare she usurp your rightful position beside Kao Tsung?"

"You have lost face, older sister." The other sister said quite calmly. "If you do not rectify this insult, our whole family will have lost stature."

"Don't you think I realize that?" Lady Wang hissed. "We must act, act soon, before that she-devil conceives a child, a boy that will threaten the succession of my son. Now here's what I plan to do . . ."

The tallest litter bearer listened intently. He was young and determined not to spend his life as a litter man to this particularly unpleasant woman. Perhaps the honorable secretary would be interested in this conversation and might see to it that he was rewarded for his perception of importance? Yes, it was worth asking for an audience as soon as they arrived at the palace. Who knew what advancement might occur?

55
An Unexpected Ceremony

RAIN. AN UNSEEMLY RAIN FOR AUTUMN. TORRENTIAL, SUMMERTIME RAIN. Twilight at noon. Thunder at night... I'm heartily tired of it... my heart is as sodden with grief as the earth is from this constant downpour. The emperor, my beloved Sire, is failing before my eyes... sitting here, beside him, I watch his sudde *retreat from this world, moment by moment... if only there was some magic I could call up to strengthen his hold on life...*

"Tsien..." the emperor woke abruptly, pushed himself up on his pillows, "Tsien, call my inner council, summon Kat Kat Zanggi, invite my son, Kao, to attend... I know now what must be done!"

Surprised out of her dolorous reverie, Tsien jumped up and pulled on the long, tasseled cord that hung beside the door, which opened immediately to a pig-tailed, bowing servant. She gave him the command, then turned back to the high, carved bed. "Perhaps I should leave you now, Sire?"

"No!" he thundered with his old vigor. "No, I want you here, beside me when they come, but while we wait, you may want to freshen up a bit from your night's vigil. You may go, but come back within three quarter hours looking like your usual glowing self."

As Tse Tsien left to cross the hall to her own apartment, she was smiling. *I wonder what that old dragon has in mind—mischief of some sort, I'll wager, judging by that rascally look on his face. But oh, how good it is to see him awake and so lively!*

Takla Makan and Su Chi were asleep, curled up together on the window seat as she entered. Su Chi jumped to her feet and bowed deeply. Takla Makan just yawned and stretched, an old brown cat at ease in the world.

"What can I do for you, Madame?"

"Not Madame—not married yet, little one—you can help me into a more fitting costume in which to greet His Majesty's ministers. The blue chiffon, I think, and find the silver hair ornaments that Kao Tsung gave me last year, the ones with tiny pearl flowers that sound like fairy bells. Now hurry, please!"

She tossed on long silk petticoats: the first, white cotton as fine as moonbeams, the second, pure silk with the iridescence of pink clouds at dawn. Her maid held the last layer high, to float it down, as blue as the everlasting sky at noon, over her head. Tsien pushed into the tight sleeves that were puffed high at the shoulders, then took the other end of a long, embroidered, purple sash held on one end by Su Chi, and turning into the tight end of the scarf, wrapped her waist round and round, leaving the last to knot and trail down her back. The tight sash pushed her breasts into the low neckline of her bodice. An ivory satin, stand-up collar framed her face and lent a certain majesty to the whole ensemble..

Tsien sat while Su twisted her thick, red-gold hair into a looped and braided topknot, finishing the whole elaborate hairdo with the two long ivory hairpins, where tiny silver bells in the shape of flowers dangled over her ears. Lastly, she carefully arranged the long, wide arm sleeves—brocade of blue phoenixes lined in red silk—over her wrists. She slipped bare feet into high, wooden platform sandals, and then clitter-clattered out the door to meet the men across the red-tiled hall.

WHILE TSE TSIEN DRESSED, THE EMPEROR'S MOST TRUSTED ADVISORS WERE ASSEMBLING,

"But Shih-min, I wonder," Chang-sun Wu-chi was speaking in the familiar way that he and Tai Tsung used together, "I wonder if this action will not cause the very trouble it is meant to forestall?"

"Perhaps you are right, Brother-in-Law, yes, you have often given me good counsel throughout the years since our boyhood together, but in this case, I feel...aahh, Fang Hsuan-ling, there you are, thank you for coming so quickly, you have such an admirable grasp of State affairs that I need your presence just now."

The smell of eucalyptus was strong in the room; the lines of the emperor's incense clock were almost burned through and the quarter chimes were beginning to ring when the other ministers—dour Confucianist Wei Cheng, pragmatic librarian and historian Chu Sui-Lian, and Chang-sun Wu-Chi—all old campaigners with the emperor, arrived together, all rather breathless. Striding behind them with his usual panther-like grace, was Head Secretary Kat Kat Zanggi, followed by the newest and youngest council members Li Shih-chi and Li Ching, both equally at home as court officials or as commanders-in-the-field.

"Now, don't stand around looking as if you were at a death bed—any reports you may have heard in this regard are to be *dis*regarded!" the emperor chuckled at his own joke, and the others, following his lead, smiled and relaxed, settling themselves on small stools in a half-circle.

"Some of you are aware of the quandary I've been in to name a successor. With my despicable eldest son Li Cheng's banishment, I am left with a son who has no interest, possibly no talent, for governing. He should, incidentally, be here shortly—as will Wu Chao Tse Tsien."

He looked around, searching each familiar face for reactions. Noting little response, he continued, "It has been my *Chen Kuan* vision for all of Chian that I have planned and lived for, my *True Vision* that must have a capable leader, one who is astute, fair, decisive, and above all, not bound to any one powerful family who would rule only in their own favor.

"The common thread for a successor to follow must be the *T'ang Code of Law* that has been my constant endeavor to write and to follow for the good of our country. My successor must understand and respect its wisdom, must follow the paths toward peace universally, for enrichment and well being of all our people."

Several white heads nodded in agreement. The warm wet smell of bamboo and rain-drenched mushrooms drifted in through the open window. Wei Cheng, as he was wont to do, cleared his throat often, a punctuation to the emperor's words.

"I know that you have noticed, and some of you," he smiled, "have objected to the increasingly important function Wu Chao Tse Tsien has played in my administration."

A murmur, like bees humming before flight, passed around the circle.

"You see, I am an old soldier, strong in the ways of warfare, wise only in the ways of recognizing the right arrow to choose which will hit the mark. Tse Tsien is that right arrow—but the question in my mind has been: How to incorporate her profound talent for governing without defying the very Code that we have sworn to uphold? Imagine my elation this morning when I awoke with a remedy!"

Warily, the ministers turned to each other, seeking reassurance, wanting unity.

"Kao Tsung and Tse Tsien have agreed to be married—there is mutual respect and some affection from each of them. But state weddings take time to execute and can be prone to delays. And I may not have enough time to... well, oversee the transition. There are jealous forces at work, I'm told..." He looked across at Kat Kat Zanggi as he twisted the jade seal ring on his thumb, "Certain factions are fomenting division and discord within the Four Families, who may try to obstruct a large state wedding for longer than I'm willing to wait. Unseemly violence is to be avoided, however possible, so I have called us all together to witness..."

"But surely you cannot..." "Do you mean..." "Most Luminous, I believe that..." "We'll need to..." "Fei fei fei..."

"It is expressly stated that The Ruler may, in times of crisis," his voice boomed out, brooking no interruptions. "The Ruler may perform whatever ceremonies necessary to secure the smooth transition of power without bloodshed. I am choosing this path. My son Kao and my companion and confidante Tse Tsien will be here any moment. By now you realize, I'm sure, that I intend to marry them immediately, a civil ceremony that will be made law by your witnessing. Zanggi, did you bring the scroll you have readied? Does anyone have any comments at this time? Comments, that is, that are constructive for I expect your immediate adherence to my wishes...no?"

A stunned silence ensued. Into that silence, Tse Tsien walked, head held high, smiling like the sun shafting through clouds.

"Good morning, Noble Ministers, it's always a good day to be in your illustrious company." She curtsied, then perched on the end of the emperor's bed and looked around at the counselors gathered there—one from each of the main branches of government.

"S-s-so sorry, S-Sir," stuttered Kao Tsung, bursting through the open door, still tying his embroidered indigo sash. "I w-w-was in the observatory and t-t-time just disappeared, y-you know." He bobbed his head to each of his father's advisors, greeted Tai Tsung with an apology for lateness and sat on the other side of the bed.

"Children, it is my desire that you two shall be wed...and you have agreed to do so. I am grateful for this and am anxious for you to be married this morning so that a new generation can soon begin. I need to know the succession of my *True Vision* will continue. The Lady Wang has two young sons, of course...though it sometimes seems odd to me, with many women who have been in my bed, that there are so few boy babies that survive. Well, that is as it is, and *you,* dear Kao are my son and heir.

"Now I am aware that you are reluctant to be the head of state, to be burdened with all the responsibilities and decisions that implies, and I must say that there are many days I agree with your position," he turned his head to look at his son, stroking his long mustaches thoughtfully. "But I believe that, with Tse Tsien as your wife, beside you in court as in more personal times, that you may find those duties to be less onerous and confusing than you fear."

Tsien sat very still, hardly breathing. Workers' voices from the gardens below fluting above the cicadas' increasing song, drifted in through an open window. Sunlight skimmed through sheltering curtains, shimmered across Tai Tsung' silver hair, and illumined dust motes hanging in the air.

Kao Tsung sat up straighter, reached across the bed, took Tsien's hand, and whispered, so he would not stutter at such a solemn time, "With you, each day will be the best day of my life. With you, Tsien, I will not be afraid, but will cherish our lives together...come what may."

"Peach Flower?" the emperor prompted. "Can you add your own declaration?"

"Yes, Sire. I am deeply honored by your trust and even more, by your devotion to your vision and the *Tang Code of Law* that we have worked so hard on together, through the years. I promise you that I will do all that I am capable of to hold true to these, and to be the best wife I can to your son, who is dear to me.'

"In my power as Supreme Ruler of all Chian and its surrounding hegemony, I pronounce you husband and wife." Tai Tsung nodded in satisfaction and gestured to Zanggi to bring a scroll and the imperial seal.

"Let us all here bear witness to the present day marriage of my son, Kao Tsung, and my ward, Wu Chao Tse Tsien. After I have stamped this official scroll, please pass it around so that each of you, my august ministers, can add your *chop* as witness to this happy day. All the pomp and pleasures of a state wedding will still take place, just postponed now, until the ordained auspicious time for public celebration.

"Thank you all for attending with such patience and consideration to an old man's wishes. We will convene again very soon. Tsien and Kao, see to it that you are living in the new wing of the palace together by nightfall. "

Soft footfalls, soft undertone of discussion as, two by two, the council filed out. Impetuously, Tse Tsien threw her arms around the emperor and gave him a hug. Kao Tsung laughed unexpectedly. They left together as if they had not a care in the world.

"How short life is, a flicker of summer lightning." Tai Tsung murmured.

56
A Banner Of Horses: A Dragon: Love Surprises

WHAT DO YOU SAY TO YOUR BEST FRIEND WHO HAS SUDDENLY BECOME your husband? Do you still talk about polo? Discuss the weather? I thought this was to be a marriage of convenience...to establish the succession, and to ease his mind about my safety... but he made it quite clear that he expects grandchildren... that he has set us together to... to play in the rain and clouds, but I know so little of all that, only Pirjhan, my Jhani...so very long ago. Perhaps Kao Tsung and I might just...

Tse Tsien, holding Takla Makan, in her arms, walked quickly down wide halls that led from her room to where a more spacious apartment had been readied for her. A dozen or more servants laden with her personal possessions hurried along behind her. At each door of the recently completed wing an official greeter, part of her new household staff, stood and bowed as she passed.

I wonder what they're thinking...what do they say about Kao Tsung and me? Are they happy with us, their new masters? I must make friends with them soon...get to know them, so they can be my eyes and ears as well as merely servants...

She came to the end of the long passage, opened the double door and stepped back in amazement. It was a very large, semi-circular room filled with embroidered pillows on blood-red Turkish rugs and, in the center, a raised bed curtained with blowing gauze. Through tall open windows she could see beyond to a formal garden complete with roses and a maze. The walls were painted with herds of multi-colored horses racing, cinnamon, umber, dun, and a few of perfect white, like punctuation marks in the flowing manes and backs. Beyond them were the ice fields of craggy mountaintops and a strong sun beating down.

Aaaahhh, look what the emperor has had made for me... the banner of horses I lived with and loved... so I'd feel at home here... so thoughtful. So, once again, we begin... right, Takla Makan? How many years now since you wandered into my life...thirteen? fourteen? So much is different now...yet you are still here and that makes me glad for us both, right, pussy cat?

She put Takla Makan down in a pool of sunshine where her old bones might soak in the warmth and she'd be able to move better. The next hours were spent rearranging, unpacking and exploring, settling in. Then, tired from so much excitement after an early rising, she curled up on the bed and fell asleep. And sleeping, dreamed. And dreaming, found herself in her dragon dream again. But this time, she wasn't *riding* the dragon, feeling its power beneath her, this time she *was* the dragon, awesomely aware, ebulliently strong, surging skyward toward the stars, her long tail streaming behind her like a comet. Fearful darkness filled the spaces between the stars, a blackness that pulled her, inexorably, into itself.

The rasp-click of the door latch awoke her. Already it was twilight, but the night's lamps had not been lit. For a moment she was disoriented, not recognizing the room she was in, so new in its light and shadows. But she watched, quietly, as the familiar shape of Kao Tsung went over to the high windows and stood looking out.

"Beautiful, isn't it?" she murmured.

"Hello, my dear," he said, walking over to sit on the bed beside her. "I looked in an hour or more ago to see you sleeping so peacefully that I went away. Now you are rested?"

"Oh yes." She stretched and sat up. "This must seem as odd to you as it does to me—you and me—married, living together."

"Not odd, no. Rather wonderful, actually," he whispered and smiled at her. "Do you like the wall murals I had painted for you? The horses are the kind you knew?"

"You? You brought this banner of horses to life for me? I thought that he had done it...I mean, I didn't know you remembered, that you even..."

"Tse Tsien, my little one, I remember every word you have ever spoken to me. You are so lovely...a bright star in the heavens of my life... you must have sensed how happy you make me...how happy I am that my father has cleared the way for us to love each other. Now I know that there is an order to our universe, an order, a *justice* even, that I've never dared to hope for...I used to wish that you could love a bumbling fool like me...at least that's what my other wives think of me. But you have always been kind, and I know it's too early to ask you to love me, but perhaps...perhaps we could enjoy each other in small ways? A bit of rain and clouds as a simple delight?"

I have never heard him speak so long, so personally...how could I have missed this? How could I not realize...? Love him? Well, maybe I do...in a way...he has been such a part of this life, first on the polo field, then in state functions. Oh, Sky...it would be nice to feel again, to be...loved again.

He moved closer and pulled her into his arms, rubbing his short beard into her sleep-tumbled hair. He smoothed stray hairs from her forehead, then lifted her chin, tipped her head back to look into her eyes. A current of recognition surprised them both.

Tsien felt a ripple of awareness skim along her skin, making her deliciously aware of her body, its yearning, its quickening to his maleness, answered with such eagerness by her female longing. Longing to be touched, to be held, to surrender to this suddenly, wonderfully exciting man.

He felt himself filling, growing long and hard with passion for this precious woman whose arms entwined his neck, nuzzling his shoulder. In the base of his belly, a shivery hum began to build. He hugged her. Hard. And laughed with immoderate freedom, and was pleasured even more by her answering giggle.

He reached beneath the bodice of her gown, molding her breast with his slim hands. Slowly he leaned down to her, tasting her skin, his lips hungry on her throat, her shoulder. Lifting her arms from his neck, he laid her back on the coverlet.

She felt the world move in slow motion, liquid, molten. He smelled of incense and sweat, of leather and sandalwood. She melted under his caress, feeling a newborn heat rising from her center—a fire that flared into life, let out of its long imprisonment, free to burn with dancing delight.

"Mmmnnnn, Tsien, little love...now? Is this all right for you?"

"Yes, yes! Oh yes...now...only now!"

Her skin was flushed, her eyes slanted and sultry. He had never seen her so beautiful. His mind tangled and spangled, swirling like a cluster of stars, sweeping all before it. He slipped out of his kimono and slowly, so slowly undid the sash on hers, exposing her whole body to his kisses.

Her golden body melted beneath him. She felt herself arch to meet him, light as air, sweet in a blue-purple singing sweetness that flowed through her, flooding everything in this timeless moment. She heard fluting bird sounds and realized that it was her own voice.

Her apricot scent pulled him into her, thrusting and riding the mounting power of the two of them...becoming one.

Higher into the clouds they came. A slim aching cry of memory from her heart, a deep moan of satisfaction from his, and they pulled apart, floating back into their own skins like a gentle rain.

57
TAKLA MAKAN: A KUNG-SPARROW-EYED CAPE

AFTER THIS, EVERYTHING WAS DIFFERENT; EVERYTHING WAS THE SAME.

Every *day* was the same for Tse Tsien—consulting with the emperor and ministers before official audiences in the Great Hall, meeting with underlings who needed direction on this project or that—listening deeply, evaluating, always Tai Tsung's shadow. A Tai Tsung that, much to everyone's amazement and delight, seemed to have gained a fresh grasp on life, vigorous, full of ideas and his old energy—and that was both different and the same.

KaoTsung's days, too, were the same, deeply engrossed in his charts of wheeling stars, suns and moons, changes and seasons observed and postulated in his tower observatory on the other side of the palace.

At the end of the day, they came together. Nights were an enchanting exploration of each other in wondrous, sensual ways. And that was very different for them both.

TSE TSIEN RAN ALONG THE POLISHED STONE FLOOR and nearly ran into Faina as she turned the corner.

"Oh, Faina, you are grown so big bellied! Don't you think you should slow down a bit before the baby comes? The housekeepers surely can manage without you for a little while."

Faina rubbed her hard, swollen belly with happy satisfaction. "I don't mind, Tam, I like to be busy, it makes the days go faster."

Because Tse Tsien had moved her living quarters, Faina, too, had to move in order to stay close, as her friend insisted. This time there was room in the new wing for both Camel and Faina, with a nursery for the expected baby.

"Does Camel mind moving into new quarters? I know he loved the others, so near to the gardens and greenhouses, but this is all right with him, isn't it?

"Oh, good gracious, yes—well, he says he feels a strangeness, with all the fancy things we have now, but I see him smile that happy grin of his! What we're both looking forward to is the birth of our first child—think of it, Tam! Our own *family!*"

Faina hugged Tse Tsien, who, caught up in her friend's joy, laughed delightedly. Late afternoon sunshine glowed through an open window.

"Soon there will be little ones filling these silent halls with their patter and play—aaahh, how good that will be, Faina."

"Tam? You said once that you have been told that you could not conceive, carry, a baby—is that still true? D'you think that…maybe now that…I mean, you and Kao Tsung might…?"

"No, my dear, a great sorrow scoured me out, Mistress Feng says so, even though you wisely observed," she smiled, "that the ordinary ways of a man and a woman together might result in a child—no, it's not in our stars this time."

"But…"

"It's just the way things are. It is as Kat Kat Zanggi says, quoting from the *Tao Te Ching:* 'Know contentment and you shall not be disgraced, know satisfaction and you shall not be imperiled; then you will long endure.' A wise man, that Lao Tzu, and I am *quite* satisfied—or at least hopeful. Better than merely satisfied, really, like a newborn myself! Everything seems so different and…so sweet.

"We will keep right on. All of us. Together, come what may—I'm expected in the Great Hall, want to walk along with me?" So accustomed was she to being followed by only half a dozen guardsmen, Tse Tsien hardly noticed the addition of more black-clad warrior monks.

I wonder where that delightful Shaolin healer is? Wherever Sun Simao is, his skills have worked a miracle with Sire, thank the Everlasting Sky, may his health continue!

Unusual sounds of laughter came from the hall as she grew closer.

Now what? She thought.

The sedate chamber, usually filled with solemn petitioners and courtiers, was alive now with children and their parents. The great open space and shining floors had excited toddlers barely able to walk, as well as taller children of seven or eight years who were running after each other, hooting and hollering, sliding sideways into each other, caroming around and in between laughing grownups. As Tse Tsien walked in, there was a shout from a tall guardsman with his arm around a dainty woman dressed in country riding clothes, at the center of it all.

"Tam! Look who we've brought for you to get acquainted with!" He swept his arms out in a wide circle that encompassed all the children flitting around him.

"Batu! And Juchi! Are all these *yours!*"

"Oh no, some are good friends and *their* children as well as our own. It's been several years since we were all in Changan together and now that we've just been posted to Loyang, we thought this would be a splendid time for us to pay a visit. Children, come here, meet this beautiful lady, my old chagan's daughter that I've told you so much about."

She stood heron-still in the doorway, hardly breathing. Memories flooded through her. Then, as Batu and young Juchi and their wives ran toward her, she took a deep breath to bring herself back into the present, and ran to meet them.

From the small balcony above the hall, Kat Kat Zanggi stroked his mustache with his soft hand and smiled. *Splendid—one more layer of people between my Spitfire and those who would disgrace or harm her.*

TSE TSIEN STEPPED OUT OF HER STEAMING, SCENTED BATH ONTO THE COOL SLATE FLOOR, wrapped herself in a cotton kimono and walked into the bedroom. Bamboo lattices were pulled down over the windows leaving the room in a kind of twilight glow.

Mmmnnn, a few hours of nothing to do except get ready for the party tonight—rare and delicious, don't you think, kitter-kat? Takla Makan? Wake up you sleepy head, you can't sleep all the time. She reached down to pet her cat who was curled up in the center of the wide bed.

Its body was still. Very still. Too still.

Takla Makan? Oh, you are so cold . . .you are...oh Sky!...you are... gone. She gathered the cat up in her arms and buried her face in its body. Her tears glistened on its brown fur. She lay down on the bed and cuddled it like a little child. Sorrow for all passing life engulfed her.

And that's how Kao Tsung found her when he came in. "Tsien? Tsien wake up, we need to dress for the evening," he said in a kind of singsong, so he wouldn't stutter.

"I'm not going. I can't go now—can't you see? Takla Makan is *dead!* And oh, Tsun, I miss her so already."

"My dear, of course you'll miss your kitty, but she was *quite* old, wasn't she? Her time to move into a new life, I expect. We really must go, even though it's informal, not a state appearance, but father will be there, and your Tai Yuan family—and it's to be in honor of your Igren friends joining us here. I think you really must go, dear one."

Gently, he picked up Takla Makan and helped Tsien sit up. "We'll call Su Chi to make arrangements for her burial. Tomorrow...when you can be there. Now come see what I've had made for my bride."

He put a small bundle wrapped in green and blue brocade, tied with silk ribbons, in her lap. "Open it—now, please."

Tse Tsien wiped away tears with the ends of her sleeve, sniffled and smiled up at him. She opened the package and watched a splendor spill out, an iridescent crowd of k'ung sparrow feathers—violet red purple, a glowing green blue, of tail-feather eyes looking up at her.

"Why Tsun, they're *beautiful!*" She sighed, amazed.

"Put it on! It's something you can w-w-wear tonight."

"All right, oh, it's a short cape—a capelet of feathers!"

"Yes, just for you, my d-d-dear, now dry your t-t-tears and let's get ready." Kao Tsung was so pleased with her pleasure that he just stood there, watching her, grinning at the success of his gift.

Su Chi answered her summons, bowed, wrapped Takla Makan in a towel and left the room, calling as she went to her mistress's dressers to come quickly.

The dining hall was a merry hubbub by the time Tse Tsien and Kao Tsung entered quietly. Even so, all heads turned to look at them—he as massive and dark as his father, wearing a long-sleeved poppy-colored tunic over mulberry silk trousers—she, her hair tied loosely back with an ivory clip, kingfisher blue earrings, a slim shaft of turquoise silk with the feathered cape over her shoulders.

"There you are, daughter!" Her Tai Yuan mother hugged her, then held her at arm's length. "My, you *are* splendid! I can hardly imagine that you are the same travel-worn waif you were when first I laid eyes on you...how many years ago? Fifteen? Sixteen? But what a lucky thing for the whole family when you came into our life Wu Chao Tse Tsien!"

"Thank you, mother of mine, for all you gave me then, for all you continue to watch out for me now." She put her arm around the older woman's shoulder and walked toward the serving table where dozens of colorful dishes of food and sweetmeats waited.

"Come, Tsien, have a glass of wine before all these rascally men drink it all...we brought a wagonload of our best from the vineyard this year."

"So, the mare's teat grapes we asked Serindia to send as tribute are doing well in your province?"

"They certainly are—we, that is, your father thought—that it was a waste of time to plant those spindly little sticks, but la! It's been a wonderfully worthwhile endeavor. Camel Kuo, the Imperial Gardener, d'you know him?"

"Indeed I do, he married one of my closest friends...Faina, you may remember?" Tse Tsien sipped the smoky umber wine from an almost transparent porcelain cup.

"Well, Camel came to us last year for some cuttings and knowledge of what to do with them, and you know...I just saw him in the garden when I came...he told me of his success in creating the Grape Gardens in the Imperial Park in Changan. Soon you'll have plants from all over the world in your palace gardens at the rate he's going, won't you?" She shook her head and all the tiny crystal beads hanging from her headdress tinkled.

"Camel *is* a wizard...in addition to the delicious peaches of Samarkand that he's grown, there's blue lotus blooming in the bell tower pond now... and he tells me that he's hybridized roses into tight, fragrant blooms that last longer than the single-petalled wild roses."

"When you come for a visit, perhaps you could..." She was interrupted by Lady Wang's sister elbowing her way between them.

"So!" She shrieked "Don't we think we're grand in a feather cape that only royalty is allowed to wear! I suppose you scraped up all those feathers from the birds your greedy cat killed, eh? Well, it won't be catching any more birds *now,* will it?" Her shrill cackle crackled around them like summer lightning.

"Ching Yueh, lower your voice, please. Calm down. How much wine have you had to drink?" Tse Tsien reached out to take her arm and lead her away.

"Don't you touch me, you witch! I'm not drunk. You've bewitched my sister's husband or he never would have stooped to marrying you!" She pulled away, then turned back and began clawing at Tse Tsien in a mad fury.

Tse Tsien ducked and tried to get away, but Ching Yueh grabbed her hair and began to yank her around.

Feathers flew.

Many-eyed feathers were torn loose, tossed into the air, floating down over everyone, looking for all the world as if eyes, everywhere, were watching. Within moments, guardsmen took hold of the wild woman who now was screaming obscenities and threats as she was hustled out the door.

Tse Tsien was surrounded by other guardsmen who formed a living wall around her. Over their shoulders she could see Kao Tsung standing very still, looking worried.

The emperor immediately took control of the situation. "All right everyone, let's not let one unruly person ruin such a pleasant celebration, please continue on. Zanggi, will you accompany me to my apartment?"

"Shall I come with you, Sire?" Tse Tsien called out to him.

"No, no, my dear, I'm just weary tonight...terribly tired all of a sudden. Carry on..."

A rather subdued crowd, but still in good spirits, stayed for a little while, telling stories, reminding each other of long ago family ties. Finally, they came to say goodnight and wandered out into the night.

"At last, I don't think I could go on much longer," Tsien murmured to Kao Tsung.

"We can leave any time now, I think...let's go," he whispered back.

58
A Crooked Path: More Light!

LATER THAT EVENING, TSE TSIEN, IN AN INDIGO-PATTERNED COTTON SHIFT and Kao Tsung in chrysanthemum silk pajamas, were lying on their bed, re-living the party before they could go to sleep. They gazed out at the garden where stone lanterns glowed like giant fireflies.

"It turned out to be a good party after all, didn't it?" Tsien sipped from a cup of warm milk. "This reminds me of the mare's milk, warm and frothy, that I used to have as a child."

"Yes, yes it did, due to the good spirits of *your* family. I will apologize for mine, for Lady Wang and her sister—she has always been rather mean-spirited."

"And yet, you have three children by Lady Wang—you must have liked her at one time?"

"I did my duty. You may have noticed that our youngest child is already ten years old. After he was born, I made myself scarce in that wing of the palace, alone with my books and star-measuring devices. And playing polo, of course, where I met you—a happy day for me. You were such a mystery to me then! So daring!"

Tsien laughed. "And now?"

"Now you are still a mystery, but one that I hope to learn about more and more as our days together continue. Oh, my dear, have you any idea how much I love being with you? Holding you like this?"

Tse Tsien was silent. *How sweet it is to feel the warmth of his body on this cool evening...looking back at my life, there's that crooked path again...when I was little, I knew exactly who I was, what my life would be like until I joined the Everlasting Sky...and now, lying here beside my husband who is heir to all of Chian, it's as if I've been several different women...the harum-scarum Igren girl who thought she could do anything. Escaping from Mazar Tagh, the intense months across the mountains, the Buran, and...falling in love. Aieee!*

A Jade Garden girl, Faina and Takla Makan—oh, I shall miss you so, kitten... learning to write in the Forest of Pencils...how important my good ghost Zanggi has been to me in so many ways, all ways but that one terrible one...will I ever be able to let go of that black time? Then, the emperor's friendship...the river god's wife, father's death and the decision to stay here. Sometimes I feel like a piece of thistledown blown by the wind into worlds I didn't even know existed before... and now... all the politics of the court, the many currents of life in the palace... I know who I am now, Kao Tsung's companion and the emperor's shadow in whatever he does, wherever he is...didn't get a chance to talk to him at the party tonight though...wonder why he left early?

"Little one, you are so lost in reverie, come back to me."

"You know, I was just thinking, what d'you suppose Ching Yueh meant when she said that my cat wouldn't be killing any more birds—how did *she* know that Takla Makan died?"

"Hmmnn, is that what she said?" He murmured and brushed hairs back from her face. "There was such confusion just then, I didn't hear."

"And oh, Tsun, my beautiful feathered cape...gone! All gone!"

"Never mind, my sweetest...I'll get another one for you."

"You *are* good to me, Tsun, you'll be a good emperor, too, kind to your people, gentle."

"Hmmnnn, I'm not so sure...I feel so *unsure* of my abilities in that regard, being emperor, I mean...I'm not much interested in governing, you see, I really dislike all the picayune problems that must be decided upon, I'd rather let myself roam the universe of sky and stars. I'll tell you, and only you, Tsien, I don't feel strong enough to be emperor."

Tsien sat up quickly, turned to face Tsung, and said, in a voice vibrant with conviction, "Oh, Tsung, that doesn't matter, truly! I'm strong enough for both of us! Your father—and mine, too—have trained me well, and we'll just go right on...together!"

She looked up, put her hands on either side of his head and kissed him. Softly, slowly, pulling back a moment. "We will have a good life together. . . ."

The outer door slammed open. Four guardsmen burst into the room.

"You must come immediately." The first man commanded.

"His August Majesty summons you both!" said the second.

"Sire? Is he all right? One moment, I'll get dressed."

"No time, you must come *now,* just as you are!"

"But..."

"See here, w-we-we only need a little time to..." Kao Tsung sputtered.

"The emperor, sir, is dying. There *is* no time."

Two guardsmen on either side, they ran down the long corridor, into the starry night, across the courtyard, racing up the long stairs to the emperor's suite, high on the third floor of the main palace.

Heart pounding, Tsien stopped for a moment at the door, flanked by Tai Tsung's most honored personal guardsmen, took a deep breath to center herself, and went in. Kao Tsung followed close behind.

The high-ceilinged, spacious room was lit by a single hanging lantern. Incense smoke swirled along the slanted rays it cast. Curtains covered the tall windows. Black-clad, silent servants, nearly invisible, stood or crouched against the walls, waiting for summons. One slender bed, raised slightly from a blood red Sassanian carpet, was in the center of the room; only its intricately carved headboard gave hint that the ruler of the most vast and progressive country in the world lay there.

The swansdown coverlet was scarcely rumpled, so wasted had the emperor become. Tsien knelt at his side and reached for his large, bony hand.

How could I miss how thin he is? He seemed to be as strong as ever and yet his heart must have been failing him more and more...and he never said a word to me...

She smoothed his gnarled fingers and murmured, "I'm here, Sire, and so is your son."

"Aaahhh, Peach Blossom, it's this old warrior's last stand," he whispered.

"Oh Sire, don't leave us yet—I still have so much to learn...and you have been the best teacher, father, friend I could have ever wished for... stay."

"I'm tired, my dear, thought I'd never say that, but yes, I'm tired. I want to go. Kao Tsung? Son? Where are you?"

"Here, F-f-father, right here, beside Tsien." He put his hand over the joined hands of his wife and father.

"Ah, yes, there you are, both of you. Now, carry on, make my *Chen Kuan* a true vision."

"W-we'll *try,"* agreed Kao Tsung. "We *will,"* stated Tsien.

"And, Tse Tsien? Be careful…be very careful…and….love…. each… other." The words ended in a long sigh.

Tsien looked across the bed and realized that many people had been coming in quietly, circling them, filling the room. Waiting.

There's really nothing more to be said, is there? My heart hurts, I feel it must be breaking…I didn't realize how deeply I loved him…

She put her left hand over her aching heart. She watched as the rise and fall of the emperor's chest lessened, then stopped. She held her own breath. *Is this how it ends? This great man? Gone with one small breath? No…he's breathing again now…*

And so they sat. Transfixed, listening to the slight rasp of the emperor's ragged breath…in, out… in…out. Silence lengthened between his breaths.

Suddenly, he opened his eyes and whispered, "Let there be…more light!"

Tsien snapped her fingers. A servant came forward. "We need candles. Quickly!"

A dozen candles appeared and were lit. Their light flitted shadows across the faces gathered there.

"More light!" the emperor rasped.

Again, more candles, until those persons closest to the bed had to step back to avoid being burned. Tse Tsien and Kao Tsung did not move, holding Tai Tsung's still warm hand.

Air…the first act of a newborn is to breathe…and now the last act is only breath…

Counting the time between breaths now, the whole room seemed to be breathing in unison, in harmony with the emperor. In…out..…in…… out……….in……………

"Light! More light!" he said, quite audibly this time, breathing out hoarsely.

More candles lit, row upon row of candles, lighting up the dark night. Filling the room was the smell of burning wax and the slow wheeze and rattle of the emperor's breath. Trying to live, trying to die—a stubborn wind rattling through dry, desert canyons.

The bitter taste of death in her mouth, Tsien put her arm around Tai Tsung and laid her head down on the pillow beside him. Time ceased to have meaning. Only watching, only waiting existed, only life existed still. With his every breath, Tsien felt and heard, in the dwindling beat of his heart, her beloved mentor's waning strength. As she accepted and let go of mounting grief, she became aware of a stream of unknown energy beginning to creep along her body; an energy that began as a mere hum, increasing in volume and intensity until her whole body vibrated and sang with a presence full of vigor, wisdom, compassion; hot, passionate, undeniable...recognizable in spirit form.

And then, a soft slurry of breath and Tai Tsung's weary old body sagged, lifeless. A sudden breeze blew the curtains aside, guttered the candles and blew them out.

A brief moment of absolute silence before Tse Tsien's high, keening ululation shattered the air, before the moans and cries of all those in attendance, joined her.

A rose-colored light suffused the room. It was dawn.

59
Tse Tsien Carries On The True Vision: Ti Li Comes

"TSUN? ARE YOU AWAKE?" TSIEN TURNED OVER AND PUT HER ARM AROUND HER husband's broad back.

"Mmmnnn, now I am." Kao Tsung replied, shifting closer.

"The forty mandatory First Days of Observing Death are over, and the Great Memorial for the emperor can't take place yet for a year and even though our mourning will be longer. I think we must begin to carry on, to continue as he would want us to."

"In what way?" he mumbled.

"Yesterday, remember, three ministers brought us all the petitions that have piled up? And there are the ambassadors from Sogdia, Kucha and particularly, Silla, who have been waiting for an audience for months, and..."

Kao Tsung turned toward her, nibbling her ear, reaching beneath the covers to stroke her long, lean legs.

"You smell so good, Tsien, like m-musk and smoke and dark places I'd like to enter..."

She felt the warmth of his body along hers, his soft hands like smooth ribbons of electricity along her skin.

"Aaahhh, Tsun, I do love lying here in bed, early in the morning, no one else around...it's the only time we have together, isn't it?"

"Mmmnnn, never thought it could be s-so grand. Y'know, my dear I'm far more interested in our lives together than I am appearing in court and all that entails."

"I know, but we have to, don't we?"

"I detest it—all those whining people needing this, wanting that, complaining, accusing...how do you stand it?"

"Well, I guess I've been trained to do it and it never occurred to me not..."

"And I admire you for it, I'd just rather ride polo, study stars, be in bed with you...like now." He smiled, and began to fondle her breast.

"Oh, Tsun, you're trying to change the subject...I just have this feeling that Sire is looking down on us and saying 'get on with it—be the emperor!'" *What can I do to awaken his interest in governing? Somehow, we must do what is necessary or the country will fall into chaos...if only he could feel the delight that Sire—and I—know of making things happen. Many parts of governing are rather boring, just routine, of course, but then there are times so exhilarating...I think he needs a project to get involved in...something he might get excited about...let me think...*

"Tsun? I have an idea!"

"Hmmmnnn?" He nuzzled her throat.

"Two ideas, actually." Tsien twisted out of his arms and sat up in bed, pulling the covers close around her.

With a sigh, Kao Tsung, sat up also. "All right, Tsien, since there seems to be no stopping you—what are these ideas of yours?"

"Well, first, I think we should enlarge the palace here in Loyang—I like being here better than Changan, and with all the children...Faina's new baby, Batu and Merket's three, Juchi and Mei-li's four...little children running tumbling around, all over the place...I love it, but it's getting too crowded. We could build new wings from the main palace and have a large garden and courtyard in the center for the children to play in together and..."

"And I can just hear the loud objections from the Secretary of the Treasury, that it's too expensive, unnecessary...let all these young families live on their own..." Kao Tsung brushed back his long, black hair in exasperation.

"But wouldn't *you* like to do it, my husband? This is one of the things you could simply *do*, now that you're the emperor yourself." She took hold of his hand and slowly stroked his palm. "Wouldn't you find pleasure in designing a new palace, one that reflected what you admired? Watching it grow and become beautiful...for us?"

"Well...maybe...would you like that, Tsien? Would you like to live here most of the year...just visit Changan in the spring?" He looked at her, trying to understand her intensity.

"You do understand, don't you, Tsun? I want us to be remembered for doing important things, lasting things."

Kao Tsung shook his head and smiled at her, "I can see that this is important to *you*...all right, we shall propose it. Now, your second idea—I think I'm awake enough to consider two." He smiled indulgently.

"It's the university system, Tsun...it needs changing, don't you agree?" Eagerly, she got up and began to pace around the bed.

"I know absolutely nothing about the university—or its system. Why don't you enlighten me?"

"Really? Right now the university is small, only about 40 students at most. And all the students are sons of the Five Families, and mostly, they just fool around until graduation and then fill a government job at good pay and prestige—and they're usually not very good at that even. Some can't even write!"

"I love it when you get so excited about things, you know, your eyes seem to spit fire!"

She stopped, still. "Zanggi used to say that," she said thoughtfully. "Anyway, my idea is to require an examination before admittance to the college...perhaps a written essay that would demonstrate their education level, their ability to read and write and understand ideas that would have some bearing on important tradition and values, to eliminate those who would not be useful or skillful in running the government...don't you see?"

"What would they write about? I'm one of the few of any of the nobility that knows anything about the stars and planets..."

"Oh, Tsun, I don't mean things like that...they would have to have some knowledge of our *Tang Code of Law* of course, and then, reasonably, the canons of Confucius and Lao Tzu and some of Hsuan Tsang's Buddhist texts—if he ever gets them all translated from the Sanskrit."

"A big order!"

"Yes, but just think...if they really studied, really became educated, I'm sure we'd have many, much more qualified young people and much less corruption because they would understand these important concepts."

"Examinations, eh? Not just a family connection?"

"Definitely. What d'you think?" She began to braid his black hair into one long braid. "Sit still, please, or you'll look all fuzzy if I don't get this braid tight enough."

"I suppose that young Yuan brother of yours would be one of the first to qualify, wouldn't he?"

"Li-Shih? He'd be first class, truly, such a smart one, he is!" *I think it's working...he's got a glint in his eye for a change...what fun it could be! We could make such a difference.."*

"Tsien, I admire your daring—as always—since the first days we played polo together—no fear. Not like me, I must say, but..."

A knock on the thick wooden door. "Come!"

Su Chi walked in carrying a tray that held a pot of tea, two porcelain cups and a dish of tiny, fragrant bean cakes. She bowed and put the tray down on a low table in front of the windows. The first morning sunlight, shining through trees, stippled the pillows and thick rug with light and shadow.

"Mornin' Madame, morning Most Illustrious, Secretary Kat Kat Zanggi said to tell you that he would like an audience at your convenience. No, that's not exactly what he said and you said to always be truthful, Madame, did you not?"

Tsien looked across the room at Kao Tsung, lifted up both her hands, shrugged, and grinned at him. "Yes, Su Chi, of course. So what did the honorable secretary say?"

"He said to tell you he wanted to see you as soon as you woke up. There." She bowed low and then stood by the door she had just entered.

"Very well, then...shall we see him now, Tsun?" At his assent, she motioned to her maid to leave. "Tell him we shall be ready in a quarter hour."

Kat Kat Zanggi came through the door as if marching to music only he could hear. Immediately behind him, a tall, thin man dressed in the burgundy robes of a Tibetan monk, slipped along carrying an ornate covered basket over his left arm.

"Greetings Most Illustrious Couple, it is good to see you in such good health this morning," Zanggi bowed. "I have a serious matter to lay before you—a decision I've made that I hope you'll accept."

"Decisions so early in the d-day?" grumbled Kao Tsung.

"One which I trust will give you pleasure in the long run."

"I'm not sure that you're serious, Ghost, you look too happy," Tse

Tsien shook her finger at him. "What are you brewing now?"

"I have decided that you need this." He gestured to the monk, who extended the basket toward her.

"For me? A present, Zanggi?" She took the basket, set it down, cautiously lifted the top, and peered in. A moist, black petal of a tongue licked her nose. She jumped back in surprise as a small fawn-colored puppy popped out, its feather-duster tail wagging wildly, its whole chubby body wriggling with delight at its new freedom. It leaped into her lap, straight up as if pulled by a string, reached toward Tsien's laughing face and snuggled into her shoulder, making happy puppy sounds.

"Sky! Zanggi, what kind of exuberant little creature *is* this?" She was fending off its busy paws and tongue, giggling so hard she could scarcely speak.

"This, my lady, is a *Shih Tzu,* which means *lion*—a small lion dog, sometimes called the chrysanthemum-faced dog, the girl half of a pair sent as tribute by K'iu Tai, the king of Viqur, part of the vast mountainous country of Tibet." The honorable secretary looked smug.

Tsien lifted the puppy down and watched her begin to frolic all over the room, leaping, pirouetting, and prancing. "Look how proudly she holds herself! Zanggi, how did you even think of this? I've never had a dog before. A falcon, a swan, a kitty, yes—but never a small, fluffy lion. What a wonderful gift!"

"Fei, fei, fei—just a thought I had."

"If I didn't know better, I'd think I could detect a blush behind that impassive face of yours," Tsien teased.

"On a more serious note, I thought you might need...I wanted you to have an extra pair of eyes and ears with you at all times, to alert you to...to let you know if there were someone near you who shouldn't be... who might not be...well, *friendly.*" One slim hand massaged the other absently.

Tsien picked up the puppy and held it out at arm's length, where it squirmed and kicked. "What shall we call you, little one?" Tsien cocked her head to one side. "You're very frilly—and more than a little, silly. Hmmnn, what would you think about being called Frilly Ti Li? Would you come to that? Well, we shall see, shan't we? Ti Li, Ti Li Ti Li—look, she knows her name already!" She put the frisky puppy down and looked at Kao Tsung.

"Tsun? Isn't she smart? Tsun? What's the matter? You look as if you'd seen a ghost!"

Kao Tsung was standing rigidly, eyes wide open, arms straight down his sides, immobile.

"Tsun! Look at me! Say something!"

He shook his head as if waking up suddenly and looked around in a rather dazed fashion. "Aaaahhh, wh-where? Wh-wh-who?" He took hold of the table to steady himself.

"Are you all right?" Tsien went to him quickly and held his arm.

"Yes, yes, I'm fine—a little dizzy is all." He patted her hand reassuringly.

"Does this *dizziness* happen often, Your Majesty?" Zanggi looked worried.

"Once in awhile, usually when I'm tired, or angry, or..."

"Hmmnnn, we must have the royal astrologer cast your chart—maybe there is some sort of a spell at work here."

"Now, Zanggi, don't put ideas in his head—maybe bean cakes don't agree with you anymore, my dear." Tsien led a reluctant Kao Tsung over to a chair and helped him to sit down. "Now rest a bit. I think you and the monk better go, Zanggi—thank you both so very much for Ti Li—we'll be fine. Say nothing of this to anyone."

"Of course, My Lady." Looking troubled, he bowed low and left, his wide sleeves fanning out behind him.

It was a bland, quiet, no social engagements time in the palace. No frivolities allowed for a full year in homage to Tai Tsung's memory. But the business of governing began, slowly, to resume. Kao Tsung reluctantly appeared each morning in order to hear grievances and petitions, sat solemnly on the peacock throne, flanked by at least two of his inner council ministers, who took turns attending.

Slightly behind him, behind a wood filigree screen, Tse Tsien sat, close enough for her to whisper comments and advice to Kao Tsung. Usually, Ti Li was curled up asleep in her lap, except for the rather disruptive times when she would toddle out to chew on a minister's brocaded slipper. Since she was, however, the emperor's dog, no one dared to say an unkind word to her and she quickly became petted and indulged, a welcome distraction to the often dreary recitations of real or imagined wrongs, a court favorite.

60
Something Momentous: Kao Tsung Rallies

TSE TSIEN WATCHED WITH INCREASING IRRITATION AND FRUSTRATION AS, day after day, Kao Tsung lay in bed, sleeping or gazing out into the garden, his formerly full, ruddy face grown sallow and grey. He only roused from his torpor when Ti Li bounced up onto his chest and began to lick his face with her small, exuberant tongue. Then he would smile, rather sadly, and murmur to her as she snuggled into his shoulder.

Without him, all the court duties fell to Tsien. *In a way, it's easier this way—I don't have to pretend that Tsun is actually deciding, but how can we go on this way? Already the ministers are beginning to demand more answers—when will the emperor return? What exactly is wrong with him? 'Sky! I wish I knew!*

They want to know what shall we do about...the army conscription? the belligerent envoy from Silla? the county tax collector's dereliction of duty? I'll simply have to take control openly and let the chips fall where they may. But first, I need to consolidate those who will back me... the followers of The Tao will most certainly be on my side, and probably the young group of Buddhism's adherents as well. Will these factions be strong enough, I wonder...to allow me to govern until... well, until some coalitions can be formed? The Confucian ministers, of course, will wrangle over any suggestion of mine and block them all whenever they can...they think it wrong for a woman to have authority—the only authority they respect in a woman is her ability to bear and raise children.

Tsien sighed and poured herself a cup fragrant tea from the iron teapot that her maid had just put on the coals of the standing brazier.

A strategy is needed, but I am so tired these days…wish I felt better in the mornings. Mornings used to be my best time…perhaps I'll talk to Sun Simao. He at least would keep our conversation to himself and not add to the abundant rumors of the court…yes, I'll do that.

Having decided on her next action, she sent the attending servant for Sun Simao, telling her that she was dismissed after delivering her message. Three quarter-bells later, Simao strode into the reception hall. The smell of horses and fresh meadow grass came with him, replacing the stale incense air, jogging Tse Tsien's memories of long ago.

"Aaah, Simao, you make me long to be riding out into the hills—is the grass growing long already?"

"It is—green and splendid, Your Majesty," he bowed his head in greeting. "It's been a long time since I've seen you…you are well?"

"Clever of you to ask so quickly," She smiled. *How good it is to talk someone I can trust.* "I am not ill, but I tire easily—which is unlike me, you know—and mornings are unusually difficult."

"Difficult? How?" Sun Simao, looked at her keenly.

"Oh, I seem unable to eat an early meal, rather nauseated, actually. It's probably nothing, but I thought you might know of something…"

"Tsien, would you think me rude if I asked a very personal question?"

"How personal?"

"Something that might be about your life with Kao Tsung." He said, watching her as he spoke.

"I think it would be all right, only between you and me, of course."

"Nothing that happens between us, Tse Tsien, ever goes further."

"Thank you, Sun Simao, I know that, but I just wanted to emphasize it because there are ears everywhere, the health of Kao Tsung is already conjecture, so my health must not be added to the stew. So ask away, my friend."

"There are certain symptoms, including morning nausea, that might indicate a…well, a change. For instance, have you had your monthly flow lately?"

"Hmmnnn, nooo…no, I haven't, now that I think of it, not since…" She lifted her head quickly, the way a golden eagle alertly scans for danger.

"In my relatively meager experience with women in the village, that always means that they have begun to carry a child." His voice was so soft, so tender, that the explosive words he said did not register immediately on Tsien's awareness.

"A child? Me? I don't think so—I've been told that child-bearing is not a possibility for me!"

"Perhaps, but I would venture that whoever told you that, is wrong. Your face has that certain look of a woman with child."

Trembling, with a sudden intuitive acceptance, Tsien sank down on the chair. Wide eyed, she had no words.

"This startles you, my dear?"

"It's…overwhelming!" *A baby? Kao's baby? Our baby! Amazing!* "What should I do?"

Simao threw back his head and laughed, "Do? Why, enjoy it!"

"Oh, yes, but I must tell Tsun right away! Such a surprise! Perhaps he'll wake up, take some interest in life again!" She jumped up. Ti Li, who had been asleep in her lap, went sprawling onto the marble floor, a most unhappy look on her face.

A thoughtful Sun Simao watched her go.

WITH TI LI LEAPING AND PANTING AROUND HER, TSIEN RUSHED INTO THE BEDROOM where her husband rested. She sat on the bed beside him as Ti Li snuggled happily between them.

"Tsun, I have something momentous to share with you! I've just been talking with Sun Simao and he thinks—oh Tsun, he thinks that I may have happiness within me!"

Kao Tsung opened his eyes. Quietly, he gazed up at a point beyond Tsien without smiling or speaking.

"Did you hear me? Do you know how amazing, how wonderful it would be—for us, for all of Chian? An heir, Tsun, think of it! Please, say something, tell me that you understand."

"Yes, I understand. You think that you may have a baby in your belly."

"Doesn't that make you pleased? Make you proud?"

"Is it real? I don't seem to be able to tell the difference these days—between what is real and what is a dream—I have so many dreams…"

"This is *very* real, a chance for *our* baby to carry on your father's True Vision—a baby that we can raise like a warrior for all that is good and true! " Tsien picked up his limp hand and held it tightly between her own, willing him to feel, to respond.

'Sky—what can be the matter? Neither Mistress Feng nor Simao seems to have an answer for his dwindling life force—is he poisoned? or drugged? Ever since he lost consciousness that time, after the trial, where that evil man kept lying to him, and he was so angry, he's seemed strange, often distracted...

"Come on—get dressed, please. Come outside with me—let's walk in the garden together. Court is not in session, gather your strength today so you can be there tomorrow."

Slowly, Kao Tsung sat up. Gradually, Tsien helped him to dress. Reluctantly, he let her lead him through the doors and outside, into the exuberance of early spring.

WHETHER IT WAS THE RESULT OF SOFT SPRING WINDS, INTEREST IN THE NEW PALACE being built, Tsien's insistence or Sun Simao's foul-smelling herbs, Kao Tsung began to rally. He was unable to move his left arm, and sight in his left eye was nearly gone, but somehow, he began to take an interest in the world around him, even talked of getting back on his pony for a game of polo. All of which relieved Tsien and allowed her to double her attention to revising and writing the new Code of Law begun with Tai Tsung ten years before.

Faina and Merket, new babies and toddlers in tow, came often to interrupt her.

"You're working too hard—you should be walking idly around the lily pool—or painting water colors—or calligraphing perhaps," declared Faina, looking at her friend in a worried-mother way.

"Batu said to remind you that Igren women were excused from much of their work, weren't supposed to even boil felt when with child." Merket added.

"Well, I'm no longer an Igren woman," Tse Tsien smiled at them indulgently, amused that they assumed because *they* were mothers that they now knew better, and that *they* were now her elder sisters.

"I'm fine, my dears, work is good for me."

"Is the baby lively? I mean, can you feel it kicking yet?

"Oh, yes! And such a funny, fluttery feeling! I told Kao Tsung and he was as proud as if he alone had done something wonderful." They all laughed affectionately.

"You *have* stopped being at court though, haven't you?" Faina continued.

"Soon. We have one major case to hear in the next month, then I'll cut back on that for the last little bit before the baby comes." Tse Tsien went to the sink to wash out the brushes she'd been using, scrubbed at the black ink on the last joint of her middle finger—the "black chrysanthemum" of all calligraphers—and joined her friends with a cup of green tea.

"Tell me all the news that's flying around the palace. I've been too absorbed lately to notice, and besides, no one tells me anything, fearing that I'll snap their heads off—admittedly, I've been a little snarly lately. Even Tsun tells me to lighten up."

"Our children are so enjoying the new rooms you have given us, Tse Tsien, thank you so much."

"And ours—Camel says that our children now occupy enough room for a dozen village families in this sprawling Loyang palace."

"Actually, did you hear, Faina, what happened to young Mei Lin?"

"Who is Mei Lin?" asked Tsien.

"She's the incredibly beautiful young wife of one of Batu's lieutenants."

"I saw her crying in the garden last week, just sitting on a bench by the duck pond sobbing—what happened?"

"It's Lady Wang's uncle, Wu Shih. Mei Lin says he lured her into his house and raped her."

"No! He must be crazy!"

"Crazy? Perhaps. He of course, being the high-minded Minister of Justice that he is, claims she's just an ignorant girl who misinterpreted his kind attention—that he was sorry she took offense, and so on. And then, she says, he offered her a small bag of cash if she would simply forget all about it!"

Tse Tsien was intensely quiet. "This is highly disturbing news—will you bring Mei Lin to me as soon as possible? If what you say is true, we must find out more. For the Minister of Justice to behave in such a manner will wreak havoc with the harmony of us all.

"Odd, really, I've just been writing that section of the Code that deals with a higher official having illegal sexual conduct with a younger person—much heavier punishment meted out than as if the two involved were of the same class—minimum sentence, if proven guilty, would be 500 blows with the heavy stick—but compounding it with bribery! Standard sentence in such a matter is death by strangulation or decapitation...yes, I must see Mei Lin quickly to *hear* what truth lies in her story."

MEI LIN LEFT THE ROOM, SWAYING SLIGHTLY ON HER PLATFORM SHOES. Kao Tsung turned to Tse Tsien and said in a sort of singsong, "Well? Her story was certainly vivid and full of rather disarming detail—do y-y-you think she was telling the truth?"

"I *know* she was," Tse Tsien replied quietly. "Ever since I was a little girl, I've been able to *hear* truth in what someone says—or untruth, either way. Your father always relied on this gift..."

"Still...Wu Shih is not a stupid man. Why would he do such a thing?"

"Oh my dear husband—you saw how extraordinarily beautiful she is..."

"Hmmnnn...b- but he is such a prominent Confucian! Statesman, scholar, in addition to being head of the Ministry of Justice!"

"Yes, that's what makes it so difficult. We must convene the council immediately—inform them of this scandal before Wu Shih has gathered outside support."

"This is as explosive as those *ground rats* that naughty children play with." Kao Tsung remarked.

"Ground rats? What kind of creatures are *they?*" She picked up Ti Li and absently stroked her silky fur.

Kao Tsung threw back his head and laughed heartily, a deep rumbly sound.

"What's funny?"

"I f-f-forgot that you did not grow up here, Tsien—it's the mischief-making of little boys to catch a rat and put it—and a small amount of dynamite and a bit of fuse—into a hollow bamboo stick, then light the fuse and, as the rat tries to run away, the whole thing blows apart... pouf...very messy!"

"Ooof! That's awful!"

"But an apt image for this particular mess, wouldn't you agree, Tsien?"

"Sadly, yes. I'll send for Zanggi."

"If you will permit me to make a suggestion, Highness?"

"Of course, my Good Ghost, I am asking for your view, your advice, in this, this abomination!"

"So, so...yes. We need to consult the ancient oracle, the I Ching, for the correct course of action. Its advice has never failed me—but in this case, *you* must cast the stalks and I shall read them for you. Is that agreeable to you, Mistress?" He reached into his sleeve and brought out a bundle of dried yarrow stalks. He put two stacks of cushions on the floor, pulled a small black table between them and sat down, gesturing Tse Tsien to sit opposite.

"What is it that you wish to ask from the Book of Changes, Spitfire?" Zanggi smiled as he lit incense, placing it precisely in the middle of the sand-filled bowl on the table.

"Hmmnnn, I want to know what the best course of action will be to resolve this danger, to protect the community, to bring back harmony to those around us."

"Very well put, now take the stalks and let them drop on the mat at our feet—you remember, don't you—how to hold them?"

"You showed me once, those many years ago, after I first came to Changan." She began the ritual division of stalks, four by four, taking a stalk from alternate piles, placing it between the ring and little finger of her left hand, dropping it, three times for a line, six times in all, until the pattern of trigrams became evident.

"Fei, fei fei...indeed, perfectly appropriate, and on the first throw. You were well focused I see." Zanggi nodded.

"What is it then, tell me!"

"It is the hexagram, *Resolution.* You see here, *ch'ien* in the first three lines, then, in the ruling fifth line, *tui,* surmounted by *kuai—Resolution* it is!"

"But what does it *mean?"*

"I'll quote from the book. 'The forces that may threaten you are now in a position to be eradicated. No compromise is possible. Your relationship to society at large may require you to announce the truth openly.'" Zanggi sat back and continued to look at the arrangement of stalks before them.

"'Open truth can lead to danger—so you must be constantly vigilant. Remember, you are dealing with truth and therefore, all else must be discredited. When attempting to overthrow adversaries or obstacles in powerful positions, great resolution and determination are necessary. Unless *completely* eradicated, this danger may spring back to power.'"

"Well, that does correspond to the Code—leaves me little choice does it?"

"No. You must tell the emperor to convene the council. I'll speak to some of the ministers immediately. You were right to act swiftly."

As he stood, Ti Li came racing in, scattering the yarrow stalks in all directions across the mats. Without a murmur, Zanggi reached down, collected all the stalks and bound them with a ribbon of silk.

"Come here you small rascal! I hope she hasn't broken any stalks, Zanggi...such a mischief!" Tse Tsien held the puppy on her shoulder and went out to find Kao Tsung.

61
Affairs Of State

IT HAD BEEN AN AGONIZINGLY LONG DAY. WU SHIH'S NOISY EXTENDED FAMILY lined the Great Hall, apprehensive, knowing that they would all be punished in some way if the verdict came down against him.

Tse Tsien no longer sat behind a screen at the emperor's back. She sat on an ornate chair slightly back, but alongside Kao Tsung. They were both dressed in formal robes. His heavy silk kimono, tied at the waist with a tasseled orange sash, was royal yellow. Chrysanthemums, symbols of longevity, were embroidered down the front. On his head, he wore a filigree crown that sparkled with many-hued jewels. Tse Tsien's outer robe, embroidered with imperial five-toed dragons that twisted from shoulder to hem and held pearls in their claws, was a silken peach color, sashed with cerise, which parted when she moved to show the under pantaloons of dark red. Her hair was piled in an elaborate frenzy of braided loops, pinned with long gold hairpins, from which dangled intricate jade flowers.

Ringed around them on the dais were all the council members but one—the irate Minister of Justice, who stood before them, red in the face, furious, frightened. The exquisite Mei Lin sat below on the main floor, her husband by her side. On both sides of them, a phalanx of guardsmen supported one of their own.

Adamant against Wu Shih's rant, Tse Tsien was reading from the *Code of Law,* "...for a person in authority to have unwelcome sexual conduct with a person of lesser status is an Abomination and subject to fifty blows from the heavy stick—or exile, depending on the degree of difference of mourning between the two. If the lesser person is the guilty party, he or she will be subject to exile, redeemable by payment of copper.

"If the guilty party is of higher rank, and particularly if bribery is involved whereby the injured party has been offered cash to remain quiet, the harshest penalties will and *must* prevail—to be strangled or beheaded—this is the punishment for those of superior rank, who bear the burden of upholding the highest ethical conduct...those who have disregarded their station and cast themselves and their families into the dust. There are to be no remissions for this offense, as the order of society has been disregarded and the harmony between Heaven and Earth has been cast into chaos.

"Furthermore, the wives and children of the miscreant are to be sent into exile to the jungles far to the south, the relatives to the fifth relationship to be stripped of all privileges and wealth. It is so written." Wu Chao Tse Tsien rolled up the scroll with a snap.

Charging into this solemnity, sleeves and hair flying, came Lady Wang, who threw herself down in front of the emperor.

"No! You can't do this, my husband! This is my uncle. He has done no harm, you cannot believe this, this *inferior* person, this commoner, and not believe my august uncle!"

Kao Tsung looked down, obviously annoyed. "Get up, my lady. Do not make a spectacle of yourself in this way."

"It's that harlot!" She screamed, pointing at Tse Tsien, "She's addled your wits! Cast a spell on you!"

"The *facts* have spoken against him. He has sullied the harmony of our society. He must be eradicated. You need not fear, however, because you are my wife you have first mourning rights and you and your blood sisters, will be exempt from his punishment, even though you are, legally, in his family."

Tse Tsien was amazed to hear Kao Tsung speak so clearly and simply.

"You'll pay! I'll bring the whole Wang family against you! You'll be vilified and cursed—unfit to be the emperor! I'll see to it that your children by me, by *me* will inherit this title and then watch, my unfaithful husband—I'll see you damned to hell."

"Remove this person from the court!" Zanggi's voice roared out across the room. Several of the assembled guardsmen rushed up, took Lady Wang by her arms and marched her out of the room.

Wu Shih, now totally deflated and quivering with fear, was led out behind her.

Oh dear, baby mine, you are jumping about in dismay and I don't blame you. Such an exhaustive day for us, little one. Soon, we'll leave and rest quietly, I promise. She smoothed her belly as if to comfort the baby within.

Walking gracefully together, the emperor and his empress left the Great Hall.

An unnatural quiet pervaded the palace for several weeks thereafter while the affairs of state were carried out with much less drama. During their customary early morning walk together, Tse Tsien and Kao Tsung stopped at the moon bridge to watch a mother duck lead a ripple of ducklings trailing behind her.

"Tsun, I've commissioned a sculptor to create all of Sire's favorite bayards, the horses he named and loved the most...to line the road to his tomb. I'm hoping he'll be able to finish them in time for the memorial celebration next autumn.

"But I'm getting restless...our plans seem to be happening so slowly... I'm going to send for my old teacher in the Forest of Pencils—he was so beloved by his students, so organized in their behalf... I would like to move ahead with plans to change and enlarge the university system...I believe he'd be a wonderful help in setting this in motion, don't you think?"

Before he could answer, they saw Faina, her new baby bundled across her breast, with two toddlers skimbling along behind her.

"Greetings on this beautiful morning, Your Majesties. Sir, it's good to see you looking so well again."

"So it's to be a formal morning, dear friend?" Tse Tsien smiled. "I see you have Merket's little one with you today."

"Isn't he adorable? We, Merket and I, are taking turns with the babies in the morning so we can have a few hours of peace...of course there are always servants, but somehow...we like it better this way."

"I'll leave you ladies to your woman-talk if you don't mind. Tsien, I think your ideas are excellent, do send for your old friend, tell him to come to Loyang right away...that may help you to be patient with your, *our,* many projects." He nodded to them both and walked away, putting each foot down as carefully as if he were walking on ice.

"My goodness, Tsien, your belly *is* getting big! Can't be too much longer can it? What does the midwife say?" Faina leaned down to say hello to Ti Li, who was circling and jumping in welcome.

Tsien laughed and patted her swollen belly, "She says, be patient! Be grateful that you have such good health...and other such words of comfort."

"She's probably trying to reassure you...it is unusual for a woman of your age to be having her first child, you know."

Tsien slipped her arm around Faina's slender waist. "Thirty three is not *old,* my dear, even though it may seem ancient to a young filly like you."

"I'm sorry, I didn't mean that you were old...just old for a first time birth...just a little worried about you and the baby. But, actually, what I wanted to ask you about was for after the birth—have you engaged a wet nurse?"

"A wet nurse? Aaahhh, no. I'd thought that I would..."

"As busy as you are all the time, you'll not be able to nurse the little one as much as it will want. Now, Camel has a younger sister who had a baby a few months ago so she still has an abundance of good milk—her baby's fat and happy. She's a sweet girl and I know it would be an honor for her to help you. Would you like me to send for her?"

"That would be fine, then we could get acquainted ahead of time. Thank you, Faina, for thinking of these things. It's always best to be prepared, of that I'm convinced more and more as the years go by."

With the toddlers and Ti Li playing hide and seek in and out of their long skirts, the two friends dallied a little longer before leaving in separate directions as different duties called to them.

62
A ROYAL BABY AND A COMET

"TSUN, WAKE UP PLEASE...SEND FOR THE MIDWIVES, I think this baby is coming!"

"R-r-right now? It's not even daylight!" Kao Tsung's sleepy voice sounded alarmed.

"I know—but it feels like...maybe soon, I do believe. Please hurry..."

Tsien swept aside the bed curtains and got up. She walked awkwardly to the window and looked out into the garden where cherry blossoms looked white in the moonlight.

What a lovely morning for my baby to be born—moon of first fruits, pomegranate moon. Aahhh, whew, so much pressure down there! She could hear Kao Tsung's voice shouting to the servants.

And suddenly the room was filled with other women, midwives, nurses, Mistress Feng and both her attendants, servants—all milling around excitedly, laying out cloths and blankets in preparations for helping a baby—an imperial baby—to be born. There was very little talking, they all knew their part and what to do.

Only Tse Tsien was at a loss to know what to do until Lu Chi, the head midwife took over. "Come here, Majesty, we will bathe you and I'll time your contractions which will tell us how far the baby has traveled down the narrow tunnel, how soon we might expect it to push beyond that final gate. Has your water broken yet?"

"My water? Ummnn, I don't think so."

"You will know when it does...no mistaking that flood, y'know." A broad-faced countrywoman, Lu Chi smiled.

As if on cue, Tse Tsien gasped, "Aieee, it's pouring out of me...right now!"

"Good, the little one will come more quickly now."

Servants rolled in the birthing bed—a high, slanted bed that allowed the mother to be held in squatting, semi-upright position, braced against padded armrests on either side. Tse Tsien was helped up and into position by many willing hands, each eager to be part of this royal birthing. Her feet were placed in soft leather stirrups so that she could not slip down. Now Lu Chi took up her own position at the open foot of the bed.

"Breathe steadily and deeply, Majesty, don't hold your breath when the pain comes, breathe into it, in, out...yes, like that...no, don't push yet, even though I know you want to...that's right, relax, relax fully whenever you can. The time of great effort will come soon...drink this elixir of ginger and citragandha—it will help to open internal passages."

Obediently, Tse Tsien drank in-between spasms, then lay back, only to contract her whole body again and again several times each quarter hour. Sweat slicked her throat and swelling breasts. Hours passed.

Time ceased to have meaning. There was only the imperative of birth, the rhythm of breathing, the nowhere else but here, sense of life, of being, that comes with the labor of helping and patience, waiting for a baby to swim its way through a too-tight tunnel into the world of air.

Lu Chi's voice grows faint...I hear only the breath of dragon... rasping, roaring... heavy wings pulsing high... glistening tail streaming out behind...higher...higher...now a raw, shrill cry of triumph...soaring, pushing through clouds...pushing...everything I've got, ***everything...NOW!*** *My arms reach out... to pluck one...one brilliant star, a perfect, shining pearl tucked beneath my wing... floating down...and the world burbles into being...*

The lusty cry of a baby sucking in air hungrily. An ecstatic moan of delight from the attending women and a sigh of completion with the chorus of "It's a girl child!" began this new life.

Faina took the newly swaddled baby from Lu Chi and nestled her between Tse Tsien's breasts. She watched with an understanding smile of affection as her friend's eyes widened in wonder, filled with tears.

Ohhh, didn't know it would feel like this...I feel so empty, so scoured out...and here she is, my daughter, my pearl-without-a-price...brought back from the farthest reaches of the Everlasting Sky...a treasure...

"Please send for Kao Tsung, brush my hair...bring me a clean gown... I want to get up."

"No, not yet, a little more time, my Lady," warned Lu Chi. "The afterbirth must come out first. Girls, bring a lined basket to catch it while I massage her belly a bit. Play with your little one until we're finished here."

"Aaahhh, Faina, she's so small...but so finished, so perfect...such little fingers, complete with fingernails...a wonderment, truly! I never thought I'd be this lucky...I feel as though my heart just got three times bigger...is this the way all new mothers feel? As if they've reached into a magical realm and brought back a *baby?* A magical little creature that is all your own?...to cherish and love...."

"I don't know whether all mothers feel that way, Talima, er...Tsien, but I do, too." Faina brushed Tsien's hair.

With a last contraction, and a gurgle, the afterbirth flopped into the waiting basket. "Where would you like us to bury the baby's leftovers, Majesty?"

"I think...under the flowering cherry tree outside the nursery, that way it will nourish a tree that she will see as they both grow strong, yes?"

A breathless servant brushed aside the curtains. "I can't find His Majesty, Madame—I've looked all over the palace!"

"Did you look in his observatory?"

"Oh no, I didn't think of that."

"Well, that's probably where he's comforting himself while the baby was coming. So go. You all may go. I'll just rest now...with my baby." She lay back in her clean bed, a sleeping babe beside her. She looked out into a garden radiant with sunset color—puffy rose clouds floated across the still-blue sky. Golden light seemed to come from inside everything, everywhere. Small birds twittered their twilight songs.

There's a stillness in my whole body...a kind of humming...my skin feels different...I feel different...I'm a mother! I never thought I'd be a mother...dear little one, I'll be the best one I can be...you'll see, we'll do things together, ride together...perhaps one of Shira's offspring...

Quietly, she lay still. Tired, she felt fulfilled. She drank strong, spicy chai from her favorite celadon cup, savoring the invigorating steam.

By the time Kao Tsung arrived, Tse Tsien was peaceful and glowing, cradling the baby close to her. Ti Li, wearing a new pink ribbon, curled up, guarding the foot of the bed.

"Tsien! My d-d-dear, a d-d-daughter, they tell me!" Kao Tsung disheveled and breathless, sat down gingerly beside her.

"Here she is, a pearl without price, husband." The baby woke as she picked her up and laid her in Kao Tsung's arms.

His large, soft hand gently touched the dark fuzz of her hair. The baby reached up and curled her tiny hand around one of his fingers, then met his gaze with light gray eyes.

"She's amazing," he whispered. "I thought that I had exciting news for *you,* Tsien, but I had no idea how exciting it would be to see our baby. I think she not only holds my finger, she holds my heart in her hand."

"Mmmnnn, I'm glad you feel that way, Tsun. What was *your* exciting news? Tsien smiled radiantly at the two of them.

"Oh, yes! Well, it's the comet! I've seen the comet up close through my big telescope...it must be the comet that's been expected all these years—the one in the great prophecy—the one that signifies the coming of a Prince of Wu who will be the next emperor!"

I do remember being told about that prophecy—was it Li Bo or Hsuan Tsung? Long ago in the garden one night...

"You must be so happy to have seen it."

"I am indeed, but it's a bit unsettling, you see—who is this Prince of Wu? How and when, will he appear?"

63
CHIA AND THE NEED TO BE FEARLESS

THESE HAVE BEEN SOME OF THE MOST PEACEFUL WEEKS I CAN EVER REMEMBER...*the baby is such a joy...don't know what to call you yet, do we, little pearl? The astrologers tell me they'll have a name any day, then we can have a small Naming Day ceremony...not quite a year since Sire died so celebrations must still be small, but we'll manage, won't we?* Tse Tsien covered her breasts and gave the baby, her rosebud mouth still wet with milk, to her *ayah,* Camel's little sister.

"Thank you, Mi Kuo, she's yours for the remainder of the day as I must welcome the ambassadors from Serindia, who've come so far across the northern Silk Route. I hope those milk-siblings, yours and mine, are not tiring you?"

"Not at all, My Lady, sweet and good they both are."

"I'll go and dress...she's made a rather sodden mess of this tunic, I fear!" Laughing, Tse Tsien hurried away.

BEFORE SHE CAME INTO THE GREAT AUDIENCE HALL, SHE MET KAO TSUNG in deep conversation with several of the court astrologers.

"Aaahh, Tsien," he sang out. "They have arrived at a name for our baby! Tell her, please, gentlemen."

"Most Noble Lady," the leader, in a plain, old-fashioned black tunic over loose pantaloons, bowed. "We wanted a name that said many things—first born, precious, beautiful—but one, also, that might, in some way, speak to the future.

"Ahem, to that end..." one of the other astrologers, this one dressed in brown monk's habit, broke in.

"We have decided on..." the third, also in brown, chimed in, not wanting to be left out.

"Oh, do tell us, we've waited long enough!" said Tse Tsien, impatient with their self-importance.

"Very well...her name will be Chia Wu Shin Kan Tsung, incorporating some part of both your names, you see. Giving her this name should be done on the most felicitous day—the longest day of the year—next week, that is."

"And here is a calligraphed scroll of our process to arrive at this most auspicious name." The monk held out the small scroll to Tse Tsien and bowed very low.

"Well...Chia, then...a lovely name for our lovely baby, don't you think, Tsun? Tsun? What are you staring at?" *Oh, Lord! It's the sickness again... he's starting to shake...* "Come sit beside me on this bench. Thank you, Astrologers, he'll be all right in a few moments. You may go."

Kao Tsung shook his head from side to side like an old lion and gulped air several times before he spoke. "W-what happened?"

"You were just a little dizzy. Go back to our apartment now and rest. There's no need for both of us to greet the Serindians. Why don't you begin to think of what you'd like us to do for Chia's naming day?"

AT DAWN, THE LONGEST DAY WAS ALREADY HOT AND MUGGY. By mid-morning, it was blisteringly hot, and thunderheads massed above swelling crowds that filled the Great Square. But not one of the thousands wanted to be anywhere else than here, here where they could see and hear the emperor proclaim the name of the new baby born to him and Wu Chao Tse Tsien. They waited patiently under the hammer hand of sun and were finally rewarded as two trumpeters came out onto the balcony and began to play a loud fanfare that silenced even the birds.

Eight of the ministers, including the secretary, came out and stood at either side of the broad balcony. A great cheer rose up as the emperor and his wife walked into the center. Both were dressed informally in new Serindian outfits given as tribute. Kao Tsung wore a scarlet peaked cap whose flaps stood out like ears, a long, indigo tunic fastened with a studded belt, dark blue pantaloons and black, knee-high boots. Tse Tsien had tucked her copper hair under a wide-brimmed hat from which a scarf fluttered. Her tunic was saffron-colored, belted with an orange sash, beetle-blue pantaloons, and high, soft red boots.

Faina, dressed in a patterned indigo kimono, came next in honor of her closeness to the queen. She carried the baby who was wrapped in a blanket embroidered in every color of the rainbow. Small yellow tassels rippled from the blanket's edges. Faina bowed and gently passed the baby to Kao Tsung.

He says he feels fine today...so odd how it just comes over him suddenly, and then is gone...just as swiftly...only his vision grows worse, only that leg seems to get stiffer...please let him be steady for these next moments...don't let our people see him being weak...

"My countrymen, on this auspicious day, I welcome you here to share with us..." he gestured to Tse Tsein at his right side, "with us, yes, the name giving of our new daughter."

He held her out so that those closest could actually see the wide-awake face of a bright little being. "All the stars have been consulted by our expert astrologers, and they have agreed that our first-born shall be known as Chia Wu Shin Kan Tsung!"

How amazingly clear he's speaking! He must have practiced a great deal to be able to say all that without stuttering at all...so that's done...I'm grateful that Chia did not cry...she must be terribly hot all wrapped up like that...well the garden near the lake will be cool...as soon as we can get away...

"And now," Kao Tsung looked around and smiled, "now I'd like you all to bear witness that Princess Chia Wu Shin Kan Tsung...is my heir, the official heir to the peacock throne of all Chian...show her your tribute!" He held the baby high over his head and the throng shouted and cheered with astonishment and delight.

Looking triumphant, Kao Tsung gave the baby to Tse Tsien, turned and walked back inside the palace. Tsien, holding her baby closely, surprised and pleased by his announcement, followed. One by one the rest of the aristocracy and council filed out.

Faina heard Kat Kat Zanggi muttering to himself, "Fei, fei, fei, 'tis great danger we're in now! Why couldn't he wait a little longer? That she-cat will be sharpening her claws again as soon as she hears."

The sky opened just then, spilling a flood of rain over all, while thunder rumbled from horizon to horizon. The monsoon season had begun.

"OH SUN, HAVING SOLVED THE MATTER OF SUCCESSION, it's as though he feels there's nothing left to live for...he retreats deeper and deeper into his own private world..." Tse Tsien sighed and smoothed the thin, airy cotton of her summer skirt. "Well, some days he does go to his observatory—gazing at that comet that he says fulfills the prophecy of the Prince of Wu—but many days he never even leaves our bed. He's become so thin these past months...and now more immovable on his left side than ever...he still takes pleasure in Chia, though...asks for her every morning...smiles and plays with her a little...but by noon, he's asleep with Ti Li curled under his chin...do you have any idea what's happening to him? Can you tell me?"

Sun Simao, sitting on the opposite side of Kao Tsung, was holding his wrist lightly, feeling his pulse, counting the beats. "Not exactly...it's as if his *chi,* his life energy, is simply fading away, but what the cause of that is..." He looked out the window, with rain sluicing down, as if the answer were written there. "Years ago, I saw someone wasting away like this...she'd been poisoned with tiger's whiskers...by a jealous suitor, I believe, but..."

"Poisoned! But who would want to poison a gentle man like Tsun?"

"Many people, I suspect, Tsien, he is, after all, the emperor, and that means that many envy and wish him ill. Yes, tiger's whiskers act like ground glass within a human body, you see, and gradually all the systems break down...or it could be something else. Whatever the cause, my dear, unless we are visited by a miracle, I think you should prepare yourself for his death."

Only the underwater liquid sound of rain filled the room. "He's not that old, Sun, only a bit into his fourth decade..." Tse Tsien protested.

"We are all old enough for death, Tsien...as soon as we are born," he said gently, releasing Kao Tsung's hand back to the silk sheet that covered him. Kao Tsung's eyes opened, looked from one to the other dreamily, and smiled.

"There's been so much death in my life...so many gone..."

"True, we are impermanent...regardless of how fixed, how *real* and substantial the existence of our bodies, our palaces, the green and golden land itself *seems* to be, they're not permanent. Everything comes into being and passes out of being. At Shaolin, our teacher often reminded us of this…" The sharp bones of his face softened as he looked down at the peaceful emperor.

"There is an ancient *sutra,* a written teaching from India, called the Diamond Sutra, that my teacher had us commit to memory…it's said to be the Buddha's very own words to his followers…Tsien?"

Tears flowed down Tsien's face, wetting the collar of her tunic. She tried to wipe them away with the back of her hand. "I'm listening, Sun, don't stop…"

"Yes, all right, this sutra is often spoken of as the perfection of wisdom—'Thus shall ye think of all this fleeting world…a flash of summer lightning, a cloud, a dream, a bubble in a stream…'"

"Hmmnnn, each so very real in that moment, each so insubstantial, gone in an instant, real only in memory, of a past that no longer exists." Tsien said slowly, thoughtfully. "I understand."

"Yes, this impermanence we're experiencing here…this moment…is a challenge to accept fearlessly…to deny it is to deny living fully…you will need to be fearless in the time to come, Tse Tsien. As regent for Chia, heir to the throne, you will be terribly visible to the entire world. I will help in whatever ways I, and the other warrior monks of my order can, to keep you and the little one safe."

Tsien looked at her fleeting husband, leaned over and took him in her arms, rocking him in the same way as she did Chia before sleep. She felt the rhythm of his heart pulse against her, falter, and begin again. She smelled the wisps of scent from the incense he always burned as he hunted the skies for stars at night. She remembered the indomitable horseman she had first known, playing polo alongside his fearlessness, and the fearful reluctance he'd shown when realizing he would be emperor after his larger-than-life father. All that he was, she held in her arms.

Then the rains stopped. Birds sang. The sun blazed out as it sank into the horizon. As twilight spread across the cooling land, Kao Tsung drifted into his final sleep.

When she could no longer feel his heart beating, Tse Tsien laid him down tenderly and covered his face with the sheet. She stood, took a deep breath, and said, "I'll go now to be with Chia, Sun. Thank you for giving me something to guide me while we go through this time of deep sorrow."

She brushed her hand across Sun Simao's shoulder and strode out of the room, calling to servants as she went.

64
Lady Wang Brings Regrets

THE NURSERY WAS FILLED WITH CHILDREN'S LAUGHTER. Faina and her baby boy, now almost a year and her two-year-old girl, Mi Kuo with her chubby 14-month-old son, Merket with her two boys, one and almost three, and Tse Tsien with Chia, now a sturdy five-month old, sitting up, gurgling at the older children.

How lovely it is, just to be a mother with all these babies, watching them grow together...touching their silken baby skin, the milk-sweet smell of them, their bright-eyed curiosity about everything, everyone... the world all new each moment...if this were all I had to do, my days would be perfect, it seems to me...but then, I do enjoy all the rest of governing—most of the time... Tse Tsien watched and smiled.

The doors opened to admit one of the eunuch guards, dressed as usual in an orange-yellow cotton tunic and loose pants, with the heavy medallion of honor for the guards of the women's quarters, hanging from his sash. He crossed between the children and bowed low before Tse Tsien. "Most Illustrious, a visitor requests admittance."

"Yes? Who is it?"

"Lady Wang, Madame, requests your favor."

"By the Everlasting Sky! This *is* unusual...I wonder what she wants? Well, gather several more guards, station yourselves quietly around the room, just in case, and when you're ready, invite her in."

"No! Tsien you can't let that harridan in here where the children are!" Faina leaped up with alarm.

"Be easy, my friend, she can't harm us, let's just see what she wants."

"I suppose so, but I hope you won't let her touch any of our children!"

"Patience, Faina...let's be kind."

Lady Wang, with her customary mincing steps, came softly into the room, walked over to Tse Tsien and made a perfunctory curtsy. "Good morning, Wu Chao Tse Tsien, thank you for seeing me. We have not had a pleasant past, but now that we are both widows, I would like to turn that around." She smiled rather shyly at each of the women. "I am so sorry about some of my outbursts before, please understand that it must have been my change-of-life misery that I'm definitely in the midst of and I hope it doesn't affect any of you as badly as it has me...when it's your turn.

"You see, all four of *my* children are in their second decade and therefore not interested in their mother anymore—you know how willful they get at this age—and I miss the babies. There are so many little ones in this part of the new palace...and I'd just like to be part of it—if you'd let me. " She made a conciliatory gesture with both hands, lifted her shoulders and waited.

"You surprise me, my Lady, I've always been under the impression that you...that you *hated* me."

"Hated you? Oh dear me, no, Wu Chao, I can't imagine why you should think that...do you know of anything I've ever done to hurt you? I've never been very nice to you, it's true, I guess I just didn't understand... surely you won't hold that against me, Second Wife?"

"Well, I don't know that..."

"I'd only come to play with the babies once in awhile, dandle them a bit...it would make me feel young again. Surely, you're gracious enough to allow this small request, to make things more pleasant between us?"

Ti Li woke up from her spot in the sun and bounced into their midst, skidding to a stop in front of Lady Wang. The hair down the middle of her back stood on end and her ears were back. Small eyes riveted on Lady Wang, she began a low growl.

"Hush, Ti Li, that's not very nice, come over here and be quiet. I'm sorry, Lady, but Ti Li doesn't like strangers sometimes, particularly when she just wakes up."

Lady Wang shied away from the little Shih Tzu and cleared her throat nervously.

She seems to genuinely regret past differences and I can see that she might be lonely with her children grown and now, not even Kao Tsung to talk with occasionally on his way through to his observatory...but can I trust her? I suppose there's no harm in her visiting as long as there are always other people around—guards and servants, as well as children and their mothers—with Chia at all times...but she makes me uneasy somehow...yet she, too, is grieving and I should not hold the past against her...

"We should welcome your company, Lady. Just let one of the guards know ahead of time, and we'll be happy to have you here with the children. I, too, regret that we were unable to know each other better while my husband...while Kao Tsung was alive, so maybe this can be a new beginning. Merket, why don't you let Lady Wang sit next to you... we'll send for some tea and cakes for all of us and we'll have a little time this morning together."

The ladies' conversation resumed. Lady Wang smiled and nodded while drinking her tea silently.

Faina and Merket exchanged rather grim looks, clearly suspicious of Lady Wang's about-face. Later, as they gathered up their babies and toddlers to go, they agreed, in a quick whisper, to talk to Kat Kat Zanggi as soon as possible.

In the next few days, as the monsoon flooded paths and alleys, Tse Tsien was busy with affairs of state and with family, for her Tai Yuan family—father and son—came to enroll the youngest son in Loyang's new university. Since she had enlarged the whole university system, the old practice of enrollment, made up only of sons from the Five Families, had changed. Now students from all over the country could take an examination to see if they were qualified to learn from the best teachers in classes of history, medicine, science, literature and the arts—all requirements for higher office that Tai Tsung laid out in his *True Vision*—that Wu Chao Tse Tsien had put into effect the past year and a half.

"Youngest son has proved himself a good student under his tutors' guidance and is eager to be away from home and in the company of other young scholars," said his father when they met with Tse Tsien. "We are most proud of him, Your Majesty.".

"Come now, Father, no majesty between us, please," Tse Tsien smiled and took both their arms, leading them past the ranks of omnipresent guards who parted for them, down the wide, shining hall to her private apartment. "Come and meet your beautiful granddaughter, Father, and your tiny niece, Little Brother. I'll call some servants to get you settled in your rooms."

"WHAT EXACTLY DO YOU MEAN THAT IT'S IMPRACTICAL?" Tse Tsien sat in an ornate, low chair at the head of a polished table. Her hair was pulled back and her creamy white robes flowed around her, their color reminding everyone of her first-mourning position with the dead emperors. Seven councilmen, like somber blackbirds perched on a fence, sat around the table.

The Minister of Transportation, his face red, his eyes wide and flustered, coughed and continued. "Well, the canals only go so far—in order to connect them *all,* from the Yellow River, here, to the far reaches of Nam—we'd have to conscript *thousands* of workers, and that would put a drain on the treasury, wouldn't it?" He turned to the Treasury Minister, hoping for reinforcement.

"I intend for the canals to be connected in order to speed the transport of food, materials and people from the north to the south, and south to north, to make us here in Loyang quickly in communication with the whole country, not just our immediate surroundings. I feel sure you recognize the wisdom of this, and as for the treasury...Commissioner? What do you have to say about this?" Tse Tsien gestured to him.

"Hmmmnnnn well, I suppose if you, if you..." Before the Treasury Minister could finish, the door burst open and a distraught Mi Kuo ran in, screaming, crying, holding a baby out in front of her as if it were an offering to Tse Tsien. The ministers jumped up in alarm.

"Madam! Oh my mistress! I cannot wake her! I cannot wake Chia! I only left her a minute and now she will not wake up!" She lay the baby in Tse Tsien's lap.

Tse Tsien lifted Chia up to her face, caressed the baby's face with her finger, then bent her ear to the child's mouth and nose, listening. Chia's eyes were closed, her long black eyelashes accenting her baby rosiness. "Bring a mirror...let's see if her breath will show...I can hear nothing!" Tse Tsien's voice was flat and faint.

"Chia's been fussy all day...new teeth...and I had to get clean diapers from the laundry and she said to run and do it that she'd keep watch over Chia, and then I knew there were the guards outside if she needed them and when I got back, I saw she was asleep finally, so I didn't disturb…oh, by all the gods…*what* have I done?" Mi Kuo wailed and collapsed on the floor at Tse Tsien's feet.

"Who? Who did you leave her with?" Tsien's voice was deadly calm.

"With First Wife, Majesty…with the Lady Wang…she said she'd rock Chia until I returned and I was only gone a minute…and there were guards just outside the door…" A fresh outburst of sobbing from the ayah.

"Get Sun Simao and Mistress Feng. Tell Zanggi to report here immediately…and bring the Lady Wang to me." Tsien ordered. As the two doctors hurried into the room, she gave Chia to Sun Simao. "Examine her, please, tell me she'll be all right…she *must* be all right…she's all I have…"

Within minutes, the Lady Wang, also in white, wafted into the council chambers, between two saffron-uniformed eunuchs. "Dear Second Wife…you wanted to see me?"

"What happened when you were with Chia?" Tsien demanded without preamble.

"Why nothing…she'd been fretting so I rocked her until she fell asleep, poor blossom, then I put her in her bed…is something wrong?"

"Why did you leave her alone when you said you'd wait for Mi Kuo to return?"

"I knew she'd be back soon and I had to meet my sisters…why, you sound like you're accusing me of something! How *dare* you! I was only helping…" She whined to cover her sudden anger. "What has her *ayah* done? Has she harmed the princess?"

Mistress Feng and Sun Simao, walked past the Lady Wang without speaking. Sun, tears streaming down his face, gave the baby to Tse Tsien.

"I so regret to tell you that the Princess Chia's soul has flown into the Everlasting Sky, my dear Tse Tsien."

"There was nothing we could do," added a trembling Mistress Feng.

No…no…I'm dreaming…this cannot be…I'll wake in a minute and find it's all a lie…I'm so cold…

"Chia, it's mommy, wake up, my little one…smile at me…" She hugged the baby close, nuzzled her ear and began to rock back and forth, half humming, half moaning, anguish flooding her body. She wandered, unseeing, out into the rain. A shrill, keening wail went with her.

65
A Magic Pillow: No Choice

An unnatural stillness pervaded the new palace. The voices of little children were hushed, people spoke in whispers, even the birds seemed to have lost their songs. Tse Tsien had not spoken to anyone except Faina. But she was seen pacing the garden paths alone whether it was day or night. Servants and guards hovered near in case she might call, alert to anyone invading her grief, unwanted.

But in Kat Kat Zanggi's apartments, high above an inner garden, there was intense activity. An odd assortment of five men and two women sat on thick cushions in a circle. Pale incense smoke traveled the air between them.

Zanggi, in his usual midnight blue robe, Sun Simao in Shaolin black, a captain of the guard in purple and gold uniform, one man all in flour-dusted white, another in short jacket, bloused pants and high boots, and the women—one young and pretty with fashionably painted face, the other, old, wizened whose dark braids hung down to her knees—were spitting questions and answers at each other back and forth.

"The question we must answer—and quickly—is—what would cause a healthy baby to die with no previous illness, no warning? Foul play?" Zanggi looked around the circle, challenging each of them. "Come now, you are my ears and eyes in the palace. What have you seen or heard, that seemed unusual?"

The old woman spoke first, "My mistress, Lady Wang, has been less unhappy, but I can't think that is evidence of wrong doing. She has been having a good time with her sisters lately...but I haven't noticed any..."

"We found no sign of poison, if that's what you're alluding to, Zanggi, no evidence of bruising or blows on the baby's skin...she just looked as if she were sleeping." Sun Simao said.

"I feel like we're looking for ghosts here...shadows that slip and slide just out of sight." The guardsman, who had been an officer years before in Tai Tsung's rout of Silla, was puzzled. "None of my men have reported anything suspicious."

"The five Confucian ministers of the council are seeing Tse Tsien's absence as an opportunity to seize power for their faction," Zanggi tapped his bony brown fingers on the floor beside him, a staccato beat to his alarm.

"With Kao Tsung's heir, Princess Chia, no longer...alive...since Wu Tse Tsien cannot be regent any more, who will rule?" Sun asked no one in particular. "She's in grave danger, I'm sure."

"Indeed, we need to consolidate her position somehow—she is, after all, the only person with any experience in affairs of state, the only one qualified to rule. I'm calling in all my favors on the council, as well as organizing the entire force of eunuchs, ten thousand strong. As their secretary, I believe we have enormous power, when organized, to back Wu Chao Tse Tsien...there's so much chaos in the rest of the palace, both here and in Changan, we need a strong, knowledgeable leader like her." Zanggi nodded to himself.

"In the kitchen, we hear many things that aren't common gossip in the rest of the palace, as you know," the man in white, a head chef, said. "One of my assistants, a man you may remember, Kat Kat Zanggi, who was once a bearer of Lady Wang's litter during the procession to Loyang who told you then of an interesting exchange between Lady Wang and her sisters—you have used him on other occasions, I believe? Found him reliable?

"He said something the other day that comes back to me now as perhaps more important than I realized. His name is Chang, and I believe it would be good to question him at this time, with your permission to send for him?" the chef asked.

"Do so, please," Zanggi replied. "While we wait for Chang, I need to hear from each of you what the feeling in your part of the palace is in regard to loyalty to the Most Illustrious Wu Chao Tse Tsien—and also, is it generally known that the comet has arrived in the sky? The one that portends the Prince of Wu as Chian's next great ruler?"

"The prophecy *is* spoken of in the stables," the head of the imperial stables said quietly. "But none of us really knows what to make of it... doesn't seem to have a lot to do with horses."

"In the women's wing, the comet is discussed endlessly," the young woman began in her sweet, high voice, "we wonder what this great prince will look like and whether he'll favor one or the other of us and then we're not so sure that we'd like to have a man come between us as, you know, Most Honorable One, our lives up until now have been more interesting...ever since Wu Chao Tse Tsien has been in charge...at least we've been allowed much more freedom, and that has been..."

Chang, a tall, slender man dressed in kitchen whites, ducked his head as he came through the door and perched uneasily on a pillow within the circle.

"The other day, you said you had heard something that seemed peculiar when you served a meal to the Lady Wang and her two sisters... would you elaborate on that now for us?" The chef asked him.

"Well, yes, it was the day after Princess Chia died and they were talking about that, saying oh, the poor little crushed blossom," Chang paused as if remembering. "What I thought odd was because, rather than looking sad when they said this, they all began to snicker...so I went on serving them and left the room, but stood just outside the curtained doorway to hear what might be making them so merry.

"One of Lady Wang's sisters asked her what her first wish would be when her son became emperor, and they all just laughed even more! '*My* son?' Lady Wang asked, 'of course! The first thing I'd do...I'd have every mention of that harlot erased, carved off, removed from every official record—if only because our great teacher, Confucius, reminds us that the place of women is in the home, is never in the seat of power'—that's what she said.

"I was that surprised, Honorable Secretary! So then I peered through a thin opening in the curtain and saw her pick up a little pillow and hug it as if it were a baby. And then, in a kind of singsong, she said...'and it's all possible because of my magic pillow—a magic pillow with the power of life or death'...and they all went off into hysterical laughter again! I didn't know what to make of it, Honored Sirs, but it did strike me as strange." He sat back and folded his hands in his lap.

A stunned silence ensued as the full import of what he reported sank into their minds.

"Fei, fei, fei...a magic pillow, eh? Makes sense, doesn't it? At root it gives us an explanation for recent events—the ancient evils of envy, ambition, greed.

"Captain, find these three women—Simao, you might take some of your Shaolin warriors along, too—gather up the Lady Wang and both her sisters immediately. Bring them here, by way of back alleys, as soon as you can, before they can rally the rest of that Wang family. In the midst of treason, I must organize more quickly even than I'd planned." His graying hair swung around his shoulders as he stood and turned, to walk quickly out the door, clearly a man who had decided what must be done, resolve in every step.

"YOU NEED TO EAT, MY DEAREST FRIEND," FAINA SAID QUIETLY, walking beside Tse Tsien. "You'll become ill if you don't—please, Tsien, listen to me!"

"I hear you, Faina, it's just that I can't imagine eating when..." Tse Tsien paused to pick a pink rose whose petals became crimson along its ruffled edges. "Almost everyone I've loved has died...there's nothing left for me to live for." She smelled the rose and brushed it across her cheek, "Chia's skin felt like this..."

"Tsien, of all the people in the world who have lost the ones they love, you have the most important reason for living that I can think of!"

"I can't think what it could be, nor why it would matter..."

"I know it's hard—I have no idea what Camel or I would do if one of our children died suddenly," Faina slipped her arm around her friend's waist. "But *I'm* not *you,* I don't have the burden of, or the knowledge to carry out, the emperor's *True Vision*—and you have sworn to do so, remember? You must continue to rule in order to make all his—and your—projects come about. You have no choice, dear one."

"No choice. Once again, no choice..." Her voice was colorless and flat.

In silence, they walked together, around the pond where ducklings were almost as big as their parents, through a small copse of willows that whispered together in the morning sun and climbed a small green hillock.

"It's just that everything reminds me of Chia...or Tsun and Takla Makan...or Sire...or Pirjhan and Juchi...or my father...aiieee, I feel stalked by death!" She sighed, as fresh tears flowed. "Everything is itself and it's opposite...I hate the rain—I want to drown in the rain. I can't sleep—I want to sleep forever, never wake up, it's too full of pain." She paused, looked out and down across the vast palace compound to the hills beyond.

Faina stood beside her without speaking. Tse Tsien shook as if settling a yoke across her shoulders.

"Even so, I know you're right…I must get back to work. Work can be my life now, let's go in, Faina—and thank you for showing me the way back…what a long way we've traveled together…"

66
Kat Kat Zanggi Acts On The Code: Faina Worries

"IN THE COUNTRY I COME FROM, AT THE SOUTHERN TIP OF INDIA, called Kat Kat Zanggi—for which I'm named—it is known that all men and women have a godly nature as well as an animal nature—that's why we practice our great tooth-filing ritual—filing down the animal points of our canine teeth to rid ourselves of that unwelcome nature," he said, "and when a person's animal nature dominates *everything* that they do, they are punished as if they were an animal...and therefore this Abomination is to be..."

"This is certainly one of the Ten Abominations of the Code, Honorable Secretary." Wu Shih Kuo, one of Tai Tsung's most trusted generals and advisors, agreed. "There can be no doubt that they have been plotting rebellion, plotting great sedition and plotting treason—all indicated by this reprehensible crime...but I think that, in this case, the Lady Wang and her sisters, because of their first mourning status, must be either decapitated or strangled without delay, regardless of whether it's a taboo day or not."

"I don't think they deserve to die as *superior persons.*" Zanggi leaped up and began to pace the floor, his bare feet making no sound on the stone floor. "When their souls depart, I don't want them to be able to rest in peace. I want their souls to wander without rest throughout all eternity...the harshest punishment cannot bring this child back to us, nor her father, who may also have suffered from their plotting—we'll never know. And, as long as they're honored with a seemly death, there will be no deterrent to others of their relatives, near or far, against plotting Wu Tse Tsien's death next!"

"And what of Wu Tse Tsien? What does she say?" Wu Shih sat strong and erect despite his old age.

"Nothing. She does not know...she's resilient, yes, but knowing that her baby was murdered ruthlessly could destroy her until she has had more time to recover." Zanggi's face was drawn and grim.

" I see, so you plan to carry out this sentence without going through the usual judicial process?" Wu Shih said with quiet intensity. "That's a dangerous road to travel, my friend."

"Yes...but I believe that it's imperative if we are to gain the attention and allegiance of those at court and within the various temples to elect Wu Chao Tse Tsien as empress in her own right." He stopped, faced the other man, and held out his hand. "Can I count on your support?"

"You can indeed. Wu Chao Tse Tsien is a worthy empress and I will be pleased to serve under her," Wu Shih Kuo took Zanggi's hand within both of his calloused ones and smiled. "Now, tell me, *how* will you carry out the traitors' death?"

"Like animals, I'll have them bound, put on a big-wheeled farm cart and taken to an outlying farm of a faithful retainer that I know." Zanggi looked grim at the thought. "There they will be put to death like the *inferior beings* they have become, in large boiling vats, just like all the other swine."

"By all the old gods, man, I'm glad I'm not your enemy!"

"We have work to do, you and I, old friend. Let's set about electing our empress, our fearless Prince of Wu!"

"If this is to be done, 'tis best it's done quickly, as they say." Wu Shih Kuo straightened his shoulders. Together they marched out.

A BREATHLESS WAITING AND WATCHING HOVERED THROUGHOUT LOYANG. Rumors abounded about Lady Wang and her sisters, why they had disappeared, who had seen them. Some said they were witches who had simply vanished in a pouf of smoke, others claimed to have seen them in an entourage headed south. Some country people claimed to have seen three persons put to death by the lowest punishment for inferiors. Then there was talk of rivalry between the council factions. The very air seemed to seethe with speculation and fear of wrongdoing.

The rains let up at last, and with the clear sunny weather, spirits lifted, worries of the past year were left behind in the ordinary, everyday necessities of life—eating, loving, working and simply existing. As they had so many times before, the people had survived.

Wu Chao Tse Tsien continued as emperor in all but crown, an odd idea at first to traditionalists, but so rational in all, that the entire council—with some prodding by the Secretariat—voted unanimously to install her as emperor as soon as the mandatory mourning had passed.

"It's been more than two-and-a-half years since Princess Chia and Kao Tsung died, Camel, and she still seems like a sleepwalker most of the time...and actually, she *does* sleep most of the time that she's not in council or the Great Hall," Faina followed her husband as he walked through the garden. "And I hardly ever see her smile except when she's with the children."

"Now, my dear little wife," Camel pulled a few disorderly weeds and stuffed them into a sack that hung from his belt, "You worry too much, I think, I know how you grieve for your friend...and understandably so, but, other than being as thin as a blade of grass, she seems all right."

"She's like the big water clock back in Changan...just fills up with water, drip by drip, until it falls into the basin and starts all over again..." Faina fretted.

"I must speak to my new assistant," Camel mumbled to himself, "he's so eager, he's been watering these mare's teat grapes too much... plumping them up all right, but it'll only increase the juice at the risk of decreasing the quality of the finished grapes, tch, tch," his lean, sun-tanned face looked worried.

"Camel, will you stop listening to the grapes and listen to me? Help me think of something we could do to help Tse Tsien come back to life...anything to make her interested in life again...for herself..."

"Time to withhold water a bit...harden them off..." he tested a vine tip, "Yes, yes, of course I'm listening to you...well, she likes to ride, is she riding anymore?"

"Frequently. She takes that big stallion, Bagatur and Shira's offspring, for a pounding ride—out the gate and into the hills, then back to the palace again at a breakneck pace. Lucky that all her guards now are young and able to stay with her."

"Yes, that must have been them I saw the other day...a flock of blue and gold uniforms, racing like the wind." He tasted a grape, nodded in satisfaction, snipped off a bunch with his clippers, then handed them to Faina with a little bow. "Try these, my dear, I think you'll find they're even sweeter than last year."

"Those would have been the imperial guards that Kat Kat Zanggi insisted she have around her at all times...ever since, well, ever since she became so powerful," Faina put one shiny purple grape in her mouth, "Mmmnnn, you're right...delicious!"

"I remember that you told me once about your long journey into Chian, that she had wanted to visit some caves she'd heard of—the Lung Men Caves I think you said far to the northwest...such a strange name I remembered it..."

"Aaaahh yes, that's true. We didn't get to see them with all their huge carvings that the monks had made because Pirjhan wanted to keep the horses moving toward Changan...are you suggesting we get Tse Tsien to make a pilgrimage there?"

"Might be worth a try..."

"I'm not sure it would be safe, so far...some sort of distraction like that, yes, but a huge trip like that will have to wait, I'm sure, until after the crowning ceremonies, which, now that the mandatory twenty seven months are over, are being planned for, every day by a whole village of seamstresses and musicians, astrologers and cooks. Activity all around her, but Tsien hardly seems to notice."

"Well now, all the festivities might be just the thing to wake her up, don't you s'pose? There'll be parades and performances and the like won't there? Bound to be some excitement in those to interest her."

"We'll just have to expect that *something* good will come from all the weeks of festivities...it would be good to see her happy, if only for a little while...the palace is full of children right now, and when she's with our little tow-heads, Camel, she looks at them so hungrily, as if she could just sink into their baby skins and disappear..."

"I'll pick some grapes for you to take to her, my dear, maybe they'll cheer her," his rumbly voice was as sweet as the fruit he offered her.

"Camel...I *love* you." Faina reached up, put her arms around him, heedless of his familiar hunched back, and hugged him.

LONELY, THAT'S JUST IT...I FEEL LONELY...HOW CAN ANYONE BE LONELY surrounded by people all the time? She stood by an open doorway looking out into the moonlit garden beyond. It was the still of the night and like most nights, she slept only a few hours before she woke again, to toss and turn in bed, or get up, to restlessly pace the room.

Color…all the color is gone…a gray world peopled with shadows… that's what it seems like even during the day…gray, colorless…is this how my life will always be? Each day filled with possibilities and decisions, projects needing this, people wanting that…days, thank the Everlasting Sky, are busy…constant in their demands…and I must feel grateful, for the work pulls me through each one of these long days as if I were on a string that unravels behind me…

Only at night…I can remember nights filled with stars and loving… but no more, never again…only the work, Sire's True Vision to carry me into the long years that lie ahead…but oh, how I wish there were someone to share it all with…

She shook herself and breathed deeply, filling her lungs with the cool, clear air.

Enough of this, Wu Chao Tse Tsien, enough melancholy…hmmnnn, yes melancholy's the right word…wonder how that would look calligraphed with a really fat brush…never have time to calligraph anymore…need to find the time…to set my inner self in order…no color there either, just black ink and white paper…tomorrow I'll get a desk set up in here…yes, I can do that…something to do in these lonely middle of the night hours…

Soon there will be the grand inauguration…the crowning of the Prince of Wu…me… a long, long journey since I left the Pamir valley of the Igren…another world, another lifetime ago…I'm not sure I can do this…be the emperor that Chian needs. Am I bold enough? Cautious enough? Wise enough? Aieeee…it's what Tashih Shaymak, my first father, said I was born to do…well, we get to see, don't we, Tsien or Talima or whoever you are tonight…and tomorrow there will be the seemingly endless round of courtiers and dressmakers, councilors and petitioners, servants and guards…so many people, so much to manage…

She walked out into the garden, looked up to see the half sphere of a waning moon, felt the transparent veil of its light envelop her. One of the shadows stepped toward her and bowed. "Most Illustrious, is there anything you want, anything I can do?"

"No, no, I'm sorry to wake you," she spoke to the alert guard.

"I wasn't asleep, Most Gracious Lady, truly."

"That's all right, thank you for watching over me…are there others close by?"

"As many as always…about a dozen, I'd say, Your Highness."

"Yes, well, good night." She turned back into her bedroom.

Sleep…maybe I'll try to sleep a few hours before daylight…maybe even dream… possibly a phantom lover waits for me…mmnnn, I used to dream…

67
A Grand Celebration

ON THE OUTSKIRTS OF THE CITY, CAGES OF WILD ANIMALS WAITED for the grand procession that would begin the celebrations. A most exotic lion from Champa, four hunting cheetahs from Persia, two elephants, one dark gray, the other, a priceless almost-pink, from Cham, and a whole bevy of gangly, long-legged ostriches from Tocharia, were each cared for by men and boys from their country of tribute. Double-humped caravan camels were washed and brushed, then lavishly decorated with colored woven straps and tassels.

In the high-domed aviary, domestic falcons made room for hunting birds from Silla to the north, Viet to the south, the Pamirs to the west. Prized golden eagles for largest game; gyrfalcons—one of them white, the same as Tai Tsung's favorite *Army Commander*—to capture herons and other large game birds, frosted falcons from Manchuria, and peregrines for ducks and other waterfowl. There would be competitions for the finest birds at special times during the next ten days.

In the silk villages, spinners spun all night, weavers wove long swaths of shimmering silk and damask, dyed in all the colors of the rainbow, to be made into slender, high banners, scarves and ceremonial clothes for the aristocracy.

Shaolin Monastery had been emptied of all but the youngest boys and their teachers in order to perform their amazing, synchronized martial arts. Their long trek down from the mountain fastness had not daunted them at all; daily they practiced in the outer courtyards.

The army practiced for exhibitions with spears, and *vaulting the sky* with bows and arrows; the navy put their small boats up on big-wheeled, ox-drawn wagons and filled them with flowers, guardsmen drilled with long staffs and short swords.

In the palace, frenzied seamstresses sewed feathers, furs, silks and embroidered damasks. The enormous kitchens were polished and poised to produce such exotic foods as: green turtle soup; *Tam-la*, a sought-after mollusk from the Bay of Silla served with spicy leaping fish sauce, seasoned with red-hot fagara; hazelnuts of Westerners, from Sogdiana, sometimes called pistachios, that were said to increase sexual vigor; *bitter leaf* and *vinegar leaf* vegetables from Nepal; *triphala*, the Three Fruits, from India and Tocharia that are, collectively, the elixir of life—the *emblic* myrolaban, the *belleric* myrobalan, and the *cherubic* myrobalan which grow on the Perfumed Mount of the God Indra, is the most admired, and when ripe, has six tastes, eight efficacies, leaves three tastes upon digestion, accomplishes the seventeen qualities, and dispels all varieties of illness. Shang shih, the Provost of Foods, prowled the storehouses, large and small dining halls, creating a muted panic wherever he went.

An enormous, awninged tent was laced together in the far corner of the imperial gardens so that visiting dignitaries from the western provinces could be housed and feel comfortable. When the huge felted tent arrived by caravan, it had been carried in sections on the backs of thirty camels.

Musicians—playing all sizes of drums and cymbals, reed flutes, bells and zithers—practiced traditional melodies and operatic symphonies, as well as new pieces composed especially for this august event. The palace was a-buzz with anticipation. The mourning years had been almost sleepy by comparison.

The still center of all this boisterous activity was the central cause for the celebration—the Prince of Wu—Wu Chao Tse Tsien herself. Her daily life continued in its myriad details. Without rancor she interceded in domestic squabbles; without engaging, she amiably complied with the dictates of those in charge of planning each detail of the coming inauguration, without either irritation or delight, she followed the routine set out for her. She was told that there would be a day-long processional which would take up most of the opening day, to be followed for the next seven days with a succession of parties, formal and informal, some with acrobats and dancers, some with poetry and song, even one where the best of the best Shaolin monks would perform near miraculous feats of their martial art. All of it culminating in the sacred ceremonies of installing the new emperor on the last day of the inauguration.

Before dawn, a small army of hairdressers, makeup artists, dressmakers and personal attendants descended on a wakeful Tse Tsien.

"Your bath is drawn, Most Illustrious," Mei Li, promoted from being nursemaid to personal maid, told her as she held out a soft, cotton kimono. "We will lay out your clothes while you bathe."

Still groggy from a restless sleep, Tse Tsien lowered her body into the steaming bath.

"Mmnnn, it smells like all the flowers of spring. Thank you Mei Li," she sighed.

So, it begins. The great jubilation for Her Majesty...for someone else, surely...seems so distant, really, from who I feel I am...and yet... She looked down the length of her slender body—long legs, smooth concave belly. Her hair drifted around her like seaweed as she stretched, arching her back until her taut nipples rose above the water's surface.

How simple my dreams are now compared to the ones I had as a girl when everything seemed full of promise... now I just dream of being happy sometime...a dream of happiness that seems like a dream I once had...that seems so far away, so elusive...if only my love were still alive...someone to hold and be held by...it would make this all seem less unreal somehow...

She stepped out of the bath, was quickly wrapped with soft cotton sheets. She shook her hair and tossed it back, combing wet tangles with her fingers. *Oh, come on, Tse Tsien, you've never liked whiners, pull yourself together...life is good...very good...anyone in all of Chian and its vassal states would be pleased to trade places with you...so let's get ready for the beginning of the festivities...*

First, her dressers floated a light, cream-colored cotton chemise over her head, then a reed-slim, matching skirt was gathered around her waist and tied. In ceremonial succession, each one longer and more embroidered than the one before, four silk kimonos were layered and tied—first, an immaculate white one, then plum-color, rose and pink—each color showing one after the other, and at the long oval sleeves and front opening. Lastly, a wide sash striped in the same colors as the outer kimonos was tied in an elaborate knot from which a carved jade piece dangled. The silk flowed out around her feet like flower petals.

Next, the hairdressers slicked back her still-damp hair and pinned it into dozens of small curls so that the high, winged headdress could rest close to her head. With an inner core of stiffened horsehair, the headdress was braided and twined with silken cords, cerulean blue and cloud white, each strand wrapped in gold leaf so that, in all, it caught the light and glowed. Its wide, raised wings reminded all who saw her, that she, indeed, was a direct descendant of the Celestial Heaven.

Carved ivory fingernails, like eagle talons, were slipped over her slender fingers, that now wore the jade, signet-seal ring of the emperor's power. Makeup artists smoothed a soft white paste over her face and throat, painted black *dipping swallow* eyebrows above eyes that were outlined in green-black *kohl* from Sassania, a color that brought out the green flecks in her eyes.

Lastly, she was helped into the outermost kimono, the color of ripe peaches, embroidered down the front and along the padded hem with phoenix birds—feathers and tails flying like comets. She looked like a life-sized doll, molded into the formal fashion of time-honored Chian royalty—every inch an empress.

It was still early morning on the third day of the first month, the Moon of Spring Flowers, as unanimously deemed most auspicious by the court astrologers, when Tse Tsien left her apartment for the Imperial City square to the south of the palace compound. The click-click-click of her high platform sandals echoed down crowded halls, the mutlti-hued train swept behind her until they reached the outer walkways. At that point, the eldest three children of Faina and Merket picked it up and carried it high as they had been taught. As Tsien walked, her counselors, ministers, secretaries and their wives joined her, swelling into a parade of dignitaries that fanned out, as they reached their destination, filling the dais prepared for them.

The morning was pleasantly cool. Fog filled alleys of the city and the valleys beyond, lying in wait for the heat of the sun to disperse it. The sky was already blue. No wind blew. The brightly ornamented, vertical flags hung limply on tall bamboo poles

Firecrackers erupted immediately, crackling the air, signaling musicians with shrill horns, clanging gongs, and throbbing drums to march onto the wide avenue between the reviewing stand and the Gate of the Red Bird, nearly two li beyond.

Next came the army, thousands strong, arms swinging stiffly; the navy flower boats, accompanied by penny-whistle piping; the mounted imperial stable riders on high-stepping Igren horses. The wide plaza filled to overflowing with those that came to strut and all the non-performers who came to watch. Wu Chao Tse Tsien sat very still, rigidly self-conscious, while those around her pointed and whispered with amazement.

Disciplined Shaolin monks, dressed now in orange short tunics and baggy pants wrapped from the ankle with flat, black cord, criss-crossed up to their knees. As one, they halted in front of the emperor and her dignitaries and, with a cup on each outstretched arm, another on their heads, did fast kicks, thrusts and parries, without dropping a single cup.

Sighs of wonder rippled through the onlookers as ostriches, dyed pink for the occasion, gaggled their stick-spindly legs into a kind of dance. Next, the prowling snow leopards and pair of wondrous lions; followed at last by the elephants whose trainers halted them facing the dais, and swung down on their trunks onto the flagstones. Servants rushed out with buckets. The elephants drank, stood on their hind legs, lifted their knobby, thick-snake trunks, and showered everyone with a rain of perfumed water. Shrieks and laughter as everyone shook the fragrant drops off their best clothes.

Country folk hovered at the edges of the crowds; little children hoisted on their father's shoulders so they could see, and perhaps remember into their old age, this awesome jubilation. A light spring breeze sprang up, setting the flags to fluttering, banishing the fog.

Legions of musicians, some dressed as clowns, some in formal court attire, each group according to the dignity of their individual, massed instruments. A cacophony of sounds: blaring, booming, ringing, thrumming. A clangor, jangle, rattle, uproar that reverberated throughout the enormous square.

And then, to everyone's delight, came the best and finest jugglers and acrobats from all the cities and provinces. Leaping, twisting, somersaulting, they formed a giant pyramid on each other's shoulders; the topmost boy juggled golden balls that flashed in the suddenly strong sun. The dazzle speared Tse Tsien's eyes and she looked out and down across the throng. Staring, wide-eyed, unfocused, everything seemed to shimmer through tears that filled her eyes.

Aaaahh, the gossamer threads that tie us to this world...a magic *spider spinning those shining threads into a net of living beings...*She turned her head from side to side as if the motion would coalesce each part into a whole picture.

No matter where you enter...touch that web and trembling occurs throughout...one touch...and all are touched...I may not even be able to see the far side of the web, but whatever I do, or think, or feel, energizes every strand...how wonderful! Such fragility! Such resilience! Such knowingness...strength...beauty...

*I am alone...*she lifted her chest, took a deep breath...*and yet, these glinting tendrils, woven of love and honor, hold me fast, connect me in an integral way with everyone, with all in all, world without end.*

She stood, spread wide her arms...and smiled to all those upturned faces...it was the sun itself smiling on them.

68
Alive Again: A Poetry Celebration

THAT EVENING, AFTER ALL THE SERVANTS HAD HELPED HER TO UNDRESS and remove the heavy makeup; after friends had said good night and guards took up their posts outside her rooms, Tse Tsien had time to think…and wonder.

What happened today? I feel so light, so filled with light…I still grieve, but it's as if the grief itself said "That's enough…live now."

She lit a stick of incense and watched the smoke waft toward her, enveloping her in its mystery. She breathed in slowly, sensually, savoring the smell that reminded her of soft melodies and sweet promises. She began to hum a tune, one the acrobats had danced to that morning—before the world changed, before the fetters formed by disaster the past few years simply fell away. And she was free to be herself again.

Wearing only her feather-light slip, she began to sway to her own rhythm. Her bare feet slipped across the polished floor, caressing the smoothness, calling her to dance. Arms spread wide, she whirled, 'round and 'round, ecstatically.

Ohhh, it feels so good to be alive…to feel, to be excited about all that life is offering to me now…even the intricacies of the inauguration sound intriguing…of course I can do this! No one else ever doubted me—Father, Sire, Tsun, Zanggi, all my loving friends…I was the only doubter and now I'm not going to doubt either…I will *be emperor… and a splendid one, as well…the best I know how!*

She hugged herself, picked up the coverlet from her bed, wound it around her chilly body and stepped out on the terrace. A crescent moon was high in the western sky. It cradled a star…*the metal star*, she reminded herself...so brilliant that shafts of its light seemed to pierce the fluffy night clouds that scudded across the moon now and then. Cherry trees were in full bloom. Their scent made even the night smell pink and white. A nighthawk chirred sleepily. And suddenly, there was the slight lippedy-lippedy of a little dog running toward her—and there was Ti Li, so excited that her whole little body wriggled as she leaped straight up into Tse Tsien's arms.

"Ti Li, you little rascal! How did you break out of your yard? Never mind, your company is welcome." Tsien turned her face away from Ti Li's exuberant licking, her small tongue so soft and wet.

"All right then, come along, let's go to bed, you and I...and sleep... and sleep, perhaps to dream...of something wonderful!"

The next night, Shi-mou Chi-kien's high singsong voice began the evening's poetry competition. *"The mulberry pickers slowly move... engrossed in a fistful of leaves. Suppose we slipped off for a walk, and came right back, of course. There'd be some pleasure in it."* He shifted from one foot to the other. *"Beyond these plodding people, love...there's grass to lie on, songs to sing. Why not just wander off...and pass an hour or two? There'd be some pleasure in it."* He sat down and reached for his drink.

Fingers snapped in appreciation. Servants balanced lacquered trays filled with small cups of different wines and beers as they glided between the merrymakers. It was an evening for poetry and pleasure, following the pomp of yesterday. Tse Tsien had offered a length of the finest silk to the person who brought the best poems to the gathering, and there were many who thought they'd win

A tall mon-barbarian unwound his long legs from a little chair, stood, and began his poem, *"What maiden with the willow eyes,"* he smiled suggestively toward the young courtesan beside him, *"will look at this old beggar? They say the river's wide, coming and going. Hell, who calls that river wide? Why, I c'd cross it afore breakfast!"* He slapped his silk-clad knee and grinned as he heard appreciative whistles.

It was twilight. Bronze braziers stood on long legs, filled with glowing charcoal. Colored paper lanterns swayed along long hemp ropes strung between the trees. Small tables and tiny, ornate chairs were set up across the courtyard and out into the garden.

"Lady, suppose when you were sleeping...a chill frost glazed the moon...and if the air ran frigid rivulets...that shattered on your wall like...crystal goblets," this young poet had a sad countenance, "and I were not there...to fold you in my arms...and keep you from the bitterness of early winter...what then, lady, what then?"

"A heartache question, I fear, Li Heng, for those of us who wake alone," Wu Chao Tse Tsien said, but smiled at him. "Did you recite this to Tu Fu? He's always interested in the melancholy." She was reclining on large pillows, listening, looking, drinking in the vivid social life around her. Three of her *Flying Horsemen* personal guards, in their new uniforms emblazoned with eagle, hawk or tiger on short satin jackets, sat near enough for conversation with her, Batu and Juchi among them.

Faina and Merket, also lounging on pillows, were dressed as she was, in empire-style, gauzy cotton dresses, amber and lavender, with accentuated puffy sleeves that tied at upper arm and wrist with ribbons of colored silk. Comfortable together, they were enjoying the relaxed evening.

"Did I hear someone call my name?" An elderly, rather disheveled man ambled over, bowed slightly to Tse Tsien and patted Li Heng on the back. "That's all right, keep going youngster...poems come and go in popularity, don't be discouraged."

"Honorable, Tu Fu, did you bring us a poem tonight?" Tse Tsien asked, "it's been awhile since we've seen you out and about at night...drunk again?"

"Hmmn, that is so." His laugh was carefree. "I was thinking a few nights ago about the rain—how it always seems to know when to fall and..." his surprisingly deep voice began to chant:

"Come at night...ride in on the wind
make sure we all get good and wet...
and in the morning?
Flowers everywhere!"

The crackle of fingers snapping, then conversations resumed.

Tse Tsien nibbled on a tree-shaped bit of stone honey. *Mmnn how sweet...I can hardly believe I'm in the same world as I was two days ago...it's as if the whole world shifted, opened up...and I can see the radiant colors it paints itself... I feel so full of life, after what seemed to be forever, a dark forever of sorrow and suffering and grief...*

In the darkling sky, the new moon glowed.

Merket raised her cup to the moon and said, "When I was younger, I heard a beautiful poem by our friend, Li Bo. I loved it and memorized it—would you like to hear it?"

"Oh do, please, Merket," Batu beamed with pride in his accomplished wife.

"We're companions tonight—the moon and me and my shadow—may we three meet again…to dance in the silver river of stars!"

"Aaaahh, lovely, the silver river of stars, yes," sighed one of the guardsmen.

More poetry, more wine, the night grew colder and everyone gathered around the braziers to get warm.

"It will be hard to choose a winner, won't it?" Faina whispered to Tse Tsien.

"Wait and see, I have a plan," Tsien stood up. Conversation ceased. "We have heard some beautiful poems tonight, have we not? And who should receive the prize? If you have favorites, now is the moment to tell me about it." She looked around at all the interested, eager faces of people, many of whom she already knew and loved, glowing in the firelight.

"No favorites? Well then…" Tse Tsien clapped and a line of servants walked out, each carrying folded squares of silk.

"I knew it would be too hard for me to choose from so many excellent poets, so I just decided to give each one a pi's worth of silk. There are a few different colors so you may have whatever color appeals to you tonight…and if several of you want the same color…and you can't settle your differences, I'll send for more." She gestured to the waiting servants to walk through the groups, offering silk to the poets.

"This first of our celebratory parties has been a wonderfully harmonious evening, and I thank you all for your participation… tomorrow night we'll honor painters and calligraphers…music will entertain the court and the public—think of it, companions, every kind of music, every kind of music throughout the day and into the night! And the next day, an exhibition of martial arts by the most accomplished Shaolin teachers. Which leads us almost to the day of inauguration… you'll be able to tell stories to your great grandchildren about these days and nights…and now, good night all."

She wrapped a soft, midnight blue scarf around her shoulders and sauntered out of the garden, followed, as always, by several of her Flying Horsemen.

69
Shaolin Monks Perform

A WIDE YELLOW SILK UMBRELLA, HUNG WITH RED AND PURPLE TASSELS, shielded Tse Tsien and company from the morning sun, already hot and not yet midday on this eigth day of the festivities. The vast plaza rippled with flags of many colors and designs. There was an excited buzz of anticipation from the surrounding crowd. Little boys in particular, ran amongst the grownups, jumped over rope barricades that lined the performance space, played tag with each other, and restlessly asked a parent, over and over, "Are they coming yet? Can you see them yet?"

As the first group of martial arts students, aged seven to ten, came toward them, the boys quieted down, squirmed their way to the front and sat down to watch, enthralled.

Tse Tsien beamed down on all the children, performers and onlookers alike, obviously enjoying the sunny day and everything going on around her. Her hair was wound up tightly under a high turban that sparkled with jeweled pins. With all her make up, her face was an imperial mask. A loose gown of sky-blue swept the wooden floor, and over this, was a net cape of pearls that were woven into a slithering dragon along the hem. She looked, every inch, a monarch. Sun Simao sat at her side, explaining in whispers, how each event related to the overall practice at Shaolin Monastery.

The first group of boys had shaven heads, were dressed all in red-orange, both short tunics and pants wrapped in black cords. They began to demonstrate the basic moves of strength, suppleness and concentration of the classic *hung gar kung fu.*

"They look so young, Sun...and yet so experienced somehow," Tse Tsien said, shaking her head. The carved beads that hung from her turban tinkled faintly.

After they marched off, teenagers, taller, lithe, also shaven, still in red, performed with long sticks, competing with each other for mastery. Then came the 20-40 year-olds, most of whom had spent their whole lives training and meditating at the monastery. These men paraded in front of the emperor with a sense of leashed power, their muscles taut, clearly defined on their spare, bare-chested bodies.

"They'll break up into five groups now, and then..." explained Sun Simao, "one after the other will demonstrate the advanced techniques of *wu shi ji,* the five animals' play—dragon, snake, tiger, leopard and crane.

"These are long term students who, exerting the most disciplined intention and training, will show you the *external, hard-fist* form of martial art in its most explosive and dazzling forms."

Tse Tsien watched in increasing amazement as the men became the embodiment of each animal's most essential gesture...the white crane spreading its wings, the snake sliding along, then raising its head to strike with power, the tiger flexing its claws, the eagle its wings and talons, while the heavy dragon swept its imaginary enemies away with its lashing tail...aerial leaps that looked impossible, lightning strikes with extended palms. Their bodies shone with sweat under the hot sun.

"Magnificent!" Tsien remarked, her eyes bright with excitement.

All too soon, gongs and cymbals signaled the end of their performance and the five groups separated into a wide V formation in front of the reviewing stand.

From somewhere, previously unseen, an older man, carrying a long staff that punctuated his steps with a spurt of yellow dust as it tapped down, ambled forward to the center of the V. He was very tall, and large, neither of which explained the hush that fell around him as if he might even be capable of commanding the winds that blew and popped the flags around them. He bowed and saluted Tse Tsien, before roaring a challenge to those assembled. "I am Wang Tsung Yueh, an old Taoist monk who lives at Shaolin. I am of the *internal, soft-fist* practice known as *tai chi chuan,* which can destroy but does not kill. I challenge all comers to best me, here, for the glory of our new emperor, the Prince of Wu, Wu Chao Tse Tsien!"

"What does he mean by this challenge, Sun?" she whispered.

"He means that he will overpower and beat anyone who thinks they can beat him. He's a most famous master of this school. Watch what happens."

The old man, barefoot, stood totally still. Unlike all the other monks, he had a full, dark beard and wore a dust-sweeping, un-sashed robe over the usual tunic and pants, all in a yellow-orange color—the gamboge dye that came from the country of the same name. A thick strand of carved wooden beads hung at his waist.

"He doesn't look fit enough to beat any of these younger fighters." Tse Tsien commented.

"He was, as he said, of the internal school and that does not mean the fast physical warfare of the ones we have seen so far. His practice trains the chi, that inner life force that can be harnessed to do extraordinary things."

A muscular young man strode in front of the fierce old man, saluted, then without warning, stepped toward him and punched his protruding belly with all his might. His own punch staggered him, but the old man did not quiver. Next, the challenger did a back flip in order to surprise the old man, knock him down perhaps and get a leg hold on him. The Taoist hardly moved but, his hand vibrating with energy, pushed at the air that separated the two by inches and suddenly, the younger man found himself on the ground, twelve feet away. The old man had not shifted his stance or his attention.

In one furious leap, the younger man rushed back, his arm straight out like a sword, aimed at the older man's head. The old man grasped his wrist and twisted the young man's body off the ground, over his shoulder, and forward, standing him face to face, still holding his wrist with one hand. Dismay and awe was evident on his opponent's face. The Taoist monk turned the other's hand upright, leaned over and brushed his lips across the palm.

"Just as surely as water overcomes the greatest rocks, so does the weak overcome the strong—when chi is made manifest." A dazzling smile enveloped his bearded face. He threw his bear-like arm over the younger man's shoulder and they walked away.

"Whew! Hard to surpass that display, isn't it?"

"Yes, but we have one last performance, that of the dance of short swords, *chi gong,* where, I'm told, the two finest teachers of Shaolin will do mock battle with each other. And I'll tell you, My Lady, in all my years there, I've never known these two to leave the monastery before, so it should be quite something to watch!"

"Short swords? Are they less dangerous than long swords?"

"We have a saying, 'the shorter the scimitar, the greater the danger'" Sun replied. "Here they come."

Two tall men strode into the v-shaped stage created by all the other monks. They wore short white tunics sashed in black, black pants criss-crossed with red ties, and tight, black skull-caps that covered their heads. Each carried a sword the length of his thigh, cradled in his left arm. Coming to the center, they faced each other and saluted with their heavy swords before they began to circle. Lean and low they prowled around each other until, in one blazing moment, one of them leaped into the air, arm and leg extended, toward the other, only to miss by a breath as his target shifted oh-so-slightly, from one foot to the other.

Back and forth they tested each other; the clang of blades parrying, the harsh "Ha!" of breath expelled with force kept the crowd on tiptoe, kept Tse Tsien and the court on the edge of their seats.

"They're like the cloud-spotted mountain leopards I saw once," Tse Tsien said, breathlessly. "Beautiful...and deadly." As she watched, she felt a thrill shimmer through her body in a way that she realized hadn't happened for a long time.

"*Qi gong,* yes, brings perfect power, they say, and perfect peace." Sun Simao said quietly "It takes unswerving devotion to achieve this degree of excellence."

"I greatly admire their discipline, their mastery...makes me want to be more active... play polo again...I wonder if...do you suppose..."

The two combatants were flying at each other, swords drawn, feet spiking the air, blades slamming against each other as they touched down and whirled to face each other, faster and faster.

Tse Tsien was so inflamed, she stood suddenly and went quickly toward them as if she could get inside their bodies, feel the passion of combat for herself. The two warriors, weapon arm entwined with each other's at the end of a rapid parry, paused momentarily and looked up. As they did, one of them looked directly at Tse Tsien—and his sword fell, sticking upright on its point, quivering in the hard-packed dirt. The other's sword point touched his chest. A small red flower of blood bloomed on his white tunic.

She stopped, her breath ragged as she met his shocked face. She began to tremble.

Sun Simao, sensing something wrong, went to her side quickly and brought her back to her seat. "Are you all right, My Lady?"

"Yes...yes, just startled...for a moment I thought I recognized one of them, even though they look enough alike to be twins...just a silly moment, Sun, I'm all right now, thank you...was he hurt? Was he wounded?"

The monk picked up his sword with evident ease and held it out with both hands as a sign of surrender to the other. They bowed together and to their emperor before striding off. The great drums throbbed. The day's performances were over. The satiated crowds went back to their homes.

Tse Tsien and her entourage went into the palace where giant fans, swung by servants, cooled the air.

"We certainly saw some intriguing men today, Sun," Tse Tsien put her hand on his arm, "I'd like have a chance to talk with them...also I'd like to know that the one man is all right, not badly hurt...do you think a few might come to dinner later this evening?"

"If you asked it, My Lady, how could they refuse?" He smiled. "Who shall I invite for you?"

"The old Taoist monk and his younger champion...and the two swordsmen...yourself, of course...Merket and Batu, maybe young Juchi and his wife...I'd like to have Faina and Camel, but Camel won't come, I know, and Faina won't come without him, so we'll just be a small gathering...in the garden at twilight then?"

She turned and spoke to a servant who was passing by, "Tell the kitchen, an informal dinner for ten in the garden, please."

70
TWO SWORDSMEN

"MEI KUO...WHERE ARE YOU?" TSE TSIEN BURST INTO HER ROOM, flinging her gown and shoes onto a chair. "Has the seamstress brought my new Tocharian outfit...the clothes like those I wore in the Pamirs?"

"Yes, Most Illustrious Lady, they're folded in your cabinet...do you wish to change into them now?" Mei Kuo smiled as she saw her mistress's excitement.

"Yes, now...no, shortly...I'll bathe first...the heat and dust were very heavy today...but it was exceptional anyway!"

"I thought you might want a bath after such a long day, so one is ready for you and I also brought some cool water with a twist of lemon to refresh you."

"Wonderful...I'm grateful." She pinned up her hair, dropped her undershift on the floor and stepped into the tepid bath where intensely-fragrant mimosa flowers floated.

The two swordsmen...so alike it was hard to tell which was which... and yet...one was so familiar...as if I might have known him in some other life...'Sky! He was beautiful... She shwooshed her body from side to side in the water, reveling in its caress on her taut body. *It's been so long since Tsun died and I've been, well...lonely...missing what we had together, even though it was such a short time... What would it be like to know a man like that Shaolin monk? To wake in the morning with his strong maleness in bed beside me? Oh, daydreams, Tse Tsien... monks are celibate, after all...and his life is the monastery...*

She lay still, shut her eyes and tried to empty her mind of the sensual images that seemed to sprout into a life of their own. She scrubbed off her makeup and got out finally, wrapped a towel around her and called for Mei Kuo to come.

The air was beginning to cool in the late afternoon. Tsien slipped a gauzy chemise over her head, wrapped and tied dark blue pants around her waist, and stuffed the legs into soft, red-leather boots that came up to her knees. Her short, grass-green silk tunic had be-ribboned sleeves that tied at the wrist. Several sashes—blue, purple, and scarlet—intertwined around her slim waist, tasseled ends hanging down.

"How would you like your hair arranged, Mistress?"

"It's been braided tightly all day, Mei Kuo, so just brush it out and leave it loose...that will feel good tonight, I think." Tse Tsien went to her jewelry box and, after picking up and putting back several pieces, chose a link bracelet of different colors of jade—lavender, black, yellow, green and white—gold hoop earrings, and a gold ring, set with one large piece of clearest green jade, the kind that came as tribute from the mountain villages of Burma on Chian's farthest southern border.

"Your hair is lovely, Mistress, like a waterfall, all ripples and waves over your shoulders...aaahh, so very beautiful you are tonight...I have never seen you like this, so...so shining!" Mei Kuo walked around her, admiring this almost-stranger.

"Why thank you, Mei, it's just because I feel so free in these clothes perhaps...or because tonight's dinner is not a state duty, but a spur-of-the moment pleasure with a few longtime friends and some interesting new ones as well."

She stepped into the garden with a light heart and winged feet, dancing to an old tune as she hummed merrily.

A soft breeze whispered through new leaves. Cicadas began their sonorous twilight symphony. Children's voices echoed the twitter of little birds bedding down for the night. Colored paper lanterns swung above lacquered tables and sandalwood, on hot coals in the braziers, wafted a scent of mystery that welcomed Wu Chao Tse Tsien. A frolicking Ti Li followed her into an evening of welcome frivolity.

She saw Kat Kat Zanggi, barefooted, prowling around the small lake and waved to him. "Hey there, my Good Ghost, what brings you here?"

"I heard there were goings-on that sounded too good to miss," he kissed her outstretched hand. "Fei, fei, fei, look at you! There's my Spitfire of old...thought she'd disappeared forever."

Batu and Merket arrived, arm in arm. "My, am I happy to have an evening with just grownups!" Merket said, holding her husband's arm tightly.

Batu smiled, first at his wife, then at his empress. "You are looking particularly lovely tonight, both of you. I hear some of today's performers were invited tonight? That should be interesting!"

"Do you happen to know the names of the last competitors this afternoon, no?" He shook his head. "Well, Sun Simao will know and he should be here soon. Please, all of you have something to drink—there are several juices—tea, rice wine and some of Camel's new grape wine as well."

Just then, Ti Li began to scurry around and bark her shrill bark that signaled strangers approaching.

"Ti Li, hush, good evening all!" Tse Tsien greeted the four monks who accompanied Sun Simao through the vine-covered gate.

The bearded elder, dressed as before in a long yellow coat, came forward and, with palms together, bowed. "I am Hsueh Chan—an honor to be here, Majesty, for this old monk who never thought to see you so close—and this was my worthy opponent, Pu Liang." He brought forward the younger monk, who also bowed deeply in the same manner and stepped aside.

Tse Tsien felt strands of hair whip across her face with a sudden gust, obscuring the faces of the last two monks. She brushed it away and saw them both at once, close in front of her. She stopped breathing, feeling again that thrill that began in her belly and radiated out to the tips of her fingers, up to the rising flush she felt in her cheeks.

Sun Simao gestured to the first monk, introduced him as Fu-feng and the other as Jen-Ya-shiang. Without their caps, she saw that their black hair was close-cropped and curly, their faces tanned by wind and sun like fine leather. They wore the Shaolin simple tunic and pants that they had worn earlier, with one addition—the long silver chain and medallion worn only by the most skilled Shaolin warriors. Both bowed with their customary palms together gesture of respect.

"We are honored, Gracious Majesty, by your invitation," began Fu-feng, "it's been many decades since we have been in such royal company."

"We were afraid that you might be offended by our performance..." began Jen-Ya-hsiang.

"Why in heaven's name should I be offended?" Tse Tsien heard her voice wobble a bit, then steady.

"Because I dropped my sword...so totally unlike me, I assure Your Majesty."

"I hardly noticed," she said quietly. *Hardly noticed? I couldn't even think at that moment...why does this man turn my bones into water? He's the most handsome man I've ever seen...a power that just wells out from him, dissolving me in its embrace...who is he?*

"Tell me about yourselves...where did you come from?" she commanded.

"From the Land of Lions," they said, both speaking at the same time, then, hearing their chorus together, threw back their heads and laughed, a dark, free sound.

"I, ah, came to Chian for an education and ended up at Shaolin for a truly rigorous one!" Fu-feng explained lightly.

"And you, Jen?" asked Tsien, turning to him. "Did you come to be educated?"

"Not exactly," he said nervously. "My path was rather more unpredictable."

"I think you're leaving out a great deal...I'd like to know why."

"May I ask *you* a question, Majesty?"

"Come sit over here with me, we'll be able to talk better." She gestured at stone benches beneath a citron-yellow willow tree.

"Do you have a twin sister?" Jen blurted. "You look so much like a woman I knew many years ago, a woman most dear to me, my sun and moon and stars—and I find myself unable to look at you without that old passion welling up...seeing you yesterday, you as the unapproachable, distant, cool empress was one thing...set me wond'ring actually...but seeing you tonight...is like a memory that pierces my heart."

Fu-feng looked from one to the other and shook his head in disbelief. "Brother of mine, be careful...I fear you're revealing too much in a place that has unfriendly ears everywhere."

"It's all right, Feng, all here are my friends," she reassured them. "A long time ago, when I was still a harum-scarum girl from a land far away from here, I was in love with a man who also came from the Land of Lions. He was killed...and for some time, I was near death myself with shock and grief..."

"My beloved was also killed...but I have never stopped loving her, never stopped dreaming of her..."

His smile is so sad…it breaks my heart all over again…if I could only reach out, touch him… "What was her name? This woman you loved?"

Jen hesitated, looked at Feng as if asking permission, then slowly, softly, he said, "Her name…that I've not been able to say for so achingly long…her name…was Talima, my Tam."

Tse Tsien's eyes closed, tears flooded her cheeks, her back arched and she threw back her head, "Aaa-a-i-i-i…" she moaned in an old agony.

Nearby conversation faded. Cicadas stilled. The earth stopped spinning.

She lifted her head and looked at him, "Pirjhan? Jhani? Is it really you? Are we real? Or is this another dream?"

Tse Tsien reached out to touch his arm, wanting to feel the hard muscle beneath his sleeve, wanting to feel the heat of his body, so absolutely alive.

He cupped her face with both hands, gazed at her green eyes and full lips with an intensity fueled by belief that she, too, might be real.

"How? Why? What happened? Where were you when…?" They each said at once, a parry of sharp questions that needed answers quickly.

"I *saw* you killed!"

"They told me you'd been killed…because of our…you know, our loving…betraying the emperor, they said!"

"If it wasn't *you* that I saw in the summer house, who was it? It looked just like you from the back…and then I saw only Zanggi…how could you let me go on without knowing you were still alive?"

"Wait…slow down you two," Feng cautioned.

"And *you*…you must be Firuz!" she accused.

"Yes, I am…or was, before taking monk's vows at Shaolin."

Pirjhan, or Jen, was quiet a moment, then said, "I think I know what must have happened. You see, Firuz, Kilar, and I were hunting up north with the emperor when I realized that I'd not be able to get back to Changan in time for our rendezvous, so I sent Kilar back to the city to tell you…"

"But he didn't and I thought…"

"Yes, you see, he couldn't get through the palace guards to tell you, so he sent Tulak to meet you at the summer house and tell you…"

"So it was *Tulak* that Zanggi beheaded?" she breathed.

"Yes, Kilar heard of it at once—was told that you had also been killed—and rode out to warn us that a general alarm was out for the rest of 'that Igren lot' to be killed on sight. We rode hard to get away, knowing the palace guards would hunt us down…ended up straggling around in the Shaolin mountains, living off grubs and grasses, until we stumbled on the monastery."

"We asked for asylum," Feng, or Firuz added, "and they granted it on the condition that we enter into their discipline fully, with all its rigors, and remain within the monastery walls so that passing strangers might not question two western-looking men…a promise we have kept."

"For the first years, it was incredibly hard. I just trained night and day, as hard as I could. It was the only way I could begin to function, to forget…to forget *you*…and you?"

"I…I went into a long black, shadowed place…you were dead, our baby was dead…I became nothing, no one…until the emperor, Tai Tsung, took it into his head to teach me, make me his confidante…" Tsien explained.

"Confidante?" Jen-Pirjhan raised his eyebrows.

"Now don't you pretend jealousy at this time, don't you dare! Yes, his confidante, his companion, his right arm in all things…nothing more!"

"Tengri! There's that temper I had to put up with but learned to love." He grinned and reached up to tousle her hair that tangled around his fingers.

"But where is Kilar? Is he with you, too?"

"Kilar elected to stay at the monastery, not knowing, of course that we would find…" Jen said quickly. "Wait till he hears!"

"Oh, Jhani, we have so much to talk about…can you stay?"

"Jen, we told the elder monk we'd be back in quarters by midnight," Feng-Firuz reminded him.

"I could request him to release you…" murmured Tse Tsien. "Tonight is such a miracle I don't ever want it to end."

"Tse Tsien, Maitreya? We're missing your company over here," Merket's merry voice interrupted the spell that held them. The rest of the party surrounded the three of them. Introductions were made. Zanggi stared at the two monks and muttered almost inaudibly, "Fei, fei, they look like trouble to me."

The eldest monk bowed low and said, "It is late for us, Most Illustrious, we must return. Thank you for a most auspicious evening." Beckoning to the other three, he walked toward the gate. Jen-Pirjhan held Tse Tsien's hands.

"No! You can't go…I might never find you again…oh *'Sky, I'll die all over again if he doesn't kiss me…*tomorrow, come early tomorrow, in the morning, at first light…I'll tell the guards to admit you…we can have the morning together, alone…before I have to dress for the crowning. You'll come, won't you? Promise me?"

"Wild horses could not stop me…I promise. Aaah, Tengri, after all these years…"

71
Sweeter Still

Before dawn, Tsien lay in bed, wide-awake, stretching like a cat on the smooth sheets, looking out at pale mist that blanketed the sleeping garden, imagining love again.

I'm remembering what it's like to be in love...to long for the touch of heart to heart... how I yearn to be caressed by his loving hands again...hard hands to entice my breasts and belly and...mmnnn...

Almost unbelievable...that we should be within a couple hundred li of each other all these years...I wonder if he's changed greatly... or whether I have...yes, I definitely have changed, been down to hell and back again...learned Tai Tsung's True Vision, learned to write, to calligraph... have governed, birthed a child...what if he's not ready for who I am now...what if I'm *not?*

At the foot of her bed, Ti Li stirred and whimpered in a dream.

I wonder what puppies dream of...chasing illusory rabbits? Aren't all dreams illusory? Isn't everything an illusion? Will Pirjhan—or Jen—come together with me to make a new reality, will we want to? Be allowed by the fates to do so?

She smelled the fragrant tea even before the servant slipped into the room. "Ah, thank you, did you bring two cups? Put the tray on the little table by the garden windows...I'll be up in a moment. You can go."

Over her slim cotton nightgown, she put on a spring-green kimono, raw silk padded with tree floss for warmth, and cinched it tightly around her waist. She sat down, picked up a small porcelain teacup with both hands and breathed in jasmine-flowered steam. She felt the world grow light, illumined from within—each blade of grass, each bush, each tree—glowing with the coming dawn.

A lemon-colored horizon radiated up into roseate clouds in a clear sky. Birds sang back and forth, discussing the morning's possibilities. Ti Li scampered out to smell the night's stories left behind.

She saw him silhouetted against the lightening sky as he walked toward her. Everything quickened inside her. She trembled. Hot tea spilled out of the cup over her hands and she gasped out loud.

"Did I startle you?" Pirjhan-Jen asked, his voice a deep purr, "I wasn't sure you'd be awake, so I was very quiet on the garden path."

Tse Tsien laughed, "No, I am waiting for you…have been waiting for you…forever it seems…come in, sit down, tea?" She was suddenly shy, formal.

But, instead of sitting as she directed, he came behind her, put his arms under hers and pulled her to her feet facing him. The heat of his body kindled a fire that flamed through her.

""I lay awake all night, Tam, wondering what this morning would be like, worried that we'd grown too far apart…you an empress, for god's sake! And I only a monk…too much distance to traverse…would I could leap it in one bound the way we leap from pole to pole in chi qong practice!" He ran his hands up and down her silk-clad body, lightly kissed the top of her head. "I've dreamed of a moment like this…a moment in a dream in which you still lived…now that it's here, I feel unsure of what to do…I only know that somehow, in some way, I *must* be with you, for us to be a part of each other…"

"I…I know, I mean I know what you mean…but I don't know how to say it…words seem to have left my mind…I can only feel myself melting away…" And, suiting her words, she began to slip down, out of his arms, onto the Persian rug at their feet.

"I want you…god knows I've wanted you since you were a girl…now you're this incredibly beautiful woman, incredibly powerful woman I should say…and I only want you more…I want to touch you everywhere, get to know your body and your heart and your mind as I once did…"

He leaned over her, tipped her head, cupped her face in his hands, traced the bones of her cheeks with his fingertips, and slowly, gently, brushed his lips over hers. A moment's hesitation while he seemed to hold his breath before he sank down beside her.

Her eyes wide and staring, she waited, hardly breathing, as he stripped off his shirt, smiling, holding the feeling that swelled and sang, higher and higher, lifting her from all the bonds that had held her before. Propelling her into a space as light as breath, as free as clouds.

He touched her just as he said he would, smoothing back her kimono, opening his mouth on her throat, his tongue flicking her nipples until they stood up eagerly, wanting. His lips raced along her belly bidding her to answer his desire.

She caressed the broad powerful muscles of his back, arched against him, breath and body answering him. She rose with him, belly and breast to his, his heat melting her heart, his kisses harder, more demanding. She could hear the fluting sounds of birds answering the cries she heard from deep within herself. Her mouth sought his and tasted the sweetness of him as if she had been starved for years.

He moaned and rolled over onto her, the length of their bodies fusing together as his back/her back rose and fell in unison. A surging power of pleasure that transcended all he had ever known.

She sank beneath his weight, reveling in the all-encompassing acceptance of his body, his scent, his taste, his voice, all of him surrounding and compelling everything she was or could be.

He trembled, riding the waves of desire that pulled him into her spell, into the soft wetness of her body.

As one creature, strong-winged and powerful, they flew on their joined dragon-self into a blue-sky space where only loving was real, this moment, life itself, as they had known it could be, riding together in the Everlasting Sky.

She heard a wild, exultant sound, felt the rapture as he plunged into her, shuddered with the force of their union.

Unearthly stillness followed. Free, weightless, she floated down, a feather on the wind of their passion.

They felt a sense of rightness...of belonging, of coming home through space and time...at one time...together now...together, always.

Sunlight streamed over them. An ordinary spring day began—the day she would be crowned Empress of Tang Dynasty Chian.

72
SOME YEARS LATER: REMEMBRANCE OF THESE DAYS AND NIGHTS

TSE TSIEN HELD THE THICK INK STICK FIRMLY AS SHE GROUND IT, round and round, on the rectangular, hollow stone. When a spoonful of powder had collected, she took an ornately carved water dropper and squirted a few drops of liquid into the ink, mixing it slowly with her brush until the black ink was ready to use. As she continued to mix more ink, enough for the whole poem, the pattern of words that she planned to calligraph filled her mind...*For our love-in there's... a quiet hut we've made...close on the mountain torrent.*

Yes, that will work...Kao Pau might have written this just for us, even though he lived a hundred years ago...

She looked out and down along the path through tall pines that led from the small cabin in which she worked. She unrolled a large sheet of rice paper onto the wooden floor and tacked the corners down with smooth river rocks. She kneeled, picked up her brush, wiped excess ink off on the side of the stone, and began the dance of thicks and thins, dark and light. After the first three lines, she dipped her brush again and continued...

Oh, that great strong man,
stretched out and at his ease!
Alone we sleep, alone we wake, alone we talk...

How I love to see Jhani when he thinks I'm not watching him... he's like a great mountain lion...taut, strong, sinuous...all those years of training at Shaolin made his body so irresistibly beautiful...and now...The written characters flew onto the paper...

Ahhh... these stolen days away from the palace are so precious...I know the guards are all out there, but I can't see them and I can just pretend that Jhani and I are here, alone...two ordinary people...still in love...more in love, really, than I ever thought was possible that day, more than a dozen years ago, when he and Firuz came down from Shaolin to demonstrate with scimitars...

She stood and looked down at what she had written, assessing the amount of space left on the paper...*shall I finish the poem? or leave this as is?*

Humming to herself, she sang the first part of the next verse...*On this high ground, our pleasure soft, fulfilled. Oh, that great strong man—the pivot of my life...* then, deciding, filled her brush again and, taking a deep breath, leaned down and completed it...

. . . alone we cherish, each to each.
There is no name for loving
we shall do no telling. . . .
. . .remembrance
of these days and nights
shall not soon pass.

With a grand flourish of the last character, Tse Tsien stepped back, still holding her ink-filled brush, her head tilted to one side, as she appraised the finished calligraphy. Finding it to her liking, she went outside to wash her brushes in the stream that meandered along one side of the little mountain cabin. Doves cu-cu-rooed from low branches. Small woodland creatures skittered in the needle-thick duff of the forest floor. The sunlit air was crisp, dry, resinous smelling. Through the trees, on a rocky bluff overlooking the creek, she could see Pirjhan practicing his chi gong meditation.

Hmmnnn, as far as anyone else is concerned, he's just one of my select Flying Horsemen—and if he sometimes is seen leaving my rooms in the morning...well, he's just very dutiful in protecting his empress...or his woman...

She smiled as she washed the brushes she had used, turning them this way and that in the palm of her left hand, rinsing again in the water, watching the diluted ink journey into the clear stream's vastness, drifting like smoke over stones and grasses.

It's different...being older...being companions, someone to talk things over with at the end of a busy day with audiences and ministers and all...having this is more important even than making love...it's more like being love itself...surpassing anything I could have imagined...

She laid the clean brushes down on the bank, then sat on a large, slanted boulder, warm from the sun, and watched bubbles in the stream bounce along in the swiftly moving water. Thoughts of love, like the bubbles, floated in her mind...

Sometimes love....is a filigree that traces patterns throughout your body, heart, and mind...a web of such delicate tendrils...that you're scarcely aware...that it holds you in this net of shimmering sweetness...when Jhani comes, I'll tell him, all over again, how much I love him...love our life together, court intrigues and all...

She dabbled her bare feet in the water and thought about a swim, later, together.

Sometimes love...is a great sea that sucks you out into depths you cannot fathom...and at others, a thunderous, all-encompassing tide that floods over you...drowning in an exhilarating rapture...and ohhhh, when it does...

Reflections off the water dappled her skin. She could see Pirjhan in the distance as he turned and began to amble down the path, coming toward her.

But always this love...is the song that sings you...the deep thrum of every day...a time-defying memory...however, whenever, it comes...it creates...that undeniable bond...with god...

She stretched back on the sun-warm rock, knowing that he would find her here. While she waited, she gazed at the mountain-blue sky above. Dreamily, she watched blowing clouds form, shift shape, and disappear...only to reappear in a different form in another part of the Everlasting Sky.

EPILOGUE, 705 A.D.

According to written history, Empress Wu Chao T'se T'sien was a woman endowed with broad vision, a keen intelligence and boundless energy. How she became empress is also a matter of record: After Emperor Kao T'sung died, the Council of Eunuchs set about building a solid political base of support for Wu Chao T'se T'sien. They cited the *Mahamegha Sutra's* prophecy and made public the news of the comet that Kao T'sung had noticed in conjunction with Venus. They reminded the ministers that it had been foretold generations before, that a comet would appear at the time of a magnificent woman ruler's ascendancy to the Peacock Throne. There were more than 20,000 signatures on the petition they circulated to elect her, the promised Prince of Wu, as emperor.

Rival factions within the palace drew up on lines of conservative Confucians, who despised the thought of a woman in power, and more open-minded Taoists and Buddhists, a split that was to continue until Wu's death in 705 A.D. She never made more than an uneasy truce with Confucian precepts or with those that adhered to them—and it was these same Confucian scholars who wrote the history of her reign, of which they so outspokenly disapproved, the same faction that tried to obliterate her likeness and accomplishments, allowing only one incident to be repeated down through the ages: during her reign three traitorous "superior" women were put to death in the manner proscribed for "inferiors", and therefore could not be reborn—a sin, as they believed, that they could not forgive. Ever.

As Empress Wu, China's first empress, and the only one elected in her own right, she accomplished much that has endured through time.

As a competent calligrapher, she invented twelve new characters that are still part of the classical language.

She directed the revision of *The Tang Code of Law* and saw to its completion. It was the basis of Chinese law until the 20th century.

She opened up enrollment at the universities and civil service examinations to young people from all parts of the empire, not just those of the First-Five families. During her reign, persons from classes other than hereditary aristocracy were allowed to study for the state-run examinations thereby increasing the number of graduates from about forty to more than four hundred each year.

She enlarged the canal system so that there could be swift communication from one end of the country to the other.

She continued T'ai T'sung's policies that encouraged freedom of thought and religion throughout the country.

She increased opportunities for free expression of opinions to the Peacock Throne, and was an eager listener to all who journeyed to the court from places as distant as Rome, Turkey, Persia, Tibet, Nepal, India, Burma, Cambodia and Viet Nam.

In many ways she reduced taxes, thus freeing the enterprise of common people. She did raise revenue by selling dung from the palace stables! During her reign, trade, agriculture and sericulture (the production of silk) were stabilized and increased throughout the empire.

She did move the capital from Changan to Loyang, set thousands of artisans to work building in Loyang, but forbade the *Chung-shang*, the Department of Public Works, to indulge in extravagances.

It *was* rumored that one of her Flying Horsemen, her personal guardsmen, may have been closer to her, in a possibly intimate way, than others. And children were everywhere in the palace, but I chose to believe they were surrogate children for Wu, children from the marriages of Faina and Batu, both fictional characters.

Toward the end of her reign, Empress Wu was accorded the great honor of Feng and Shan Sacrifices, previously given to only five other emperors. The Feng and Shan, most ancient and holy of rites, involved the entire country in purifying and harmonizing every aspect of their lives—spiritual as well as material. Held on the top of a sacred mountain, these sacrifices were the most magnificent of ceremonies. They were also magnificently expensive. They came close to bankrupting the country's treasury.

Except for a few skirmishes with the always-troublesome northern

Sillans (Koreans), Empress Wu ceased most military operations and sought to transform the empire by virtue of adherence to the Taoist *Way*. In this she was largely successful, for her reign was peaceful—from the Tien Shan Mountains to the sea, from the Great Wall to the Sea of Pearls.

She was an outspoken advocate of women's rights, writing both a history of women and a law which ensured that mourning for one's mother would be the same number of respectful years as that of mourning for one's father. She could also be quite gullible, superstitious and blind to the faults of those close to her.

During her long reign, there was a veritable explosion in the arts. She sent dozens of artists to the caves in Lung-men where they carved and painted for decades. Poets, philosophers, calligraphers, sculptors, painters and potters, known as her *Scholars of the Northern Gate,* were honored by her court.

She commissioned life-sized portraits of T'ai Tsung's horses, replicas of his favorite bayards, to stand along the entrance of his tomb. Many of these stone horses remain.

WHEN SHE DIED IT WAS AUTUMN, IN THE MOON OF HUNGRY GHOSTS, and the heartache call of wild swans skeined across the sky, following their ancient way against the stars. At that time, few still lived who had known, and the empress herself could scarcely remember, a wild young girl from the steppe lands of Central Asia.

Only the Everlasting Sky remembered…

In Case You Were Wondering...

The Following Are People Of Historical Record:

The Igren Chagan, although Tashih Shaymak himself is fictional, his words, in the main, aren't. They are the recorded sayings, a few generations later, of his heir, Genghis Khan, leader of the Golden Horde. Blondes and redheads with fair skin and blue/green eyes still live in Pamir villages near the borders of eastern Afghanistan, said to have inherited these genes from Alexander the Great.

The Bequi - there was often a neutral-gender person in Igren clans similar to those of the Crow Indians in this country, who held this traditional role of shaman and healer.

Chang Chen, the T'ang ambassador to the mon-barbarian West.

The aristocratic bride-to-be, (Ssu in my story, whose writing ability lit a fire in Talima's mind) who traveled west to Persia over the Silk Route, lived in Persia for many years, bore at least two sons and eventually returned to China where she wrote poetry that survives. She may have been the woman who smuggled silk worms in her hat as a bride present to her husband, thereby giving away the carefully guarded secret (death was swiftly meted out to anyone caught taking the magical worms out of the country) of how silk was made.

T'ai Tsung, this is his "tomb name". His name while alive was Li Shih-min. The majority of his dialogue and the stories he tells are as he spoke, as recorded in written history. A great warrior, he gained power in a military coup in which his father, the first T'ang Dynasty emperor, and brothers were killed. He extended and consolidated a far-flung empire through wars and diplomatic ties. During his reign, he did rescind the requirement of tribute from vassal tribes of their chieftain's virgin daughter.

T'ai Tsung's horses, his *bayards'* names and their coloring were documented as they are here.

Crown Prince Li Cheng, who loved Sassanian (Persian) ways and music, was truly banished for his excesses, to the extreme south, 2000 miles away from the capital, in what may have been the jungles of Annam.

Prince Kao Tsung, who became the third T'ang Emperor, *was* an astronomer. There was a comet that purported to announce the ascendancy of the Prince of Wu at that time. There are also some indications that he may have stuttered.

Wu Chao T'se T'sien, fourth emperor of the T'ang Dynasty, elected in her own right after Kao Tsung's death, who ruled the empire for decades. She carried out T'ai Tsung's *Chen Kuan True Vision*, making the early T'ang Dynasty one of China's greatest, a confluence of philosophies, economies, religions and peoples. Her accomplishments as outlined are a matter of historical record. Her intimate relations with certain members of her elite personal guards, her Flying Horsemen, is also alluded to, but unsubstantiated.

Duke Wu Shih-kuo of Tai Yuan and his family.

Li Chang Chao, writing master who taught in the renowned *Forest of Pencils.*

Lady Wang, Kao Tsung's ambitious wife, a member of the aristocratic Li-Tang family.

All of the Ministers and Secretaries, their titles, functions and philosophic loyalties

Prince Firuz from Persia, who came for an education and never went home again.

Mistress Feng, the Healer Alchemist. Her herbal remedies are as recorded in the great encyclopedias of Chinese medicine. She was known to always wear green.

Hsuan Tsung, the pilgrim traveler to India, who brought back Buddhist texts written on the original bark scrolls and who then translated them from the Sanskrit for years.

Camel Kuo, the hunchback gardener who raised blue lotus flowers, and was in charge of the vast Imperial gardens and forests of Kuo.

Ho Hsien-ku, the Faina of my story, was one of the Eight Immortals, who fed upon moonbeams and seashells and who disappeared into the palace during the reign of Empress Wu. Her symbol is the blue lotus. She is now a household goddess who helps maintain the home.

The Following Are Also True:

In most cases I have used the ancient names for countries and places. I have also omitted apostrophes that are most often seen in the spelling of Chinese names because they are difficult for Western readers, and do not change the sound nor the sense of the story.

The *Mahamegha Sutra*, one of those brought back to China from India by Hsuan Tsung, *did* prophesy a woman ruler for China, to be called the Prince of Wu.

All the geography, places, rivers, etc. are historically correct.

The Yasa and *The T'ang Code of Law* exist. Ku poison is one of the Ten Abominations of the Code, and was considered a "woman's crime". All points of law, whether Igren or T'ang are accurate and clearly delineate the formal society of those times.

Pirjhan's songs are translations of ancient hymns to Inanna.

Translating from the ancient Chinese is a tricky job. There is a wide difference, amongst scholars of this era, as to dates and persons involved in some of the events. Arbitrarily, I chose dates and persons that correspond best to my story.

The Feng and Shan Ritual, an extravagance of amazing proportions, was held for the Empress Wu, one of five rulers so honored.

After Empress Wu's death, in 705 A.D., a series of rulers dedicated to the more rigid principals of Confucius, held power. They made a concerted effort to discredit Wu and, in many ways, to falsify or obliterate her considerable achievements similar to the slanders about Richard III by his successors, or the effacement of Queen Hatshepsut's name and accomplishments from Egyptian monuments and records.

Empress Wu did have a peacock (k'ung sparrow) feather cape made. The last Empress of China had a net of pearls cape—such a charming idea—that I have included it here for the first Empress.

Ice, insulated by straw, brought by wagonload from northern "chous" or provinces, was stored and used extensively as described.

Cosmetics, as named, were in widespread use by the aristocracy.

All the poets and their poetry, although I have juggled the sequence of their lives. Not all these famous poets would have been alive, and at court, at the same time.

The method of obtaining, spinning, dyeing, and trading silk is extrapolated from known fact. Silk at this time was in demand everywhere, but particularly in Egypt and Rome. It has even been speculated that it led to the decline of the Roman Empire because of their enormous trade imbalance and subsequent indebtedness to China.

Cash money was not actually in common usage until nearly 25 years after the Empress' death. A pi's worth of silk, approximately one foot wide, 40 feet long, was the standard measure of currency at this time. Barter flourished.

The conflict between Confucians and Taoists or Buddhists began at this time. Buddhism was new, Taoism was old. Together they formed powerful and peaceful alliances at court. The Confucians, however, were more militant and prevailed, writing history, as most conquerors do, to discredit and vilify those of whom they disagreed.

Years after this story ends, both Chang-an and Loyang were burned completely. In the meantime, both Korea (Silla) and Japan had grafted the T'ang culture and philosophies onto their own, as well as emulating their art and crafts. Today, the greatest number of existing artifacts of the T'ang period exists primarily in Nara, Japan, some in Korea.

Legends, proverbs, rituals, games, jewelry, dances, clothing, foods, wines, celebrations, weights and measures, festivals, commerce, navigation, transportation, military action, medicine, science, and philosophies have been carefully researched and are correct for the Chinese section, nearly all of the

Igren section, and based on known fact as well as archaeological findings in that remote area of the Tagh Clan section.

In general, the stranger or more unusual something is, the more likely it is to have its source in recorded fact.

Bibliography

Many books touch on this story. Some are highly biased, written from a rigid European viewpoint that considered all Asian cultures inferior, all religions other than Christianity, as "cults". Although some of these are considered classics in the field of Ancient Chinese studies, I did not include them here.

Among those historians who delineated a vivid time most splendidly, Lamb, Schafer, and Twitchett are outstanding. The love and erudition they hold for their subject and their craft is obvious. I am most grateful to them.

Here are a few of the books I liked and used the most as source material are starred in the order of their importance:

Atlas of China, by Herrmann

Ancient China, *Time/Life Books,* edited by E. Schafer * *

Chinese Symbols and Superstitions, by H. Morgan

Early Chinese Poems, by Don Berry**

Four T'ang Poets, edited by D. Young

Inanna, by Wolkstein and Kramer

March of the Barbarians and ***Genghis Khan,*** by Harold Lamb * * *

Science and Civilization in China, first five volumes, edited by Joseph Needham * * * *

Sexual Life in Ancient China, by Van Gulik *

Silk, Spices, and Empire, by Owen Lattimore

The Cambridge History of China, vol 3, by Denis Twitchett * * * *

The Golden Peaches of Samarkand, Shore of Pearls, and ***The Vermilion Bird***, all by Edward Schafer * * * *

The Gobi Desert, by Cable and French *

The I-Ching, by Baynes

The T'ang Code, editor and commentator, Wallace Johnson * * *

To the Ends of the Earth, by Franck and Brownstone

Women Poets of China, edited by Rexroth and Ling Chung

Glossary

Aerial cars ~ a conveyance or carriage that flew by means of horizontally rotating propellers, mentioned in the ancient story of mythical strangers who arrived in China by air many centuries before. Drawings of the men who came out of these aerial cars, who had three eyes and heads that reflected, etc. look remarkably like present-day astronauts.

Ahatou or 'hatou ~ a Pamir greeting, like hello.

Alabolo ~ an early form of polo, played by Central Asian horsemen to this day using an animal head or balled-up goatskin as the puck.

Annam ~ Vietnam.

Bequi ~ a shaman, often a transsexual person

Bian ~ a city in China, 70 kms from Zhengzhou.

Buran ~ a viciously cold northeast wind, that sweeps across the Gobi Desert.

Chams ~ a kingdom once in the southeast coast of Vietnam.

Chang ~ a unit of measurement, see Table of Measures.

Chapars ~ Pamir cowboys, horsemen.

Changan ~ an old capital of Chian.

Chen-Kuan ~ the name of Tai Tsung's *True Vision* that he based the T'ang Dynasty on, which Wu Chao T'se T'sien carried out and made real.

Chian ~ the old name for China.

Chous ~ a distinct area with boundaries, similar to counties or states.

Chukkas - intervals of time during which the game of polo is played, similar to periods or quarters in other sports.

Citragandha ~ a fragrant, yellow mineral, when ground used for medicines.

Clepsydra ~ ("water thief") a clock run by water as early as 2000 B.C., sometimes created in bronze, some one or two feet high, some six feet tall.

Cup-companions ~ close friends or initiates who drink together "from the same cup"-of wisdom or social connection.

Druze ~ an old derogatory name for someone of inferior status or no worth.

Earth-kelet ~ there are many kinds of kelets, or spirits, earth, water or air, that inhabited the natural world of Igren.

Fagara ~ a hot Szechuan pepper, used in foods and medicines; also used as slang for hot stuff.

Ferghana ~ a wide valley area at the foot of Mt. Burkhan Kaldun in the Pamir Mountains of Central Asia, northwest of modern India.

Fiddles ~ two-string fiddles called "erhus", already recorded in China by the previous Sung dynasty, 420 A.D.

Flic-flacs ~ jumping with energy.

Fourth or first mourning ~ see mourning rights, below.

Frogs ~ the soft underpart of a horse's hoof which resembles the shape of a frog.

Ger ~ a round, domed dwelling or yurt made from layers of boiled, matted yak fur, spread over willow poles.

Get ~ from beget, now most often used for the offspring of an animal, usually a horse.

Gobi desert ~ a northwesterly region in China and Southern Mongolia, variously sandy, rocky, or hilly, and often cold enough for snow, where there were the lakes as described.

Hat-and-girdle ~ Pamir phrase for townsmen, non-horse-nomads.

Horses ~ the T'ang Dynasty horses, from nomad horse herds in Central Asia were prized for their beauty and stamina. Drawings and carvings show them to have an erect, arched neck, powerful hindquarters and alert head and ears. They were in many colors, but valued mostly highly for white, or palomino.

Hrom ~ Rome, Italy.

I-Ching ~ an ancient method of divination, of seeing the pattern in events and their outcome.

Igren ~ People of the Ger who lived in and around the Pamir Valley; their laws and culture were the ancestors of the Golden Horde, let by Genghis Khan and his brothers 1000 years later; a Caucasian peoples of light-colored hair and eyes that still live in this area.

Inanna ~ Queen of Heaven and Earth, (known to the Semites as Ishtar), the ruler-wife-lover-redeemer whom all Sumerians worshipped and from whom all life flowed. She combined the older Fertility Goddess with the attributes of the Goddess of Love.

Kara - a Pamir word for white.

K'ung sparrows ~ peacocks.

Karakhoja ~ a country between Kazakhstan, Tibet, and Mongolia, famous today for its tombs.

Kat Kat Zanggi ~ the name of a large island and port in the Indian Ocean, presumably Sri Lanka from whence *Zanggi* came.

Kibitkas ~ huge, flatbed wagons that often carried the ger and personal belongings of Igren as they moved from winter to summer pasture and back again.

Koguryo ~ an advanced empire of Northeast China, Manchuria and northern Korea, begun in 57 B.C., in decline by time of the T'ang.

Kucha ~ a faraway kingdom, possibly Egypt.

Kumiss ~ a slightly alcoholic drink made from fermented mare's or camel's milk.

Kuo ~ an old township in China.

Kuriltai ~ a yearly rendezvous of tribes and their chieftains: from the 1st century A.D. onward, where there was great feasting, games, races and merriment, as well as resolving tribal issues.

Land of Lions ~ present day Ethiopia, or African countries of the eastern seacoast southward.

Lungmen Caves ~ on the Yellow River, near Loyang, containing many sculptures of Buddha and Bodhisattvas.

Memorialize ~ a memoranda from a ruler recommending a person and giving him status and protection; also used in remembering someone after death .

Merket ~ a Pamir word for swift.

Mon-barbarians ~ the Chinese phrase that was used for non-Chinese who came from the far west.

Mou ~ a tiny paste-on shape used in elaborate facial fashions by noble ladies or courtesans.

Mourning rights ~ first, second, third, fourth, etc., the degrees of closeness to the emperor or empress by which it was determined which privileges or punishments pertained according to *The T'ang Code of Law,* revisions begun in the 600's by Emperor Tai T'sung, and completed by Empress Wu Chao T'se T'sien, which was the basis for Chinese law until the twentieth century.

Myrlobans ~ a particular mushroom,

highly revered for its medicinal properties.

Nestorian monks ~ named for the Catholic bishop Nestor, of Syria, who died around 450 A.D.

Ophiogon ~ a grass-like lily with black leaves and seeds, used medicinally.

Osun ~ a spirit-Goddess of beauty, wealth and love.

Paekche ~ early southwest kingdom of Korea.

Pippala ~ a type of Ficus tree.

Punt ~ an exotic country possibly in modern Eritrea or Ethiopa; a source of incense.

Red Hats ~ Catholic cardinals came from Rome to study in the more advanced culture of China.

Samarkand ~ an ancient and sophisticated city of modern day Uzbekistan.

Sanderswood ~ a precious, aromatic wood, usually of reddish hue, possibly sandalwood.

Sapphire Isle ~ Burma, where many if not most of the sapphires and jade come from.

Sassanian, Sassanid ~ the brilliant culture of Persia until the 7th century, which gave architecture, dance, music and fashion to the known world.

Serindia ~ China's Turkestani highlands.

Sha ~ an honorific, a term of respect.

Silla ~ Korea.

Sixes - a game of dice.

Skin pipes ~ bagpipes, smaller than the Scottish ones.

Sogdians ~ the inhabitants of the area near Samarkand.

Stags ~ large male deer with many-pronged horns.

Stoop ~ a falconry term, meaning a bird's steep dive from a high altitude at terrific speed.

Sudde ~ an individual's spirit or soul.

Tajik ~ the Tajik were the Persian-speaking native culture of Samarkand, also home to the smaller, fine-boned Arab horses of the time.

Tengri - a great god of thunder from Central Asia.

Tenassarim ~ Altai region of Western Tibet.

Tien Shans ~ the mountains of Kyrgyzstan, habitat of snow leopards.

Tocharians ~ an Indo-European people near Xinchiang.

Tun Huang Caves ~ renowned for their 1000 Buddhas and wall paintings, begun in 4th century A.D.

Uighur ~ people of far northwest China.

Wari ~ a game for two people played with beans or small stones in a board, or earth, of carved-out hollows played in many different cultures under different names.

Wether-drum ~ a small lacquered drum.

Yasa ~ the Law of the Igren nomad tribes of Central Asia, said to have been written by the pre-history goddess, The Blue Wolf.

Zulgur ~ a derogatory term for worthless meat.

Weights and measurements

Length

10 *tsun* = 1 *ch'ih* (slightly less than 1 foot)

5 *ch'ih* = 1 *pu* (a double pace)

10 *ch'ih* = 1 *chang*

1800 *ch'ih* = 1 *li* (approximately 1/3 mile)

Area

1 *mou* = a strip 1 *pu* wide by 240 *pu* long (approximately .14 acre)

100 *mou* = 1 *ch'ing* (approximately 14 acres)

Capacity

3 *sheng* = 1 ta-sheng (a standard pint)

1 *ta-sheng* = 1 *tou*

10 *tou* = 1 *hu*

1 *hu* = 1 *shih* (approximately 1 3/4 bushels)

Weight

3 *liang* = 1 *ta-liang* (a standard ounce)

16 *ta-liang* = 1 *chin* (approximately 1 1/2 pound)

Cloth

1 *p'i* of silk = a length 1.8 *ch'ih* in width, by 40 *ch'ih* long

1 *tuan* of hemp = a length 1.8 *ch'ih* in width, by 50 *ch'ih* long